ALSO BY SUSAN REBECCA WHITE

Bound South

A Soft Place
to Land

SUSAN REBECCA WHITE

A Touchstone Book
Published by Simon & Schuster
New York   London   Toronto   Sydney

Touchstone
A Division of Simon & Schuster, Inc.
1230 Avenue of the Americas
New York, NY 10020

First Touchstone trade paperback edition April 2010

TOUCHSTONE and colophon are registered trademarks of Simon & Schuster, Inc.

For information about special discounts for bulk purchases,
please contact Simon & Schuster Special Sales at 1-866-506-1949
or business@simonandschuster.com.

The Simon & Schuster Speakers Bureau can bring authors to your live event.
For more information or to book an event contact the Simon & Schuster Speakers
Bureau at 1-866-248-3049 or visit our website at www.simonspeakers.com.

Designed by Akasha Archer

Manufactured in the United States of America

20 19 18 17 16 15 14 13 12 11

Library of Congress Cataloging-in-Publication Data

White, Susan Rebecca.
  A soft place to land / by Susan Rebecca White.
    p. cm.
1. Sisters—Fiction. 2. Parents—Death—Fiction. 3. Loss
(Psychology)—Fiction. 4. Life change events—Fiction. 5. Domestic
fiction. I. Title.
  PS3623.H57896S64 2010
  813'.6—dc22
                              2010005679
ISBN 978-1-4165-5869-9
ISBN 978-1-4165-6062-3 (ebook)

To Mom and Dad, whose love remains legendary.
And to Lauren, who taught me to play.

We have not made mud pies for nothing.
                                    —Robert Farrar Capon

A Soft Place
to Land

Prologue

In the months following the accident Ruthie and Julia imagined and discussed the last days of their parents' lives so often it was almost as if the girls had been there, had accompanied them on the trip out west. Except of course they had not. That had been the whole point of Phil and Naomi's vacation.

Their plane crashed at approximately 3:00 P.M. on Wednesday, March 24, 1993, during the girls' spring break from the Coventry School, where Ruthie was in seventh grade, Julia a sophomore. Most of the well-to-do families from Coventry, which is to say most of the families, were taking vacations together that week, to the mountains to ski, or to the beach to relax by the ocean. Ruthie's best friend and sometimes nemesis, Alex, was going all the way to London with her parents. But Phil's caseload at the firm was especially heavy that year, and Julia had so many late and incomplete assignments to finish that she needed an unscheduled week at her desk just to get caught up.

And so no trip for the Harrisons was planned, until Julia's theater friend Marissa Tate casually mentioned that Julia could come with her to her family's beach house on Pawleys Island. Phil and Naomi made a show of extracting promises from Julia that she would spend at least two hours a day catching up on her assignments, but they readily agreed to the trip. Freed of one child, and with Mother Martha—Phil's stepmom—willing to come stay with Ruthie, they began thinking of a romantic destination for just the two of them.

Phil and Naomi lived for time alone with each other.

Naomi's favorite place in the world was Paris, in the Sixth Arrondissement, where she would sit for hours in the cafés, drinking espressos, eating pastel-colored macaroons, and observing the sophisticated people around her. In Paris, unlike in Atlanta, caffeine didn't bother her; she could drink espresso all day and still fall asleep easily at night. Phil's favorite place was wherever Naomi was happiest, but nearly equal to his love of pleasing his wife was his love of a good bargain. And since there were no bargain plane tickets to be found for a last-minute trip to Paris (he checked), he booked them on a trip to Las Vegas instead, where he got a tremendous deal on their stay at the Mirage and secured tickets for them to watch Siegfried and Roy tame the tigers.

They planned to stay put in Las Vegas for three days. The city's slightly seedy element was not a deterrent. In fact, it added to the allure of the vacation. How much further could they be from their mortgage-bound life of duty and responsibility in Atlanta than to be playing craps in a flashy casino in the middle of the day after spending the morning in bed? On the fourth day of their vacation, they would venture out of the city, renting a brand-new 1993 cherry red Mercedes convertible that they would use to drive the 270 miles to the Grand Canyon, where years ago Phil and his first wife, Beatrice, had (rather uncomfortably) camped during a cross-country drive to visit his sister, Mimi, who lived in San Francisco.

Naomi would be seeing the Grand Canyon for the first time.

Julia and Ruthie speculated that Phil was probably more excited about driving that new Mercedes than he was about any other part of the trip. Phil was a sucker for cars, trading in his old one every couple of years for whatever was the latest, fastest model he could acquire for a good price. Once he took his wife to look at a BMW he had bought for a tremendous bargain, many thousands below its Blue Book value. It turned out that the original owner of the car had been killed while driving it, in a multiple-car crash that brought traffic to a stop on I-85 for hours. All his widow wanted was to get rid of the car, fast.

Naomi told Ruthie about accompanying Phil to the body shop to see the car while it was being repaired. Its windshield was shattered and there was a little bit of human hair poking out from one of the cracks. Naomi said that she could never ride in that car without feeling queasy. It was a huge relief, she said, when two years passed and Phil traded the car in for another, newer one.

Phil had made other sketchy deals. Ruthie remembered a time when Phil was late coming home from work and Naomi was agitated because he had not phoned to inform her of the reason for the holdup. Ruthie was already dressed for bed by the time Phil finally pulled into the garage, driving a new black Jaguar. He walked into the kitchen beaming, and to an incredulous Naomi he explained: a Middle Eastern man who had once been his client had phoned him at the office, saying that he needed to sell the car within forty-eight hours, and he needed to sell it for cash.

"I had the cash, babe," said Phil, standing in his blue suit in the red-tiled kitchen while Naomi glared at him, not even saying a word. "You won't believe the deal I got."

The thing about Phil's deals was this: they usually didn't save him any money. He would often end up buying even more expensive items than he ever intended to purchase, simply because they were offered at a price below retail value. That was why Julia, at sixteen, was given a brand-new Saab 900. Phil had been planning to buy her one of the old Hondas listed in the automobile section of the *Atlanta Journal-Constitution* when his eye hit upon the lease deal advertised by Saab. At the astonishingly low rate of $288.99 a month—no money down—how could Phil not lease a new Saab for his daughter, who was actually his stepdaughter but whom he claimed fully as his own?

Julia was embarrassed by the car, which highlighted her

self-consciousness about being a rich girl at a rich prep school. The friends she hung out with at Coventry were mostly boys, smart stoners who wore black and loved to make fun of their privileged classmates. (Somehow they were able to overlook their own privileged lives.) They had a field day with Julia's Saab, and when she told them to shut up and leave her alone—she hadn't asked for the car in the first place—they told her to please stop with the "saab story."

As for Phil, he proclaimed Julia a reverse snob, adding, "I can't wait until the day you have to support yourself. Then you'll *really* miss your old man."

When speculating about their parents' last days on earth, Ruthie told Julia that she hoped they had ordered dessert after their last dinner, the night before they drove out to see the Grand Canyon, the night before they decided to board that ancient Ford Trimotor—known as "The Tin Goose" to airplane aficionados— that was supposed to fly them into the canyon itself, revealing the canyon's details up close. Julia assured Ruthie that yes, dessert was ordered, for Naomi loved chocolate above all other foods. Indeed, she was forever breaking her diet by eating chocolate and drinking champagne with Phil, after a dutiful dinner with the girls of overbaked chicken and steamed broccoli, or turkey meat loaf and a microwaved potato, or sometimes Lean Cuisine. During the day, too, she would be diligent, drinking a Slim-Fast for lunch, or having a fruit plate with cottage cheese. But if Phil opened a bottle of bubbly after dinner, she could rarely find the willpower to say no. And loosened by the champagne, how could she refuse chocolate?

The night before they drove to the Grand Canyon, Phil and Naomi had eaten at Kokomo's restaurant in the Mirage Hotel. Julia and Ruthie imagined that their mother wore the emerald green raw silk top she had purchased from Isaacson's in Atlanta, that and a pair of wide-legged black satin pants that swished when she walked. She would have worn heels, of course. Tall ones. She always wore heels when she dressed up, and the feet she slipped into them would have been creamy and free of calluses, the toenails painted with Estée Lauder Vintage Cognac. The girls both knew that Phil had a thing for pretty hands and feet, that he encouraged his wife to get a manicure once a week and a pedicure every other week, and that Naomi, though she often spoke of feeling guilty about the extravagant lifestyle Phil provided, loved to be pampered and happily, guiltily, obliged.

Phil would have worn a dark suit and white shirt, not unlike what he wore to the office most days. His tie was most likely the green one with minute white polka dots that Naomi had bought for him at Mark Shale. It would have matched Naomi's outfit, and the girls knew that he had that one with him on the trip, for it was found, curled up with the others, in one of the suitcases that were returned to their house the week following the accident.

He would have been freshly shaved; he would have smelled like Tsar cologne, which Julia had given him for Christmas to replenish his supply. His glasses might have had a speck of dust or debris or even food on them—they often did—but Naomi would have taken out the special wipes she kept in her purse to clean them. Before they left for the hotel restaurant, she probably pulled out the lint roller from her suitcase and used it on the front of his suit, too.

Phil would have been ready before Naomi, would have been dressed and waiting to go, sitting on the hotel bed and watching a basketball game on TV while she finished applying her makeup, while she dabbed the hollow beneath her ear with Chanel No. 5. Had he been waiting for her to finish getting ready in Atlanta, Phil would have sipped from a can of beer, from whatever brand was on sale at the grocery store. Naomi wasn't really a beer drinker, and so he didn't have to suit her tastes when he made his beer purchases. But in Las Vegas, Julia and Ruthie were sure, Phil would have waited until he was at the restaurant to get a drink. Phil's attitude toward the price of items in a minibar most clearly resembled moral outrage.

"But don't you think he might have bought a bottle of

champagne at the grocery store or something, and surprised Mom with it when she came out of the bathroom?" asked Ruthie. This was during one of their early discussions about what happened the night before, during those first few months when they were still living in Atlanta, supervised by their aunt Mimi, Phil's sister, who had moved into the house on Wymberly Way for the time being, leaving her husband and her interior design business unattended to in San Francisco, just until everything got sorted out.

The girls were sitting in Julia's room, on her queen-sized bed with the green and pink floral coverlet.

"That's possible," said Julia. "Especially because the trip was such a fuck fest for the two of them."

"Don't say that!" said Ruthie, hitting her sister hard on the thigh with her open palm. Ruthie did not want to think of her dead parents disrespectfully. Plus, she hated it when Julia said "fuck." There was a strong evangelical contingency at Coventry, and Ruthie had been swayed enough by the proselytizers to purchase a necklace with a small silver cross dangling from it at James Avery, the Christian jewelry store at Peachtree Battle Shopping Center, just a mile away from their house.

It wasn't that Ruthie believed Julia was going to hell for saying such words, but she worried that every time Julia cursed, God turned a little further away from her. And with Julia on the verge of failing out of Coventry, Ruthie felt strongly that her sister needed God on her side. Had Ruthie expressed these thoughts to Julia, she would have snorted, would have asked, "Where was God when Mom and Phil were on that plane?"

Ruthie wondered the same thing.

"I'm sorry, my darling, delicate one. Sorry for springing the 'f' word on you, but do you not remember the sound of the train?"

Ruthie was ten years old the first time she heard her mom making the train noises. Her bedtime was hours past, but she was awake, reading the thriller *Daughters of Eve* by a compact flashlight that she kept under her pillow. She could not figure out where the high, rising sound was coming from. She decided it must be a train barreling down the tracks over by Ardmore Park off Collier Road. Which was strange, considering that the park was miles away. She turned on her side, placed her pillow on top of her exposed ear to block out the sound, and managed to keep reading, holding the flashlight with one hand while turning pages with the other. Pretty soon the train noise stopped.

The next day she asked Julia if she had heard the train that last night. Wasn't it strange, Ruthie mused, that the noise would travel so far, all the way from the tracks on Collier? Julia looked at Ruthie as if she were a total idiot.

"That was Mom you were hearing, dummy. She and Dad were having sex."

"But the noise was so *loud.*"

Julia shrugged. "Don't ask me," she said. "I've always found that noise during sex is optional."

Ruthie covered her ears with her hands. *"Kittens and puppies and bunnies,"* she chanted. *"Kittens and puppies and bunnies . . ."*

Ruthie didn't know whether to laugh or to cry at Julia's allusion to "the train." Ever since the accident she did both—laugh and cry—at unexpected moments. In the four weeks since her parents' death Ruthie had already been sent out of the room for getting the giggles in the middle of Bible class, during the discussion of *The Hiding Place,* a book by Corrie ten Boom, a Christian woman who was sent to Auschwitz after it was discovered that she and her family had helped hide Jews.

There was nothing funny about *The Hiding Place,* and yet every time someone said "Corrie ten Boom" Ruthie began to laugh. It reminded her of something her uncle Robert once did when she was little. Uncle Robert and Aunt Mimi were visiting from San Francisco, during the summer. One afternoon all of the grown-ups put on bathing suits and went to sit by the pool. It was the first time Ruthie had ever seen Uncle Robert with his shirt off. He had a hairy chest and back, and his belly bulged over the waist of his swim shorts.

"Meet my chubby hubby," said Mimi. Robert slapped his stomach and said, with gusto, "Ba boom!"

Corrie ten Boom, her uncle Robert's "ba boom." This was not a connection Ruthie could explain to her Bible teacher. She didn't get in any real trouble, though. After the accident all of her teachers were cautious around her.

Even more often than laughing at inappropriate moments, Ruthie cried. During the dumbest times, too, when someone sitting beside her in homeroom complained about what a bitch her mom was, or the math teacher Mrs. Stanford used "Mom's meat loaf" as a subject for a word problem. Ruthie discovered that the best way to avoid crying was to sit as still as she possibly could and think only about immediate things, such as: would the spider making its way across Jason Purdy's desk climb up onto his arm, and if it did, would he notice? (Once a bug crawled out of his hair and Jason seemed only pleasantly surprised.)

When Ruthie was home, finally, and alone in her room she cried and cried, all the while trying not to make noise, because it would have embarrassed her to have Aunt Mimi overhear her distress. Even though Aunt Mimi was always telling Ruthie that there was no wrong way to grieve. Especially because Aunt Mimi was always telling her that there was no wrong way to grieve.

Alone in her room after school, Ruthie prayed. Though she wore the cross from James Avery around her neck, her belief in God was not bedrock, and more often than not her prayers to God were pleas for him to exist, for him to be real. If he did not, if he was not, that meant that Ruthie would never again see her parents.

Most afternoons Julia was away at play practice. She had always been a gifted performer, but after the accident her talent deepened, her interest intensified, and she was given the lead in the spring play, even though the lead was usually reserved for a senior. Julia was happiest during rehearsal, happiest inhabiting another person's life. She would remain this way throughout her life, always writing about others. Only once, in her memoir about rehab, would she focus her gaze almost exclusively on herself. After play practice she would often go to Steak 'n Shake or the OK Cafe with other cast members, or meet up with her stoner friends who wore black and avoided sanctioned extracurricular activities.

Mimi did not keep a tight rein on Julia, and so Julia was not usually home until 8:00 or 9:00 P.M. She would have stayed out even later had it not been for Ruthie. Sometimes Julia would swing home after play practice, pick her little sister up in her Saab 900, and take her out to dinner with her friends. And somehow, even though she, too, had lost her mother, she, too, had lost Phil (he was "only" her stepfather, yes, but she was closer to him than she was to her real dad), Julia was able to give Ruthie comfort.

Whether it was allowing her little sister to accompany Julia to Mick's for chocolate pie with her stoner friends, or allowing her little sister to sleep in her bed at night because it comforted both of them to be near each other, Julia alone made Ruthie feel better. Sometimes at night Ruthie would wake up crying and Julia, more often awake than not, would wrap her arms around her sister, would hold her tight, would use enough pressure to contain the radiating loneliness Ruthie felt.

It was funny. Ruthie wasn't used to hugging Julia. As close as they had always been, as much as they had always relied on each other, they had never been huggers. No one in their family was. Even Phil and Naomi, who were so much in love, were not big huggers. Phil always embarrassed Ruthie to death by sensually massaging Naomi's neck during parents' events—award banquets and such—at Coventry, and every night while watching TV Phil would rub Naomi's feet, but they did not hug good-bye in the morning before Phil left for the office. Phil would give his wife a wet smack on the lips, announce, "I'm off," and be gone.

Before the accident, the only time Julia and Ruthie hugged was while playing Egg and Biscuit. Egg and Biscuit was a game that Julia created, and because she created it, she got to make up all of the rules, the primary one being that Julia was always the Egg, Ruthie was always the Biscuit. Julia would stand on the far side of the room, looking forlorn, casting her eyes about but never resting them on anyone or anything until they rested on Ruthie, who stood across the room, her back to Julia.

"B-B-Biscuit?" Julia would ask, disbelieving.

Ruthie would turn, would look at Julia, would squint her eyes. "E-E-Egg?"

"Biscuit?" Julia would say again, hope creeping into her voice.

"Egg!?" Ruthie would ask.

"Biscuit!"

"Egg!"

Finally the two girls would run toward each other, screaming, "Biscuit! Egg! Biscuit! Egg!" They would meet in the middle of the room, Julia lifting Ruthie off the floor and twirling her around and around in a hug while each of them cried, "Oh, my yummy Egg! Oh, my fluffy Biscuit!"

They never really outgrew this game, continuing to play it even after Julia began high school. Of course, it was a private thing for them. Nothing they would play in front of others.

For Ruthie, it was easier to imagine the night before the accident rather than the day of. The night before, her parents were still safe, still tucked inside their fancy hotel with the glittering, flashing lobby and a myriad of overpriced restaurants to choose from. And even though their hotel room was on the twenty-sixth floor, they were, for all practical purposes, grounded. They would not plummet from the sky at the Mirage. And what they did there—the gambling excepted—was not all that different from what they did on Saturday nights in Atlanta. Get dressed up. Leave Ruthie at home with a sitter. Go somewhere expensive for dinner where Phil would order them each a glass of champagne to start and Naomi, temporarily unburdened from her motherly responsibilities, would lean back in her seat, would begin to relax.

Julia was unlike Ruthie in that she obsessively imagined the details of her parents' final day and she seemed to relish doing so. They did not know yet, during the months that followed their parents' death, that Julia would one day be a successful writer, would indeed one day write the story of her mother's early adulthood: her decision to leave her first husband, her young child—Julia!—in tow, in order to marry Phil, the man who had captured Naomi's heart during their brief romance when she was a freshman at Meredith College in Raleigh, North Carolina, and he was a senior at Duke. Phil would head to Nashville to begin law school shortly after his graduation. And because she was angry at Phil for dashing off to Vanderbilt without seeming to give a speck of thought to their budding relationship, Naomi finally agreed to go on a date with Matt Smith, a North Carolina State sophomore who had already asked her out three times.

It was Matt she would marry, Matt who would give her Julia, and Matt whose heart she would eventually break when she left him for Phil.

And so it made sense, retroactively, that Julia the writer was able to imagine Phil and Naomi's last day in such unflinching detail. And while Ruthie did not want to imagine the details herself, she allowed Julia to tell of them, because it fixed a story to the horror, which somehow made it less random. (Nothing chilled Ruthie more than the possibility that the world was a random place where parents could die for no reason.) Julia's story, which she embellished with details plucked from the encyclopedia about the Ford Trimotor, was comforting—to an extent—because it had a defined villain, Dusty Williams, the pilot. In Julia's version Dusty had started his day with a six-pack of beer, followed by a little weed. In Julia's version, Dusty's plane had twice failed inspection.

(In truth, Dusty had possessed a clean flying record, and was by all accounts a model pilot. His plane had recently been inspected. Yes, it was old, but it was in good shape. It should not have crashed. Why it did remained a mystery. Maybe there was a bad fuel load? Maybe Dusty had a heart attack once the plane was up in the air, and no one else on board knew how to fly the old Tin Goose? No one would ever know. It wasn't as if Dusty's Trimotor was equipped with a black box.)

"Well," said Julia. "You know that they got off to an early start. That Phil woke first and went down to the lobby to get a cup of coffee for Mom."

"With cream and Equal," said Ruthie. Her mother always took her coffee with real cream and Equal, an incongruity that Julia and Ruthie used to tease Naomi about.

"Right. Mom would have gotten out of the bed and pulled back the curtains, revealing a gorgeous day, the rising sun still a little pink in the sky. She would have looked out the window at the empty hotel pool, blue and sparkling all of those many feet below, too cold to swim in but nice to sit by. She might have wondered why they were leaving the hotel, were driving so many miles only to see the canyon and return to Las Vegas that night. She might have even considered asking Phil to cancel the trip, telling him that she had a headache and that the drive across the desert might make it worse."

"No," interrupted Ruthie. "She was looking forward to seeing the Grand Canyon. She told me before she left. Plus, Dad was so excited about driving that Mercedes."

"I know, I know," said Julia, impatient. "I'm just thinking that maybe that morning she had second thoughts about all of that driving. You know how bad a driver Phil was. But then he would have burst into the room holding her coffee in one hand, a Danish in the other, looking so eager, so excited, that she would have abandoned her misgivings and gotten dressed for the trip."

"It was a cool day," said Ruthie. "That's what the newspapers said."

"Cool but not too cold. Perfect for her brown linen pants and crisp white sleeveless shirt that she wore with a thin black cardigan. Phil was wearing khakis and one of those white linen shirts Mom was always buying him, a sweater tied around his waist."

"Alex's mom says you're really not supposed to wear linen until the summer," said Ruthie.

"You think they gave a shit what Alex's mom thought of them way out in the desert?"

Ruthie shrugged. No, of course not. In Buckhead, their tony Atlanta neighborhood, and among the other Coventry mothers, Naomi worried about all of the rules she didn't know, but she wouldn't have cared out there.

"They would have kept the windows of the convertible rolled up, even though the top was down, so Phil's shirt wouldn't get dirty from all of the dust kicked up on the drive."

"They were on the highway," said Ruthie. "It wasn't like they were driving *through* the desert."

"They would have had the windows rolled up anyway. To protect Mom's hair from getting all windblown."

Their mother, like Julia, had been a natural redhead, auburn, really. But while Julia's hair grew in loose curls, Naomi's was straight like Ruthie's. Naomi, who had been self-conscious about her looks, about her long nose and the little gap between her front teeth, always said that her red hair was her best feature.

"She would have wrapped a scarf around it," said Ruthie. "One of the silk ones she and Dad bought in Florence."

"Right. That's right. A Ferragamo. So they were all dressed and ready to go—no need to pack the luggage; they were coming back late that night—but just before they left the room Mom suggested that they call home, just to check on you, just to say hello."

In fact, her parents had not called the morning of the accident, and the possibility that Naomi had considered doing so caused Ruthie's throat to tighten, caused her to have to lay her head on Julia's bed to account for the heaviness she suddenly felt.

"But Phil said no. If Mother Martha answered they would have to talk with her for at least ten minutes—she was so hard to get off the phone—and besides, they had spoken with you just the night before. Plus, it was already nine A.M., they had a long drive ahead of them, and they did not want to waste away the morning in the hotel room. So Mom said fine, she'd call tomorrow when she could tell you all about seeing the Grand Canyon.

"Phil would have already arranged to have the rental car

dropped off at the hotel, and so they would have stepped outside the lobby doors to find the cherry red Mercedes convertible waiting for them, keys in the ignition, top already down."

"Otherwise Dad wouldn't have been able to figure out how to do it," Ruthie said.

(Phil's lack of mechanical know-how had always been a running joke between the two girls. They used to tease him mercilessly about his habit of watching *This Old House* every Saturday afternoon.

"Do you even know how to hammer a nail?" Ruthie would ask her father.

You had to be careful about teasing Phil, because if his feelings were hurt he might lash out fiercely. But he always had the same response to his daughters' jokes about his devotion to *This Old House*.

"I need to know what to look out for when I supervise the help," he would say, and Julia and Ruthie would groan and roll their eyes.)

"They would climb in the car, which smelled of new leather, and Phil would slip *The Eagles—Their Greatest Hits*, brought from Atlanta, just for the occasion, into the CD player. Mom would check and make sure he had his driving directions with him, and he would wave away her concern but then go ahead and pat his breast pocket to make sure the directions were there. And then they were off."

There was not too much they could imagine about the drive to the Grand Canyon, besides the wind whipping around their parents' hair, despite the windows of the convertible being rolled up. Neither Ruthie nor Julia had been anywhere out west besides San Francisco, so they didn't really know what the scenery looked like. They imagined that the road was empty, the sun was big, and there were cacti everywhere.

The noise from the wind would have made it too loud for their parents to talk during the drive, but Julia imagined that Phil slipped his hand onto Naomi's leg once they made their way out of the city of Las Vegas and onto the open road. And both girls imagined that Phil drove way too fast, for he always sped, even when his daughters were strapped into the back of the car. Ruthie remembered one time when they were driving to Union City, Tennessee, to attend Naomi's parents' fiftieth wedding anniversary and Phil took the car up to 100 mph. Naomi was asleep in the front seat, her head leaning against the window, but Julia, who was sitting behind Phil in the back, noticed where the needle on the speedometer was and pointed it out to Ruthie, who screamed, convinced that they were all going to die in a fiery crash.

"Phil must have driven even faster than normal to the Grand Canyon, because they arrived at Grand View Flights by two P.M. And we know they stopped for lunch before doing that."

That detail had been revealed in the front-page story about the accident that the *Atlanta Journal-Constitution* Metro section ran. Of course, you had to read past the jump to learn that Phil and Naomi last dined on huevos rancheros at a gas station in Arizona that housed within it a breakfast counter known for good Mexican food. The owner of the gas station, Javier Martin, a white-haired man with a waxed mustache, said the couple stood out to him, and not just because they were the only folks eating.

"They just seemed real in love, is all," Javier was quoted as saying. "Making googly eyes and touching their knees together like they was on their honeymoon."

To Javier Martin, Ruthie and Julia's parents must have seemed like a couple from a movie: Naomi with her vibrant red hair, her silk scarf, her linen pants and crisp white shirt; Phil with his linen shirt, Stetson hat—surely purchased sometime during the vacation, for it was mentioned twice in the newspaper article, but neither Ruthie nor Julia had ever seen it—and cherry red Mercedes.

Perhaps even Phil and Naomi were aware of the cinematic nature of their jaunt to the Grand Canyon; perhaps that was why they readily signed the pages of release forms at Grand View Flights, agreeing not to sue should anything happen to them on their flight. Perhaps the whole day felt a little unreal and so they took a risk that they might not normally have taken, because, hell, they were on vacation, it was a beautiful day, they were dressed so elegantly: what could happen?

"You know Phil talked Mom into it," said Julia. "You know she would have been nervous about boarding that rickety old plane, she would have suggested they just look at the canyon through a telescope, or even ride a donkey down into it. And Dad would have thrown his hands up in exasperation, said, 'Naomi! You look for a snake under every rock.'"

This was something Phil often said to Naomi, who was a worrier like Ruthie. Or he would say, "See what I have to put up with?" when Naomi scolded him about driving too fast, or told him Julia was absolutely too old to order off the children's menu, despite the deal, or refused to use the "nearly new" Kleenex he dug out of his pocket when Naomi sneezed, the folded halves of which were stuck suspiciously together, even though he promised he had not used it to blow his nose. He would grin at his daughters, repeating himself: "See what I have to put up with?" While everyone—Phil included—knew it was Naomi who had to put up with him.

"He might have talked her into it, but she wouldn't have boarded the plane if she didn't really want to do it," said Ruthie. "She liked adventure."

"And so they got in, waved to Dusty at the controls, his headphones already on, his eyes a little bloodshot from the six-pack of beer he had finished at his trailer earlier that day. The plane's interior was elegant if antiquated, its wicker seats bolted to the floor. There was room for ten passengers on the plane, but there was only one other couple besides Mom and Dad on board. A childless couple in their fifties, on vacation from Canada. The rows were only one seat wide, so Mom and Phil had to hold hands across the aisle. They fastened their safety belts tightly against their laps. They waited to take off, excited. And then the engine noises intensified, and they were moving forward, picking up speed until the plane was going fast enough to lift off the ground.

"Everything was so loud around them, louder even than it had been on the convertible ride across the desert, and then they were going up, up, up, toward the clear blue sky. And Mom would have whispered, 'Off we go, into the wild blue yonder,' because she always whispered that at takeoff on airplanes. And her heart would have lifted at the excitement of what she and Phil were doing, she would have felt light and free and alive, and then she would have heard a terrible noise and the plane would have shook—"

"Stop," said Ruthie. "I don't want to think about that. I don't want to think about the actual crash."

But clearly Julia was feeling devilish, was feeling charged. She wanted to finish her story; she wanted to tell all its details, including the conclusion: the nosedive that ended in an explosive crash against the side of the canyon, the crash that left all five of them, the childless couple from Canada, Dusty, Phil, and Naomi, dead. To tell the story was to control it somehow.

"What did Mom think about during those last few seconds? Did she think about what would happen to us? Was she furious at Phil for pressuring her into boarding the plane? Did she try and pretend that everything still might turn out okay, that the plane might touch ground lightly, despite all evidence to the contrary? Did she pray? Did she cry? Did she and Phil kiss?"

Ruthie could not listen to her sister anymore. She banged her fists against her sister's chest and shoulders, yelling, "Shut up, Julia. Just shut up!"

Part One

Chapter One

Spring 1993

When the call came from Grand View Flights in Arizona, Ruthie was in the kitchen fixing dinner while her grandmother—stepgrandmother, really, but she had served as Phil's mother since he was three—was sitting in the sunporch, sipping from an Amaretto sour that Ruthie had prepared.

Ruthie loved to prepare and serve food. She had been doing it since she was a little girl and would squish Cool Whip between Nilla wafers and invite Julia to a tea party. More often than not Julia said no, preferring that the time she spent with her little sister be on her own terms. Naomi would come to Ruthie's tea parties, when she wasn't too busy cleaning up around the house or fixing dinner. Some Saturdays when Naomi was off getting her nails done, Ruthie was able to talk her father into joining her, though he often acted bored, and would bring the newspaper to read while she poured tea and served him Nilla sandwiches.

Mother Martha, who had a black maid named Gwen in Tennessee who prepared and served her meals, was delighted for Ruthie to fill Gwen's place. Indeed, the meal Ruthie planned to serve—chicken breasts cooked in cream of mushroom soup, baked beef rice, and steamed broccoli with cheese—was not all that different from what Gwen would have fixed.

Using the back of a wooden spoon, Ruthie spread the soup over the skinless chicken breasts, which she had arranged in an eight-inch-square Pyrex dish. The soup was so gelatinous that when Ruthie first plopped it out of the can a ringed indentation remained around its middle. Ruthie knew from past experience that once heated the soup would loosen and turn into a yummy sauce.

The phone rang twice and then stopped. Mother Martha must have answered. That was okay. Ruthie's parents usually called later in the evening—it was only 5:30—and all of her friends were out of town with their families, on spring-break vacations that had been planned months in advance.

Then it occurred to Ruthie that it might be her sister, Julia, calling. Julia was spending spring break with her friend Marissa Tate, at the Tates' beach house on Pawleys Island, and had not yet phoned to tell Ruthie "hi."

Ruthie walked toward the phone. She would rescue Julia from Mother Martha, who was notorious for never letting anyone hang up. Even if you said, "I've got to go; I'm going to be late" for a birthday party, ballet practice, youth group, whatever, Mother Martha would ask you a new question, would refuse to let you say good-bye.

Ruthie picked up the phone. "Julia?" she asked.

"Hang up, dear," said Mother Martha, a little sharply. When Ruthie hesitated—was her grandmother crying?—Mother Martha said, *"Now."*

Ruthie hung up the phone with a sinking feeling. Julia must have gotten in trouble. Julia was always getting in trouble, and the problem was, her getting caught was almost always unnecessary. At least that was what Ruthie thought. Like the Saturday night that Julia came home from a cast party drunk. Had she gone straight to her room and closed the door, neither Naomi nor Phil would have bothered her. But instead she approached Ruthie's room, waiting in the doorway while Naomi said good night. Julia pretended to read while she was waiting, but she was so tipsy she didn't realize that she was holding her book—*Zen and the Art of Motorcycle Maintenance*—upside down.

Naomi noticed.

And once Naomi noticed that, how could she not notice the fact that Julia smelled of alcohol? And so Julia was busted, grounded for two weeks, the use of her Saab limited to driving to and from school. In a way this pleased Ruthie—it meant Julia would be forced to spend more time with her—but also, it scared her. Ruthie hated for her sister to be in trouble, hated that her sister got drunk.

Ruthie couldn't worry about Julia. She would think about dinner, about the chicken. It would take about forty-five minutes to cook, and the rice an hour, so she would put the breasts aside for a moment. She went to the refrigerator to take out a stick of butter, then to the pantry for the rice and the beef consommé. To a yellow porcelain pot her mother had bought in France Ruthie added a cup of uncooked rice, a chopped onion, the can of beef consommé, four tablespoons of butter, and a dash of Worcestershire sauce. Following her mother's instructions, written in perfect script in a black-and-white-speckled notebook Naomi had filled with recipes when she was in the tenth grade, Ruthie would bake the ingredients, covered, in the oven at 350 degrees. The ingredients would meld, and an hour later the rice would be tender, rich, and buttery.

She was sliding the yellow pot into the oven when Mother Martha walked into the kitchen, her face pale and drawn. The pink rouge she wore stood out against her white skin.

"Ruthie dear," she said.

Ruthie closed the oven door and turned to face her grandmother.

"Ruthie, I need you to sit down with me," said Mother Martha, her voice strange, choked.

Concerned, Ruthie hurried to her grandmother, whose legs were shaking, on the verge of collapse. She put her hand on Mother Martha's forearm and guided her to a seat at the kitchen table.

What had Julia done? Ruthie sat in the chair next to her grandmother, already thinking up excuses for her sister's bad behavior. Mother Martha just sat there. Twice she opened her mouth, but no words came out.

"What's wrong?" Ruthie finally asked.

Though Mother Martha was looking at Ruthie, her filmy blue eyes seemed focused on something far away. "Oh God," she said.

This was shocking. Ruthie's grandmother never took the Lord's name in vain.

Tears pooled in the old woman's eyes. "Oh, my poor, poor baby."

"What? What is it?" asked Ruthie, her heart rate increasing.

Mother Martha reached a shaking hand out to her, and Ruthie grabbed it, more because she wanted to steady the hand than anything else. Her grandmother's hands, which she rubbed with cocoa butter every night, were smooth and soft.

"There was an accident."

"Is Julia okay?" asked Ruthie. It was hard to get out the words. Her mouth was dry.

"It's your parents, dear. They were in an accident."

Ruthie's first feeling was relief. Julia was not in an accident. Julia was not in trouble.

"Are they okay?" asked Ruthie, not even imagining that they might not be.

And then Mother Martha started crying, tears spilling over her eyes, running down her cheeks, and taking her makeup with them so that her pink cheeks were streaked with pale lines where the skin showed through.

"Oh, you poor, poor baby," cried Mother Martha.

Ruthie shivered involuntarily. "What happened?" she asked. "Where are they?"

Mother Martha could not keep it together. She was crying so hard now she couldn't speak. She was pressing her fist into her mouth, as if trying to press back words she did not want to say.

Ruthie had to speak for her, trying to narrow down the

possibilities by asking the right questions, as if they were playing a game, as if her next question should be, "Is it bigger than a bread box?"

"Are they in the hospital?"

She imagined her father driving too fast on some desert highway, not slowing for the curve. She imagined Phil losing control, the car spinning, sliding off the road, finally stopping when it hit a lone tree. She imagined a tuft of hair through broken glass, blood. And then she saw them lying on separate hospital beds, banged up, bruised and bandaged, separated from each other by a long hall and cold, efficient nurses, like the nurse in that movie Julia made her watch, *One Flew over the Cuckoo's Nest*.

Mother Martha opened her mouth but again said nothing. She blinked her eyes several times in a row. "Get me a napkin please, dear," she said.

Ruthie stood, walked to the counter, opened a drawer, and grabbed a paper napkin for her grandmother, a heavy white one with a scalloped design along its border. She sat down again at the table, handed the napkin to the old woman. Mother Martha dotted her eyes with it, swallowed hard, and spoke.

"They died, sweetheart. In a small plane that crashed into the Grand Canyon. Everyone on the plane died. Your parents, the two other passengers, the pilot . . . all lost."

Ruthie was trying to listen, trying to understand, but Mother Martha's words just did not make any sense at all.

Ruthie was upstairs in her sister's room, burrowed beneath the pale green bedspread flecked with tiny pink flowers, waiting. She told herself it was all a mistake. Her parents were not dead. Mother Martha was old and had been confused. Julia would straighten things out. As soon as they figured out where she was, Julia would make things okay.

Except they could not find her. When Mother Martha phoned the Tates' beach house, asking to speak to Julia, Mrs. Tate had sounded confused. "Why, Julia couldn't come," she said. "Marissa invited her, but Julia said she had too much schoolwork to catch up on and her parents wouldn't let her go." Next Mother Martha had called Julia's father, Matt, in Virginia. He had not heard from her, either, and then Mother Martha had to explain everything, had to tell Matt that in addition to the fact that his daughter was missing, his first wife was dead.

Mother Martha asked Ruthie if there were any friends of Julia's they could call. Ruthie knew that Julia hung out with a group of boys who wore black, but she didn't know any of their real names. She only knew the nicknames they called each other: Roach, Wanker, Dickhead, and Guido. She thought about Dmitri, Julia's first boyfriend, but decided there was no way she could be with him. Dmitri was too straightlaced, too good, to allow Julia to hide out with him when she was supposed to be at the Tates'. Mother Martha was starting to panic, was walking up and down the tiled kitchen floor, wringing a red dish towel in her hands, muttering, "I just don't know what to do. I just don't know what to do."

The raw chicken, surrounded by the cold gelatinous soup, still sat on the counter in its eight-inch-square Pyrex dish.

"I need to lie down," mumbled Ruthie. "I'm feeling sick."

She had slunk out of the kitchen, not even sure if Mother Martha noticed.

There was a pink Princess phone in Julia's room, on the bedside table. That night the phone rang often. Ruthie would lift the receiver and listen in after she was sure Mother Martha had answered. She had to make sure the caller was not Julia, calling to say where she was, calling to explain why she had not been with Marissa. But it was always someone else, someone who had heard about the accident and was calling to express sympathy, to ask, "What can I do?" Relatives. Old friends of Naomi's. Colleagues of Phil's. Even the *Atlanta Journal-Constitution* called. They were running a story. They wanted a current photo of Phil and Naomi. They wanted a photo from Phil and Naomi's wedding day.

The wedding had been at city hall. Naomi, who was only beginning to show, had worn a pale blue pants suit over a white blouse. Julia, in a blue and white plaid jumper and white collar, stood by her side. Phil wore the black pin-striped suit he had worn that day to the office. Naomi used to say that she felt so guilty for leaving Matt to marry Phil, she didn't think she deserved a real wedding. Not for the second time around.

Ruthie heard Mother Martha walking up the front stairs, slowly. Pulling the bedspread over her head, she closed her eyes. She would pretend she was asleep. She heard the flick of a switch as Mother Martha turned the hall light on. Ruthie heard a soft knocking on the door. She did not answer, but Mother Martha opened it anyway.

"Dear," she said, standing in the doorway. "Dear, I'm going to have to call the police if we don't locate Julia soon. You don't have any idea where she might be, do you? She won't be in trouble, I promise. We just, we must find her."

Ruthie slowly lowered the bedspread from over her head.

"I don't know where she is," she whispered.

She pulled the cover back over herself so that all Mother Martha could see was a bit of her dark hair.

Where could her sister be? Not with Marissa, not with Dmitri. Possibly with other friends of hers from the theater group, but wouldn't most of them be on vacations with their families? When she heard Mother Martha close the door to her bedroom down the hall, Ruthie pushed away the covers, got out of bed. Julia had given Ruthie dire warnings not to touch her stuff, but it wasn't as if she were here to get mad. Ruthie opened the single drawer of the bedside table, looking for clues as to where her sister might be. There were some scattered matchbooks, a Bic lighter, some safety pins, a bunch of blue pens without tops, some folded-over notebook paper that when opened revealed several poems that Julia had started.

Ruthie walked to the chest of drawers. Opened the top left drawer where Julia kept her underwear. Ran her fingers beneath the panties and bras. Came up with several quarters and some price tags clipped from new clothes. She opened the top right drawer, the one where Julia kept her socks. Pushed the balls of socks around. Found a box of Altoids. She opened it, and inside was a thin white cigarette. A joint.

Ruthie closed the box, quickly, as if its contents were contagious. Looked at herself for a moment in the mirror above the dresser. Looked at her straight, flat brown hair. The two pimples on the lower half of her face. The circles under her brown eyes, circles that had mysteriously appeared within the past few hours, as if her body were marking itself for grief. As if her body had decided to proclaim to the world: Here is an unlucky girl.

Ruthie noticed something in the corner of the mirror. A strip of four photos, taken in a booth. Photos of Julia—her mouth open wide in every one, as if she were dying laughing—with a straight-faced boy with long blond hair that came past his shoulders. Jake. Jake Robinson. Jake the senior who wore a black leather jacket atop glaringly white T-shirts, who wore his long blond hair pulled back into a ponytail during the day—per Coventry's rules—but let it loose as soon as he left campus. Julia had pointed him out to Ruthie, said he burst through doors at school as if he were storming out of a bar after a fight.

Julia had told Ruthie that his mom had died when he was little and now he lived alone with his dad in Ansley Park, a pretty neighborhood bordered by the High Museum on one side and Piedmont Park on the other. Julia said that Jake and his dad acted like bachelor roommates. If no one answered when you called their home, the answering machine told you to leave a message for "the Robinson boys." They would drink beers while watching sports on TV; they would make sure to knock before entering each other's rooms.

Ruthie knew her sister had a crush on Jake but hadn't realized they were actually hanging out. But here was proof, Julia's laugh captured on film. She would call his house, see if he knew anything about where Julia might be. See if she might possibly be there, hanging out with "the Robinson boys."

Ruthie looked under the bed for the Coventry directory. For some reason, her sister always kept it there, as if it were a thing to be hidden. She found it beside a box filled with photos of Julia and her theater friends, plus Phil and Naomi's copy of *The Joy of Sex*, stolen from underneath their bed.

Under normal circumstances Ruthie would have taken the time to flip through its pages, to ogle the drawings of the woman with the hairy armpits, the man with the scraggly beard. But not tonight. Tonight the strange pictures held no allure. Ruthie flipped to the "Rs" in the Coventry directory and found the listing, Jake Robinson, 22 Westminster Drive. She dialed the number. The phone rang and rang. On the sixth ring, a man picked up. His voice was low and scratchy, and he sounded confused, as if she had woken him in the middle of a dream.

"This is Ruthie Harrison—may I please speak with Jake?"

Her best friend Alex Love's mom had taught her that this was the correct way to introduce yourself on the phone, after Ruthie once called and simply asked, "Is Alex there?"

The voice on the other end coughed. Then it was silent for a minute. "May I please speak with Jake?" Ruthie asked again, louder this time.

There was silence, a silence that lasted so long Ruthie was about to hang up, but then she heard rustling and another male voice said hello.

"Is this Jake?" she asked.

"Who wants to know?"

"It's Ruthie Harrison, Julia's sister," she said, wondering as soon as the words were out of her mouth if Jake would be confused. She and Julia did not share the same last name. Julia's last name was Smith, same as her biological father's.

"I really need to speak with Julia. Is she there? It's an emergency."

Jake, or whoever it was on the other line, mumbled "fuck."

"Hang on," he said, and then he whispered, "Jules, I think you need to take this."

"Tell them I'm not here," Ruthie heard Julia whisper back.

"I think it's your little sister."

And then Julia was on the other end, her voice higher than normal, as if she were trying to disguise it. "Hello?"

Ruthie started to cry. Disguised though it might be, it *was* her sister's voice on the other end of the phone. And this meant that she was not in another state, not far away. Indeed, Ansley Park was fewer than four miles from Ruthie and Julia's home in Buckhead.

"Is that you, spaz? What the hell are you doing? Why are you calling me here?"

Ruthie cried harder. There was too much to say.

"Sweetie, what is it? I'm sorry, I didn't mean to be a jerk, it's just—I'll be up shit creek if Mom and Dad find out I'm here. You can't tell them. Promise?"

"Mom and Dad are dead and you have to come home," said Ruthie. "You have to come home."

And then something happened. Suddenly. She dropped the phone and she was on the floor by Julia's bed choking and crying, crying so hard it was difficult to breathe. She was a baby in the crib, crying for milk. She needed her mother. She needed her mother. Her mother whose gentle voice could soothe her after a nightmare, whose fingernails were always kept long, perfect for scratching a daughter's back. She needed her mother.

Her sister would come.

Within twenty minutes Julia was pulling up the driveway in the Saab 900, jumping out of the car and slamming its door shut, walking briskly around to the back of the house, since the heavy front door could only be opened by the turn lock inside and not a key. Ruthie heard Julia moving through the kitchen, heard Julia running up the back staircase, the staircase that included a "moving" chair that chugged up and down a metal ramp, a leftover from the time an old invalid woman had lived in their house. Julia was opening the door to the upstairs hall and then Julia was there, in the doorway of her room.

Julia. Julia. Her lips were red and swollen, probably from kissing Jake Robinson all afternoon. The rims of her eyes were red, the whites bloodshot. She wore a filmy shirt with a swirly purple design, hippie looking but sexy, too. She did not have on a bra; her nipples poked out from the thin fabric. Her jeans, Levi's, were well worn, faded. Beneath them she was barefoot. She always went barefoot, drove barefoot, too, and though this made Phil crazy, made him go out of his mind, she kept doing it anyway.

Ruthie stayed on her bed, her back toward her sister. She wanted to jump up, to rush toward Julia, to bury her head against her shoulder, to not look up again until everything was straightened out, but she was not able to make herself move. To move, to run, to embrace Julia would make it all true. The moment of impact, Ruthie's body against her sister's, would mean her parents really had died.

Impossible.

Julia climbed into bed with her. She smelled of cigarettes, alcohol, and something else, something that reminded Ruthie of bleach but did not seem entirely clean.

"Scoot over," Julia said, for Ruthie was lying in the middle. Ruthie obeyed. Usually when she and Julia slept in the same bed Julia would draw a line with her finger, marking which side was hers, which Ruthie's. Julia usually allowed herself three-quarters of the bed while Ruthie had to fit within the remaining quarter, which she was happy to do, as long as her sister let her stay.

Julia lay close beside her, let her little sister spoon into her, put her arms around her, and whispered in her ear, "It's going to be all right. It's going to be all right."

The funeral was held the following Monday, a funeral with no bodies. The plane had exploded after impact, and the bodies had burned.

Nearly everyone came. Relatives drove from Tennessee, including

Naomi's sister Linda, who brought her mother, Granny Wigham, whose mind had deteriorated rapidly since the death of her husband. Aunt Mimi and Uncle Robert flew in from San Francisco. Many of Ruthie's and Julia's classmates from Coventry attended, let out early from school, along with a handful of teachers who had arranged for substitutes to teach their afternoon classes. Julia's old boyfriend, Dmitri, showed up with his parents, but Ruthie did not see Jake Robinson. The staff, associates, and partners from Phil's law firm were there, along with Addie Mae the housekeeper, and a sizeable percentage of the Trinity Church membership. Friends of Naomi from her hometown of Union City, Tennessee, came, along with friends of hers from Virden, Virginia, who had never before forgiven her for leaving Matt for Phil. Beatrice, Phil's first wife, who lived in Nashville with her second husband and their three sons, did not come.

Matt and Peggy did. When they first arrived at the house on Wymberly Way, Peggy, wearing a blue denim jumper over a white T-shirt, her shoulder-length blond hair in a tidy braid, had asked to speak to Julia alone. They went into the formal living room, a baronial space with wood-beamed ceilings. Ruthie listened outside the door as Peggy lectured Julia, told her that while she knew now was not the time to discuss it, she did not want Julia to think that no one cared that she had lied about where she was going for spring break and had stayed for four nights at the home of an eighteen-year-old boy.

"From now on I am going to keep a close eye on you," said Peggy. "Because I love you too much not to. Now come give me a hug."

The funeral. The funeral. Ruthie's memory from that day was so fuzzy. Years later, in the first waking moments after having the abortion, she would be reminded of the fuzziness of the funeral while waiting in the recovery room at the clinic in San Francisco. The world was both sharp and blurry. The pain sharp, the details blurry.

At the funeral there were so many people and they were all touching her, hugging her. Even her mean math teacher, Mrs. Stanford. Ruthie was trying not to cry. Aunt Mimi and Naomi's sister, Linda, who lived in Memphis, had sat down with the minister the day before to tell him all they remembered about Phil and Naomi. Mimi said she wanted to give a tribute, but she thought she would be too broken up to do so. The minister did a good job. Spoke well of Ruthie's parents. Wove in funny details, like what Phil wrote in Naomi's college yearbook, so many years ago: "I wish I could leave you with a better impression of me, if that were at all possible." Spoke about the gift of married love, of how well Phil and Naomi had loved each other. Told them, "The Lord is my shepherd, I shall not want."

Julia held Ruthie's hand during the ceremony. Her aunt Mimi sat on Ruthie's other side, her husband, Robert, beside her. Mimi cried while prayers were said for the souls of Phil and Naomi. Ruthie watched Mimi cry, wondering how it was that Mimi could look so pretty, even in these circumstances, her manicured hand periodically swiping at the corners of her eyes with a delicate cloth handkerchief.

After the funeral everyone was invited back to the house. Mimi had arranged it, said it was necessary to provide a place for the many mourners, to let them drink, eat, maybe even laugh a little over their memories of Phil and Naomi. There was not much laughing. The guests stood in solemn little clusters, drinks in hand, talking quietly, stealing glances at Ruthie in the straight black skirt that came to her knees and a white button-down oxford shirt of Julia's. It occurred to Ruthie that she looked like a very young caterer. Her feet hurt from standing so long, but Mimi had cleared out the chairs in the dining room to make the table into a buffet and all of the sofas in the living room were occupied. A makeshift bar had been set up in the sunporch, and Walt, who lived in the garage apartment behind the house, was serving beer and pouring wine and bourbon for whoever wanted it.

Mimi must have arranged beforehand for Walt to come pour drinks. Either Mimi or Alex's mom, Mrs. Love, who always knew exactly the right thing to do in any circumstance, who had called the night before, telling Mimi to please let her know how she could help. Who, like Aunt Mimi, wore a sleeveless black sheath and a pearl choker. Only Mrs. Love's hair was not pulled back into a chignon, like Mimi's, but was instead swept back with a wide yellow headband. To the house she had brought two beef tenderloins, four packages of Pepperidge Farm rolls, and little dishes of mayonnaise mixed with horseradish to spread on the meat.

Someone had brought a HoneyBaked ham, someone else a pound cake. There were cut-up vegetables and dip from Publix. At first the vegetables were placed on the dining room table still arranged on the black plastic Publix tray they came on, but someone (Mimi? Mrs. Love?) had intervened and placed the vegetables prettily on a large silver platter. It was not Ruthie's mother's platter—the only silver Naomi had owned was her Rose Tiara flatware, which Julia would inherit—so the arranger of the vegetables was probably Mrs. Love. She probably had brought over a stack of silver platters, knowing they would come in handy.

Ruthie wanted to go upstairs to her room, close the door, and lie down on the bed. But how could she, with so many people, so many mourners come to witness her grief? Everyone who walked by her touched her. Gave her shoulder a squeeze, patted her on the arm, or pulled her in for a hug. She stationed herself by the dining room table, fixing beef tenderloin sandwiches with the horseradish mayonnaise. She had barely eaten anything before the funeral. Just a frozen honey bun, heated in the microwave. The meat was so good, so soft, so rare. She ate four sandwiches, quickly, stuffing them in her mouth to discourage anyone from trying to talk to her.

Mrs. Love, in her sleek black dress and pearls, came and stood behind her, put her long fingers on Ruthie's shoulders, rubbed. She smelled of Joy perfume, of bottled roses. Ruthie wondered, briefly, if Mrs. Love would let Ruthie and Julia come live with her, with the Love family. Life at the Loves' house would be so different. Alex had so many rules. No TV during weeknights, only one dessert a day, no white shoes after Labor Day, thank-you notes to be written promptly, no later than one week past receiving a gift.

Julia would never survive.

Where *was* Julia? Ruthie glanced around, while Mrs. Love's fingers continued to massage her shoulders. There she was in the sunporch, talking to Walt, the makeshift bartender. Julia, wearing a black peasant skirt made of fabric that looked like crumpled tissue paper, did not look all that different from how she usually appeared. Ruthie noticed that Julia was holding a coffee cup discreetly by her side. Ruthie guessed that the cup was filled with bourbon, which Julia once told Ruthie was a mourner's drink, a drink for sorrow.

She turned to face Mrs. Love, who smiled sadly before wrapping her arms around her, pulling her in for an embrace.

"You don't know how sorry I am, sweetheart," Mrs. Love whispered into Ruthie's hair.

Ruthie felt tears forming. She nodded as politely as she could while trying to avoid eye contact with Mrs. Love. If Ruthie looked straight at her, she might start to cry.

"I'm going to go see how my sister is," she said.

"It's so good you two have each other," said Mrs. Love.

Ruthie walked across the dining room and down the three steps that led to the sunporch, where Julia stood with Walt.

"Hey, spaz," said Julia.

Ruthie shot her a mean look.

"Sorry, sorry. Hey, Ruthie."

"Do you have any Sprite?" she asked Walt.

He shook his head. "All I've got is beer, white and red wine, and the stuff that was in your dad's liquor cabinet."

It must have been Mimi who had arranged for Walt to bartend, because Mrs. Love would not have forgotten to include drinks for the kids.

"You want to go get one?" asked Julia. "I can drive you to the BP on Peachtree."

Ruthie was torn. On the one hand, there was nothing she would rather do than leave this gathering of people who felt sorry for her. On the other hand, she was not sure if that was allowed. Also, she was almost positive that Julia had been drinking, and she did not want to be the victim of a drunk-driving accident. Just that year she had read *Izzy, Willy-Nilly*, a novel about a girl who was paralyzed from the waist down after being in a drunk-driving accident.

"Will you let me drive?" Ruthie asked.

"You're thirteen."

"You've let me drive in the Baptist parking lot before," said Ruthie. "It's easy."

Walt covered his ears with his hands. "I'm going to pretend I know nothing about this conversation," he said.

Julia motioned toward the side door with her head. "First let's get out of here," she said.

Telling no one besides Walt that they were leaving, Ruthie and Julia slipped out the door in the sunporch that led to the side yard where Naomi had her herb garden, which was overrun with rosemary and mint. Ducking past windows, they walked to the front of the house and then ran as fast as they could down the driveway.

"Which way?" asked Ruthie at the foot of the drive.

"This way," said Julia, a little breathless but still running. She turned right on Wymberly Way, and they ran down the street to where Julia had parked her car. Ruthie wondered if her sister had purposefully parked the Saab far away, where it wouldn't be noticed, if she had been planning to sneak out of the memorial, to visit Jake Robinson perhaps, though he had not even bothered to show up for the service.

It was a sunny day, blue sky, warm. The tall trees overhead had tiny buds on their branches, and all over birds were calling back and forth.

"You really want to drive?" asked Julia, winded from running.

Ruthie nodded emphatically. Suddenly there was nothing else she would rather do.

Ruthie was creeping down Wymberly Way going 15 miles an hour, her seat pushed so far up that her body was scrunched against the steering wheel. Julia had insisted. Otherwise, Julia said, Ruthie wouldn't be able to reach the pedals.

"I'm as tall as you," Ruthie had said.

"*Au contraire*, my *frère*," said Julia.

Ruthie was scared to be behind the wheel, to be controlling Julia's Saab, but also, she was thrilled.

"Sweetie, you are going to get pulled over for going this slow," said Julia. "You've got to speed up."

Ruthie pressed hard on the accelerator and the car leapt forward.

"Jesus," murmured Julia. Ruthie smiled. In a weird way, she was enjoying herself.

"Do you know where your turn signal is?" asked Julia.

Ruthie nodded.

"Okay, slow down—no, not like that. Don't slam on the brake. Be gentle. Gently press on the brake. Okay, good. We are going to come to a complete stop. Now put on your turn signal. We're going left."

Ruthie did as she was told.

"Look both ways. Do you see any cars coming? In either direction? Okay, repeat after me: S-T-O-P-one-two-three. That's what my driver's ed teacher said to say every time you reach a stop sign."

"S-T-O-P-one-two-three," said Ruthie.

"Now you can turn."

She turned, driving slowly down Peachtree Battle Avenue, passing gracious homes and old trees, women in shiny warm-up outfits walking speedily along the sidewalk, their arms curling weights while they moved.

"There's a car behind you, Ruthie, and he's not driving like a ninety-year-old lady, so you are going to have to either pull over or speed up."

Ruthie pressed on the gas and the needle on the speedometer

climbed to 40. She was driving, really driving, on a real road, not in the parking lot of the Second Ponce de Leon Baptist Church.

"They're going to make me live with Dad and Peggy," said Julia. "In Virden. And Aunt Mimi is going to take you with her to San Francisco. At least that's what Mimi thinks is in the will. She says we'll know for sure tomorrow, once the lawyer comes to read it."

Ruthie felt dizzy, nauseated. She was breathing fast little breaths, like she still did every time she was on a plane that hit turbulence. She lifted her foot from the accelerator, let the car coast on its own, losing speed. A driver behind her laid on the horn, honking for her to accelerate, but she did not. Without Julia even instructing Ruthie to do so, she put on her right blinker, steered the car over to the side of the road, and pressed hard on the brake.

"Put it in park," said Julia, her voice calm, soothing.

Ruthie obeyed.

The two girls sat in the car, not saying anything.

They switched seats so Julia could drive. First she drove them to the BP on Peachtree so Ruthie could get a Sprite and then back up Peachtree Battle until they reached Memorial Park, which occupied several acres of land. Sometimes she and Julia would run along the park's perimeter, Ruthie always tiring out before her sister. Deep in the park itself was an area with swings and a slide, wood chips on the ground. It was empty. Julia and Ruthie walked to it, sat on the swings.

"Remember how you used to tell me not to swing too high or I'd flip over the bar?" Ruthie asked.

"That once happened to me," said Julia, smiling. "I had red marks from gripping the chains so tightly when I flipped. Otherwise I would have come slamming to the ground."

"You are so full of it," said Ruthie.

Julia smiled.

"The moon didn't follow you, either," said Ruthie.

"What are you talking about?"

"At night, when we were in the back of the car while Dad was driving us back from dinner or something, you used to tell me that you cast a spell on the moon to make it follow you wherever you went. Then you'd point the moon out to me through the window, and the whole drive home I would watch it follow us."

"Face it," said Julia. "I'm full of magic."

"Ha," said Ruthie. "You couldn't really cough up money, either."

Julia used to amaze Ruthie with that trick. She would cough, hold her hand to her mouth, and pull away a ten-dollar bill.

"You forget I'm part Mattaponi," said Julia. "On my dad's side. It gives me mystical powers."

"Okay, so if being, like, one-sixteenth Indian gives you mystical powers, use them to tell me where Mom and Dad are right now."

Julia sighed, and Ruthie thought she might not answer, that Ruthie had annoyed her by bringing up the subject they were trying to avoid. Ruthie pushed against the ground with her feet and started swinging in earnest.

"Honestly," said Julia. "I think they're gone. I mean, maybe some of their ash floated into the atmosphere, and in a billion years will become a part of a star. But other than that . . ."

Julia shrugged her shoulders, defeated.

Ruthie felt an ache in her chest. "You don't believe in heaven?" she asked, remembering afterwards one of her father's favorite lawyer sayings: "Never ask a question if you don't want to know the answer."

"No," said Julia. "I'm sorry, but I kind of think this is it."

Ruthie wondered why, given her sister's capacity for storytelling, Julia couldn't believe—or even just pretend to believe—that their parents were more than dusty, weightless things.

Ruthie felt so strange swinging back and forth with her sister. Swinging made her realize, in a way that she had not before, how thoroughly the laws of physics had been changed. Before the accident, before the funeral, before Julia told her that she was to go to Virden and Ruthie to San Francisco, she had been anchored so securely to the world. What a terrible thing to now be loosed.

Chapter Two

The day after the funeral one of the attorneys from Phil's firm, John Henry Parker, arrived at Julia and Ruthie's house to read the will. It was raining outside, raining hard, and he was wet, smiling apologetically at Aunt Mimi as he stood in the entry hall of the house, his overcoat dripping.

"I usually carry an umbrella," he said.

"You poor thing," said Aunt Mimi. Though she was Naomi's age, Mimi looked younger. She was wearing slim black pants and a bright green button-down shirt, her blond hair pulled into a girlish ponytail that twisted into the shape of an S. "Let me take your coat and get you a towel."

Ruthie was standing in the front hall by the marble table with the antique music box, watching. Mr. Parker put down his brown leather briefcase before sliding out of his coat. She knew that a copy of her parents' will was inside that briefcase, the document that would soon reveal her future. Hers and Julia's.

"Sweetie, can you run upstairs and get Mr. Parker a towel?" asked Aunt Mimi.

"Sure," Ruthie said, pushing a lock of her straight brown hair behind her ear, which was newly pierced, the gold starter ball still the only earring she was able to wear. You had to wear the starter ball for six weeks, and her ears had only been pierced for five, since her thirteenth birthday last February 22. That had been one of Naomi's few unbendable rules: no pierced ears until the girls were teenagers. Naomi herself never pierced her ears. She always wore clip-ons, which Ruthie and Julia would divide among themselves when they sorted through Naomi's "costume" jewelry. The real stuff, the three gold bracelets, the emerald necklace and earrings, the long chains embedded with tiny diamonds, the rings, all would be split up according to the will.

Ruthie walked up the front stairs. The banister scrolls were made of wrought iron. Once when Ruthie was four she put her head between two of them and got stuck there. Naomi tried everything to get Ruthie out, including spreading butter behind her ears, but Ruthie's head was firmly lodged. Luckily, their house painter arrived that day. A strong man, he was able to pull apart the scrolls and slip Ruthie's head back through.

She walked up the stairs, covered in a burgundy Oriental runner, thick bronze bars securing the rug to each stair. Phil loved Oriental rugs and had covered the floors of every room downstairs with them. At the top of the stairwell the house became less fancy, more utilitarian. The floors up here were covered in wall-to-wall beige carpeting. Phil loved to tease the girls about the first night after the carpet was installed, when they both sat up in bed and vomited the strawberry milk shakes they had drunk that evening for dessert. At the time, Phil had been angry with the girls for throwing up. He had felt the girls' sickness was a sort of sabotage, and while Naomi cleaned up the mess he seethed, muttering that the carpeting he paid good money for, the carpeting he did not even want to install in the first place, had already been marred. In both Julia's and Ruthie's rooms there was still a pale brown stain by the side of each bed.

The linen closet was at the top of the stairs. Ruthie opened it, revealing shelf after shelf of neatly stacked towels and sheets, her baby blankets with their satin edging on the very top, perfectly folded. On the bottom shelf were toiletry supplies: multiple packs of Ivory soap, two huge bottles of Scope, a three-pack of Crest, and two containers of Reach floss.

Ruthie stared at the shelves, blinking back unexpected tears. Her mother had always been so neat, so organized, so prepared. The smell of clean linens and Ivory soap was redolent of her. She could see her mother, in the den after dinner, sitting on the sofa and folding laundry while she and Phil watched TV.

Ruthie grabbed a blue beach towel from the middle rack, closed the door, and brought it to the lawyer waiting downstairs.

Now toweled off and dry, Mr. Parker, slim in his black suit, sat with Aunt Mimi in the study, making polite conversation while they waited for Matt and Peggy to arrive from their hotel so that Mr. Parker could read them the will. Matt and Peggy had been in town since the day before the funeral but were headed back to Virden tomorrow. Though everyone pretty much knew they would be returning to Atlanta in the near future to fetch Julia, for now they needed to get back to their twelve-year-old son, Sam, who was staying with Peggy's mother.

Julia was upstairs in her room, listening to Morrissey's *Viva Hate* again and again. When Ruthie knocked on her door earlier that morning, Julia had barked, "Not now," with such menace that Ruthie had backed away, stung.

Ruthie hovered in the doorway of the study, listening to her aunt and Mr. Parker make small talk. Mimi had gone to Vanderbilt as an undergrad, and Mr. Parker seemed to have lots of friends who went there, so they had plenty of names to exclaim over: Skip Ball, Holden Avery, Margaret Strickland.

"Maggie was in Tri Delt with me," said Mimi.

"Did Vandy Tri Delts answer the phone, 'Delta, Delta, Delta, can I help ya, help ya, help ya?'" asked Mr. Parker.

"Not if I answered," said Mimi. "But that's not saying much. By no stretch of the imagination was I a model member."

"I imagine you were pretty enough to be a model," said Mr.

Parker. Ruthie noticed a quick change in his expression, a flash of intensity.

Mimi blushed and made a little *tsking* sound with her tongue.

Just the other night Mimi had mentioned to Julia and Ruthie that while she generally disliked the politics of southern men, she enjoyed their audacity. Ruthie didn't enjoy Mr. Parker's audacity at all. She knew that Mr. Parker was married, with two cute kids who went to Coventry. His wife, Mrs. Parker, was one of those women whom Naomi was intimidated by. One of those women who seemed to have memorized that elusive handbook that explains the correct thing to do in every situation, just like Alex Love's mom.

And now Mrs. Parker's husband was flirting with Aunt Mimi.

Married men shouldn't flirt, Ruthie thought. She walked away from the study, hoping that Aunt Mimi and Mr. Parker could tell by her receding heavy footsteps that she disapproved.

She wandered through the house. Rattled, really. Rattled about, like a bony old lady, like a ghost. She walked into the dining room, with its formal wallpaper left over from the previous owners of the house, its heavy silk curtains, the antique sideboard where Naomi kept her Rose Tiara silver flatware, the long oval table that could extend even longer. Their family hardly ever ate in here, dining instead at the round wood table in the kitchen that had been hand-painted by a local artist with curling vines and flowers.

The dining room was reserved for holiday dinners, plus occasional parties for Phil and the other members of his firm. Naomi only deigned to host when it was an absolute necessity for Phil's career. She strongly disliked entertaining. There was a reason for that, and Naomi would explain it any time Phil pestered her about throwing an open house. "You don't remember what happened the last time we did that?" she would say. Eventually Ruthie had heard Naomi's story so many times *she* could repeat it to her father.

When Naomi and Phil first moved into the house they threw a big Christmas party for all of the neighbors. Naomi, late in her pregnancy with Ruthie, wore a red maternity dress with a big white bow at the neck. She looked like she was wearing a red tent, she said, but at least she knew Julia would look cute, wearing the red plaid taffeta dress with the wide sash that Naomi had sewed for her for the occasion.

Naomi had also prepared all of the food, prepping for weeks in advance. She made chicken and ham pinwheels, little pizzas with black olives, meatballs in sweet-and-sour sauce to be eaten with a toothpick. She made chicken liver pâté with cognac and lots of butter, pigs in a blanket, miniature quiche lorraine. She made two cheesecakes with blueberry sauce, marshmallow cream fudge, oatmeal date cookies, and homemade boiled custard, which required hours and hours of stirring at the stove.

Naomi set the food out buffet-style on the fully extended dining room table. On the antique sideboard she placed three stacks of plates next to two red straw baskets, one filled with white paper cocktail napkins, the other filled with cutlery. In Virden she would have used plastic forks and knives, but she didn't want to seem too informal. Also in Virden, parties were often dry, but Naomi knew Atlantans were drinkers. So Phil bought a case of André champagne.

Naomi spent the evening sliding trays of appetizers in and out of the oven, replenishing the platters she had arranged on the dining room table. Phil walked around with a bottle of André in hand, refilling glasses. Even little Julia had a job. She was to circulate downstairs, carrying a red straw basket of M&M's, offering them to guests. At one point Julia tripped, scattering the candy all over the floor, a pattering of hard, bright confetti. Julia gathered the M&M's up quickly, put them back in the basket, and continued serving, until someone told Naomi what had happened and Naomi came and whisked the M&M's away.

"I'm not done," said Julia, indignant.

"Sweetie, everyone's had enough candy," said Naomi.

The next day at breakfast, Naomi looked tired but pleased. Phil, in his robe, ate leftover chicken liver pâté spread on toast for his breakfast, while Naomi and Julia ate Product 19 brand cereal, Julia's with a big spoonful of sugar dissolving on top.

"Any other funny stories besides Julia and her spilled M&M's?" Naomi asked Phil.

"That story's funny?" asked Julia, grinning. Naomi said that even as a little girl Julia had liked to entertain.

Naomi nodded at her, smiling.

"Bob Tingle locked himself in the study and watched the game," said Phil.

Naomi made an exaggerated motion of rolling her eyes. "Funny stories, not stories that demonstrate rudeness."

"A group of ladies laughed really hard. They said it was funny that you served André champagne," said Julia.

"Who said that, honey?" Naomi asked, her voice a little too high.

"I don't know," said Julia. "They were pretty. One of them had on a long gold skirt that was very shiny."

Naomi glared at Phil. "That's Elizabeth Spencer she's talking about. Oh, what a bitch!" She squeezed the bridge of her nose with her thumb and forefinger. "Oh God. I can't believe we served André. What was I thinking? This is Wymberly Way, not Virden."

"What does 'bitch' mean?" asked Julia.

Phil laughed heartily. This laugh was one of the things Naomi loved about him; she said it showed how he embraced the pleasures of life.

"Ask your mother," he said, before taking a huge bite of his toast and pâté. However invested he was in living where "Old Atlanta" resided, he had never been particularly invested in impressing anyone from it.

"It's a bad word, sweetie. Mommy shouldn't have said it."

"But what does it mean?"

"It means someone whose nose is stuck so high in the air, when she spits her saliva lands back on her face," said Phil, his mouth full of pâté.

"That's really more the definition of a snob," said Naomi, her voice sad, tired.

• • •

Ruthie wondered what would happen to the house. Would they sell it? And if so, who would do it, Aunt Mimi? The lawyer?

Maybe—Ruthie hoped—the house would just be put aside until she and Julia were all grown. Ruthie knew her father would not want the house to go on the market. Nothing made him prouder than owning a Philip Schutze–designed house on Wymberly Way, arguably one of the most beautiful streets in Buckhead. Julia referred to its purchase—which Phil spoke of endlessly—as her stepfather's greatest triumph.

The funny thing was, when he and Naomi first started looking for houses their Realtor wouldn't even show Phil ones in town.

"The public schools have gone to hell," she said. She was sixty years old with the posture of a ballerina; her name was Dot and she had silver hair.

"We'll do private," said Phil, unconcerned. He and Naomi sat in the back of Dot's Cadillac holding hands while she drove.

"The suburbs are really the place to be," Dot said. "You can zip in and out of the city on the freeway and have your own acre or two just outside the perimeter. Often on a wooded lot."

"Dot, how many times have I told you I don't want longer than a fifteen-minute commute?" said Phil, pressing against his seat belt as he leaned forward to make his point. "Now I know you have listings in the city, so why aren't you showing them to me?"

Dot glanced back to look at Phil before saying in the most gracious tone, "I have found that my Jewish clients tend to be most comfortable living in Sandy Springs or Dunwoody."

Phil threw back his head and laughed. Naomi did not. She stared out the window at the other cars on the freeway.

She always said that at that moment she wondered: What in the world was she doing in this car, with this man? Why wasn't she in her ranch house in Virden on Fairwoods Road, sharing coffee with her next-door-neighbor, Sharon?

"Dot, did I ever tell you about how Naomi and I first met?" Phil asked.

"You did not," said Dot.

"It was at a Wesley Fellowship event at Duke. Wesley Fellowship as in John Wesley, the founder of the Methodist church."

"Oh," said Dot, glancing back at her two clients. Giving them a brilliant smile of inclusion. "Well. I do understand your concerns about commute time from the suburbs. Why don't we just turn around at the next exit? There might be time for me to show you a listing I just got in Buckhead, on Wymberly Way."

Phil grinned at Naomi. She did not smile back. She was three months pregnant with Ruthie. She felt sick. She would have low-grade nausea for the entire pregnancy, a learned detail Julia used to tease Ruthie about, as if it were a mark against Ruthie's character.

Ruthie headed back upstairs, to her room, but this time she used the back staircase. On a whim she decided to ride the moving chair. Just because it had been so long since she had. The chair was covered in cracked yellow leather and looked slightly ominous. Julia always called it the electric chair.

Ruthie sat down on it and pressed the button underneath the right arm. The button looked like a doorbell, but instead of ringing when pressed it began the chair's slow ascent up the rail. There was also a doorbell-shaped button on the wall that operated the chair. When she was little, the only thing Ruthie's friends ever wanted to do when they came over to play was ride the moving chair. It used to bore Ruthie to tears. It used to drive her crazy.

When the chair reached the top Ruthie hopped off, then turned the handle on the door that opened to the upstairs hall. Once in the hall she saw that the door to Julia's room, which was catty-corner from the back stairwell, was still closed, Morrissey's melancholy lyrics slipping through the cracks.

Looking at the closed door angered her. There was no reason for Julia to shut herself away so meanly. And so Ruthie marched up to it and knocked loudly.

A moment passed before the door opened, a crack. Julia peeked out, her long curls loose and tumbling over her shoulders.

"Is anybody else around?" she asked, her voice an urgent whisper.

Ruthie shook her head.

"Okay, come in. Make it fast."

Julia opened the door just wide enough to let Ruthie slip in before closing and locking it again.

"I take it the solicitor is here," Julia said. What should be the whites of her eyes were streaked with red lines.

"What's a solicitor?"

"A lawyer. A scumbag."

"Dad was a lawyer," Ruthie said.

Julia shrugged. "I'm not saying Dad was a scumbag, just that it's a corrupt line of work."

"What about lawyers who defend innocent people? What about that guy in *Inherit the Wind*?"

Coventry had staged a production of that drama. Julia played Rachel Brown.

Julia waved away Ruthie's rebuttals. "None of the members of Phil's firm defend innocent people," she said. "Believe me."

And then, "Want to see something cool?"

Ruthie looked around Julia's room to see what might be new. There were the two pink lamps attached to the wall, each decorated with a pink metal bow below a white shade. Dangling from the arm of the lamp closest to the door was a card with the Playboy bunny symbol printed on it. There was the antique sleigh bed that had cost Phil a fortune and that Ruthie and Julia once broke by doing flying somersaults on top of the mattress. There were the posters of Janis Joplin and Jimi Hendrix that Naomi had forbidden Julia to hang—for fear of messing up the paint—but that Julia had hung anyway.

"What am I supposed to be looking at?" asked Ruthie.

Julia pointed to her ear, which was covered by her auburn hair.

"I don't see anything," said Ruthie.

Julia lifted her hair, holding it away from her face in a ponytail, her hand the rubber band. In addition to the dangly beaded earring Julia wore, there was a safety pin stuck through the middle of her lobe. Bits of dried blood crusted around the needle of the pin.

"Ew," said Ruthie.

"Shut up. It's cool," said Julia. "Want me to do it to you? You just have to ice down the ear and then stick the pin in real fast. You'll barely feel it."

"I think it's against Coventry's dress code," said Ruthie.

She wasn't joking, but Julia responded as if she were.

"Ha. Very funny. Come on. We'll be the only two people in the world who have them."

"But it's ugly," said Ruthie. "And it looks like it really hurt."

"No pain, no gain," said Julia, quoting her least favorite PE teacher, a petite blond woman who favored all of the popular kids and was always eager to jump in with stories about her days as a Theta at UGA.

Ruthie looked out the window, saw Matt's white Ford Taurus pulling into the front drive. "They're here," she said.

"Oh fuck," said her sister. "Time for our execution."

Ruthie knew what the will would say. Julia had told her. Still it was shocking to hear the words read aloud, shocking to hear the lawyer John Henry Parker decree that the girls would be split up: Julia to live with Matt and Peggy in Virden, Ruthie to live with Mimi and Robert in San Francisco. It was like a harsh sentence being handed down at a trial, though no one had yet been found guilty.

Chapter Three

Though Ruthie had been warned, she was still shocked that she and Julia really were going to be separated. A date had even been set, June 10, a week after Coventry let out for summer break. Peggy, Matt, and Sam would drive down from Virden the day before. Early the next morning, they would load all of Julia's belongings into their minivan and Julia would follow them back to Virginia in her Saab 900. Two days later, Mimi and Ruthie would board a plane that would take them to San Francisco.

Until then, Mimi would stay with the girls in Atlanta, supervising them as well as the sale of the Wymberly Way house. She would let her husband, Robert, take care of things at home, while her business partner, Marc, handled the interior design needs of wealthy San Franciscans.

It had been a week since the will was read. Ruthie and Julia were in bed in Julia's room whispering in the dark. Before the accident it had been a special treat for Julia to allow Ruthie in her bed, but now the girls almost always slept together. They lay on their backs, a printed cotton sheet, soft from years of washing, pulled up to their necks, the blanket and comforter in a messy pile by their feet.

"I mean, I like Aunt Mimi," said Ruthie. "A lot. But I don't really know her. And now I'm supposed to move all the way to California and live with her and Uncle Robert? I just don't understand. What were Mom and Dad thinking?"

"They weren't," said Julia. "Do you think Phil ever believed—for a moment—that he could possibly die before he reached, I don't know, age ninety-five?"

She was right. Phil had always expressed extreme confidence in his longevity. It had something to do with the fact that he was in a terrible car accident as an infant, had flown through the front windshield—he had been sitting on his mother's lap—after another car smashed into the side of the one his father was driving on that rainy day in rural Tennessee. When the ambulance came, the medics pushed the broken baby, his blood streaked by the rain, away from the middle of the road but did not tend to him, for they thought he was dead and others could be saved.

Except Phil was still alive. His father, too. Indeed, Phil's father walked away with only scratches, while the others, Phil's mother and two of her cousins, were dead.

The doctors at the hospital nicknamed baby Phil "Lazarus." Because of the apparent miracle of his recovery, he was told by the aunt who helped raise him that God had spared him for a reason, that he was put on this earth to achieve mighty things. His father went off to Korea, to fight in the war, enlisting just a few months after the car accident, perhaps hoping to die over there, too. He did not die but instead returned home with a new bride, Martha, whom he had met when he was in basic training at Camp Breckinridge, and who wrote to him faithfully while he was overseas. Martha would give Phil his sister, Mimi. Phil's aunt argued that the arrival of Mimi—a companion for the lonely Phil—was further proof of God's special love for the boy.

Phil told his daughters that for a long time he believed in the divine specialness that his aunt attributed to him. As a teenager he even considered going to seminary. But during college Phil traded in his religiosity for skepticism. He still attended events sponsored by the Wesley Fellowship, in an attempt to meet girls, but he no longer believed. It was enrolling in a class on the history of the Holocaust that did it. How could he have faith in a God who would choose to snatch one baby in Tennessee from death but would turn a blind eye to the tens of thousands of babies snatched from their mothers' arms by Nazi soldiers and killed in front of them? Still, Phil held on to one steadfast tenet or, rather, one steadfast superstition: having faced death so early, he would not face it again until he was an old, old man.

"At his core, he didn't believe he was vulnerable," said Julia. "He might not have believed in God, but he sure had a God complex. Remember that dream he told us about, his dream of driving through Atlanta in a bright, white car?"

Ruthie did not remember, so Julia—whose ability to recount past events was almost creepy—told it to her in exacting detail. It was several years ago, and they had all been in the kitchen, eating a breakfast Naomi had prepared of soft scrambled eggs, crisp bacon, and hot buttered toast, when Phil told them he had a dream to share.

In the dream, Phil found himself on the open road, speeding along, until suddenly and unexpectedly he came upon miles and miles of stopped traffic, six lanes wide. Phil had no choice but to stop, too. People honked their horns and shook their fists out their windows, but not one car moved, not one inch. Phil was frustrated, annoyed, until he realized that he and his car were somehow shrinking, shrinking until they were both so small that he was able to drive underneath all of the other cars stalled in traffic, just drive right through, until he was past the traffic jam and once again on the open road, where he sped off.

"What do you think it means?" Phil had asked his family.

"I think it shows an inferiority complex," said Julia. "I mean, the fact that you were smaller than everyone."

They all knew that Phil did not have an inferiority complex. Julia was just goading him.

"Wrong," said Phil, as if Julia were a contestant on a game show and he, its host, had access to all of the answers.

"It means you really like cars," said Ruthie.

"That's part of it, squirt," said Phil. "But go deeper."

"What it means of course," said Naomi, after swallowing a bite of egg, "is that deep down you believe that you have the ability and agility to get out of tough situations that others can't."

Phil beamed. "You girls have a smart mother," he said.

The girls did have a smart mother, or rather, they *had* a smart mother, and her interpretation of Phil's dream stuck with them.

Their father could get out of anything.

"Which is why," Julia explained to Ruthie in the dark of her bedroom, "the instructions in the will are so absurd. They're like . . . they're like a recipe for a cake no one will ever bake. They don't need to work."

"But what about Mom?" asked Ruthie. "She worried about everything. And she was always giving us her little 'cautionary tales.' Like if I told her I was going to walk to Peachtree Battle Shopping Center, she'd tell me about the girl who just the week before was kidnapped while walking there. How a van pulled up to her, and a lady leaned out the passenger window and asked for directions. How the girl couldn't hear what she was saying and so she stepped closer, and suddenly someone jumped out of the back of the van, grabbed the girl, and whisked her inside before the van took off at a hundred miles an hour, never to be seen again."

"But think about it, Ruthie. Mom never worried about her own death. She worried about ours. She probably worried so much about ours that she forgot that she could die, too."

"I still can't believe she'd send you to live with Peggy."

"I don't know what choice Mom had. Peggy's married to my dad."

"But you don't even know him," said Ruthie. "Not really. I probably know Robert and Mimi as well as you know him."

"That's not really Dad's fault. Mom's the one who left."

"But Peggy is so—so awful. Think about the first time you met her."

"Don't remind me."

"Tell the story," Ruthie demanded. "About that first time."

It was a horrible story, deliciously so, and one that Julia told well.

"I'll tell it only if you'll tickle my arm while I do, and scratch my back afterwards."

"For how long?"

"For as long as it takes me to tell it."

"No, I mean how long do I have to scratch your back afterwards?"

"Ten minutes."

"Five," said Ruthie.

Because Julia never took off her black Swatch, wearing it even to bed, she was the one to keep track of time whenever Ruthie agreed to scratch her back. The hands of the watch did glow in the dark, making it easy for Julia to count the minutes, but Ruthie was pretty sure that her sister cheated, counting one minute for every two.

"Eight," said Julia.

Ruthie gave an exaggerated sigh and then agreed to the deal.

Julia stretched her arm out on top of the sheet and Ruthie began running her nails up and down it.

"Dad and Peggy had just that spring gotten married, and none of us had met her yet, though we had heard from Mom's old neighbor in Virden that Peggy was really pretty and really young. She was twenty-two, which was actually two years older than Mom was when she married my dad. She had just graduated from college, from Radford University, and she was already pregnant with Sam.

"The plan was for me to spend the first week of July with Dad and Peggy in Virden. So July first Mom, Phil, me, and you all drive up there. Of course you were only a baby, so you mostly just slept and pooped. I remember Mom insisting we take the Volvo wagon instead of the Mercedes. She didn't want to be flaunting Phil's wealth. Phil pooh-poohed her of course—claiming she was a reverse snob—but he went along with her wishes."

Phil was always proclaiming his wife and daughters reverse snobs.

"It was a long drive from Atlanta to Virden, despite the fact that Phil terrified Mom by driving really fast. Along the way he made three stops, once for McDonald's and twice for a bathroom break. He wouldn't have stopped that many times, but Mom insisted."

"He loved to make good time," said Ruthie, remembering the uncomfortable sensation of holding her pee during car trips to visit their relatives in Union City, Tennessee.

"When we were getting back into the car after lunch at McDonald's, Mom glanced at me while fastening you into the car seat. 'Damn it,' she said, which was surprising because she rarely cursed. I had a ketchup stain across the pretty little ruffled T-shirt she had dressed me in. She sighed—you remember those sighs of hers—but then she said, 'Oh well. Peggy is going to have to get used to the fact that young children are messy.'

"Which is all to say that I arrived looking a little out of sorts. Phil pulled the Volvo into the driveway of the little brick ranch on Fairwoods Road, and before Mom had a chance to fix my hair or help me find a new shirt this pretty pixie of a woman opened the door and came and stood on the front porch, looking toward the car.

"'There she is,' said Mom. 'And she certainly is attractive.'

"Peggy was wearing a bright yellow blouse tucked into a wraparound denim skirt with a big butterfly embroidered on its side. She was so tiny and cute. She didn't look pregnant at all. She wore her blond hair in a long braid down her back. She looked like a preschool teacher, like someone who would greet you at the classroom door, hold your hand, and lead you over to the table where the apple juice and cookies were all set out.

"When Mom saw Peggy standing on the porch, she put the pink plastic Goody brush back in the glove compartment. 'I guess we should go meet your new stepmommy,' she said.

"Phil had already gotten out of the car. He opened my door. I stepped out and started walking on the front grass toward Peggy.

"'Sweetheart, use the path, please,' she called, in her melodious, tinkling voice. And so I walked over to the brick path that wound from the driveway to the door. Phil and Naomi hung back, hovering by the Volvo, as if planning to take off as soon as they saw me safely enter the house. I was so anxious that they were going to leave that I kept turning around, checking to make sure they were still there.

"Finally I reached Peggy. I remember being overwhelmed by how pretty she was, with her shiny blond hair, the light dusting of freckles over her cheeks, her heart-shaped lips.

"She studied me for a moment and then said, 'My goodness, for all the child support Matt sends, I would have thought you'd come better dressed!'"

Ruthie squealed in horror. Peggy was like someone out of a fairy tale, but with a twist. From her looks and general cheerfulness you would assume her to be a good witch when really, underneath, she was awful.

Or at least, that was how Julia painted her to be.

"Of course then she blushed, realizing she'd been rude, I guess, and said, 'Well, this just means we can go shopping at the mall and get you some cute new things!'"

"God," said Ruthie. "What a mag." "Mag" was a word that Ruthie had invented. It meant "bitch," but you could say it without swearing.

"I think she was actually trying to be nice at that moment. Trying to be chummy."

"Okay. Then what a dumb butt."

"Yep," said Julia, "I think Mom scared Dad out of marrying smart women. Not to mention women his own age."

Peggy was only five years Matt's junior, but even though she was now thirty-five she seemed younger. There was just something so girlish about her, so hopelessly naïve. She was someone who adored the idea of projects—but was horrible at follow-through. Julia loved to tell Ruthie about all of the unused appliances in Peggy's kitchen: the Cuisinart that was purchased so she could make homemade baby food for her one and only biological child, Sam; the pasta roller; the ice-cream maker; the juicer.

They all went untouched. Gerber, Mueller's, Breyers, and Tropicana filled Peggy's grocery cart instead.

"She's an overgrown, very pretty child," said Julia. "And now she's supposed to be my mom."

Julia turned over and lifted her shirt around her shoulders. Ruthie still owed her eight minutes.

The next afternoon when Julia and Ruthie arrived home from school—they had returned to Coventry that Monday, after taking the week of the funeral off—Mimi was sitting at the kitchen counter, drinking a glass of white wine and flipping through a Horchow catalog.

"Hi, beauties," she said, smiling sadly.

During the week and a half that Mimi had been with them, her moods had been erratic. Sometimes she was all spirit and energy, as if it were up to her to replace her nieces' grief with joy. Other times she would burst into a little crying jag, apologizing between shakes if either Ruthie or Julia was around.

"Hi," said Ruthie, dropping her L.L. Bean backpack—heavy with books—onto the floor. Julia, who carried her books in a woven Guatemalan bag that Dmitri had given her back when they were dating, placed the bag on the counter. Judging from its drape, it didn't look as if it had much in it.

"Ruthie, you want a Coke?" Julia asked as she walked toward the refrigerator.

"Okay."

Julia prided herself on drinking regular Coke and not Diet, and she impressed upon Ruthie that this was an important choice for girls to make, so they wouldn't appear to be vapid, only concerned with looks and calories. Julia also told Ruthie that it was necessary for every woman to know how to drive a straight shift. Jake had taught her how, using his dad's 1974 BMW 2002.

Julia retrieved two red cans of Coke from the middle shelf of the fridge, along with two packages of string cheese. She handed one of each to Ruthie, then sat beside Mimi on one of the bar stools by the counter.

"So, Meems, I have a question for you."

Mimi raised her brows a little but didn't say anything about being called Meems.

"Say my dad wasn't around. Say something awful happened to him and he was dead. What would have happened to me? Do you think Mom and Phil would have had me go live with you? Or with Aunt Linda, or what?"

Linda was Naomi's older sister who lived in Memphis. She had gotten pregnant at age sixteen, which had scandalized Naomi's parents, as well as their fellow members of First Methodist Church in Union City, Tennessee. But Linda had made it work. She married the boyfriend who impregnated her, had the baby, finished high school, had another baby, and proceeded to earn her BA in elementary education. By twenty-four she was a second-grade teacher. By the time she was thirty-eight both of her sons had left home for college and she and her husband started taking backpacking trips through Europe every summer, reveling in their long-awaited freedom.

Surely Linda would have resented being asked to finish raising another child after forfeiting her adolescence in order to raise her own. Plus, she and Naomi were not close. Linda had been unsympathetic regarding Naomi's decision to leave Matt; when Naomi tried to explain to her sister that she was *driven* to leave Matt for Phil, that it was as if she had no choice, Linda told her that she was acting like a child, and that for her own child's sake she should "just snap out of it." Naomi used to tell her daughters that she was happy that the two of them had each other. That it was important to have a sister you could trust and confide in.

Ruthie, who had also settled on one of the stools and was halfway through her piece of string cheese, did not say anything about the unlikelihood of Linda's taking Julia, fearing that her sister would feel unwanted. Instead, Ruthie teased Julia.

"Say something awful happened . . . ," she echoed, attempting a deep Jersey accent, as if she were a member of the Mafia. "Jeez, Julia, what are you going to do, put a hit on your dad?"

Ever since the accident Ruthie had found herself full of a sort of dark, inappropriate humor.

"Sweetheart," said Mimi, ignoring Ruthie's joke and placing her manicured hand on Julia's forearm. "If your father was not around to care for you, of course you could come live with us. That would be optimal, wouldn't it, for you and Ruthie to stay together? I hope you know that even though you are going to be moving to Virden at the end of the school year, we want you to come visit us as often as possible in San Francisco. Maybe we can even talk Peggy and Matt into letting us have you over the summer."

"Really?" asked Ruthie.

"If it's okay with Peggy and Matt, it's okay with Robert and me."

Ruthie turned to beam at Julia—this, finally, was good news—but Julia was staring straight ahead, her forehead wrinkled, as if in anger. Or concentration.

Julia took off in her Saab early that evening, so it was just Mimi and Ruthie at dinner, which was not unusual. They each ate a Lean Cuisine—Mimi apologizing for not cooking, saying that in San Francisco it was usually Robert who fixed all of the meals. Mimi had another glass of wine while Ruthie drank milk. Afterwards Ruthie went up to her room to finish her homework, which she had already started on the car ride home with Julia.

She sat on her bed, her books spread about her, reading *The Wizard of Oz*. They were reading it for history class, because it had something to do with American politics and populism. According to their teacher, the Cowardly Lion stood for William Jennings Bryan, whom they had just discussed that day in class. Ruthie kept forgetting that she was supposed to be reading the book symbolically. She just found it thrilling to read an interesting book for history, especially one whose story she already knew so well from having watched the movie starring Judy Garland countless times.

Ruthie heard a light tapping on the door frame. She looked up and there was her sister, back from wherever she'd been. Julia walked into the room and closed the door behind her. "We need to talk," Julia said.

When she sat beside Ruthie on the bed—after pushing her books out of the way—Ruthie was overwhelmed by the smell of cigarette smoke. Though Julia hadn't told anyone where she was going for dinner, Ruthie guessed that she had been with Jake Robinson. Jake smoked Marlboro Reds, a habit Ruthie had declared disgusting, though Julia justified it by saying, "Hey, if you're going to smoke, you might as well go full throttle."

"You want me to come with you to California, right? And not just for the summer?"

Ruthie looked quizzically at her sister. Did Julia even have to ask?

"Of course," she said.

"I think we're going to be able to do it, then. Mimi convinced me this afternoon. I wasn't sure if she and Robert would really be up for having the two of us move in with her, but I don't think she was bullshitting when she said she'd take me if she could."

"Yeah, but she also knows that you have to go with your dad, because—you know—he's still alive and he loves you."

He was still alive. Ruthie's parents were not. How long before that knowledge would seem real to her? Before it would seem normal to think of them as dead?

Never, Ruthie hoped. She hoped the knowledge of their death would always seem wrong.

"Look, Dad loves me, I'm not doubting that, but what you said last night was right. I haven't been a part of his life for fourteen years. And I can guaran-damn-tee you that Peggy is not thrilled about me moving in with her."

"You don't know that," said Ruthie, feeling protective of her sister. "She kept hugging you at the funeral. Throwing her arms around you, telling you not to forget that *you are loved.*"

Ruthie said those words in Peggy's accent, deeply southern and concerned.

"Peggy loves her some drama," said Julia. "Did you see her clutch that cross she wears around her neck when they got to the part in the will about me living with them? That was a clutch of martyrdom, my friend, not a clutch of joy."

Peggy *had* grabbed for her cross when it was announced that Julia was to come live with them, which had seemed unnecessarily dramatic to Ruthie, considering that everyone in the room was already pretty sure of what the will would reveal.

"Your dad loves you. He's always sending you those bowls."

Matt and his son, Sam, had a workshop out back, and for the past few years Matt had been carving bowls out of single pieces of wood and then shining them to a high gloss. He had sent Julia four so far, gorgeous things that nearly rivaled the Philip Moulthrop bowl Phil had bought Naomi for their tenth anniversary.

"This afternoon I realized what I have to do in order to convince Dad to let me live with you in San Francisco. I have to make him understand that he's making a noble sacrifice by letting me go, by letting us stay together. Make him feel like the true mother in the story about King Solomon and the baby. Remember that one? How two moms were fighting over a baby, each saying it was hers? And Solomon said to cut the baby in half because he knew the real mom would relinquish the baby before she would let that happen to it? Well, pretend you and I are Siamese twins or something, and King Solomon just decreed that we must be cut in half, so that Mimi gets one half and Dad gets the other. But Dad can cry out, 'No! Let her go as long as she can go whole!' And by doing that he'll show how much he really loves me."

"But the real mom ended up getting the whole baby. That was the point of the story. Once she proved her love she got him."

Attending Coventry had made both of the girls well versed in the Bible.

Julia waved away Ruthie's logic. "You're being too technical. You've got to think about the spirit of the example, not the actual outcome. Anyway, I wrote Dad a letter. I realized I needed to say it in a letter and not over the phone, because if I try to explain it with Dad on the line I'll just get all flustered and go off point. So I went to Café Intermezzo after you and I talked to Mimi. Just sat out on the back patio drinking coffee and smoking while I wrote. And I have to say, Ruthie, the letter is fucking brilliant. My most persuasive work so far. I don't say a word in it about not wanting to live in Virginia, or not wanting to live with them. I just convince them that you and me staying together is best. Anyway, here it is. See what you think."

She thrust a folded letter at Ruthie, which Ruthie opened and began to read:

April 7, 1993

Dear Dad,

I know you are not used to receiving letters from me. I'm thinking the only one I ever sent you, besides holiday cards, was when I was a little girl, soon after Mom and I had moved to Atlanta. Just "I love you" written unevenly on a sheet of white paper in crayon, along with a stack of pictures I had drawn at school. I remember Mom bundling them all together and sending them to you in Virden, saying, "Won't your father be pleased to get all of this beautiful art."

You telephoned as soon as you received the letter, told me how you had taped the pictures to your bedroom wall, how you planned to look at them every night before you went to bed and each morning after you woke. How having those pictures was a little like having me there.

"This is really sad," said Ruthie, looking up from her sister's words.

"It's good isn't it?" asked Julia, her voice animated, excited.

Ruthie imagined Matt alone in his house in Virden, peeking into his daughter's old bedroom with its permanently made bed and empty closet. How lonely Matt must have been after Naomi took Julia and moved to Atlanta! Ruthie wondered, how come she never thought about this before? She had always viewed her parents' story through their eyes, the eyes of the victors; she had always thought it wonderfully romantic, fated. A happy ending to a difficult beginning.

But there were others involved who would not view her parents' rekindled romance as beautiful and inspiring.

Matt, for one. And Beatrice, Phil's first wife . . .

Ruthie returned to the letter.

> *Oh, Dad. It makes me so sad to think of us back then. I missed you so much when Mom and I first moved to Atlanta. I cried every night at bedtime because you weren't there to read to me and help me say my prayers.*
>
> *I still remember what it was like living in Virden when you and Mom were married. I still remember the feel of riding high above everyone on your shoulders, when we would walk to the park. I remember feeling so safe being carried by you.*

For the first time it occurred to Ruthie that Julia was not exactly a winner in this story, either.

> *I can only imagine how you ached for me—for us, when Mom left and took me with her. I suppose I'm better able to imagine how you felt losing Mom now that she is gone from my life, too.*
>
> *Mom and Phil sure bounced our lives around.*
>
> *But you found Peggy! And you had Sam! Sam, who came into your life only a year after Ruthie came into mine. Sam and Ruthie helped heal things, didn't they?*
>
> *I've had friends ask if I resented Ruthie when she was born—always assuming that I did. After all, I had been an only child with an intact family, and then quite suddenly my parents were divorced and here was a new sister. And not only a new sister, the child of my new stepfather. (And I grew to love Phil, I did, but I hope you know he never, ever took the place of you.) It's funny. Maybe I should have resented Ruthie, but I never did. She was—is—the most important person in my life. Maybe I shouldn't say that, Dad, but I'm trying to be truthful here. It's not that I love Ruthie most; it's just that Ruthie is the one who needs me most.*

"You don't love me the most?" asked Ruthie, outwardly indignant though inwardly moved by Julia's declared devotion.

"Of course I love you most. But that's not the point of the letter, spaz. The point is we need to engender sympathy for you from Dad. We need him to see you as someone who needs my protection and guidance."

"Your guidance about what? What kind of cigarettes to smoke?" Ruthie teased.

Julia slapped her sister on the thigh, hard.

"Ow!"

"Keep reading!" Julia ordered.

Ruthie rolled her eyes but obeyed.

Ruthie and I have been so connected from the very beginning. When she was just a tiny, fussy baby—

"I was not fussy," said Ruthie.

"Read!" said Julia.

I could make her stop crying by talking to her through the slats in her crib. As she got older, more often than not it was me she came running to any time she was upset. I was sort of like a little mother to her. When she was a toddler and would act up at dinner, banging the bottom of her knife against the table, or shaking salt all over her food until it was covered in a sheet of white, Phil would sometimes send her away until she could "behave properly." And Ruthie, who hated nothing more than to be singled out, to be in trouble, would flee from the kitchen, wailing.

"Go on," Mom would say to me, in that resigned, tired voice she adopted when dealing with difficult children. And I would run to find Ruthie. Usually she was flung on the sofa in the living room, a mess of shame and tears. I would rub her back. I would gently tease her out of crying.

"Whatever you do, don't smile," I would say. "Don't smile. Do not! I'm warning you."

Eventually she would smile.

As she grew older we became even closer, because now we could play

together. Summers were an endless series of games: trying to make perfume
by simmering rose petals in water—

"Oh my gosh, do you remember the time we dumped all of Mom's Chanel No. 5 into the sink so we could use the empty bottle for our rosewater perfume?" Ruthie asked.

"We? *You* did that, Ruthie. You were the one who poured out the perfume, and I was the one who got in trouble. I wasn't given my allowance for two months. Two months!"

"We both got in trouble," said Ruthie.

She didn't remind Julia that she, who at that time did not yet receive an allowance, had been spanked. Even though her mother's spankings were more symbolic than painful, it shamed Ruthie deeply to admit to having ever received one. It shamed her deeply to be punished.

"Why aren't you reading?" asked Julia.

Mom and Phil were so occupied with each other that we became each other's world.

Just like you and Peggy and Sam have created your own world. Of course I'm a part of that world, Dad, I always will be, but the three of you have lived together for Sam's entire life without me, save for a few weeks every summer, a few days over the holidays.

I think it's going to be difficult—for Sam and Peggy especially—for me to come live with y'all this late in the game. I think it might disrupt the world y'all have created.

Oh, Dad. I hope I'm not hurting your feelings. The last thing I want to do is to hurt your feelings. I love you, and I need you. You are the only father I have—the only parent I have. But please hear me when I say that instead of living with you and Peggy, I think it would be better for every-one—Ruthie especially—if I were to live with her in San Francisco at Mimi and Robert's house.

Aunt Mimi says she is willing to have me, if you are willing to let me go.

I know this is different than what Mom and Phil's will stated, but maybe we need to apply some of the wisdom of Solomon here and realize that the deepest expression of your love would be to stop the splitting of Ruthie and me. We wouldn't be going against their wishes, not really. You would still have custody, still be my legal guardian. Still be my dad. I would just live with them. It would be as if I were at boarding school. And I could come and visit every summer, just like always, and spend Thanksgiving and Christmas with you, too.

(I could even send you drawings, like I did that time when I was little, and you could hang them on your wall. To have a part of me always near . . .)

I cannot imagine being separated from Ruthie. I cannot imagine what that is going to do to her. I am the only immediate family she has left. And she doesn't know Mimi and Robert at all. How is she expected to go all the way to California by herself and be their only daughter? After losing <u>both</u> of her parents. Imagine that, Dad. Becoming an orphan at thirteen, and then being separated from your only sister.

"Gosh, you make me sound pathetic."

"It's called creating pathos, Ruthie. And it's absolutely essential for us to do so if we want my father on our side."

"I'm an orphan." Ruthie's face scrunched up, the way an infant's does, just before he is going to howl. She started crying, loudly, overwhelmed by the loneliness the letter had brought forth.

Julia put her arm around her sister, let her head fall into her lap as Ruthie cried and cried and cried. It was such a hard cry that it was over in a few minutes. For that moment at least, she had simply cried herself dry, and now she remained in Julia's lap, her face red and tearstained.

"Let me finish reading it to you," said Julia.

She read in her loud, clear voice, enunciating every syllable as she had learned to do onstage.

"'I don't know how to make sense of all of this loss, Dad; I really don't. But for me to come live in Virden, without Ruthie, would be a loss that doesn't have to happen.

"'Please, Dad. I love you. Please. Please, please love me enough to let me go to California with my sister who needs me.

"'Your daughter, Julia.'"

Ruthie remained buried in her sister's lap. Julia was right. The letter was brilliant.

"I don't see how he can say no to this," Ruthie said. But Julia did not hear her, because Ruthie's voice was muffled by her leg.

"What?"

Ruthie sat up, gingerly, the way you do after a round of throwing up, when you seem to be emptied out yet you're not sure the vomiting is over.

"I said, 'I don't see how he can say no to this.'"

Julia nodded slowly, like an ancient sage. "Behold the power of my pen."

Chapter Four

Ruthie awoke to the panicky cry of her aunt: "Girls! You overslept. Get up! Get UP!"

As if in cahoots with Mimi, the alarm clock started beeping. Julia, without opening her eyes, lifted herself up enough to smash down the snooze button. "Five more minutes," she mumbled, her head collapsing against her pillow.

Mimi started shaking Julia's arm. "Come on, sweetie, wake up! You are so late."

Ruthie, still drowsy, sat up. "What time is it?"

"Seven twenty-one," said Mimi.

Ruthie whacked at her sister, whose body was hidden by the covers. "Oh my gosh. Julia, get up!"

Ruthie had been planning on taking a shower. Julia had been planning on finishing her math homework. Instead they dressed as quickly as possible, smeared their tongues with Crest, and grabbed breakfast on their way out the door—a silvery package of Pop-Tarts for Ruthie, a cup of coffee for Julia.

Once in the car, Julia sped down Wymberly Way. They were just so late. They were late so often. Julia probably wouldn't have cared, but another late meant a major detention. They came to the intersection of Wymberly Way and Habersham Road, where there was a stop sign. Julia slowed to a rolling stop, glanced over her right shoulder to make sure no one was coming, then turned left and revved the engine.

"So when are you going to tell Mimi?" Ruthie asked, trying not to look at the speedometer.

"Tell Mimi what?"

"What you wrote in the letter you sent your dad."

"Why would I say anything to Mimi before I hear from Dad?"

Julia balanced a paper cup that was half-full of coffee between her legs. As she drove, the coffee sloshed against its sides. Ruthie recognized the cup as one from the Cherokee Club. Cherokee was the most "new money" of the good Atlanta country clubs, as opposed to Capital City, or the Piedmont Driving Club. Phil hadn't cared. Cherokee's grounds were beautiful, its food was good, and it was near their house.

Phil used to exercise at Cherokee's gym three mornings a week, and would always grab a cup of coffee from the hospitality bar on his way out. When he returned home he would rinse out the cup that the coffee came in and save it for a second, or third or fourth, use. Phil hated to waste.

"Because you need to get your story straight with her. It's been almost two weeks since you sent that letter, and your dad is going to call soon. What if he talks to Mimi before you do? I mean, in the letter you told him that Mimi said you could live with her if your dad was okay with it. But she didn't actually say that. She said *if* something happened to your dad you could live with her."

Julia shrugged. Made a left onto West Wesley. From there it was almost a straight shot to Coventry, just one more turn onto Chapel Lane. Julia was flying. A major detention would mean she'd have to go to school on Saturday and pick up any trash that was strewn about campus.

Ruthie eyed the speedometer. They were going nearly 60 miles an hour.

"Spaz, you have to trust me on this," Julia said, attempting to make eye contact with Ruthie, which made Ruthie even more nervous.

(Again and again Naomi had told the story about the two brothers who were killed in a car accident because one kept making eye contact with the other while he drove. And Ruthie and Julia would always say, "The brothers died. How could anyone have known what the driver was doing before the wreck?" And Naomi would tell the girls that they hadn't died immediately. That the brother who was driving had lived long enough to whisper a warning to the doctor at the hospital.)

"There's an art to what I'm doing—it's called the art of negotiation. I can't say anything specific to Mimi until I hear back from my dad. That way I can tailor my argument to her based on his response to me."

"You sound like a lawyer," said Ruthie. "Like Dad—my dad. You're driving like him, too. Can you please slow down?"

In response Julia pressed on the accelerator.

"Julia!" cried Ruthie, alarmed. "Stop!"

"Chill," said Julia. "Jesus. I know this road like I once knew Dmitri's dick."

"Oh gross! Why do you have to say things like that?"

(The truth was, Ruthie actually wanted to know more about Dmitri's penis. Or not Dmitri's specifically, just any boy's. Ruthie was curious about what one—a grown one, not a baby's—looked like in real life. The only grown one she had ever seen had been a quick flash of flesh that made its way through the scrambler on the Tuxedo channel.)

Julia roared through the green light at Howell Mill, rounded a corner, and picked up even more speed as she drove along a straight section of road. Ruthie felt powerless and about to cry.

"Slow down! God! If you do I'll shut up about the letter—I'll let you be the 'master negotiator.'"

Julia tapped the brake, slowing down to 50. "If I get a major detention, I'm blaming you."

•   •   •

Ruthie was new at Coventry that year, having attended St. Catherine's—an Episcopal elementary school known for its nurturing attitude and wealthy parents—from pre-school through sixth grade. St. Catherine's was a sort of feeder school for Coventry, though Coventry was certainly not known for its nurturing attitude. In fact, Coventry was notorious for being the toughest school in Atlanta, both socially and academically.

Many of the students at Coventry had been there since kindergarten and would be there through the twelfth grade—barring expulsion, sudden poverty, or the discovery of a severe learning disability. These students were called "lifers," and they seemed to take a personal sort of pride in their parents' decision to have enrolled them at Coventry back when they were five. The girl lifers especially seemed to resent the influx of new blood that was admitted in the junior high, forty new students in sixth grade, thirty new ones in seventh.

Before Ruthie matriculated at Coventry she imagined that she would be popular there, same as she had been at St. Catherine's. Being popular at St. Catherine's was really no big deal. There were only fifty students in her sixth-grade graduating class, and besides Gabriel Schwartz, the classroom pariah who left in the middle of fifth grade, everyone was more or less accepted.

Especially after the sixth-grade trip to Jekyll Island, where they got to sleep in tents and roast marshmallows over campfires built by their teachers. It was on that trip that Ruthie allowed Derrick Bridges to kiss her, during a forbidden game of Truth or Dare. Instead of pecking her on the lips, Derrick darted his tongue expertly into Ruthie's mouth. She developed an instant and overwhelming crush on him. At St. Catherine's, such crushes were easy to explore: she sent word to Derrick through Alex Love that she wanted to "go" with him; he said yes, and for two months, though they never spoke a word to each other—or, for that matter, kissed again—they were a couple.

Figuring out the social equation at Coventry required a much higher skill set. It was like going from the multiplication tables to algebraic equations. Except instead of manipulating numbers, you had to learn how to manipulate people. Mostly this seemed to hinge on the ability to detect and administer sarcasm, even when you were dying for someone just to be nice.

It was 7:53 when Julia and Ruthie pulled into the back gate of Coventry. Homeroom started at 8:00.

"I'm too late to drop you off at the junior high," said Julia. "You're going to have to walk with me."

Julia was a sophomore, and while sophomores at Coventry were allowed to drive to school, they had to park by the back tennis courts, a good half mile away from the main campus. And there was a campus-wide rule that forbade anyone—parents or students—from stopping their car to pick up sophomores trudging up from the back lot. The school claimed this was to keep its morning traffic flowing smoothly.

Ruthie thought that Julia was being a pain to make her walk, because Julia was going to be late regardless. Dropping Ruthie off at the junior high building wasn't going to change that fact. And besides, it was Julia who had punched off the alarm clock that morning. Still, Ruthie wasn't going to argue with her sister. What leverage did she have? Her sister had the license, the car, the keys.

"Fine," said Ruthie.

At least she knew her homeroom teacher, Mr. Roman, wouldn't mark her as tardy. Ever since the accident, all of her teachers had been letting things slide.

Julia parked the Saab in one of the last spots in the sophomore lot, and they began the long trudge to the main campus. It was a pretty walk, actually. It was late April and everything was in bloom, including the pink and white dogwood trees that grew on the periphery of the woods that surrounded the campus.

Julia's auburn curls were loose, wild. She wore a pair of used Levi's, cowboy boots, and a short-sleeve black T-shirt. Around her neck hung a long strand of tiny red beads. She looked cool, even though she had thrown on her clothes in less than a minute.

Ruthie, on the other hand, in her khaki pants from the Gap and blue polo shirt, did not look cool. She looked fine—acceptable— but she did not stand out in any particular way. For the millionth time she wished that she looked more like Julia, that she, too, had her sister's sense of style. That she, too, had inherited her mother's vibrant auburn hair. Instead Ruthie's hair was plain and flat and often full of static. And of all of her mother's features, the most prominent one she had inherited was Naomi's long nose.

Julia took a last sip of her coffee before chucking the empty cup into the bordering woods.

"Julia!" chided Ruthie.

"Chill. I'll be back here Saturday morning to pick it up."

Ruthie watched as car after car passed them, mostly moms driving car pool. She imagined Naomi behind the wheel of her Volvo station wagon, the radio station tuned to 90.1—NPR— even though Ruthie preferred listening to Z93 and Julia claimed to like the college station Album 88.

It occurred to Ruthie, while walking, that it was hypocritical of Coventry to have a rule against people in cars giving lifts to pedestrians. Didn't the school claim to be Christian? And wouldn't Jesus have pulled over to pick up the least of those amongst him, which surely would have included the sophomores who had to park in the crappy lot?

Just then a tiny vintage BMW 2002—the color of butter— slowed down and came to a stop beside the girls. Ruthie recognized the driver as Jake Robinson, his blond hair pulled back into a pony-tail, a Marlboro Red hanging from his mouth, even though being caught with a cigarette on campus was grounds for suspension.

"Get in," he said.

"Um, that's okay," said Ruthie. "We're almost there."

But Julia was already opening the passenger door. "We are *not* almost there. We've still got a quarter of a mile to go."

Ruthie hesitated. She didn't want to walk the rest of the way by herself. But she didn't want to sit in the back of Jake's car, ei-ther—most notably because he was smoking but also because she associated him with her parents' deaths. After all, it was his house she had to call in order to tell Julia the news about Phil and Naomi.

"Come on," Julia said to Ruthie. "Squeeze in the back."

Ruthie sighed, then walked to Julia's opened door. She slid behind the front seat and sat in the cramped back, where there were no seat belts. The car smelled like stale smoke and the song Jake was blasting was disturbing, its singer stating, again and again, that sex was violent.

Julia adjusted herself in the passenger seat while Jake started driving toward Allen Hall, the junior high building.

He glanced at Ruthie in his rearview mirror, and she realized he had just asked her a question.

"What?" she said. "I can't hear you."

He turned down the music, just a little. "You're Ruthie, right?"

"Uh-huh," said Ruthie.

He whispered something to Julia, something about Julia being the sexy one.

"Shut up," said Julia. But in the rearview mirror Ruthie saw her sister's private smile.

Sometimes Ruthie hated her sister.

They were almost to Allen Hall. Ruthie did not want Jake to pull up in front of it. Usually there was a teacher stationed by the front entrance, making sure drop-off ran smoothly. Ruthie did not want to be caught in the car of a smoking student.

"This is fine," said Ruthie, pointing to a curb a good three hundred feet from the entrance. "Just drop me off here."

Jake pulled over to the curb Ruthie had indicated. Once the car was stopped Julia got out of the passenger seat so she could tilt it forward and let Ruthie squeeze through. As Ruthie was walking away from Jake's car, her L.L. Bean backpack swung over one shoulder, she heard Jake ask her sister, "Want to get out of here?"

"Fuck yeah," said Julia, and before Ruthie could say anything Jake was swinging a U-turn, then peeling down the main drive, headed toward the back gate of campus.

They were going to get caught. Ruthie knew it. Dean Hasher

made a point of hiding out in the woods by the back gate, on the lookout for students trying to get away.

Ruthie was so occupied thinking about Julia and the hell she would catch—if not from Mimi, then from the school—for leaving campus to cut class with a smoking, speeding boy that at first she did not notice the commotion taking place in the turnaround in front of Allen Hall.

And then suddenly Ruthie was upon it, looking down at Laney Daley along with twelve or so other students. Laney was scrambling around on the sidewalk on her hands and knees, wearing jeans so tight they squished her rear flat as an ironing board. She was picking up what looked like little white cigars rolling about. But of course they weren't cigars; they were tampons. Somehow they had fallen out of her purse, which lay open and abandoned a few feet away.

There must have been twenty tampons on the loose. Ruthie could not fathom why Laney would choose to bring twenty tampons with her to school. Then again, most everything Laney did was unfathomable. Laney, who was also new to Coventry that year, was so awkward, so earnest, and so nakedly desperate that sometimes Ruthie wanted to pull her aside and just give her a few tips for survival. Like that tampons were a private thing, a shameful thing, something to be zipped away in an inner pocket of a backpack or a purse. And you only brought two to school—at the very most!—on days when you had your period.

Ruthie registered the looks on the faces of those observing Laney. Their expressions were short on sympathy, long on scorn. Within the half hour, everyone would know about this.

But now the second bell was ringing and so the gawkers rushed inside.

Ruthie was on her way in when she saw a familiar burgundy diesel Mercedes wagon pull up to the curb. It was Mrs. Love's car, the same one she drove when Alex and Ruthie started pre-school together at St. Catherine's.

Ruthie hadn't seen Mrs. Love since the funeral.

Alex stepped out of the front seat of the wagon, wearing a button-down pink-and-white-striped shirt over a short khaki skirt, Keds, tiny ankle socks. Ruthie smiled at Alex, and waved at Mrs. Love through the closed passenger window. Mrs. Love rolled the window down. She was wearing tennis whites. Atop her blond hair was a visor with the words "The Cloister" spelled across it.

"Hi, Max!" said Mrs. Love, her face taking on an expression of delight, affection, and perhaps a little pity.

Max was what she had called Ruthie ever since Ruthie had changed her name to Ellen, her middle name, when she was four years old and then decided to change it back to Ruthie when she was in the second grade. Upon this second name change Mrs. Love had declared, "I'm so confused I'm just going to call you Max!"

"Come here, sweetheart; let me see you up close," said Mrs. Love.

Ruthie poked her head in the window and felt the spring of unexpected tears. It was the smell of Mrs. Love's Joy perfume that brought them on, the essence of rose that brought back so many easy afternoons of playing at the Loves' house with Alex, dressing up in Mrs. Love's old clothes, pulled from the spare closet in the guest room, before Mrs. Love would finally shoo them out of the house and into the backyard, proclaiming that "wild Indians need a little sunshine."

"How are you doing?" she asked, her voice leaking sympathy.

Ruthie swallowed. Blinked. "I'm good."

"We are going to have you and Julia and your sweet aunt over to dinner soon."

"Okay," said Ruthie. "Great."

"You take care now, sweetie." Mrs. Love waved good-bye and drove off, the tailpipe of the wagon blowing black diesel smoke.

Alex walked over to Ruthie, her brows raised in a question.

"What the heck is going on?" she whispered, pointing to Laney, who was trying to reach underneath a parked car in order to gather the last of the tampons.

"I guess she brought an entire box of tampons with her and they fell out of her bag."

"Should we help her?" asked Alex, her tone indicating that was the last thing she wanted to do.

"No! People might think they're ours."

"Gosh, you're right," Alex said, clearly relieved.

"Anyway, the second bell already rang."

The girls hurried inside, where they split off, each headed to her own homeroom.

It was the first quasi-normal conversation that Ruthie had had with Alex since the accident. Actually, it was the first quasi-normal conversation they'd had in a long time. They had been so excited the year before when they both were admitted to Coventry. But soon after classes began, Alex and Ruthie became socially competitive. Each yearned to be friends with the Eight, that elite group of pretty white girls, all of whom had been at Coventry since kindergarten, who had grown up splashing in the Piedmont Driving Club pool together and smacking their tennis balls back and forth on the club's courts.

It didn't matter that the Eight seemed to have no idea that either of them existed; in Ruthie and Alex's desire for popularity, they had turned against each other. Alex began pointing out pimples on Ruthie's skin, asking sweetly if her mom had considered taking her to the dermatologist. And Ruthie's teasing about Mrs. Love's many rules—no R movies, no TV during the school week, no soda—took on a mean, bullying edge.

And then after the accident, Alex's attitude shifted toward Ruthie again. Alex became alarmingly sweet. She developed a habit of smiling encouragingly at everything Ruthie said—the way one would with a crazy person—even if Ruthie was just complaining about Mrs. Stanford giving them a pop quiz in math, or the fact that it had rained for five days in a row. Alex would just beam at Ruthie, her eyes widened as if in perpetual surprise, her lips stretched upward, her long white teeth prominent.

Sometimes she would give Ruthie's arm a little squeeze of encouragement and Ruthie would yell "Ow!" just to startle her.

Ruthie definitely preferred the scheming, plotting, competitive Alex of the pre-accident days, rather than this saccharine version. Ruthie wondered if future interactions with others would always feel so fake, if no one would ever again know how to strike up a conversation with her for fear of accidentally reminding her that—oh yeah—her parents had died.

As if she could forget.

When she finally made it to homeroom, which was also her English classroom, Mr. Roman gave her a squinty look of concern and motioned for her to come to his desk.

Being summoned by Mr. Roman was cause for much stomach fluttering. He was just so gorgeous, with his green eyes, his square jaw, his light brown hair that he kept just an inch past respectable. He was a young teacher, twenty-six or twenty-seven. He had been in the Navy after college, and the girls in his class—at Coventry the middle school English classes were segregated by sex—would whisper about how cute he must have looked in his Navy blues. He had been in an a cappella group in college, and on special occasions he would sing to the girls.

She walked over to his desk, where he sat with his attendance book in front of him. Ruthie noticed that he had marked her on time for that day, as well as on Monday when she had also been tardy.

"Is everything okay?" he asked.

"My sister accidentally turned off the alarm clock, that's all. I'm sorry."

Mr. Roman smiled, revealing his dimples. "Don't worry too much about it. I know there's a lot on your plate right now. A lot on your sister's, too. Just check in with me, okay? Let me know how you're doing."

Since the accident all of Ruthie's teachers had been really kind toward her, which felt weird. The middle school teachers at Coventry were in general a cranky, prickly bunch. But Mr. Roman's kindness was different. It did not feel fake. It did not seem to be a cover-up for his own discomfort with grief.

• • •

Just as Ruthie had predicted, by the end of first period everyone in the seventh grade knew about Laney's loose tampons. But the rumors didn't end there. People were saying that when Laney got on her hands and knees to retrieve them there had been blood on the seat of her pants. The fact that the back of Laney's jeans was perfectly clean was irrelevant. The stain existed in everyone's mind, and that was all that mattered.

Laney Daley. What a cautionary tale. Laney, by negative example, had taught Ruthie everything not to do when dealing with the popular kids at Coventry.

Lesson one: Do not appear to be trying too hard. This was Laney's gravest sin. Waving frantically at the Eight whenever they walked by, sitting near them during assemblies, attempting to sit at their table in the cafeteria, despite the fact that day after day they chirped, "Sorry, that one's taken," at whatever seat she tried to claim. And every day Laney acted surprised by their rejection.

Lesson two: Be wary of sudden, unexpected friendliness, especially from Eleanor Pope, the prettiest and the meanest of the Eight. That past February Eleanor had slipped Laney, through a crack in her locker, an invitation to a slumber party at her house. Only the invitation was a joke, a gag, listing a fake address on Valley Road, giving a fake telephone number to call to RSVP.

Did Eleanor intuit that Laney would be so thrilled to receive the invitation that she would forego the formality of phoning to say she could come and would instead rush up to Eleanor, surrounded by friends at her locker, and tell her that yes, yes! She would be there. If only she had phoned, it would have been an automated operator who announced, in a cheerful voice, that the number she was trying to reach was not in service. Or maybe the number Eleanor gave Laney did work, was some stranger's number, was perhaps the phone number of an old man who would answer on the fifth ring, confused and disoriented. Would that have been enough to clue Laney in? Would that have prevented her from having her mother drive her up and down Valley Road—one of the ritziest streets in Buckhead—searching for an address that did not exist?

Lesson three: Never show your pain.

The Monday after the alleged slumber party Laney Daley marched up to Eleanor Pope and, in what surely was a line provided to her by one of her parents, demanded, "What, exactly, was the big idea behind all this?"

Eleanor, so pretty in a black dress that looked like a polo shirt, only longer, raised her brows slightly and said with mock surprise, "Oh my gosh, you didn't get that it was a joke? You really thought I'd invite you to my house? That's so funny."

Ruthie, whose locker was two down from Eleanor's, had witnessed the interaction. And when Eleanor smiled at her, a smile that expressed both pity and contempt for Laney's cluelessness, Ruthie smiled back, and rolled her eyes in agreement.

She was rewarded that afternoon. Eleanor said "hi" to her as they passed in the hall. But Ruthie had learned not to expect any promises from small gestures of friendliness (lesson two). Just because Eleanor said hello one day did not mean she would do it again. It was all so tricky. It was all so exhausting. More exhausting even than making good grades at Coventry, which simply required a tremendous amount of study.

When Ruthie returned to school after the funeral, she surprised herself by feeling grateful to be back in the midst of Coventry's strange social labyrinth. She was grateful for any distraction from the haunting thoughts that had lodged themselves in her brain. She thought obsessively about the last few moments of her parents' lives, when they realized the plane was going down. A loop of images ran through her head—her mother screaming, her father trying to shield Naomi with his arms before the pilot barked for them both to put their heads against their knees. And with those images came a series of unanswerable questions:

Did they know they were about to die, or did they fool themselves into thinking that somehow things would turn out okay, that once again Phil would cheat death? Did they think about her and Julia, about what would happen to them? Did they regret the instructions left in the will? Were they scared of death itself or just the pain of dying? Did they wonder if there might be a heaven or a hell? Did they pray? Did they kiss? Did they cry?

Compared to this echo chamber of her own imagination, Ruthie welcomed returning to the land of the bitchy girls, the land of the cranky, demanding teachers.

But the accident had a ripple effect even at Coventry. When Ruthie returned to school after the double funeral, everyone was kind and solicitous. Teachers and students alike. The members of the Eight smiled at her sweetly in the hallway. Her math teacher, Mrs. Stanford, who once had asked if she was "trying to sound stupid," started calling her "dear."

The last class of the day was English with Mr. Roman. Both Eleanor Pope and Laney Daley were in the class with Ruthie. Ruthie was a little surprised to see Laney still at school. If it had been she who was caught picking up twenty rolling tampons, she who had been rumored to have blood all over her pants, she who had been asked loudly at lunch, by Trevor Jackson, whether or not she had anything he could use to stop up his bloody nose, Ruthie would have gone home sick.

But there sat Laney, in her assigned seat in the second row, wearing acid-washed jeans—which went out of style years ago—and a Coventry T-shirt.

Eleanor walked in just before the second bell, her long dark hair pulled into a high ponytail. Still tan from spring break in Barbados with her family, she wore a white denim miniskirt and a turquoise scoop-neck top with three-quarter-inch sleeves. Around her neck was a half-inch-thick silver chain. In her ears, big silver hoops. She was chewing gum. She was wearing heels. She looked about eighteen years old, her blue eyes widened by liner, her angular cheeks even further defined by blush.

They were reading the *Odyssey*. Not the modernized version, but the classic. It was a seventh-grade tradition at Coventry,

God knows why. The language was so dense, so confusing, that Mr. Roman only assigned three pages per night. Still, Ruthie struggled. It was like reading a foreign text without having taken any language classes. And the print was so small, the pages so thin. And what did she care about the adventures of Odysseus anyway? The only character she liked was Penelope, who promised her unwanted suitors that when she finished weaving a shroud for her dead father-in-law she would accept that Odysseus was dead and choose one of them as her new husband. But every night she secretly undid that day's weaving.

Mr. Roman was talking about the sirens who sang to the sailors, making them veer off course, making them crash against the rocks. Wise Odysseus, knowing the lure of the siren song, told his sailors to lash him to the stern of the boat so he would not give in to the seductive music.

"Do y'all think there are still siren songs today?" asked Mr. Roman. "Temptations that steer us off course?"

Ruthie thought about Julia in the front seat of Jake's car early that morning. "Fuck yeah," she had said when he asked if she wanted to get out of there. Everything was a siren song for Julia: boys, cigarettes, alcohol, pot. They all called to her. They all made her veer off course. But what could she tie herself to that would keep her from turning toward danger?

Ruthie. If Julia could be tied to Ruthie, Ruthie would make sure her sister stayed on track.

Casey Floyd, who was not a member of the Eight but sometimes sat with them at lunch, raised her hand. "What's your siren song, Mr. Roman?" she asked.

He grinned, raked his hands through his hair. "Ladies," he said, "I never stray off the course."

"Yeah, right," said Eleanor.

"My wife would probably say Häagen-Dazs ice cream. I always tell her I'm going to cut out sweets and then I pass by those pints in the freezer section of the grocery store and I just can't help myself."

"What's your favorite flavor?" asked Suzy Branch.

"Chocolate chocolate chip," Mr. Roman said. "Gets me every time."

A buzz was felt in the room. Mr. Roman was letting them get off topic. This was something he usually curtailed the girls from doing, but it was a warm spring day and maybe he was as ready to be done with school as they were. Maybe he would even sing for them.

"Will you sing us a siren song?" asked Casey.

Mr. Roman grinned, flashing his ultrawhite teeth.

"Come on," said Casey. "Sing us a song that will veer us off course. It will be like a real-life example." She was famously bold.

"Well, I've got one that kind of fits." Mr. Roman stepped out from behind the podium where he had been lecturing, tucked his hands into the pockets of his chinos, fixed his gaze somewhere above the girls, and began singing in a clear, unwavering voice about a desperado who needed to come to his senses.

The girls burst into giggles and scattered applause.

Laney turned and grinned at Eleanor, as if they were friends. "I think he's wicked cute!" she said.

"I think you're wicked dorky!" Eleanor whispered, exactly matching Laney's breathless tone.

Mr. Roman was still singing. Ruthie wasn't sure if she was supposed to keep smiling or just watch him the way she'd watch a movie, straight-faced but interested. He was singing something about the queen of diamonds, the queen of hearts.

"I want to bear his children," whispered Casey.

"Dare you to tell him," whispered Eleanor.

He kept singing, his gaze just above the girls, his eyelids half-closed.

"No way."

"I'll do it!" volunteered Laney.

Oh my god. She would. Ruthie knew it in her bones. Laney would tell him that she wanted to have his children. On the day that she dropped twenty tampons in front of the junior high, she would declare her desire to be impregnated by her seventh-grade teacher. Ruthie wanted to lean over and tell her to shut up, just shut the hell up. Just keep your head down and get through this year and things will get better.

Julia said that in high school everyone calmed the fuck down.

Ruthie squinted her eyes, looked at them, at Eleanor and Casey smiling wickedly, encouragingly, at Laney. At Mr. Roman, in his button-down oxford shirt tucked into chinos, crooning at his seventh graders. Singing the entire song, slowly. At Laney, in her terrible acid-washed jeans, her Coventry T-shirt. Her permed hair, which might have been the style at her prior suburban public school but was certainly not in fashion at a place like Coventry. Her use of the adjective "wicked" to mean good.

Laney was going to yell out that she wanted to bear Mr. Roman's babies, and no one would ever, ever stop talking about it.

Except Ruthie wouldn't be around to hear. In less than two months, she was going to be out of this place. All of these people, so real in this room right now, would be reduced to memory.

She squinted so that everyone looked blurry, fuzzy. She imagined them receding into the distance as she boarded a plane that took her away from Coventry, away from Atlanta, away from this world. She had a glimmering realization: Soon none of this would matter. These people, these sadistic girls, they would be so far away.

Mr. Roman had (finally) reached the apex of the song, the repeated line, sung with gusto, demanding that the desperado accept love.

There was a brief moment of silence, as Mr. Roman stood, having offered himself before them. And then Casey stuck her fingers in her mouth and wolf-whistled and someone began clapping and everyone followed and Ruthie saw Laney's hand shoot up—oh God, she was going to ask to be called on before saying it—and before that could happen Ruthie heard herself shout, "I want to bear your babies!"

It didn't matter what she said. She was soon to be gone.

And everyone was laughing, as if Ruthie had just cracked the funniest joke in the world; everyone was laughing besides Laney, who looked annoyed that Ruthie had stolen her line.

And because it was Ruthie who said it, the poor girl who just lost her parents, Mr. Roman only blushed and shook his head and told the girls to stop being silly.

"Let's get back to the book," he said. "We've gotten way off course."

Chapter Five

When Ruthie and Julia walked in the back door that afternoon, Mimi was waiting for them at the kitchen table.

"Hi," said Ruthie, dropping her backpack on the floor as always.

"Hi," said Mimi. She did not smile at Ruthie like she usually did. "Julia, we need to talk."

Ruthie glanced at Julia, who looked a little roughed up. Her hair was loose and flattened a bit in the back, and her nose and cheeks were red from the sun. She did not look like someone arriving home from a diligent day of study.

Julia slipped her bag onto the center island, then walked to the refrigerator and opened it. She pulled out two Cokes.

"What about?" she asked, handing a Coke to Ruthie.

There was a crack and a hiss as Julia popped the top. Ruthie opened hers slowly, barely making a noise.

"Dean Hasher called. Said he's the Dean of Boys at Coventry? Apparently you didn't show up for any of your classes today."

Julia rolled her head slowly from one shoulder to the next, as if she were trying to stretch out a crick. "Oh yeah," said Julia. "He's right."

She walked over to the kitchen table and sat in the chair next to Mimi, placing her Coke on the hand-painted table without using a coaster. Had Phil been around, he would have insisted she use one. He had been fanatical about the use of coasters on anything that cost him money.

Ruthie remained by the center island, drinking her Coke and watching her sister respond to her aunt. Julia did not appear to be nearly as concerned as Ruthie felt she should be.

Mimi looked directly at Julia, raised her hands imploringly. "Honey, what's going on? I can't be getting calls from Coventry saying you're a no-show. I mean, what the hell did you do all day?"

Julia put the Coke can, beaded with condensation, to her forehead. She let it rest there a minute, and then pulled it away. "I'm sorry. I'm an idiot. I'm impulsive. It was a beautiful day and sometimes I just get so depressed about what happened to Mom and Phil it's hard to be at school, hard to be where everyone has such a normal life. I just couldn't take it today. I went to the park."

Ruthie gave Julia an incredulous look. Was she not going to add the fact that she went to the park with Jake Robinson? Wouldn't Mimi already know that anyway, if Dean Hasher had called?

As if she read Ruthie's mind, Mimi asked, "Did you go to the park by yourself?"

"No. I went with Jake. Look, I know everyone thinks he's bad news, but he's actually a really good guy. His mom died, too, you know, when he was little. Had an aneurism and snap, she was gone. He's the only person I really know how to talk to about all of this."

Ruthie wanted to scream, "What about me? You can talk to me!" And she knew that Jake and Julia didn't spend their time talking about their mothers. Ruthie bet Jake hardly thought about his mom anymore at all. What kind of a person plays a song about how violent sex is and then goes to the park to cry about his dead mom?

Mimi pushed on the tip of her nose with her pointer finger, a nervous gesture Ruthie had seen her do before. "You don't know what a shitty position you're putting me in, Julia. I honestly don't know what to do here. I guess I'm supposed to scream and shout and ground you. But I just don't have it in me to do that right now. And frankly, I don't know how much good it would do. Seriously, though, I need you to fucking go to school and stay there."

It was the first time Ruthie had ever heard a grown woman use the word "fuck" except for in the movies. Southern mommies just did not use that word. At least not the ones Ruthie knew. She bet Mimi didn't use to use that word, either, back when she was growing up in Tennessee.

Julia looked embarrassed, and Ruthie was glad.

"I'm sorry," Julia said. "I was being an asshole. I won't skip class again."

Apparently it was free curse day at Wymberly Way.

"I know you're angry about having to move to Virden. But maybe some good will come out of it. Maybe you and your father will build a really strong relationship. And it's only for two years. Afterwards you can apply to wherever you want for college. We all know how smart you are. You've still got time to buckle down, to apply yourself. And if you do that—and you quit skipping classes—you'll get in somewhere really top-notch. And you know what? A letter came from your dad today. It looks like he's really trying to reach out."

Julia looked suddenly very alert. "Today? Where is it?"

"It's on the marble table in the front hallway. With all the other mail."

"Are we okay? Can I go read it?"

"To be completely honest, I'm still annoyed. But sure, go ahead."

Julia sprang from her chair, kissed Mimi on top of the head, and hurried out of the room. Mimi pulled two long clips out of the back of her hair, freeing it from its chignon. She ran her fingers through her scalp for a full minute, her eyes closed. When she opened them they landed on Ruthie, who was trying to decide whether or not she could sneak out of the kitchen to follow Julia, to read her dad's letter with her.

"Do me a favor, sweetie," Mimi said. "Keep your innocence for as long as possible. I'm not good with teen drama."

"Julia and I are very different," said Ruthie. She felt disloyal saying it, but she also knew it was true. "Besides," she added. "You did great."

Just then Ruthie heard Julia screaming in the hallway. "Fuuuuuuuuuuuuck! I hate that goddamn fucking bitch!"

They heard a loud thudding as Julia ran up the stairs.

Mimi looked at Ruthie, her eyes wide. "She's not talking about me, is she?"

"I think she's probably talking about her stepmom. About Peggy."

"You want to go talk to her?" asked Mimi.

As Ruthie hurried off to find out exactly what had made her sister scream, it occurred to her that she and Julia had switched positions. That it used to be Julia who was running out of the kitchen to comfort a hysterical Ruthie, crying on the living room sofa, having been banished from the table for doing childish things.

Ruthie found Julia in her room, sitting on her bed, knees curled up to her chest. She was playing INXS, loudly.

"Can I turn this down?" Ruthie asked.

Julia shrugged. Ruthie walked over to the stereo, turned down the volume.

"Aunt Mimi wants to know if she's the g.d. f-ing mag you were talking about?"

Julia pushed a little breath of air out of her mouth, shook her head at Ruthie, as if she were hopelessly naïve.

"I got my response from Dad. They're not budging. He thinks San Francisco is not an appropriate place for a 'spirited teen' like me. It's straight out of Peggy's mouth. God, I hate her."

"Let me see the letter," said Ruthie, walking to the bed with her hand held out.

"You can read it, but bottom line, they're making me go to Virden."

Ruthie read it anyway. She wanted to see for herself.

April 16, 1993

Dear Julia,

Peggy and I received your letter the other day, and we both appreciate the care you put into it. After I read it I rummaged through the boxes I've got stored in the attic, looking for those pictures you sent me when you were a little girl. We took them down when Peggy first moved in. She noticed that the edges were curling and said they would be safer in an album. You'll be interested to know that I found five of your drawings. Three are of cats, one is of a dog, and one is of you. The cats are orange, black, and brown and white striped. The dog is brown, and you, of course, have that beautiful red hair that you got from your mother.

I suppose you sent me pictures of all of those animals because you imagined I was lonely and you wanted me to have some companions. Well, I was lonely, sweetheart. You were right. It was a hard time. You are also correct when you say that Peggy coming into my life was a blessing. Peggy followed by Sam.

Julia, it's always been one of our wishes that you knew your half brother better than you do. Please remember that you are as related to him as you are to Ruthie. Someday you might even feel as close to him as you do to your sister.

I know it is going to be hard to be separated, but we want you to know that Ruthie is allowed to visit any time she wants. If she would like, she can come spend a few weeks with us every summer, just as you used to do. In your letter you spoke about applying the "wisdom of Solomon" to your situation. Well, Peggy and I have been talking about it, and we think that the wisest decision is for you to come live with us in Virden. We believe we can offer you a steadier environment here than you would have in San Francisco. There are many reasons for this, and here are just a few: Neither Mimi nor Robert are your blood relatives, and they might not feel as responsible toward you as we will. Neither Mimi nor Robert have ever had children, and we are not sure if they know what it takes to be a parent. Plus, sweetheart, from what I understand, they live in the middle of the city. I am sure that is an exciting place to be, but I'm not sure it's best for a teenage girl. Especially a spirited teenager like yourself. Peggy in particular feels strongly about this.

I imagine this letter will be greeted with some disappointment, but I hope you are soon able to see that you coming to live with us in Virden is really the best solution. I think you are going to like living here. Not only will you be able to develop your relationship with Sam; you will be able to develop your relationship with Peggy, too. She always wanted a daughter, you know. And now she can be a real mom to you.

If you would like to talk about this more on the phone, that's fine. Just call us. Call us anyway; it is always good to hear your voice. And we'll be seeing you soon. On June 10 as planned.

With love,

Dad

Part Two

Chapter Six

All was lost, all was changed, and Ruthie could not get warm.

The morning of their departure from Atlanta, Mimi had suggested that Ruthie dress in warmer clothes than a tank top and shorts, but Ruthie politely ignored her aunt. Atlanta was so muggy and hot it was impossible to believe she would ever feel cold again. Simply walking from their taxi to the entrance of the Atlanta airport caused little beads of sweat to appear on Mimi's upper lip. Hours later they landed in thick fog, the temperature forty degrees cooler. Ruthie shivered as she and Mimi stood on the sidewalk in front of SFO, scanning for Uncle Robert's silver Audi.

"Mark Twain said the coldest winter he ever spent was summer in San Francisco," Mimi said.

It was the first time Ruthie had ever heard that saying, but it would not be the last. It turned out everyone said it in San Francisco, everyone delighted in rolling it out to any newcomer surprised by the cold summer.

Not just cold. Bone-chilling. Ruthie's bones were chilled, even though Mimi immediately bought her thick scarves to wrap around her neck, a fleece jacket, a puffy down vest, mittens. In the room where Ruthie slept, which overlooked the tiny backyard garden where calla lilies bloomed, the window was leaky, a half-inch gap between it and the pane.

"Robert jokes that all our windows are nailed open," said Mimi, when first showing Ruthie the flat. Ruthie stood in the doorway, surveying the space, which was half the size of the bedroom she had left behind. "It's wasteful, I know, but don't you think the old wavy glass is beautiful?"

Mimi claimed she loved beauty even more than her brother, Phil, had. Though she could not be such a purist with her clients, when decorating her own home, anytime she had to choose aesthetics or function, aesthetics always won. So instead of cluttering up the living room with a boxy TV, Mimi chose simply not to have one. (Later, when flat screens came along, she relented.) Instead of putting a washer/dryer where the outlets were in the kitchen, which would have taken up precious space and jutted into the area where beautiful foods were to be prepared, Mimi used the wash and fold down the street. (Or, to be more accurate, she dropped her laundry off there on her way to her office in Hayes Valley and had someone else wash and fold it.) Mimi even used her sterling silver as her everyday flatware.

"We have it, it's gorgeous, why not?" she said. "I suppose if we had been able to have children we would have been more practical, but we couldn't, and so . . ."

She waved a tarnished repoussé fork in the air to finish making her point. A lover of beauty or not, Mimi rarely got around to polishing the silver. Of course, Ruthie's mother never polished her silver, either, but Addie Mae the housekeeper did.

"Addie Mae *loves* polishing silver!" Phil used to say.

Once Julia added, "Just like she *loves* ironing your shirts!"

Phil had glared at her. "Don't be a smart-ass," he barked.

He was a man who, though he loved to tease, was not so good at being teased himself.

Maybe it was better that everything was so different in San Francisco. Maybe if Ruthie had stayed in Atlanta, had, say, lived with the Loves while Julia went to Virden to live with her dad and Peggy, things would have been even harder. Ruthie would have forever been *near* but never *at* home. Whereas San Francisco, San Francisco was a different planet, with its rolling fogs and cold summers, its eucalyptus trees that made the air smell medicinal, its houses packed so close together, and none shaded by one-hundred-year-old white oaks, as Ruthie's house on Wymberly Way had been.

Almost all of the houses on Mars Street were attached on each side, with only front and rear windows. Mimi and Robert's house (they co-owned the property with friends, the Woodses, who lived in the flat downstairs) was rare in that it was freestanding, but it stood so close to the house next door that Mimi could reach her hand out the kitchen window and rub it against her neighbor's siding. Ruthie wondered if this, plus the fact that they only owned the upstairs half of the property, meant her aunt and uncle didn't have much money. But that didn't make sense, because the inside was filled with old rugs and gleaming wooden chests of drawers, upholstered sofas and chairs topped with bright silk pillows, vibrant paintings preserved behind thick glass, lined silk curtains on the windows. Robert and Mimi had money. It was just that like everything else, money in San Francisco presented itself differently than it did in Atlanta.

The worst moment of every day was waking up, opening her eyes, and remembering where she was. The bathroom was down the hall, not attached to her bedroom, and her uncle Robert might well be using it, as there was only one toilet in the entire flat. Ruthie was terribly anxious during those first few months that she might stop up the toilet and only Robert would be home to help her clean up the mess.

Her sister was thousands of miles away, at her father's house in Virden, VA, not across the hall in her queen-sized bed, big enough for Ruthie to share if Julia deigned to let her. Her parents—she did not know where her parents were, but she knew she would never see them again except in photographs. Naomi was not about to wake her, to tell her with forced cheer (Naomi had not been a morning person) *to rise and shine, breakfast will be ready in ten minutes!*

It was summer, and Aunt Mimi believed that with all she had gone through, Ruthie deserved to sleep in. So no one would appear in the doorway at all. Each night Mimi would tell Ruthie to help herself to anything in the kitchen when she woke up, that there was cereal in the cabinet, juice and milk in the fridge.

"We're out of regular milk, but there's soy milk. Do you like soy milk?"

Ruthie did not. She found it too watery, too sweet. Yet what was the point of telling Mimi she did not like it? Everything had changed. She might as well get used to another new thing.

"Do you want to go to the museum this weekend?"

"Walk across the Golden Gate Bridge?"

"Take a ferry to Sausalito?"

Ruthie did not, did not, did not. She did not want to do anything that forced her to leave the flat, to go outside into the strange cold air.

Ruthie's refusals did not seem to bother Mimi. The only requirement she had of Ruthie was that she meet with a therapist. And so, once Ruthie was more or less settled into the flat, and once she more or less knew her way around the neighborhood streets (walking down the hill took you to the Castro, up the hill and to the right to Cole Valley), Mimi arranged for Ruthie to see Dr. Cooper two days a week, Tuesday and Thursday mornings at 10:00 during the summer and, once the school year began, Tuesdays and Thursdays at 5:30.

It was Dr. Cooper who saved her, not because he helped her unearth buried feelings of grief and rage, but because he told her it was okay to pour all of her energy into external concerns: reading during the summer, and sometimes helping Uncle Robert cook, and, once school began, studying.

That past spring, when it was determined that Ruthie was coming to San Francisco to stay, Mimi had managed to enroll her niece at the Eleanor Hope Hall School for Girls. Hall's had been around for almost a hundred years. The middle school girls—the oldest of the students—wore sailor uniforms, blue skirts and white middies with blue flaps. Hall's was in the ritzy Pacific Heights neighborhood, in a pink marble building that overlooked the bay.

Ruthie was embarrassed when Mimi showed her the babyish sailor uniform she was required to wear, yet she was also relieved that she did not have to figure out what the styles were for eighth-grade girls in San Francisco, at least not immediately, not until a "free dress" day or a weekend spent with a friend.

During the fall of Ruthie's eighth-grade year at Hall's, a weekend spent with a friend seemed increasingly unlikely. Most of the girls had attended the school since they were kindergartners. Eighth grade was it; the following year they would splinter off, heading to various private day schools in the city and Marin, boarding schools on the East Coast, or the magnet public high school, Lowell.

No one was exactly unfriendly, but Ruthie definitely felt like an interloper and an oddity at Hall's. She shocked her fellow classmates one morning in homeroom when she admitted that she had never been to a Bar or a Bat Mitzvah. And they giggled at her use of the word "y'all," asking her to say it again and again.

But besides a casual interest in her southern exoticism, no one reached out to be her friend. No one, that is, besides Dara Diamond, who had purple-tinted hair and wore black lipstick, a girl who claimed to dress "full-out grunge" on the weekends. On the third day of the school year, Dara had sat down next to Ruthie in the outside courtyard during Snack, the fifteen-minute break in the middle of morning classes. Ruthie was sitting on the low wall of the courtyard, watching the little kids play kickball, eating a hard-boiled egg. Though the cafeteria menu changed daily, during Snack you could always get an egg.

"You know the yolk is yellow because that's the color the chick would have been, right?" asked Dara.

Ruthie glanced at her, and then looked at the crumbly yolk of her half-eaten egg. "Gross," she said.

"I know. Totally gross. My sister is always telling me crap like that because she's a vegan and she wants everyone else to be a vegan, too. Which drives my mom crazy. I mean, my mom is like practically best friends with Alice Waters, so she totally worships food and thinks nothing should be forbidden. Except, you know, junk food. And going to school with boys."

Ruthie knew about Alice Waters because of Robert. He had told Ruthie that Alice was an "important" chef, possibly the most important chef in America. He said that sometime soon they would drive over to Berkeley to eat at her restaurant, Chez Panisse.

Dara swept her arm from left to right, as if she were a tour guide at a museum, making a pronouncement about an entire collection.

"Smell the estrogen," she said, widening her nostrils for effect.

"That's dumb," said Ruthie, focusing her attention on Dara, wondering what it was that made some people just *spill* everything.

"I know. Veganism *is* dumb. It's like, I'm sorry, but she wants me to give up cheese? I practically live on cheese. Especially the *queso* dip they serve at Chevys. Oh my god, that stuff is so good, maybe sometime—"

Ruthie looked at Dara so coldly it was as if she dried the words up in her mouth. "What's dumb," she said, "is your saying you can smell the estrogen at Hall's. Hello? You don't have estrogen until you have your period, which means that at most maybe half of the seventh grade and most of the eighth grade has it. That's *not* the whole school."

Ruthie felt a little thrill at her rudeness. (How polite she was at Robert and Mimi's house! How much like a visitor she felt, even though it had been three months since she moved in.)

"You're telling me Mrs. Lowery doesn't get raging PMS?" asked Dara.

Ruthie laughed, despite herself. Even though she'd only had

her for two classes so far, Mrs. Lowery stood out. Yolanda Lowery (who allowed the girls to call her "Yo Lo") was the acting teacher. Every eighth grader was required to take her class because at the end of the year the entire grade put on a musical, complete with costumes and set design created by the girls. Yo Lo's flamboyant dress—she was especially fond of flouncy skirts and all things purple—and her utter belief in the girls' talent made her popular with the students, but the rumor was, God help you if you got on her bad side, which Dara apparently had. It was said that Yo Lo, who was in her late fifties and had been teaching at Hall's for over thirty years, used to whap the tops of distracted girls' heads with a yardstick, back when such things were permitted.

"Even if you count the teachers, that's hardly the majority of the school," Ruthie said primly.

"Hardly" was not a word Ruthie usually used. It was a Phil word, one he pulled out when he was trying to win an argument. "That's hardly relevant," he would say, or, "I hardly think that matters. . . ."

"Do *you* have PMS?" asked Dara. "Not to be a jerk or anything, but you kind of act like a snob."

"Not to be a jerk or anything," mimicked Ruthie. "God."

Ruthie tried not to show it, but she was a little pleased. Being labeled a snob was much better than being labeled a clueless southerner.

The truth was, she wasn't trying to be snobby, at least not toward anyone but Dara. It was simply that Ruthie didn't have her bearings. Just last spring she was firmly ensconced on Coventry's campus, its white-columned brick buildings lined in perfect geometric order among rolling green lawns and towering trees, the leaves of which shaded the students, who trotted from building to building in their collared polo shirts, their L.L. Bean backpacks hanging off one shoulder.

Now she was enrolled in a school housed in a pink marble mansion that towered above the sea, where girls wore sailor uniforms and her French teacher was a lesbian—no secret about it!

Where every morning at 10:15 Ruthie stood in line in the cafeteria to have a Spanish-speaking woman in a hairnet hand her a hard-boiled egg, still warm. Where her classmates were the children of famous people: a mystery writer who sold so many books she owned three houses all on the same block overlooking the bay, an economist from Berkeley who last year was given the Nobel Prize. One of Ruthie's classmates was from a family who had a whole wing named after them at the San Francisco MOMA.

How was she to act among these people? She had barely broken the code at Coventry and now here she was, completely alien to California culture, just as she had been alien to Coventry culture the year before.

"I guess I act like a snob because I come from Mars," she told Dara, relenting.

"You mean Mars the planet or Mars the street?"

"You know Mars Street?" asked Ruthie, surprised. Most of her classmates did not live near the Castro. Most lived in the Avenues, or in Pacific Heights or Sea Cliff.

"Dude, we live on Uranus," said Dara.

"Hardy, har, har," said Ruthie. "That's so funny I forgot to laugh."

"No, I'm serious. My mom's house is on Uranus Terrace. We're neighbors."

"Oh wow," said Ruthie. There was a Uranus Terrace in her neighborhood.

She was briefly excited by the fact that they both lived on streets named after planets. Then she noticed how absolutely eager Dara looked, how she was leaning toward Ruthie as if they were about to share confidences, as if she believed they were on their way to becoming fast friends.

Ruthie needed a friend. But she wasn't sure if she wanted a friend who seemed to need her just as much.

Ruthie buried herself in schoolwork. During lunch she would go to the library, preparing her assignments for the next day. Before the bell rang and classes began, she did not laugh and talk with the other girls, did not discuss who might or might not be at that weekend's dance at the Jewish Community Center, did not plan trips to Union Square to buy new jeans. She sat quietly at her desk. She reviewed her notes from the previous day's lesson.

She liked most of her teachers at Hall's, and they liked her. Most were fairly traditional in their pedagogical approach, and that suited Ruthie just fine, reminded her of Coventry in fact. But in one class the students were encouraged to sit in a circle on the floor and "let it all hang out." That was Zeigfeld's—"call me Mr. Z"—class, eighth-grade English, and Ruthie hated it. During the second week of class Mr. Z gave the girls an assignment to bring in an object from their childhood that they cared deeply about and then talk about why that object held such significance. This proved hard for Ruthie, who did not want to dig through the boxes of childhood artifacts she had brought with her from Atlanta. For comfort that first week in San Francisco she had dug out the rag doll Naomi had sewed for her when she was four, whom Ruthie had named Crystal Bell.

But Ruthie could not bring Crystal Bell to class. There was an unseemly quality to her, primarily because over the years the doll had developed dark stains on her pink cotton skin. Naomi used to say that Ruthie loved Crystal Bell "just a little too much." Julia used to call the doll Melanoma Bell. Certainly she was not the type of thing to bring into a group of eighth graders, many of whom had probably played with dolls with real hair and porcelain faces in their homes in Pacific Heights.

Instead Ruthie brought in an orange, purchased the night before at Eureka Market. When it was her time to share with the circle, she said, "When I was a kid my favorite snack was always an orange. Even if my mom offered me ice cream, or cookies, I usually chose orange slices."

"How did your friends react to that?" asked Mr. Z.

Ruthie knew that he wanted her to add some drama to the story, to say that she was teased, or people assumed she was a suck-up, or that she devised a clever method to barter her desserts for oranges *plus* cash.

"No one really cared," she said.

She looked down at her lap. Usually when she did that Mr. Z left her alone. Which he did, calling on Deena, who had lugged in the first saddle she ever owned, a tiny though substantial thing that smelled of leather and animal sweat.

While Deena spoke lustfully about riding her mare, Silky, Mr. Z kept looking at Ruthie, even cocking his head to the side at one point. As soon as the bell rang he told her he wanted the two of them to have a "powwow."

"I'll write you a tardy excuse," he said. "Don't worry."

Being tardy was the last thing Ruthie was worried about. The punishment for tardiness was to receive a notice. Two notices equaled a detention, which meant you had to spend an hour after school helping the office ladies make copies. That in itself did not sound too unpleasant, and besides which, she had never actually seen anyone receive a detention. The girls at Hall's were good at talking their way out of things.

"Ruthie," said Mr. Z. "I don't mean to pry. But I know that something very difficult happened to you not so long ago, and I just want you to know that this classroom is a place where you can share some of your sadness."

Ruthie nodded and Mr. Z pressed on. "Isn't there some object from your childhood more meaningful than an orange?"

Ruthie wished she felt composed enough to tell him that she also liked apples, but she did not. She felt like she was going to cry, and she really didn't want to cry in front of him. To do so would bring him too much satisfaction. She looked down at her feet.

"Okay, kiddo," he said.

There was nothing she hated more than being called kiddo.

"You don't feel like sharing. I understand. Take your time. No pressure from me. Just know that whatever feelings you shove down are going to have to come up again sometime. And some people think it's better to control when it comes up than to have it just one day boil over and take you by surprise."

Ruthie imagined a boiling mess of green grief bubbling out of her mouth the first time a boy tried to kiss her. She smiled at the image.

"May I be excused now?" she asked.

"One more thing." He walked over to his desk, looked around for a scrap of paper, and scribbled her an excuse for being tardy. "You don't want to forget this, do you?"

Talk. That was all people did in San Francisco.

Talk, talk, talk, talk, talk, talk, talk.

Talk at dinner, talk on the phone, meet for coffee and talk, take walks in the morning up and down the hills, talking.

Processing was what Aunt Mimi called it. That or unpacking, as in "let's try to unpack your feelings about this situation."

Mimi told Ruthie that everyone was trying to be conscious.

Everyone was trying to be intentional.

Everyone was trying to be honest.

Ruthie just wanted to be left alone.

She wanted nothing more than to retire to her tiny bedroom after dinner, do her homework, check it twice, and, if there was time afterwards, read a book. (Actually, what she really wanted to do was watch TV, but in Mimi's house, that was not an option.)

Uncle Robert seemed to understand Ruthie's desire for alone time. He was quiet by nature, a writer who sometimes got so lost in his head Aunt Mimi would resort to snapping her fingers in his face to get his attention. Sometimes Robert snapped back. Once he told her not to treat him like a dog. Other times he smiled, sheepishly, and called himself an absentminded professor. Except he wasn't a professor; he was a writer of self-help books for business leaders, his most successful titled *Chi Your Mind . . . and the Rest Will Follow.* When Ruthie first saw it—along with a row of foreign editions—on the bookshelf in Uncle Robert's office, she pronounced "chi" like the Greek letter, like Chi Omega sorority. But

Robert said it was pronounced "chee, like you're almost saying 'cheese' but not quite."

Ruthie asked Robert what "chi" meant. He told her that it was a Chinese term that stood for balance and well-being.

"To be honest," he said, "I'm no expert on Chinese philosophy. But the book's point is this: If you live from a generous frame of mind, if you train your psyche to assume abundance instead of scarcity, success will follow. But you can't only be generous when dealing with the top dogs. You have to be generous with the little guys as well, your server at a restaurant, Amelia who rings you up at Alpha, the Muni worker who drives the streetcar."

"Have *you* cheed your mind?" asked Ruthie.

Robert shrugged. "Sure, I try. But at the end of the day, I'm just the scribe. And the more of these books I write, the more often we can get roast chicken at Zuni."

Zuni Café was Robert and Mimi's favorite place to eat. Located in a strange, angular building on Market Street near Franklin, the restaurant initially confused Ruthie, because she knew it was supposed to be a special, fancy place and yet it was nothing like the special, fancy places in Atlanta. It had no tablecloths; the stairs leading to the second floor were steep and unwieldy; the diners were seated as close together as the houses on Robert and Mimi's street. Yet no matter what night of the week, Zuni was always packed. Even though Mimi always made a reservation, they usually had to wait at the bar for a few minutes before being shown to their seats, which Mimi said was part of the fun because that allowed them to people watch.

And people watch they did. The most interesting people ate there! Older men and women who did not dress as if they were older, who dressed instead as if they were characters in a strange, abstract play. Women with cropped hair, spiked hair, bleached hair, crazy hair. Men in T-shirts that read: ACT UP; women in three-piece suits. One crazy-haired woman argued so fiercely with her male companion over whether or not Mia Farrow was a fashion icon that Ruthie thought they were going to get in a fistfight.

At the restaurant, there were women with women. Men with men. Ruthie had never seen so many gay people in her life. In Atlanta Naomi had once rented the garage apartment behind the house to two women, but when Ruthie asked her mom if they were lesbians Naomi had grown irritated and said it was rude to make assumptions. And once Ruthie's parents had dragged her to see *Torch Song Trilogy*, because they had read a good review of it in the *New York Times* and they couldn't find a babysitter. Ruthie, who was in the fourth grade at the time, had been utterly mortified by the whole thing.

Except now—only months after moving to San Francisco—she couldn't remember why she was embarrassed by it. *Everyone* was gay in San Francisco. Or if they weren't gay, they were weird—punk, pierced, androgynous. Even at Hall's, which was one of the more traditional private schools in the city, several of her class-mates had two moms and Abigail Stevenson had two dads. And there was Ruthie's French teacher, Madame Dubois, elegant in her tailored pants and tucked-in blouses, who spoke openly about her partner, Isabelle.

Sometimes Ruthie felt as if she had been swept into a vortex, a Twilight Zone. Sometimes it seemed hard to believe that Buck-head actually still existed. It was so very different from where she was now; it was as if it spun on a different axis.

Robert loved to eat raw oysters, which Ruthie thought was dis-gusting until she overheard the two most popular girls from her class at Hall's rhapsodizing over how much they loved Kumamoto oysters, which were small and surprisingly sweet. (Another differ-ence, another change. At Coventry Eleanor Pope and the Eight had loved iceberg lettuce and unbuttered French bread.) And so Ruthie joined Robert in the first part of his Zuni ritual: the slid-ing of a half-dozen raw oysters down the throat, while Aunt Mimi sipped a glass of champagne and nibbled on Acme bread. For the next course, Robert and Mimi would split a Caesar salad, ordering extra anchovies on the side. During the salad course Ruthie always ordered shoestring French-fried potatoes, which were thin, hot, and salty.

And finally, the three of them would split the Zuni roast chicken. Unlike the oysters, the roast chicken took no getting used to. Ruthie loved it from the beginning. Salt-brined for days, stuffed with herbs, and then roasted in a hot wood oven, the chicken was served with a salad made of cubes of toasted sourdough bread, pine nuts, currants, and arugula, then tossed with a champagne vinaigrette and juices from the cooked chicken.

Eating the salty meat with the flavored, warm bread made Ruthie feel inordinately comforted. It seemed to have the same effect on Ruthie as drinking had on Mimi, whose shoulders relaxed and eyes softened as soon as she took the first sip from her champagne flute. For Ruthie, taking that first bite of chicken made her forget about the strange and lonely new life she had somehow fallen into. Or rather, not so much forget as momentarily not mind.

At night, once the lights were out and she was lying in her bed, not sleeping, she ached for Julia, missing her even more than her parents, for Julia was still alive, Julia was still, technically, reachable, although Ruthie found it harder and harder to connect with her on the phone. It was the three-hour time difference that made things so difficult, that and the fact that Mimi and Robert always ate late, around 8:00, so that if Ruthie wanted to call Julia after dinner it would be nearly midnight Virginia time. And calling before dinner was tough because there was therapy two days a week, plus homework. Not to mention the fact that Uncle Robert, who worked from home, often made business calls in the late afternoon.

The first week after Ruthie moved to San Francisco she did call Julia after dinner, figuring that it was summertime and Julia would probably be up late.

The phone rang three times before someone picked up. Ruthie heard Julia say "hello," but then she heard another voice, the voice of an irritated woman, Peggy.

"Who in the world is calling at this hour?" she asked.

"I got it, Peggy," said Julia in her most insolent tone. "You can hang up now."

"Julia dear, I don't need for you to tell me what I can and cannot do. Who is calling?"

"It's me, Ruthie, from California." (How strange it was to say she lived in California.)

"Okay? So hang up the phone now," said Julia.

"Ruthie, honey, it's good to hear your voice," said Peggy. "It would be even better to hear your voice before nine P.M."

Ruthie, near tears, apologized for the late call.

After Peggy hung up, Julia spent the rest of the conversation detailing what a bitch her stepmother was. Every weekend Peggy would make a long list of chores for Julia to do, and if she didn't finish with them by nightfall, she couldn't go out. Peggy threw away Julia's favorite pair of ripped jeans, saying that "there was no need to go around deliberately dressing like trash." Worse, Peggy implied that it was Phil and Naomi's fault that they were dead, that they were utterly foolish to have boarded the Ford Trimotor.

"Those two never thought about the consequences of their actions, did they?" Peggy said.

"Of course the real reason Peggy hates me is because I look like Mom," said Julia. "She knows Mom left Dad and not the other way around, and she resents that I resemble the woman who broke his heart."

"Gosh, Julia," said Ruthie. She really didn't know what else to say. Peggy sounded horrible.

"How's Aunt Mimi?" Julia finally asked.

"She's good," said Ruthie. "She's really nice."

"Well, lucky you."

"Yeah, I sure am lucky," said Ruthie, irritated.

For a moment neither of them spoke, and then Julia said she had to get off. Hanging up the phone, Ruthie was more aware of the distance between her and her sister than she had been before the call. Their lives had taken such different turns.

Somehow the difference in their lives was easier to accept through letters. In writing, Julia presented the details of her new life in Virden with humor and irony. In fact, Ruthie heard her sister's voice clearer in letters than she did on the phone. It was like being in bed with Julia, late at night, when Julia would tell Ruthie stories, or play Seven Steps to an Unlikely Outcome, a game she had invented. To play, Julia would come up with a far-fetched ending to a story that had yet to be told, something along the lines of, "Phil quits his job, gives away all of his money, and becomes a Hare Krishna." And then Julia and Ruthie would have to create the story in seven steps, starting with step one ("Phil notices a homeless man holding an 'I will work for food' sign on his way to work . . .") and going back and forth with the telling until they reached step seven, where the story had to end with Julia's prescribed resolution.

"And it has to be logical, too," Julia would instruct. "Each step has to work with the one that preceded it."

Only now, it was as if their *lives* had become the game. All of Julia's letters to Ruthie contained details that could have been taken straight from a round of Seven Steps. And though many painful things were happening to her, Julia wrote of her new reality with a certain bemused acceptance. She told of her two paternal grandparents, Rhubarb and Elsie, who only had twenty teeth between the two of them but still ate Milky Ways every day, sucking the candy bars like Popsicles. She told of being pressured at church not only to sign a virginity pledge ("too late!" Julia had written) but also to attach a small pink plastic baby to her key chain to show her support for Operation Rescue.

As for Ruthie, writing letters to Julia allowed her to share her new life without feeling so self-conscious. Without feeling as if she were bragging about the fact that she landed the better deal. She wrote of eating Kumamotos—knowing her sister would wrinkle her nose—and taking long walks with the overweight uncle Robert, who would always buy the two of them some sort of treat in the course of their outing, making her promise not to tell Mimi, who, in general, did not approve of processed sugar or snacking between meals.

"But what's the point of a walk without a destination?" Robert would ask, usually as they were nearing Tart to Tart, a bakery in the Inner Sunset.

And Ruthie would say that there was no point, no point in walking at all, unless you were rewarded with cake. And with that agreed upon, they would push open the door of the bakery and stand in line along the display case of sweets.

"You won't believe how many cakes there are to choose from," Ruthie wrote. "We'll have to try to taste them all when you come for Thanksgiving."

Chapter Seven

October 1, 1993

Dear Biscuit,

Man, do I miss you! And man, do I wish that I was in San Francisco, or you were in Virden—don't laugh—one or the other, so long as the two of us could hang. I mean, I wouldn't need you to be my shadow or anything. We wouldn't have to spend *all* of our time together. We wouldn't have to share baths or watch each other pee or anything like that. . . .

Speaking of peeing, do you remember the time when you were little and you got that urinary tract infection because you were wiping the wrong way—back to front instead of front to back? And you had to take those pills that turned your pee orange? You were eight at the time and every time you peed you wanted to show me because it looked so weird. Anyway, one night during The Time of the Orange Urine, you slept with me in my bed. When I got up the next morning and went to the bathroom (you, of course, were still lying lazily beneath the covers) I asked you why the cap was missing from my brand-new expensive tube of Shiseido facial wash I had gotten for my birthday. And you said, oh yeah, that in the middle of the night you had gotten up to pee, and at the same time you had taken the cap off of my Shiseido wash to smell it and had somehow managed to drop the cap into the toilet. And so you very kindly left the cap off so you would remember the next morning to tell me that it had been floating in orange pee.

Hmm, maybe it is a good thing we ended up in two different places. . . .

Just kidding. I miss you tons. Virden pretty much blows the big one. It is beyond boring here. There is nothing to do but watch TV, go to the crappy ass mall featuring the oh-so-sophisticated Belk's as its anchor store, and look out my window at the mountains. I guess my boredom will serve you well, 'cuz it means you will be the lucky recipient of my vivacious wit and wisdom, as told through my wicked pen.

Peggy is a total bitch, as to be expected. Today I made chocolate-chip cookies (told ya I'm bored), and just as I started creaming the butter and sugars she warned me that she had bought *very* expensive chocolate chips so I "should save them all for the dough and not snack on them." So I'm expecting the chips to be really impressive, right, to be made out of Jesus' dark flesh or something like that, but when I look in the pantry all I see is a twelve-ounce bag of Hershey's semisweet morsels.

Way to live it up, Pegs. No Kroger brand for you!

Dad doesn't seem to know what to do with me. He is spending a *lot* of time out back, in his workroom. He and Sam are building me a desk, which I guess is nice, though it's not really necessary. I always just sit on my bed to do my homework. Plus I don't really like the thought of Sam having anything to do with any part of my life. Remember how he was always a little creepy? Well, he's way creepy now. And way religious. He actually listens to Christian rock. It's all about lifting up your hands to praise the Lord. I bet God hates that crap. I ask you: how can "praise music" be worthy of God's ears? It is all so vapid. Makes me think about Coventry, actually, and how during one assembly this conductor dude came and talked about how you don't find God *through* books, music, art, nature. You find God *in* books, music, art nature. . . .

Jeez, did I just wax nostalgic about Coventry??? Virden must really suck.

So how are you, Goofy Ruthie? Granddaddy Rhubarb told me a joke about San Francisco. Not sure where he got it from because all he and Granny Elsie do is sit around and watch the PTL channel. (That's Praise The Lord to you, my lil' San Francisco heathen.)

Anyway, wanna hear it? Wanna hear it?

Of course you do!

Here goes: There was this mussel and this clam and they were best friends. The clam was named Sam and the mussel was named Fred. Well, one day they each die, and Fred the mussel—who was a good and noble mussel—shoots straight up to heaven, where he meets Saint Peter and is given a golden harp. Sam the clam, who was always a little naughty, shoots straight down to hell, where he promptly opens an all-night club, called Disco Inferno.

Fred the mussel misses his friend Sam the clam terribly, so he asks Saint Peter if he might go visit. Saint Peter grudgingly approves, and Fred grabs his harp and shoots down to visit Sam. They have a hell of a time. They eat fried foods, talk all night, play music, drink, catch up, etc. The next morning Fred is due back in heaven. He says his good-byes to Sam and heads back up. Saint Peter is waiting for him at the pearly gates. The first thing Peter says is, "Fred, where is your golden harp?" Fred looks all around, realizes what happened, gulps, and says, "I left my harp in Sam clam's disco."

Get it? Get it? "I left my harp in Sam clam's disco" . . . "I left my heart in San Francisco"?

Did you laugh so hard you peed your pants? Surely. (And are you crying great tears of sympathy for me that Sam the clam jokes are what pass as high entertainment in Virden? Or, at least, at Granddaddy Rhubarb's house?)

Goofy Ruthie, I miss you so much. More than Mom even, in a weird way. I mean, she's gone. And you're still here. Except you're not. At least, you're nowhere near Virden, VA. Which is great for you, sucky for me.

I think about you every day. You and your stinky farts.

Write back, write back, write back! I'll be waiting with bated breath. Hope I don't pass out.

Love,

Your older and infinitely wiser sister, Egg

October 8, 1993

Dear Egg,

That joke about Sam the clam was the worst! Robert and Mimi say so, too, but then, maybe it's not so bad, because last night Robert told it to one of his friends who came over for dinner and his friend laughed really hard at the punch line. Then again, his friend drank about five glasses of wine, so maybe he was just drunk.

Probably I shouldn't tell you this, because I know you will think it's sick, but last night I ate rabbit. Yep, rabbit. Uncle Robert, who does most of the cooking, had fixed rabbit a couple of times before, but up until last night I just sort of pretended to eat it and filled up on bread instead because, you know, I kept thinking about *The Runaway Bunny*. But last night he cooked the rabbit with mustard and cream and served it over polenta with all of these really yummy vegetables—roasted butternut squash and greens and a few roasted beets—and it just looked so good that I had to try. Julia, it was DELISH. We will have to get Uncle Robert to make it for you when you come out here! Rabbit meat actually does taste like chicken, but more flavorful, more chickeny, if that makes sense.

Shoot, I have to go. Aunt Mimi is calling me. We are going to the alteration place to have my school uniform hemmed. TO BE CONTINUED . . .

Okay, I'm back. The alteration lady is also the dry cleaner. She's Oriental—I mean Asian. (That's what Mimi says is nicest to say.) Anyway, I guess the dry-cleaner lady lost one of Mimi's sweaters a while back, because today when we walked into the shop she cried out, her voice getting louder and higher with each word: "I. Found. Your. SWEATA!!!" I've been saying it over and over again to Aunt Mimi all afternoon.

> Aunt Mimi: Should we go get a hot chocolate?
> Hilarious Ruthie: I. Found. Your. SWEATA!!
> Aunt Mimi: Do you want to eat at La Med or at home tonight?
> Hilarious Ruthie: I. Found. Your. SWEATA!!

Okay, so this is also kind of funny: At the dry cleaner's, Mimi and I fought about the length of my uniform skirt. All year she's been bugging me to get it hemmed, like five inches above the knee. She says the goal is to look cute, not frumpy. I told her about Dean Brown at Coventry, how she would walk around the school carrying a ruler in hand, measuring all of our hemlines. Mimi thought that was hilarious. "Phil certainly put you in the lion's den, didn't he?" she asked. I told her that no one took Dean Brown too seriously, that everyone made fun of her walking around with her stupid ruler, wearing her beehive from the 1960s.

Arguing with Mimi over the length of my skirt made me think about the time that Mom and I got into that big fight over whether or not I could wear a piece of her cut-up nude panty hose as a headband. Remember how we would tie our hair back with her old hose? Mom *hated* it. She made me take the hose out before she would unlock the car door so I could get out and go to school. She said if I wore cut-up hose to class everyone would think I was raised in a trailer. I remember being so mad at her, thinking that she was just so snobby and clueless. And now I can't imagine wanting to go to school with part of someone's hose hanging off my head!

But just that year Mom started going to that little shop at Phipps Plaza that sold all of those crazy sequined outfits. You said she was going through an "Adventurous Period." That was around the same time that weird client of Dad's took them to that nightclub called Lipstick, where all of the men were dressed like women. They were so giggly about having gone there! Like they were just the coolest two people on earth. Anyway, I remember being really embarrassed by the clothes she bought at that shop. There was this one outfit that I thought was super tacky. It was a black sequined pants suit and it was made of this stretchy lacy material that was see-through all the way up her thighs. I remember thinking, as she said good-bye at the door before she and Dad went to their Christmas party, that I was glad I didn't have a friend over that night, because I wouldn't have wanted anyone from school to see her.

I have a photo of Mom and Dad from that night. I'm looking at it right now. Dad is wearing a tuxedo and his hair is neat and short. Mom is about five inches taller than him because she is wearing heels. In the photo Mom is smiling really big and she looks really pretty. Really pretty and really thin. (Remember how all she would ever eat for lunch was a fruit plate? But then she said she ruined her diet every night by always having a drink with Dad and chocolate for dessert?)

It makes me so sad to look at these photos of Mom. She looks so alive.

But I know she's not.

Send me some of those expensive chocolate-chip cookies you made.

Love,

Biscuit

October 15, 1993

Dear Biscuit,

Aw, sweetie, I miss Mom, too. And I find looking at photos of her harder than anything. You're right, she looks so real, so alive, you think you can just pick up the phone and call her. For me the hardest thing about looking at photos of Mom is knowing that she's never going to age beyond the most recent ones. Knowing that her life ended at thirty-nine. That that was that.

It's so sad to think about. Too sad.

Also sad is the fact that you are eating bunny rabbit for dinner and enjoying it. Let me just take a moment here to say: EWWW-WWWWWWWWWWWWWWWWWWWW.

Forget *The Runaway Bunny*. What about that pair of hares we used to see in Granny Wigham's yard every spring? Those sweet, soft brown rabbits that frolicked together in the grass! Who were always together, who had probably mated for life. Jeez. There's probably some lonely bunny in someone's backyard in San Francisco right now, looking for his mate, having no idea that she was cooked with mustard and cream.

Cruel. Cruel.

Just teasing. Though seriously I don't think I'd do very well eating Robert's food. My imagination is much too strong to start eating bunny rabbit. I'll stick to Peggy's meat loaf and mashed potatoes, thank you very much, 'cuz meat loaf is just made of—well, meat. That already comes ground up and in its Styrofoam package. (Right?)

So guess what? I'm smarter than anyone in my class at school. I know, I know, one is not supposed to "toot one's own horn," as Peggy would say, but Ruthie, I'm not kidding. I'm a genius compared to these people. I cannot believe how different the public high school in Virden is from Coventry. I guess I was naïve. The highest math class here, which they erroneously call Trig, is pretty much all Algebra II, which I have already taken. No one in French class speaks any French, including the teacher, who has a deep and dreadful southern accent ("par-lay view France-say, y'all?"). And the big book we're reading in eleventh-grade English—I repeat: ELEVENTH-grade English—is *To Kill a Mockingbird*. Yep, *To Kill a Mockingbird*, which Mom and I read together when I was, oh, nine, and which we studied from cover to cover in Mrs. McGibbon's eighth-grade English class.

Virden Victory, yeah! (As the cheerleaders say.)

I guess I should consider myself lucky, 'cuz I don't think I'm going to have to do much studyin' to make good grades. Jesus, I could be valedictorian. (Can you imagine?) It's funny. At Coventry

we always complained that classes were really hard, but I didn't honestly believe that they were that much harder than classes at public
school. Or maybe it's just public school in Virden. Let me tell you,
this town is not a collection of Virginia's best and brightest.

On the friend front: It's kind of like that Berenstain Bears
book *The Trouble with Friends*. Did I ever tell you about the time
that I went to B. Dalton at Lenox Mall, looking for a Berenstain
Bears book to give to you for your birthday? It was a joke gift, of
course. I was just doing it to be obnoxious, debating whether or
not I should give you *Too Much TV* or *Too Much Junk Food*. So I'm
at the little display case with all of the books, and this cute but
slightly overgrown-looking redheaded girl walks over, picks up the
Berenstain Bears book *Trouble with Friends*, and says to me: "Trouble
with friends. That's what I have. Trouble making 'em, trouble
keeping 'em."

God, I didn't know whether to laugh or cry. Poor girl. I mean
what causes someone to walk through life like that, with no filter?

Speaking of filters, I've got to learn to use more of one when
dealing with La Peggy. I am, ahem, grounded right now for my
"smart mouth." Not that being grounded really changes my life or
anything. There is seriously nothing to do here.

Ah, woe is me.

Your poor, bored, supersmart sister,
Julia

October 23, 1993
Dear poor, bored, supersmart sister,

I'm sorry that you are grounded, but I'm so excited that in just
a few weeks you are coming to San Francisco for Thanksgiving!
We are going to have so much fun! Mimi, Robert, and I are planning the whole trip. We'll take you to Sausalito, which is this really
cute town just on the other side of the Golden Gate Bridge. It's on
the water and there are sailboats everywhere and places to get ice
cream, and it's just really fun. Oh, and there's this really good sushi
restaurant in Sausalito that we'll take you to that Robert says has

the best sashimi in the Bay Area. And I can take you all around Mars and Venus (streets, that is!) and we can climb the Vulcan Steps and burn a thousand calories and then go get smoothies in the Castro. And we can go down to Union Street and shop and get more smoothies and then Uncle Robert can cook each of us our very own bunny rabbit for dinner!!

I can't wait. Make the next four weeks go by fast, okay?

November 1, 1993
Dear Julia,

WHAT IS PEGGY'S PROBLEM? How can she ground you from coming to see me? What right does she have? And why doesn't your dad tell her she's not allowed to do that?

If she hates you so much, why isn't she happy that you are going to be away for a week? I don't understand. I'm so mad. I'm so mad I took a ceramic coffee cup and threw it against the wall. It didn't break, though, just bounced against the rug.

Aunt Mimi says Peggy's punishment is "unreasonable and unfair." She says it's cruel to keep us apart after all we've been through, no matter what you did. (What *did* you do?) Maybe if she doesn't change her mind you could just come out here anyway? I bet Mimi would send you a plane ticket. She's really upset about this.

God, I hate Peggy. You are right. She is a BITCH. Not just a mag. A BITCH!

November 10, 1993
Dear Ruthie,

I hate it here. I hate it here so much. Peggy does not want me. She doesn't want me in her house, but she doesn't want me to leave her house, either, because that would mean that I "win." I never knew what it meant to really hate someone until I came here to live. Nothing Mom or Phil did compares to this. Nothing. It's like Peggy has this impression that she always has to keep up, that she's a perfect homemaker, a perfect mother to Sam and me, a perfect Christian who never misses a week of church, a poor martyred woman who provides for her wayward stepdaughter no matter what.

BULLSHIT!!!

She sucks.

I don't think I'm going to be able to talk her into letting me go to San Francisco for Thanksgiving, even after Aunt Mimi's call. Truth is, Mimi's call probably even made things worse, because it embarrassed Peggy, made her storm into my room and call me a little "snitch."

You are right. Dad *should* be defending me. He should tell her to step the hell aside, that he's my father and he's in charge of whether or not I can go to California to visit my sister for the break.

So I got caught drinking. I had two wine coolers, Ruthie. Two wine coolers! I know you don't drink yet, but that's like having a glass of grape juice with a tiny bit of white wine poured in. But since Peggy doesn't drink at all (what a good Christian she is!), she thinks that this is a really, really big deal. She keeps telling me that Sam knows how to have fun without using mind-altering substances. I wanted to tell her: "Some people consider round-the-clock masturbation mind-altering."

I held my tongue. Luckily. I'm in too much trouble as it is. I had skipped a day of school the week before I got caught drinking and somehow Peggy found out about it, so now she's on this big kick that I am "headed nowhere, fast." Not like her precious Sam. Did I tell you he still does Boy Scouts, in the seventh grade?! Vomit.

God, he's such a dork, Ruthie!! He has no friends, besides the little Christian prayer group that he's a part of from church, and they have to be his friends. You can't call yourself a Christian group and then not let in the losers.

Seriously, Ruthie, Sam is such a freak. The other day I was in the shower and I just had this feeling come over me that I was being watched. So I pull back the shower curtain, and I don't see anyone, but the bathroom door is cracked and I hear someone padding down the hall. He was watching me, I swear to god he was. What a perv. It's like he's getting off on having me in the house. Which is sick. I mean, not that I'm thrilled about this fact, but he *is* my half brother. Yick.

Ruthie, I'm so, so sorry that I'm not going to get to see you for Thanksgiving. I really wanted to be in San Francisco with you. I would have even eaten a little baby bunny if you had really wanted me to.

I love you,

Egg

Chapter Eight

It was cold and wet in San Francisco on Thanksgiving Day, the first holiday without her parents, and no Julia, either.

Peggy had not been swayed.

At least the weather matched Ruthie's state of mind: clamped down, gray.

She spent the morning in the kitchen with Uncle Robert, helping him prepare the meal they would share that evening with their neighbors the Woodses. Robert had brined the turkey—which he had special-ordered from Drewes—for two days in a black Hefty bag filled with salt water and peppercorns. He took the brined bird out of the refrigerator, poured it out of the Hefty bag and into the sink, and proceeded to rinse it with cold water. He then took a bunch of paper towels and dabbed the turkey dry before placing it in the roasting pan that sat on the counter.

"We'll let Mr. Bird hang out for a couple of hours," Robert said. "It's always best to roast meat at room temperature."

Ruthie could not imagine her father ever calling the Butterball turkey Naomi roasted each year Mr. Bird, let alone going through the hassle of brining it. Not that he would have known how to do such a thing. The only food Phil knew how to prepare was fried bologna sandwiches, which he would fix for Ruthie and Julia on the rare nights that Naomi was not home.

Next Robert took out an uncooked tart shell that he had made the day before and had refrigerated. He placed the shell on the island in the middle of the kitchen. The refrigerator door still open, he took out a package of bacon. After peeling off six slices, he spaced them apart in the cold Le Creuset Dutch oven. Turning on the gas, he adjusted it so that it burned at a medium flame.

Before Ruthie moved in with Robert and Mimi, she had never seen anyone fry bacon in a pan. When her mother fixed bacon she cooked it the microwave in a paper towel-lined casserole dish, one minute for every slice.

"Was your dad a cook?" asked Ruthie, who was, as instructed, rubbing a piece of Gruyère over a box grater, the shreds landing on the waxed paper Robert had placed beneath it. (She imagined rubbing off a layer of her own skin. She wondered how much she would have to grate before she felt the cut.)

"Oh God, no. My mother wouldn't let him near her kitchen. Not that her cooking was all that great. Lots of bland pot roasts."

"Who taught you, then? I mean to do things like brine? Mimi?"

Robert barked out a little laugh. "Not Mimi. Definitely not her . . . though she loves a brined turkey, she's not going to be the one doing it. I've always been the cook in our relationship, but I really got into it a couple of years ago when I wrote a little piece about the Tante Marie cooking school for *Sunset*. Had so much fun learning professional *truques* that I continued taking classes even after the article was published."

Ruthie did not ask Robert for the meaning of the word *truque*. Ever since she had moved to San Francisco, she was constantly being made aware of how much she did not know. Sometimes her dearth of knowledge embarrassed her and she would choose to remain privately ignorant.

Stealing a glance at her uncle, who was flipping the sizzling pieces of bacon with metal tongs, she wondered if he might secretly be a homosexual, like Marc, Mimi's business partner, who was gay, though not secret about it at all.

Uncle Robert was certainly unlike any man Ruthie had ever known in Atlanta.

In Atlanta, men—daddies—wore suits and ties, or doctor's scrubs, and you didn't see them between breakfast and dinner. They were gone, off to an office where important work was being done and there were refrigerators stocked with an endless supply of free Coca-Colas. That had been the detail about her daddy's office that most impressed Ruthie, that when he went to work her father could have a Coke any time he wanted and he didn't have to pay a dime for it.

Robert didn't go to an office. Or rather, his office was in their home on Mars Street. It was the nicest room of the flat, with a gas fireplace and two walls of bookshelves. The walls were painted a deep red, and whenever Ruthie went in there she felt warmed, as if she were sitting by a fire.

It was a wonderful room, cozy, inviting, and a little old-fashioned. Robert even had one of those sliding ladders attached to the bookshelves, so that he could reach any book he wanted, at any time. There was a delicate prayer rug on the floor that he and Mimi had bargained for years ago in Morocco and an ancient but working record player on a metal cart in the corner. Sometimes Robert would play his jazz albums from college, all kept meticulously in a leather trunk beside the player, each record stored in its original paper sleeve.

Usually Cooper the cat was lying on the cleared-off section of Robert's desk, but Cooper was such a mellow cat that it was easy to overlook him. He was more like a rug for the desk. "A rug that sheds," Mimi always added.

Mimi was the first one up every morning. In that way she was similar to Ruthie's mother, who always rose early to make a pot of coffee for Phil. And same as Naomi—well, before Julia got her license—it was Mimi who drove Ruthie to school in the morning. But the similarity between Mimi's and Naomi's (former) schedules ended there, for after dropping Ruthie off at Hall's, Mimi headed straight to her office in Hayes Valley, which was filled with fabric samples, antiques, and little clippings from magazines featuring rooms that she and Marc had designed. Whereas after dropping Ruthie off in the morning Naomi would head home for her second cup of coffee before "beginning her day," which often involved waiting at the house for the various assortment of people who arrived to take care of it: the housekeeper, the plumber, the pool man.

Each morning when Ruthie made her way sleepily into the kitchen, Mimi was already there, drinking a glass of fresh-squeezed juice, the desiccated orange rinds in a pile beside the juicer. Bright-eyed, made up, her pale blond hair twisted into a chignon, Mimi was always dressed and ready to go. And just like the trace of a southern accent that she could not seem to abandon, the way Mimi dressed in San Francisco marked her as slightly different from her peers. She was more formal. Whereas the other women in their neighborhood wore soft T-shirts printed with interesting graphics atop jeans or leggings—that or something utterly unfeminine, clunky Doc Martens and thick canvas pants—Mimi always dressed up. She liked straight skirts made of natural fibers and lined with satin. She liked silky little tops with some interesting detail along the collar, tiny square buttons, say, or hand stitching. If the shirt provided no extra luxury she might throw a silk scarf around her neck.

In a way, Ruthie thought, watching Robert select three eggs from the carton and place them in the middle of the counter so they wouldn't roll off, the rhythm of life at Mimi and Robert's house wasn't all that different from how the rhythm of life at her parents' house had been. It was just that instead of the man leaving in the morning and coming home to a hot dinner, it was Mimi who left and Robert who cooked. Robert and now Ruthie.

Robert was reaching into the refrigerator again, this time pulling out a carton of whole milk.

He closed the refrigerator door, opened the carton, sniffed.

"Oh shit," he said, and then held the carton close to his face so he could read the expiration date printed on it.

Ruthie was still not accustomed to hearing adults casually curse. In Atlanta the only adult she knew who cursed with any regularity was her father, and he almost never said anything stronger than "ass" or "damn."

"Hmm. It says it doesn't expire until next week, but smell this." He offered the offending paper carton to Ruthie, who refused to take it.

"Ick," she said. "I trust you."

He glanced at the bacon sizzling in its grease. "I guess I'd better finish this and then run down to Eureka," he said. "I can't make the filling for the tart unless I have milk."

Eureka Market was a bodega just a few blocks away, at Seventeenth and Eureka Street. It was a downhill walk to the store, a steep climb coming back up. Uncle Robert, who was not in the best shape, usually drove there, double-parking if there were no spots in front.

"I'll walk down there and get some more," said Ruthie.

"Are you sure you don't mind?"

Ruthie shook her head. She really didn't. It would be nice to be alone and outside for a few minutes. Her mind kept drifting to her parents, and she wanted to think about them with no interruptions.

Seventeenth Street, which ran perpendicular to Mars, was so steep that Ruthie felt as if she were being pushed forward during the whole walk down. She studied the sidewalk as she walked, afraid of tripping on something.

On clear days you could see a vast stretch of the city from this part of Seventeenth, from the art deco sign in front of the Castro Theatre to the yellow stucco Safeway on Market, past the tall buildings downtown, all the way to the sparkling bay. But today the view was obscured by fog. Ruthie wore jeans and a long-sleeve T-shirt, a down vest, a scarf (cashmere, a gift from

Mimi) wrapped around her neck. She trudged down the hill, imagining her mother just last Thanksgiving, a little harried with her schedule Scotch-taped to the kitchen counter, which listed the casseroles she had already prepared, and, beside each one, the time it should go in the oven.

Ruthie had helped her mother. She tore apart and washed the romaine lettuce for the salad; she stirred the squash and onions that were simmering on the stove. She brushed the tops of the unbaked Parker House rolls with melted butter. Her father kept coming in and out of the kitchen, just to check on them. Just to say hello. At one point he had forked the heart out of a pot of simmering giblets that Naomi was preparing for her giblet gravy.

"Phil!" Naomi said, clearly annoyed. "I needed that!"

She had stood with her hands on her hips, an angry mother scolding a child.

"Relax, babe," Phil had said, his own contentment at having the day off evident.

He was so jolly on days off from the office, a juice glass in his hand, filled with red wine.

Holidays and weekends were the only times that Phil did not wear a suit and tie. And he never wore blue jeans. Last Thanksgiving he had worn khaki pants and a short-sleeve button-down shirt, blue plaid, tucked in with a belt. His dark hair grew a little long on both sides of his head, but he was bald on top. He had wire-rim glasses and a dark mustache streaked with silver hairs. Back when Dunkin' Donuts had run its "Time to Make the Donuts" ads featuring a short, round, mustached man resigned to making donuts in perpetuity, Alex Love had joked that the "Donut Man" looked just like Ruthie's dad.

It was a comment that highlighted the difference between Alex's father and Ruthie's. Mr. Love was tall and athletic, with a full head of hair and perfect vision. Whereas Phil was short, a little plump, and bald. And he not only wore glasses, but he also had a weak eye, one that wandered a little to the left whenever he was tired.

Despite all of this, her father seemed utterly confident, self-possessed in his Brioni suits and fancy leather shoes, purchased at Neiman's annual sale. Naomi told Ruthie that Phil's self-confidence was what drew her to him in the first place. The way his presence filled the room. The way he made the most ordinary outings fun. She said that just going with Phil to buy socks was fun. And yet . . . sometimes he shared the Donut Man's defeated air of resignation toward his work. Phil was so tired when he came home at the end of the day. His eye would wander and he would be cross.

Once after Phil had snapped at Ruthie during dinner, snapped at her over nothing, and she had run away from the table in tears (Ruthie did not like people to see her cry), Naomi had found Ruthie in her room, and had tried to explain to her why Phil could be so grumpy.

"He loves being able to send you and Julia to private school," she said, tickling Ruthie's neck with her long nails. "And you know he loves this house. But it takes a lot of money to keep everything running. There's just a lot of pressure on him, that's all."

Once Phil told Julia not to consider law school. "Being a lawyer pays the bills," he said. "But it sure is a drone."

So occupied was Ruthie by her thoughts, and by watching the ground while she walked, not wanting to stumble and fall down the steep hill, that it wasn't until she was standing directly in front of Dara, whose hair was freshly tinted purple, that she saw her. Her appearance was so sudden it was as if Dara, and the young woman standing beside her, had materialized out of the fog.

The woman standing by Dara wore baggy jeans and a Bikini Kill T-shirt, a pink plastic headband holding back her curly hair, which looked exactly like Dara's except it was dyed black.

"I've been saying your name like ten times now!" said Dara, slightly out of breath from climbing the hill.

Ruthie didn't know how to respond to that. What was she going to say: "Sorry, I was preoccupied with thoughts of my dead parents"?

"So anyway, what are you doing here?"

"Just going to Eureka Market for milk," Ruthie said. "We need it for the bacon and Gruyère tart we're making."

"Yum! We just came from there. For ice cream. But what are you doing in this neighborhood?"

Did Dara not remember any of their conversation from the first week of school? Ruthie certainly had not forgotten that Dara said she lived on Uranus.

"I live up there," Ruthie said, pointing behind her.

Dara made a show of slapping her forehead. "Of course! You live on Mars. You're a Martian. Right. I totally forgot. Well, anyway, hi! Happy Thanksgiving."

Why was Dara acting so friendly, so bubbly? Ruthie had been so bitchy to her that day during Snack, had actually taken pleasure in being rude. Since then, Ruthie had been nicer but never really accepted any of Dara's direct overtures toward friendship. But seeing Dara here on Seventeenth Street with the pink-headband woman—hadn't Dara said she had a sister, a vegan?—so far away from school and sailor uniforms, Ruthie could not remember why she had chosen to remain so aloof.

"Are you Dara's sister?" Ruthie asked.

"No, I'm her mom," said the woman. "I was a child bride."

Ruthie was confused. Headband woman looked no more than twenty years old, if that.

Dara rolled her eyes. "Ruthie, meet Yael, my sister. Who is so funny she ought to do stand-up."

"The vegan?" Ruthie asked.

"Am I that exotic?" Yael teased Dara. "That you discuss my eating habits with strangers?"

"You say 'exotic'; I say 'bizarre,'" said Dara.

Yael bumped her sister playfully with her hip and Ruthie felt consumed with jealousy.

Julia was supposed to be here.

If Julia had not been caught drinking, she would be here.

"And Ruthie's not a stranger. We go to Hall's together."

"Hi, Ruthie from Hall's," said Yael. "So back to your oh-so-appropriate question about my eating habits, I usually am vegan, but I'm going to indulge in dairy today. Can't get Chandra to stop making her crusts with butter, and can't help but eat them once she does."

"What about turkey?" asked Ruthie, even though Yael had just implied that questions about what she ate were rude.

Ruthie didn't care. She thought Yael was rude.

"Chandra got a Tofurky," said Yael.

"It looks like a turkey, but it's made of tofu," explained Dara, who seemed to intuit that Ruthie might not know what one was.

Ruthie was dying to tell Julia about Tofurky. *God. San Franciscans.*

"Is Chandra your cook?" Ruthie asked.

Many of the girls at Hall's came from homes where there was a full-time cook.

"Jesus, Dara, you really go to a ritzy school, don't you?" said Yael. Turning to Ruthie, she said, "We have no cook. No butler, either, for that matter—"

"That's not what I meant," said Ruthie, deciding she *really* didn't like this Yael person, wondering what the hell kind of name was Yael anyway?

"Chandra's our mom," said Dara.

"You call your mom by her first name?" asked Ruthie. She didn't mean to keep firing off questions. What she meant to do was act cool, erect a wall, make an excuse, and get away. Yael was too prickly, and it was too hard seeing sisters together, joking, having fun.

"We call her Mom to her face, Chandra when we are talking about her," said Dara.

"Ice cream's melting," Yael said in a singsong voice, waving the plastic grocery bag she held in her hand.

"I guess we should go," Dara said. "You want to come over later and eat ice cream with us? We've got Health Bar Crunch and Chocolate Chip Cookie Dough."

"Thanks," said Ruthie. "I don't think I can. My family doesn't eat Thanksgiving until late."

"Are a lot of your relatives in town?" asked Dara.

The question pleased Ruthie, because it indicated that Dara didn't know she was an orphan, that Dara believed her to be normal. Believed her to be the type of girl whose mom was just now brushing melted butter on the uncooked Parker House rolls. Ruthie had assumed that everyone at Hall's knew what had happened to her mom and dad. It was such a small school, and it was so rare for someone to matriculate in the eighth grade.

The teachers definitely knew. Mr. Z's constant psychological probing made her sure of that.

"Just my aunt and uncle," said Ruthie, pleased with her answer. It was not a lie, but it obscured the truth.

"We've got to go, girl," said Yael, pushing on Dara's shoulder with her free hand.

Dara growled at her sister, but in a friendly way. "Okay, I guess I've got to go . . . but call me! Let's get together over break!"

Ruthie murmured something noncommittal but was surprised, once they started climbing the hill back toward Uranus Terrace, that she was not relieved by their departure.

She was so damn lonely.

At five o' clock the Woodses arrived, exactly on time. Ruthie had returned with the milk hours earlier, and she and Robert had prepared the bacon and Gruyère tart. Still, there were lots of last-minute things to do, and Robert, pulling the perfectly browned turkey out of the oven, muttered to himself while he and Ruthie listened to Mimi greet the Woodses at the door.

"Don't they know to arrive at least ten minutes late to a party?" he whispered to Ruthie. "I haven't even had time to have a drink."

Ruthie wasn't sure what to say in response and Robert, sensing her concern, said, "Don't listen to me. I'm just being a kvetch. Go say hi and I'll finish in here."

Ruthie walked into the living room. The Woodses were still standing by the door, Tim Woods holding an oversized bottle of wine.

Tim Woods was a blond, muscled man of great height, well over six feet tall. His dark-haired wife, Nina, whose mother had escaped from Communist Romania, was tiny by contrast, her bones birdlike in their delicacy. They had one child, a girl named Tatiana, who had a preternaturally advanced vocabulary for age nine, and who walked over to Ruthie and handed her a pot holder, woven from colored elastic bands that Tatiana had strung together on a plastic loom.

"Thanks," said Ruthie, holding the pot holder limply in front of her.

"I hope you get ample use from it," said the child.

Mimi, who was so tall and blond next to Nina, was ushering in her guests. She looked casually elegant in black pants, a slinky cream top, and a gray cashmere wrap that she slung oh-so-casually around her shoulders.

Ruthie knew that Mimi must have been popular in school while Nina, sharp little Nina with her tacky skintight lace top over a too-short black skirt, was not. At least, not in the way Mimi would have been. Not in any way wholesome.

Except Nina married Tim, who was as wholesome looking as could be, with his sweep of blond hair and broad shoulders. Tim looked as if he grew out of a cornfield, as if he shot right out of the ground, ready to inherit the earth, with a toothy smile.

The sparkling wine Tim had brought was chilled, and so Mimi took the bottle into the kitchen, where Robert poured it into flutes, emerging to serve. The grown-ups settled in the living room, each with a flute of bubbly. It was a large bottle, the largest bottle of wine Ruthie had ever seen. Robert, who was still wearing an apron tied around his significant middle, told her that it was called a magnum and that it was the equivalent of two regular bottles of champagne.

"Though technically Roederer Estate is sparkling wine, since it's grown in the Anderson Valley and not in the Champagne region of France," Robert said. Encouraged by her interest in his cooking, Robert was always imparting little epicurean lessons to Ruthie.

"Roederer Estate is my absolute favorite," said Mimi, giving Robert a nonverbal rebuke with her narrowed eyes. Though Mimi loved to say that she had "gone native" when she moved out to California and was now a true San Franciscan, she would forever remain a southern woman in that she was always worried about the possibility of offending a guest.

"May Tatiana and I have a taste?" asked Ruthie.

Mimi considered the request, and then gave a little nod. "I don't see the harm in cultivating a taste for champagne. You don't mind the girls having a sip, do you, Nina?"

Nina Woods sucked in her breath so her cheeks went concave, before raising her eyebrows a little mockingly. "Why would I mind?" she asked, her tone indicating that only in coddling, litigious America would Mimi's question even be asked.

Robert poured the girls a third of a glass each, in thin champagne flutes etched with wispy flowers. They clinked their glasses together, and Tatiana said, *"Salut."*

Ruthie studied Tatiana, who took a tentative sip of the wine. She was small and delicate like her mother, with thin wrists and long fingers, her nails painted blue. But unlike her mother, she was a blond, her straight hair shoulder length and worn parted down the middle and pulled back rather severely with two metal barrettes.

"Want to come hang out in my room?" Ruthie asked.

She thought she might play big sister, show Tatiana her CDs and her makeup, which included the stuff that Alexandra Love's mom had bought for her the year before, when Mrs. Love took Ruthie and Alex to JC Penney to have their colors done at the Color Me Beautiful counter. Ruthie would determine Tatiana's colors, declare whether she was a fall, winter, spring, or summer. She would tell Tatiana about Julia, how Julia rarely wore makeup, only pinched her cheeks to give them color and coated her lips with clear gloss so they would shine. How Julia was kind of a hippie, even though the sixties had long since passed. How when Ruthie was a little girl her sister had succeeded in convincing her that she, Julia, was a witch, that she had magical powers, that she could cough up dollar bills and cast a spell on the moon, making it follow them home from dinner.

Maybe Ruthie would even teach Tatiana how to play Egg and Biscuit. Or if not that exact game—which seemed a little too sacred to share—maybe a similar game, Coffee and Cream or Croissant and Jam.

Tatiana glanced warily at her mother, who had settled on the opposite side of Tim on the upholstered sofa. It was covered in a fabric that Ruthie recognized from Mrs. Love's house, cream with dark green palmetto leaves.

"Can't we just stay in here?" Tatiana asked.

Ruthie felt deeply embarrassed. Rejected by a nine-year-old. Rejected by a dorky nine-year-old who wasn't even pretty. Whose skin was so pale you could see her blue veins.

They stayed with the adults—Tatiana lying between her parents on the upholstered sofa, Mimi in one of the two Stickley leather lounge chairs, and Ruthie on the floor, pressing the side of her face against the top of the ottoman, feeling the cool leather, trying to blink back tears.

Closing her eyes, she imagined that when she opened them she would be back in Atlanta, back in the house on Wymberly Way, sitting around the antique dining room table with her parents and Julia, sitting on Chippendale chairs that God help her if she rocked back and forth on and caused a leg to break. Smirking at Julia while their father, who every day but holidays was an atheist, declaimed his Thanksgiving prayer.

The loneliness Ruthie felt was so deep it reached all the way to her groin.

• • •

Robert disappeared into the kitchen, then returned with a plate containing thin slices of the bacon and Gruyère tart. Ruthie took a slice gratefully. It was warm, rich, and buttery, the saltiness of the bacon tempered by the sweet cream of the custard.

Soon after, Robert returned with a tray full of little white espresso cups filled with pumpkin soup, each cup topped with a dab of a triple crème cheese called St. André. Ruthie felt a melting sort of love for her uncle, this kind fat man who cooked delicious, fattening foods. She took a sip of the soup and for a moment thought of nothing besides its rich creaminess, its marriage of sweet and smoke.

"Don't I need some sort of utensil for this?" asked Tatiana.

"Drink it straight from the cup," said Mimi. "Like this."

Mimi threw back the soup with one sip.

Tatiana followed Mimi's example. "Outstanding," she proclaimed.

"It really is," said Nina. "What is your secret, Robert?"

"Bacon," answered Ruthie. "He starts the soup with six pieces of it."

"It's a nice surprise, isn't it?" Robert said, settling into the other Stickley chair. "So often people pair pumpkin with sweet ingredients, but I think it works really nicely as a savory soup. Plus everything goes better with bacon."

All of the adults agreed, and Robert made a joke about how Jews who kept kosher missed out. "The Italians are the real chosen people," he said.

It was a joke Uncle Robert made often. Ruthie had begun to notice this about him. He was very entertaining. He had good stories. But if you hung around him often enough—which, of course, Mimi and Ruthie both did—you realized that he told the same stories again and again, rotating them the way Mimi rotated the best pieces in her wardrobe, the gray cashmere wrap, the alligator pumps, the strand of pearls so long she could double it up and the two loops would still hang to her waist. Sometimes when Robert went on too long about one thing or another, Mimi started spinning little circles with her hand, encouraging him to speed things up.

Since she had come to stay with her aunt and uncle, there were occasional times when Ruthie noticed Mimi looking at Robert in a way that was far from affectionate. Mimi would study him, he who during the day was often in need of a shower. Who was unshaved, and even had hair growing out of his ears. She would study him in a detached manner, almost as if she were trying to figure out how this man got into her house. Once when he was particularly grungy, she told him he was relying too much on "pure intellectual capital."

Mimi confided in Ruthie that even though Robert was one of Phil's best friends at Duke, Ruthie's dad had initially been against the marriage. He thought Mimi was too good-looking for Robert, and though he wouldn't have stated it explicitly, he made suggestions that Mimi was lowering her social status by marrying a Jew. At least if they planned to live in the South, which Phil erroneously assumed they did.

Aunt Mimi *was* more physically attractive than Robert. She was so thin, so collected, so put together, so elegant. When Ruthie first saw the actress Gwyneth Paltrow on-screen she thought, *That's Mimi as a movie star.* A cool sort of beauty, Mimi was the type of woman who could get away with wearing an all-white outfit: white sandals, white pants, white top, gold jewelry. If Robert attempted to wear all white—a Tom Wolfe–style suit perhaps—he would spill something on it within an hour. Or let out one of his earth-shaking sneezes and land a green booger right on the lapel.

Most of the time Mimi and Robert seemed to get along, but sometimes Ruthie overheard them fighting in the master bedroom. It was just across the hall from hers, only a few feet away, not like it had been in the house on Wymberly Way. In Atlanta, her parents' room was on the other side of the house, down a long hall and barricaded by a heavy door that locked. And if her parents ever fought in there, Ruthie never heard it. The sound of her mother's "train" was the only noise that ever carried to Ruthie's room.

In Atlanta, whenever Ruthie thought she heard an ominous bump or bang from downstairs—which, imagined or not, was often—she would tiptoe down the hall and try to enter her parents' room. Sometimes the door would be locked. She was never certain enough of the presence of a robber to knock on the door and disturb her parents—that would mean serious trouble unless there really was an intruder.

On the nights when the door wasn't locked Ruthie could usually calm herself down just by going into their room for a few minutes. She would listen to them breathe, her father lightly snoring, her mother slowly inhaling and exhaling. But on the nights Ruthie found their door locked she felt panicked. Finally she convinced her mother not to lock it, ever. Instead Naomi bought a sign that read: PRIVACY PLEASE, I'M ON THE PHONE TO PARIS.

"If you see that on the door do *not* disturb us," her mother warned.

And Ruthie, who by that time had overheard the train, promised she never, ever would.

The grown-ups were talking about some city ordinance and Ruthie was bored.

During previous Thanksgivings, she and her sister would play games while waiting for the meal, Connect Four, or checkers, or maybe even chess, though Ruthie wasn't very good at it. Or Julia would rope Ruthie into being the watch guard for some forbidden thing she wanted to do: smoke a joint in the pool house, or lock herself away in her bedroom for an hour with Dmitri, back when she was dating him. If her parents' plane had not crashed, if they were in Atlanta where they were supposed to be for Thanksgiving, Julia would probably find some way to sneak off and see Jake Robinson after everyone had feasted on turkey, stuffing, and her mother's homemade Parker House rolls, which were so light and delicate it was entirely possible to eat five in one sitting.

Ruthie glanced at Tatiana on the couch. Her head was in her mother's lap, her feet in her father's. Ruthie felt a surge of animosity toward her. What kind of a nine-year-old turned down the offer to hang out with someone older? Ruthie had never turned down Julia's offers to hang out. Julia made life fun, rich with drama and intrigue.

Ruthie wondered: what was Julia doing at this exact moment? Certainly not sipping from a glass of sparkling wine with her dad and stepmom—of that Ruthie was sure. Peggy was Southern Baptist and did not drink anything stronger than coffee. Probably Julia was sitting in Peggy's living room, bored, just like Ruthie. Listening to adults talk about whatever it was they considered themselves experts on. Maybe Julia had her Discman in and was listening to The Cure or Morrissey. (As if Peggy would let Julia get away with exhibiting such obvious antisocial behavior!)

Maybe Julia was writing Ruthie a letter.

The letters Ruthie received from Julia were always mailed in envelopes the backs of which were decorated with hundreds of wavy lines and circles, like henna on the hand of an Indian bride. Even if the letters had no return address, Ruthie always knew immediately who they were from. Even if Julia didn't hand-decorate the envelopes, Ruthie would immediately know who the letters were from. Her sister had the most distinctive handwriting, impossibly slanted, like all of her letters were in danger of toppling right over.

"Do I have time to call Julia before dinner?" Ruthie asked, interrupting Nina, who had just said something about the homeless in San Francisco being out of hand.

(Terribly suspicious of the left, Nina took pride in what she coined her "unfashionable ideas." And whenever Robert tried to argue with her politically she trumped him by pointing out that *his* mother didn't risk her life escaping from a Communist country.)

"Great idea," said Mimi. "Do you want to call her from your room so you have privacy?"

Ruthie nodded, relieved. Mimi was good at intuiting her needs.

She walked to her room at the end of the flat. Even though it was half the size of her old room in Atlanta, it was pleasant, with a bay window overlooking the garden. And while Naomi had never let Ruthie hang any posters on the wall, fearing the damage the tacks might do to the paint, Mimi told Ruthie she could decorate however she wanted. Ruthie knew that if Julia had been around to help, the walls of her room would be covered with posters of the Grateful Dead, Janis Joplin, Dylan, Morrissey, and The Cure. But Ruthie wasn't really into Julia's music and especially disliked the Dead. She found Julia's Dead tapes, with their long instrumental riffs, tedious.

The walls in Ruthie's San Francisco bedroom were painted a soothing blue-green. Mimi said she had come up with the color by bringing her favorite Armani sweater to the paint mixer at Cole Hardware. Ruthie liked the color so much she kept the walls mostly unadorned, save for a corkboard with pictures tacked to it—mainly pictures of Julia—and a framed Ansel Adams print of silvery birch trees. On her desk she kept a framed picture of Naomi and Phil, sitting on the living room couch, looking at each other as if there were no one else in the world, smiling.

Ruthie's phone was on her desk, too, an old white Princess phone of her aunt's whose number buttons were stained a putty color from where Mimi's foundation had rubbed off. Ruthie dialed the Virden number, which she had memorized the first week she was in San Francisco. After two rings Peggy picked up.

"Hello, Smith residence," she said.

"Hi, it's Ruthie. May I please speak with Julia?" she asked.

Ruthie never knew what to call Peggy, so she tried to avoid addressing her directly.

"You could if she was home," said Peggy, a fleck of impatience in her voice. "I sent her to the Kroger to buy marshmallows. Her father forgot to get them when he went grocery shopping for me."

"Are you making sweet potato casserole with marshmallows on top?" asked Ruthie, a little envious.

"I most certainly am. I have to make Sam and Matt's favorite dish, don't I?"

It was Julia's favorite, too, but Ruthie felt shy about mentioning that to Peggy.

Earlier that afternoon when Ruthie had suggested to Robert that he place marshmallows on top of the sweet potatoes that he had mashed with butter, cream, bourbon, and molasses, he had looked at her as if she had asked him to please stuff the turkey with the limbs of small children.

"Can she call me when she gets home?" Ruthie asked.

Peggy sighed. "Well, we're going to eat as soon as she gets back, so she better call you after supper is finished and the dishes are washed."

"Okay," said Ruthie. "Thanks. Um, Happy Thanksgiving."

"You, too, cutie."

Besides calling Ruthie cutie, Peggy had sounded nothing like her former bubbly self. Instead she sounded both resentful and self-satisfied.

Ruthie returned to the living room to find Mimi telling Nina and Tim Woods about Julia being grounded from coming to California to celebrate Thanksgiving with Ruthie.

"What can you do?" asked Mimi, lifting her hands, palms up. "What can I do? Peggy says no, her father goes along with it. He's her legal guardian. What choice do I have but to go along with their decision?"

Mimi's voice warbled and Ruthie realized that her aunt was about to start to cry. She cried easily, especially if she was drinking. Ruthie wondered how many glasses of champagne—sparkling wine—Mimi had consumed.

"I feel so sorry for this girl. She has to go through the divorce of her parents when she's so young. And then she grows accustomed to living with her mother's new husband, my brother, who was a wonderful person—"

She glanced at Ruthie.

"But was pretty set in his ways. And then her mother and stepfather die. And now she's living with this zealot who won't let her blink without permission."

Was her father set in his ways? Ruthie supposed he was. He was always the one to drive, the one to choose the restaurant on nights they ate out, the one who set the tone at the dinner table. Indeed, his authority had been such a core part of who he was that it actually amazed Ruthie that he had died. It was hard to believe that he had allowed death to happen to him.

The zealot Mimi referred to was surely Peggy. But Ruthie's understanding of the word came from Julia, who used to spit out the name—"zealots!"—in reference to the evangelical Christians at Coventry, the kids who would slip behind the closed door of room 103 in Cushing Hall for early-morning prayer sessions. The kids who would call in sick en masse and then show up on the evening news for having taken part in the swarming of an abortion clinic by Operation Rescue. The kids who always seemed to be covertly trading notes back and forth when they passed each other in the hall between classes, notes that were signed with Christian fishes and their initials, as if it were dangerous to write out their full names.

Julia spoke most virulently about a girl named Ashley Lavelle, a serious girl with a penchant for plaid knee skirts. Ashley often volunteered to give the devotionals at Coventry, during which she would tell her fellow students that she had "a crucial message" for them about the necessity of accepting Christ as their personal savior. Again and again she told them that humans were inherently flawed, God was inherently perfect, and the only way to connect the flawed humans with the perfect God was through the divine bridge of Jesus Christ.

"I have a crucial message for her," Julia would say. "A flannel tartan skirt accented with an oversized safety pin is not attractive."

Ruthie used to laugh at Julia's wickedness but in bed at night would pray for Jesus to enter her own flawed human heart. Though Julia did not take the devotionals seriously, Ruthie did, even if she only heard their content secondhand. At Coventry, students didn't give devotionals until high school. In the junior high the devotionals were given by the teachers, the most memorable the one when Mr. Tarkenton confessed to the entire assembly that he had once murdered a man. And then at the end of his confession—the students rapt, stunned—he made another confession: He hadn't really killed anyone. He had made the story up. But if he *had* killed someone, Jesus would forgive him. That was the thing about Christ. There was nothing you could do to lose his love. . . .

And then Ruthie's reverie was interrupted because Tim Woods was saying something about how Julia could petition for emancipation.

Ruthie turned her attention to Mr. Woods. Julia had mentioned the possibility of emancipation in one of her letters, but Ruthie didn't know whether or not it was a real thing she could actually petition for or if Julia was just exaggerating, comparing herself to a slave owned by Peggy. But Mr. Woods used the word, too. And he was a lawyer, and not likely to use overblown language. At least not if he was anything like Ruthie's dad, who was always telling Julia that hyperbole weakened one's argument.

"Robert and I have discussed that possibility," Mimi said carefully, glancing at Ruthie again. "But Julia only has a year and a half left of high school. And if things get really bad—well, her eighteenth birthday is next October, near the start of her senior year . . . and while we hope she and Peggy will have worked out some sort of truce by then, if not . . . at that point she could legally come here."

"She could?" asked Ruthie.

"She could," said Robert, and it was clear to Ruthie that this was something he and Mimi had already discussed.

As if it were an inflating balloon, Ruthie's chest filled with hope.

For the first few minutes of dinner no conversation was had. Everyone just raised fork to mouth, murmuring compliments between bites.

The turkey was salty and tender; the gravy, thick and smooth. The roasted baby potatoes were enlivened with little flecks of bacon and lots of butter and salt. And Ruthie had to admit, the sweet potatoes Robert had mashed with butter, cream, bourbon, and a little molasses were even better than the ones topped with marshmallows. There were two kinds of dressing, one made from crumbled cornbread and one made with white bread, sausage, and sage. There were green beans sautéed with garlic and butter. There was a homemade cranberry sauce dotted with orange zest, and homemade biscuits that Robert had made with real lard, purchased from one of the many Mexican markets in the Mission. (The biscuits were tender and flaky, but Ruthie missed her mother's rolls.) There was a salad of bright Bibb lettuce and green onions, loaded with grapefruit, ripe avocado, and toasted pecans.

Tatiana, a notoriously picky eater, swallowed one bite of turkey and then ate three biscuits, each slathered with butter.

"Enough with the butter, sweet pea," said her dad. "Have some salad."

Nina shrugged in her dismissive eastern European way. "It's Thanksgiving," she said. "She should eat what she wants."

"Would you mind not sabotaging everything I say to my daughter?" asked Tim, and the room grew quiet in a different way than it had been the moment before.

Ruthie, hating the tension, tried to think of something to say. "Do you think Mitchell's avocado ice cream would taste good with tortilla chips?" she asked.

Mitchell's was an ice cream shop in the Mission that almost always had a line of customers out the door. Whenever Robert and Ruthie ventured there, Ruthie would sample the more exotic flavors—avocado, green tea, lychee, purple yam—before ordering her usual, a scoop of chocolate and a scoop of caramel praline.

"I don't know if my poor heart could handle ice cream *plus* chips," said Mimi, placing her hand on her chest in an exaggerated gesture, which, now that she no longer lived there, Ruthie recognized as southern.

"You had better keep in good health," said Nina. "Otherwise you're going to be in big trouble if Hillary Care passes."

Robert rolled his eyes. He often said it was unconscionable that the United States didn't have universal health care, and he was a huge fan of the Clintons.

Nina noticed the eye roll. "What do you like about Hillary Care? Is it the task force that holds secret meetings? Or the prospect of having Soviet-style hospitals?"

"That's pushing it," said Tim.

"Look," said Robert. "The closed meetings were probably a mistake, but to focus on one tactical error when there's a health-care crisis in this country? I'm just glad someone in power is addressing it."

"Oh please," said Nina. "By adding to the bureaucracy?"

"You do realize we already have a costly and inefficient health-care system in place, don't you?" asked Robert. "It's called the hospital emergency room. And if you're poor in this country, that's where you go for everything."

"Or you get motivated to find a job," said Nina.

"You have *got* to stop reading Ayn Rand," said Robert.

Tim let out a surprised laugh; Mimi glared at her husband.

Ruthie knew that Mimi agreed with him on health care but felt it was rude to invite people over only to argue politics, especially Nina, who would never be swayed. Indeed, Robert and Mimi privately joked that they had to keep Nina as a friend because otherwise they wouldn't know anyone in San Francisco who had ever voted for a Republican.

"Ruthie, why don't you tell the Woodses that funny joke Julia shared with you?" said Mimi.

Ruthie was momentarily confused. Julia had told her a joke that past weekend, during one of their increasingly rare phone calls, but Ruthie was pretty sure it wasn't a good one to share. The joke was about the difference between condoms and coffins: how they both held stiffs, but one was coming and one was going. Had Mimi been listening in on the phone call?

"You know, the one about Sam the clam and his disco," prompted Mimi.

"Oh," said Ruthie. "You want me to tell it now?"

"Please," said Tim. "I beg of you."

Robert and Nina both looked like they wanted to keep arguing, but they remained quiet and Ruthie began the joke.

Mimi beamed at her. The conversation was saved.

They were sitting in the living room again, plates in their laps, eating pie. Robert had made lemon chess and pecan, and there was vanilla ice cream to go on top. Ruthie loved the sweet-tart combination of lemon desserts, and was eating a large slice of the chess pie. It reminded her a lot of a lemon square, except there was a tang to the pie's custard, because of the buttermilk Robert had added.

She thought about her mother's lemon squares, how they were the best she had ever tasted. She remembered how crisp and buttery the crust was, how gooey the filling. She tried to imagine her mother, baking in the kitchen, and then was overtaken with anxiety, because she could not picture her mother, could not picture her with the green and white polka-dot apron tied around her waist. All Ruthie could remember was the photo from the obituary in the *Atlanta Journal-Constitution*, a formal picture that Naomi had taken for the church bulletin at Trinity Presbyterian. In the church photo she was smiling stiffly above a blue turtleneck sweater. She looked bland, conventional.

And then the jangle of metal permeated the air as someone outside twisted the old-fashioned ringer on the door. And just like that the spit dried in Ruthie's mouth because suddenly she knew. The person on the other side of the door had to be Julia.

Mimi was walking across the room to open the door, and Ruthie's heart was pounding.

When Ruthie called, Julia had not been at the Kroger buying marshmallows! She had slipped away instead, driving her Saab fast toward the Roanoke airport, thirty miles away, or perhaps even all the way to D.C., where she could catch a direct flight. She had been saving money and it was with this money that she had bought a ticket. Once past security and on the plane, she had settled back into her seat, not at all nervous, even during turbulence, because she knew it was her destiny to see her little sister. It had been five months since they had seen each other. Five months. Enough was enough and finally Julia had taken action.

As a little girl, Ruthie had believed that Julia possessed magical powers. For a moment, she believed in Julia's magic again.

Mimi opened the door. There stood Dara.

Dara.

How could she have believed that Julia could have traveled all that way without Peggy knowing she was missing?

"Hi again!" Dara said to Ruthie. "I looked you up in the Hall's directory."

And though Ruthie did not answer, Mimi invited Dara in.

She was an idiot for having believed—even for a minute—that Julia was just going to show up in San Francisco, after being forbidden to come.

"Ruthie," said Mimi, her voice in full hostess mode. "Why don't you introduce us to your friend."

Ruthie looked at her aunt, tried to speak, but her throat was so tight she couldn't.

As if Julia could just slip away unnoticed.

"I thought if you were through with dinner maybe you could come over to my house and have ice cream," said Dara.

"How lovely," said Mimi. "I'm sure Ruthie would love to, wouldn't you, hon?"

Even if Julia somehow managed to secure a plane ticket, she would first have had to get to D.C., which was over three hours away. That or drive down to Roanoke and take a small plane from there to D.C. And surely by the time the turboprop landed in the capital city there would have been a policeman waiting to intercept her as she deplaned.

"Sweetie?" asked Mimi. "Are you okay?"

Everyone was looking at her, concerned. She hated their concern. She hated being the center of their attention.

"I'm sorry," she said. "I feel sick. I'm sorry, Dara. It's really nice of you to offer, but I just need to lie down. Another time, okay?"

"Oh, sweetie," said Mimi.

"Maybe it wasn't a great idea for you to have that champagne," said Tim.

"It was a big meal," said Robert. "Everyone probably needs to lie down."

"Another time, Dara?" asked Mimi, as if she were the one turning her down.

After Dara left, Ruthie assured them all that she was fine, that she just needed to lie down for a few minutes. She assured Uncle Robert that she did not need any Pepto-Bismol, even though he swore by the stuff. She thanked him for the delicious meal, told him it was the best turkey she had ever had. She thanked Tatiana for the pot holder, said good night to Tim and Nina.

Once safely ensconced in her room Ruthie lay on the bed, staring at the bulletin board with photos of Julia and her tacked to it.

It had been five and a half months since she had last seen her sister. Five and a half months since Julia, her Saab packed with everything that had not fit into Peggy's minivan, had hugged Ruthie good-bye for the final time and gotten behind the wheel of her car, to follow her stepmother and father out of the driveway and into a new life.

Ruthie's sister seemed as far away as her parents. But she kept expecting that to change. Ever since she had moved to San Francisco, she had been on the lookout for her sister. Ruthie kept expecting her to show up. It wasn't Ruthie's fault that she held such high hopes. How many letters had Julia written Ruthie plotting just such an escape?

"What's Peggy going to do?" Julia wrote. "Ground me? Well, fine, there's nothing for me to do in this fucking town anyway. It wouldn't make a difference."

About a month ago, returning home from Rosenberg's deli, where she had gone to get a sandwich, Ruthie spotted a long-haired young woman sitting on the front steps of Mimi and Robert's building. Ruthie was walking toward the setting sun and was a bit blinded by it, so she could not make out the woman's features with any distinction. But the way the woman was sitting—Indian-style—looked like Julia; her messy red hair looked like Julia's; her peasant top with the embroidered flowers looked like something Julia might wear.

And who would sit on the front steps of someone's house un-less she was waiting, specifically, for the people who lived there to arrive?

Ruthie started walking faster up the hill that was Mars Street, her heart racing from both anticipation and exertion. She was only twenty or so feet away when the girl—woman, Ruthie realized—looked straight at Ruthie and Ruthie saw a face that was pock-marked and scarred from acne.

It wasn't her sister at all.

It wasn't even someone who resembled her sister.

It was an ugly woman who, upon closer inspection, looked like she was probably homeless, who looked like she might ask Ruthie for change. Which was exactly what she did, as soon as Ruthie got close enough to her. As soon as Ruthie was standing by the steps, holding the front door key tightly in her hand.

"I don't have any to give, but I can direct you to a shelter," Ruthie said.

This was the line Aunt Mimi had taught her to say.

"Oh, go fuck yourself, you little snot," said the woman, and Ruthie jerked back her head in surprise. Though she knew it wasn't Julia, it still shocked Ruthie to be cursed at by someone she had, just seconds before, believed to be beloved.

And now here Ruthie was again. Fooled once more. Fooled and alone, in this Armani green room with its view of the garden, its framed Ansel Adams print, its corkboard that served as a shrine to Julia. It was all so strange. What the hell was she doing here? How had life spit her into this room, in this flat, in this city, when she was supposed to be at Wymberly Way, eating Parker House rolls and sweet potatoes with marshmallows, bland turkey, and cornbread stuffing?

If they had not boarded that plane . . .

No. It went beyond that. Where the blame fell.

She stood, walked to the corkboard filled with photos. There was one of Julia alone, standing beside the Chattahoochee River, one hand pushing against the trunk of a tree. She was wearing old Levi's that she had painted designs on, flowers, a sun, a moon. Her hair was blown back from her face and she was looking rather boldly into the camera. Rather arrogantly.

Ruthie felt a rush of anger toward her sister. Why couldn't Julia do anything right? Why did she get caught drinking weeks before her scheduled trip to California? Why was she locked so tightly in battle with her stepmother? Why was she out getting marshmallows during the very moment Ruthie needed to talk with her?

And then Ruthie allowed herself to have the thought that she had been avoiding ever since she and Mother Martha discovered that Julia had not been at the beach over spring break, had instead been camped out at a boy's house, not four miles away in Ansley Park.

If Julia had not lied and gone off to be with Jake Robinson, none of this would have happened.

If Julia had not lied and gone off to be with Jake Robinson, my parents would still be alive.

Chapter Nine

Cafe Flore, where Ruthie was meeting Dara for breakfast, was midway between Ruthie's house on Mars Street and Dara's dad's house in the Duboce Triangle, where Dara was staying over spring break while her mom went on a yoga retreat in Costa Rica. It was kind of a pain to have to schlep all her stuff over to her dad's, Dara said, but ultimately it didn't bother her that much. At her dad's house she could watch TV, and he always had Cap'n Crunch cereal and Cheetos waiting for her, two of Dara's favorite foods, and two foods her "whole foods" mother expressly forbade.

Normally Ruthie would have just walked down the hill to Cafe Flore, but Mimi happened to be heading to work just as Ruthie was leaving, so her aunt offered to give her a ride.

But first Mimi had to run to the bathroom. Whenever they were leaving the house, Mimi always had to run to the bathroom. It was as if she had an irrational fear that in the fifteen minutes it took to drive from her house to her office she would be overcome with a desperate and possibly uncontrollable need to pee.

Ruthie waited for her in the kitchen, opening the door to reveal the near-empty refrigerator. Other than the carton of half-and-half, some anemic-looking parsley, a half-empty carton of chicken stock, and a stick of butter, all that was in it was the usual collection of condiment bottles that they never used but never threw away: some chowchow friends of Mimi's had brought back from South Carolina, an old bottle of Dijon mustard, a couple of different brands of hot sauce, some sort of chocolate liqueur, a bottle of raspberry jam that had become hermetically sealed and no one had been able to use now for a month.

Robert and Ruthie were planning to shop for groceries at Andronico's that afternoon. In addition to buying all of Julia's favorite foods—bagels, cream cheese, Doritos, Pop-Tarts, Mallomars, orange Fanta—they planned to buy ingredients for the feast they would cook in honor of her arrival.

Julia was scheduled to arrive the next afternoon at 3:45. She was staying for a week, not flying back to Virginia until the following Saturday, which meant she would be in town for the actual anniversary of Phil's and Naomi's deaths, March 24. Not that Ruthie wanted to make an occasion of the day. It would be enough to get through it. It would be enough to have Julia to talk to, one-on-one.

Still, Ruthie told herself not to get her hopes up too high. Just because Peggy and Matt *said* they were allowing Julia to come to San Francisco for a week—luckily her and Ruthie's spring breaks coincided—did not mean that Peggy, at the very last moment, might not hold her stepdaughter back. After all, Peggy hadn't let Julia come to San Francisco for Christmas, claiming it was important for the Smiths to take a family ski vacation to Snowshoe Mountain in West Virginia.

It was hard to believe that ten months had passed since Ruthie had last seen her sister. It was impossible to fathom that her parents had been dead for a year.

Ruthie heard the sound of the toilet flushing and then water running and soon after Mimi breezed into the room, bright eyed and ready to go. Her hair was in its standard chignon and she wore green wool trousers with just the faintest checked pattern on them, along with a crème-colored silk blouse and several long, thin gold chains. The trousers looked like money.

They walked out the back door and down the stairs that led to the garage where Mimi and Robert's Audi was parked.

"Please let Tim Woods already have left for work," Mimi intoned.

Robert and Mimi shared the garage with the Woodses, a garage that was not big enough to park two cars side by side. If Tim had already left for work, then Mimi was in luck and could back right out with few obstacles. But if Tim was still at home, she would have to back his car out onto the street (using the spare key hanging from a hook in the garage, her spare key hanging beside it), leave it parked in the street with its hazard lights on, back her car out, leave *it* parked in the street with its hazard lights on, and then pull his car back into the garage before she and Ruthie could finally leave.

They were in luck. Tim's car was already gone. Once in the car Mimi and Ruthie both put on their seat belts and Mimi started the engine.

"God, I hate backing out of here," she said, her right arm stretched so that it rested on the back of Ruthie's seat, her head turned to look behind her as she backed the Audi up the steep driveway that led from the basement-level garage. Muttering a quick prayer, Mimi stepped on the gas and shot up the driveway, over the sidewalk, and onto Mars Street with a bump, somehow managing not to hit any pedestrians or get hit by an oncoming car.

"Good job," said Ruthie.

She always said "good job" after her aunt made it out of the driveway successfully. Such a feat required some sort of acknowledgment. It was funny how the simplest tasks in San Francisco took so much more effort than the same tasks in Atlanta had. Ruthie never gave a moment's thought as to whether or not her mother would be able to back the car successfully out of the garage in Atlanta, and there was certainly never a vehicle obstructing the way, a vehicle you first had to move. In Atlanta, their three-car garage was located behind the house, where there was enough space to turn the car around before you drove it down the front driveway and turned onto the road.

No one ever *backed out* onto Wymberly Way.

"It's nice you've made such a good friend," said Mimi, turning the radio dial from KPFA—the talk station that Robert liked but Mimi said was too militant—to a station that played classical music.

Ruthie shrugged noncommittally. She liked Dara, liked her a lot, and spent most weekends with her. Yet Ruthie still harbored reservations about her. Dara wasn't the type of friend Ruthie would have made in Atlanta. She certainly wasn't like Alex Love. Dara was not preppy and pretty and athletic, her eyes gleaming with competition. Dara was odd looking, with her blue metal braces, her purple-tinted hair, her steady rotation of band T-shirts, most passed down from her older sister, Yael. Dara was both eager and subversive, and while Ruthie found that such a personality mesh was great fun, she was still sometimes struck by self-consciousness that this strange girl had become her closest friend.

Her aunt glanced at Ruthie. "Has Dara been at Hall's since kindergarten?"

"Yep," said Ruthie. "She's pretty sick of it."

"I'm sure she's thrilled to have you in class, then. You must be a breath of fresh air."

"I guess," said Ruthie, shrugging.

It wasn't that she wanted to be elusive, to hold Mimi at arm's distance. It was just, well, Ruthie was sure that Mimi thought Dara odd, and that she was just being a good sport about Ruthie having befriended her. When Mimi was in eighth grade, she had been a cheerleader.

At the intersection of Market and Castro they passed what Ruthie assumed to be the world's largest pride flag. Mimi drove one more block, then turned left onto Noe. All of the spaces in front of the café—which looked a bit like a greenhouse—were taken, so she punched on her hazards and double-parked.

"You have your quarters, right?" Mimi asked.

Mimi insisted that Ruthie carry a roll of quarters with her whenever she ventured alone into the city, so she would always have a way to phone home if necessary. Mimi also gave Ruthie a stack of her business cards, to keep in her bag and in her pockets, so that if Ruthie were to be found unconscious (God forbid) the authorities would have a way of contacting her.

"I've got them," said Ruthie, patting the side of her canvas tote bag.

"I don't mean to be such a worrywart. But do be careful. And of course have fun!"

Mimi often apologized for being a worrywart, which was comical, really. Relative to Naomi or any other mom Ruthie knew in Atlanta, Mimi was not a worrywart at all. As long as Ruthie carried that roll of quarters, and that stack of business cards, Mimi pretty much let her do whatever she wanted.

"I'll be careful," said Ruthie. "Not that I think there's that much danger of anyone bothering me here in the Castro. Unless someone wants to, you know, drag me off and make me listen to Judy Garland albums or something."

It was a joke Dara once made, talking of how she wasn't afraid to walk alone at night through her dad's neighborhood because it was primarily populated with gay men. Dara was allowed to make such jokes because her father, after leaving her mother when Dara was nine, moved in with his boyfriend, Truong, who was from Vietnam and was always bringing home strange produce from the Asian markets in the Sunset, most noticeably a durian fruit that filled the apartment with the sweet smell of rot.

"You are becoming a true San Franciscan with that wicked wit," Mimi said, then immediately looked troubled. "What I mean is, you're picking up the tenor of this town. I know Atlanta will always be your hometown."

Mimi was forever going back over the things that she said to Ruthie, combing her words for anything that might offend or be hurtful. Ruthie knew Mimi did this out of kindness, but she found Mimi's constant editing a little exhausting. Besides, Ruthie hadn't spoken to anyone from Coventry since she had moved in with Mimi and Robert, except on her fourteenth birthday, when Alex Love phoned and they shared a few awkward moments breathing into their receivers and trying to come up with things to say.

For Ruthie, Atlanta had become the past, and she didn't like to dwell there.

She found Dara at one of the outdoor tables that offered a good view of Market Street. Dara, nibbling on a muffin, wore a Sonic Youth T-shirt over ripped jeans, an olive green sweater that looked as if it once belonged to someone's granddad, Doc Martens, and black lipstick. Her purple-tinted hair was pulled into pigtails held in place with thick, pale rubber bands, the kind intended to hold together loose pens and reports, not the kind intended for hair. Ruthie felt particularly preppy compared to her friend, with her white wool rollneck sweater from J.Crew, her Gap jeans, and her yellow Converse One Stars.

"Hey, Roots," said Dara.

Whatever private qualms Ruthie had about Dara, she always felt buoyant upon seeing her friend.

"Hey, Dars. How's the muffin?"

It was 10:00 A.M. and Ruthie was hungry.

"You won't like it. It's from Safeway."

"Why'd you bring it here? They have a good menu."

"My dad bought them for me. I felt bad not taking one. He's such a Jewish mother. He's always pushing me to eat."

"Let me try it," said Ruthie.

Dara handed it to her and Ruthie took a small bite. Apple cinnamon. The cinnamon was overpowering and the apple flavor tasted artificial. Wordlessly she handed the muffin back to Dara.

"What, you don't like it?"

Ruthie shrugged. "It's fine."

"Oh my god, you are worse than my mom. Can't someone just

eat a muffin in this town and not have it turn into the Pillsbury Bake-Off or something?"

Dara was smiling.

"Like your mom eats Pillsbury products," said Ruthie.

"God, I know. She's so annoying."

"Where's the menu?" asked Ruthie, glancing around. "I'm starving."

"You have to order at the counter," said Dara. "Remember?"

"Oh yeah." She stood. "Do you want anything?"

"I'll take a hot chocolate, extra whipped cream."

"Don't you need some protein?" asked Ruthie. "Have you eaten anything besides that muffin?"

"God, you're just like my dad."

Ruthie returned to the table carrying two mugs of hot chocolate, the rims overflowing with whipped cream. A server would bring her breakfast—the spinach frittata with feta—as soon as it was prepared. She put the hot chocolates on the table, and then sat down. Dara swiped a bit of whipped cream from the mug closer to Ruthie.

"Hey!" said Ruthie, and swiped some off the top of Dara's mug.

"Thief," said Dara, teasing.

"So 'What's Happening!!'?" asked Ruthie, quoting from the title of a show she and Julia used to watch together, a sitcom about a skinny black teen, his sarcastic little sister, and his two best friends, one of whom was so fat he had to wear suspenders just to keep his pants up.

"Just playing a solo game of Who the Hell Is He?" said Dara.

Who the Hell Is He? was a game that Dara and Ruthie had come up with while waiting for Dara's mom to pick them up from the shops at Laurel Village. They had sat on a bench by the metered parking spaces, waiting and waiting for Mrs. Diamond, who was always, perpetually, late. Bored, they started inventing narratives for everyone they saw coming out of Bryan's Grocery, making a competition out of who could come up with the best story.

"Okay, who the hell is he?" said Dara, pointing to a short Asian man, walking alone, wearing jeans and a Charlie Brown-esque sweater, yellow with a jagged brown line around the middle.

Ruthie took a small sip from her hot chocolate, drawing the drink up from beneath the cream. "International pimp. Going incognito."

Ruthie had recently learned the word "incognito" during a Wordly Wise lesson in English class, and using it made her feel smart.

"Jeez, do you have a dirty mind," said Dara. "I was going to say exchange student from Japan who got out at the wrong stop on Muni."

"Oh, that's good," said Ruthie. "And his host family lives on your mom's street and he's wandering all over the Castro asking men how to find 'Uranus.'"

"Gross," said Dara. "I mean, I'm fine with my dad being gay and all, I really am. But I just don't get the whole butt thing."

"Shhh," said Ruthie.

"Then again, Yael said she did the butt thing once, with a guy."

Ruthie put her hands over her ears. "I do not want to hear this," she said.

It was just like Dara to start talking about "the butt thing" in the middle of the Castro. Ruthie guessed that most of the other patrons at the café were gay, as well as eight out of every ten people who walked by on Market Street. There were a lot more men in the Castro than women. Sometimes they walked alone, sometimes hand in hand, sometimes bunched together in a group, like fraternity boys on a college campus in their matching polo shirts.

"Okay, who the hell is he? Or is it a she?"

Ruthie pointed to a sad-looking man walking up Market wearing a feathered brown wig and white plastic hoop earrings. He had on a denim jumper over a white T-shirt and, below the dress, white patent-leather pumps.

"That is a very confused person who needs to stop taking fashion advice from commercials for Terrific Toni's," said Dara.

Ruthie laughed. Terrific Toni's was a chain of discount hair salons that ran commercials showing women with dated haircuts and perms.

A server arrived with Ruthie's food, setting the plate down before her. Her breakfast was served with toast and roasted potatoes. Ruthie shook a little ketchup onto her plate and salted the potatoes—she thought potatoes could never be too salty—and then started in on the frittata.

"You can have some if you want," she told Dara, who immediately grabbed a potato off Ruthie's plate.

Ruthie kept watching the men—and occasional women—walking past. She always hoped to see Mimi's business partner, Marc, in the Castro. The last time Marc came over to have dinner with Robert and Mimi, Ruthie asked if he ever hung out at Cafe Flore.

"I try my best to *avoid* the gay ghetto, sweetheart. There are other places in the city we're allowed, you know."

Ruthie sipped from her hot chocolate, which had cooled to the point of lukewarm. It was still yummy, thick, rich, and almost bitter, not cloyingly sweet the way Swiss Miss mix was, which was the only hot chocolate Ruthie had ever tasted before moving to San Francisco.

"She's probably going to get hammered tonight and be too hungover to get on the plane tomorrow," Ruthie said.

Dara, who had been especially heavy-handed with the black eye makeup that morning, blinked. "Who are you talking about?"

"My sister. Julia. She's coming tomorrow. At least she says she is."

"Oh my god, for a minute there I thought you were still playing the game and I was really confused."

Dara laughed with more force than Ruthie felt the confusion warranted.

"Is she a big drinker?" Dara asked.

"She drank some in Atlanta, but she wasn't a crazy alcoholic or anything. From her letters it sounds like she drinks a *lot* in Virginia. I mean the reason she couldn't come for Thanksgiving was because she got caught drinking wine coolers at a party. And then later she got in trouble because her stepmom found a bottle of vodka under her bed."

"She should totally go straight edge like Yael," Dara said.

In addition to being a vegan, Dara's sister, Yael, did not drink, smoke, or do any drugs. Still, she considered herself a riot grrrl and a punk. On one of the few occasions that Ruthie actually spoke to her, while Yael was fixing herself a lunch of quinoa, red pepper, and avocado, Yael told Ruthie that she was "totally DIY" and not "adverse to a little civil disobedience every now and then."

Ruthie didn't ask what "DIY" meant, and she had no interest in knowing what form of civil disobedience Yael engaged in. Ruthie intended to stay *way* on the right side of the law. She didn't even like jaywalking, which Robert did all of the time, any time a store or restaurant across the street struck his fancy.

Acts of civil disobedience aside, Ruthie admired Yael for not doing drugs. Admired and appreciated her for it, because it meant Dara probably wouldn't do drugs, either, which was a big relief. Ruthie had made a promise to herself that she would never take an illegal drug. It would be easier to uphold that promise if Dara made it with her.

From what Ruthie could gather, kids in San Francisco, especially at the private schools, smoked a lot of pot. Before Hall's let out for the break she had overheard Robyn and Zoe, the two most popular eighth graders, laughing about how much food Zoe's older brother and his friends would eat when they came in stoned from the pool house. Zoe said that her dad had nicknamed the pool house the Cannabis Cabana.

Ruthie figured a lot of people in Virden, Virginia, must smoke pot, too. The last three letters Julia had sent all included details about the foods she and her friend Doug Hambridge liked to consume when they were high and had the "munchies." Dairy

Queen blizzards, entire Domino's pepperoni pizzas, grilled pimento cheese sandwiches, hoagies with cream cheese, jalapeños, and mozzarella.

It all sounded really gross to Ruthie.

"Her plane could crash," said Ruthie, regretting the words as soon as she said them.

"Don't say that," said Dara, as if she were a parent scolding a small child. "Anyway, that's impossible. Your parents and your sister can't all die in separate plane crashes."

"She could meet some hot guy on the plane and, I don't know, decide to go to his house for spring break instead of ours," said Ruthie.

Dara stared at her the way that Blanche sometimes stared at Rose on *The Golden Girls*, dumbfounded by her ignorance, if a little amused.

"Your sister is going to arrive tomorrow, you are going to meet her at the airport, and the two of you are going to have a great time for the next six days," said Dara.

Ruthie liked this about Dara. How she wasn't afraid just to proclaim things boldly, to put chaos in order, to name the way that things would—by force of Dara's will—work out. It was like the time Ruthie was panicking because she hadn't memorized the quadratic formula and they were going to be quizzed on it that afternoon in Math.

"This is what we are going to do," Dara had said as they walked together across the courtyard, headed to Spanish class. "You and I are going to the library during lunch, where I am going to drill that formula into your head. If we don't have time to eat lunch, fine. Buy an extra hard-boiled egg during Snack and you can eat it for energy before Dillard's quiz."

Ruthie bought the extra egg, Dara drilled the formula into her head, and she passed the quiz. In fact, she received a perfect score on it.

"I just can't believe it's been ten months since I last saw her," Ruthie said. "Her stepmom wouldn't let her come for Christmas because she had planned this whole bonding ski trip to 'get them back on track.' Of course Julia hated every minute of it."

"Before she started college Yael went and lived on a kibbutz in Israel and I didn't see her for a year," said Dara. "She was a total stick when she came home."

Ruthie felt annoyed. "It's not the same thing," she said, though she didn't even know what a kibbutz was.

The next afternoon Robert, Mimi, and Ruthie sat in traffic on 101 on their way to the airport to pick up Julia. Mimi had first suggested that Ruthie and Robert wait at home while she went and got Julia, but Ruthie said no, she wanted to meet her sister at the gate. Though Mimi didn't say so outright, Ruthie knew that her aunt was concerned that being at the airport, hearing the flight announcements, going through security, and watching planes come in for landings might trouble Ruthie, might make her think too much about the details of her parents' own death.

Not that the huge commercial jet Julia would be arriving on from Washington, D.C., was anything like the Ford Trimotor that had killed her parents.

"I want to see her the minute she gets here," Ruthie declared. She kept private from Mimi her anxiety that if she did not grab Julia as soon as her sister deplaned, Julia might disappear.

Robert said he would park so that Mimi and Ruthie might make it to the gate on time for Julia's arrival. The two of them speed walked through the terminal. (Regardless of how late they were, Mimi would not be so inelegant as to run.) They made it to the gate just as the incoming passengers were deplaning. First the ex-pensively dressed set from business class, men mostly, with their casual suede jackets, their shiny belt buckles, their leather carry-ons. Then an exhausted-looking mother, her young child riding on her hip, his legs straddling her waist. A white woman with dreadlocks; two well-groomed men whom Ruthie assumed to be a couple; another two men who were talking in the loud, jocular way of businessmen; another family, this one made up of three blond daughters, each with her own rollaway carry-on; a couple of students with backpacks in Georgetown sweatshirts.

And then a girl, a young woman, with auburn hair, long silver earrings, a T-shirt printed with tiny flowers, faded jeans, leather sandals that looked like something Jesus might have worn. Over her shoulder was a bag woven of brightly colored threads, the bag from Guatemala that Julia's first boyfriend, Dmitri, had given her.

She was looking around, and then she locked eyes on Ruthie. Locked eyes and smiled.

And Ruthie was smiling back. All of her frustration, all of her pent-up anger toward Julia, it was slipping out of her, and what was left was pure excitement. Excitement that her sister was here. Julia was striding toward her, was hugging her hard, was grabbing Ruthie under the arms, which tickled, and lifting her a few inches in the air before putting her down with a grunt.

"Biscuit," she said. "You are no longer light and fluffy. You must have eaten too many bunnies."

"Shut up," said Ruthie. "Egg."

And then Ruthie started to cry because it really was Julia. Julia was standing in front of her. Julia whose hair looked just like their mother's. Julia who was teasing her about her tears.

"I'm only staying a week!" Julia said. "You'll only have to share a bed with me for a little while. It's nothing to cry about."

Ruthie punched her sister on the arm, smiling.

"Julia, don't you look beautiful!" said Mimi, kissing her on the cheek. "Here, let me take your bag."

Deftly Mimi unhooked the woven Guatemalan bag from Julia's shoulder and slung it over her own.

"Surely this isn't all you have, is it?"

"I checked a suitcase," said Julia.

"Wonderful. Let's head to baggage claim. And I'm sure you need to stop off at the bathroom. I certainly always do when I get off a plane."

That was Mimi, all smiles and small talk, as she glided the two of them to the restroom, where she and Julia disappeared for a moment while Ruthie waited, and then through the terminal, past security, toward baggage claim.

As they walked, Mimi asked Julia about her flight, about the food, about whether or not she was hungry.

"I hope you are," said Mimi. "Robert and Ruthie have prepared a feast."

Ruthie glanced at her sister. It was unreal to have her here, walking beside her, touchable. Ruthie realized what people meant by the expression "in the flesh." She could not stop looking at Julia. Julia! Her auburn curls pulled back with a rubber band. Her tinkly silver earrings with all of the teeny-tiny bells, earrings that Julia had bought from the mean lady at the Onion Dome. The lady who used to bark at Ruthie not to touch anything whenever she accompanied Julia into the store. In the middle of Julia's left lobe was a small red scab, evidence of where she had pierced it with a safety pin.

"I'll eat anything but bunny," said Julia, grinning at Ruthie.

Ruthie returned the smile, but not before glancing at Mimi. She did not want her aunt to think that she had complained to Julia about Robert's rabbit with mustard sauce.

Mimi appeared to be unperturbed. "What did you and Robert prepare, sweetheart?" she asked.

"Crab cakes," said Ruthie. "With rémoulade. And coleslaw—which might not sound very good, Julia, but the way Robert makes it is super yummy. Trust me. Plus a field greens salad. And I made chocolate pudding cups for dessert."

Ruthie had recently learned to make the pudding cups, using a recipe Robert had clipped from *Sunset* magazine. She had prepped the batter for the "cups" in advance—Ruthie used ramekins—and just before they were ready to eat dessert she would pop them into the oven at 375 degrees. Twelve minutes later she would pull them out and place a small scoop of ice cream into each center.

When Julia spooned into her cup the outer edges would be solid like a brownie, while the inside would be molten chocolate.

"Pudding like Jell-O pudding?" asked Julia. "I love Jell-O pudding."

"These are more like melty brownies. You'll see."

"I love melty brownies," said Julia.

"Then you'll love these," said Ruthie.

They had to wait by the baggage claim carousel for more than twenty minutes. During that time, Robert walked in through the airport's revolving doors. Ruthie saw him before he saw them.

It was funny to see him from a distance. He was small, plump, *nebishe*, to use one of his Yiddish words. He was not someone you would necessarily notice in a crowd, and if you did notice him you certainly wouldn't think, *What a hunk*. Yet he was theirs, providing Mimi and Ruthie with food, humor, warmth. He was theirs and he loved them, had seemed to love Ruthie since the moment he first picked Mimi and Ruthie up at this same airport last June, when Ruthie was so new to San Francisco and everything was so very, very cold.

And suddenly Ruthie felt a fierce surge of love toward her uncle, was so happy to see him, was waving, calling, "Uncle Robert, over here!"

And he was bounding toward them, smiling.

"Hello, traveler," he said to Julia. "It's wonderful to see you."

"Sweetheart," said Mimi. "Go like this."

She swiped a fingernail between her two front teeth, and Robert, mirroring her, did the same thing, dislodging a small bit of black bean.

Robert often got things stuck between his teeth, and Mimi always noticed.

"Hi," said Julia, smiling shyly at him.

He was a writer. Julia wanted to be a writer one day.

There was a succession of thumps as the suitcases started dropping onto the conveyer belt, which rotated round and round. A large Hartmann bag tumbled onto the belt, and Julia, pointing to it, said, "That's mine."

Seeing the suitcase made Ruthie let out a little gasp. It had been her mother's. It was the suitcase Naomi had taken with her on the trip to Las Vegas, returned to Atlanta by the Mirage Hotel, after the accident. It was such an elegant suitcase with its leather handles, its nubby tweed.

Dinner was delicious and Robert and Mimi were charming, pouring Julia a glass of white wine, asking all about her classes, her interests, her ideas. They wanted to know where she was thinking of applying to college, what she did for fun in Virden, what local politics were like there.

"I don't think there are any local politics besides 'Love It or Leave It,' and 'Don't Take My Gun.'"

"I can see you fit right in," quipped Robert, taking a second helping of coleslaw.

"There has to be more to Virden than that," said Mimi.

"I guess," said Julia, shrugging.

Ruthie was mostly quiet during dinner, only joining the conversation to tell Julia about the high schools she had applied to for the next year, which were Urban, Lick-Wilmerding, and University. She explained to Julia that Urban was on the block schedule, so you only had a few classes a day, but each was really long.

"It encourages true engagement and gives the students enough time to dig into their work," said Robert.

"Not that Robert has any preference as to where Ruthie goes," said Mimi, winking at Ruthie.

The only hiccup to the meal was dessert. Ruthie was so excited about the pudding cups, but after she pulled them out of the oven and went to the freezer to retrieve the vanilla ice cream she could not find the carton.

She checked the trash can. The empty carton of Breyers was sitting in it. Uncle Robert! He could not be trusted alone with ice cream. That was why they rarely kept it in the house. She poked her head into the dining room.

"We forgot to buy ice cream," she said, staring meaningfully at

Robert. She did not want to tell on him in front of Mimi, who was forever encouraging him to diet, telling him that they both needed to cut out sugar and snacks, even though she was admirably thin.

"I'll whip some cream," said Robert. "That should go nicely with the chocolate, don't you think?"

As he passed her on his way into the kitchen he whispered, "Sorry! I have no self-control when it comes to dessert."

And so it was with lightly sweetened whipped cream that Ruthie topped the pudding cups, not Breyers vanilla. It was still delicious, rich and dark and molten, the whipped cream just taking the edge off the chocolate's bitterness. Except Julia did not seem to like it. She put one bite into her mouth and a look of distaste crossed over her face.

"What, you don't like?" Ruthie asked.

"You do not like my crêpes Suzette?" asked Robert, but he was just making a familiar joke with Mimi, was repeating what a waiter in Paris had once said to her when she did not eat all of her crêpes made tableside.

"I'm just used to things a little sweeter," said Julia, and put down her spoon.

That night in bed, side-by-side on Ruthie's full-size mattress, Julia's curls splayed on the white pillowcase like the corona of an eclipse, Julia grilled Ruthie about Robert.

"How many books has he published?" she asked.

"Um, four I think."

"Has he ever written a novel?"

"I don't think so. He writes books for businesspeople, mostly. But he did write one book about the history of gefilte fish, which is this stuff that only Jewish people like."

"What's it called?" asked Julia.

The Carp in the Bathtub," said Ruthie.

"He really loves you," said Julia. "He looks at you the way Dad used to. Like he's just so thrilled that you are his daughter."

This talk made Ruthie uncomfortable. For one thing, she loved Robert, but he was not her father. And she didn't like Julia bringing up the old charge that Phil loved Ruthie more than Julia because Ruthie was his biological daughter.

"Mimi is always telling him he's got something stuck between his teeth, or dust on his glasses, or a stain on his shirt."

"Yeah, she's kind of a bitch to him," said Julia.

Ruthie felt suddenly defensive of Mimi. She didn't want Julia to turn her aunt into a Peggy. "He usually does have something stuck between his teeth or a stain on his shirt."

"He's allowed to be a slob," said Julia. "He's a famous writer. If I ever become a famous novelist I'm going to gain a hundred pounds and sit around all day in my pajamas, eating chocolates while I type away."

"Gross," said Ruthie. "Anyway, I don't think Robert is really famous. It's not like people stop and ask for his autograph."

"Do you think he might look at some of my stories?"

Ruthie was pretty sure that Robert would, but she suddenly had a tight feeling in her throat. She didn't want Robert looking at Julia's stories, didn't want her uncle to decide that Julia was the talented one, and not Ruthie. She didn't want Robert's attention to shift from her to her sister.

In Atlanta everyone—Naomi and Phil, the teachers at Coventry—knew that Julia was brilliant. And she had proved it sophomore year when she scored 1480 on her PSATs. That she was a bad student was simply because she was lazy, didn't do the homework, didn't turn in papers.

Ruthie had been a solid student, a hard worker who made decent enough grades but did not bowl anyone over, did not have English teachers tell her (as they did Julia) that when it came to her writing, the best thing they could do was step back and not get in her way.

"He's pretty busy," Ruthie said. And then she felt guilty. "But you can ask."

"Hmm."

"Hey, guess what?" asked Ruthie, wanting to change the subject, to make Julia laugh and not brood.

"What?"

"I am a C. I am a C-h. I am a C-h-r-i-s-t-i-a-n. 'Cuz I've got C-h-r-i-s-t in my h-e-a-r-t and I will l-i-v-e-e-t-e-r-n-a-l-l-y!"

Julia started whacking at Ruthie with the pillow. "Shut up; shut up; shut up! You're reminding me of Virden!"

It was a song Ruthie had learned the summer after fifth grade, when she signed up with Alex for what she thought was a regular spend-the-night camp but turned out to be run by fundamentalists. Unless you read your Bible every day, writing down the verses you read on a little chart above your bed, you did not get dessert. And every morning a fourteen-year-old boy wearing white gloves came into the cabin to do room inspection and everyone had to stand at attention by their beds and salute him when he walked by. And he could inspect any item in the room. Once he even looked through a girl's box of tampons.

"Maybe I'll sing that to Peggy when I get home," said Julia. "Tell her I found Jesus in San Francisco."

"Good idea," said Ruthie. And then, because she felt so bad that Julia had to live with her awful stepmother, Ruthie asked her sister if she would like for her to scratch her back.

Julia rolled onto her stomach and lifted her T-shirt so that it bunched around her shoulders. "Not too hard," she instructed.

This, if nothing else, made things feel normal. Ever since Ruthie could remember she had been scratching Julia's back, following her sister's instructions as to exactly how she liked it done.

The next morning Ruthie woke to a series of pokes in her side.

"Rise and shine," said Julia, who was already dressed in a purple tie-dyed T-shirt and used Levi's.

Ruthie put a pillow over her head and moaned. Since turning fourteen she had lost her ability to be chipper in the mornings.

"What time is it?" she asked, her voice muffled from the pillow.

"Time to get up!" said Julia. "Time to explore San Francisco!"

Julia walked to Ruthie's CD player and pressed play. Loud music filled the air, music that Julia had clearly chosen just for this moment. Seventies stuff, corny but fun, declaiming the band's urge to celebrate life.

"Oh my god," said Ruthie, sitting up as her sister started dancing to the music, raising her arms above her head, moving her hips back and forth, shaking out her auburn curls.

But then Julia was walking toward the bed, was bending down and pulling Ruthie up by the arms, was forcing Ruthie to dance with her.

"Don't you want to celebrate?" asked Julia, gently mocking the song's lyrics.

Ruthie felt like an idiot, and she wondered if they were waking Robert, who tended to sleep late in the mornings, but then something sparked inside her and she threw up her hands, started shaking her hips, too.

She was having fun.

After a breakfast of Pop-Tarts and chocolate milk (both purchased especially for Julia) the girls went back into Ruthie's room so she could get dressed and Julia could put on her makeup. While they readied themselves, Julia played "Sugar Magnolia" from the Dead's greatest hits album.

"Let's go to Haight-Ashbury," Julia said.

"It's just like Little Five Points," Ruthie said. "It's not that exciting."

"Dude, I live in Virden, Virginia. Where the most exciting thing that happens is Biscuit World's two-for-one special on Wednesday mornings."

Julia was sitting by the little dressing table Mimi had set up for Ruthie, complete with a three-way mirror and a silver tray to keep her cosmetics on. With one eye open, the other closed, Julia dusted her left lid with gold shadow, and then her right. This was new. In Atlanta Julia had hardly ever worn makeup.

"Biscuits are exciting," Ruthie said.

"Want me to do your makeup?" asked Julia.

Ruthie had already applied a little brown liner to her eyelids and Clinique blush—from a free sample Mimi had received—to her cheeks.

"I'll take a little eye shadow," she said.

She walked over to Julia, stood facing her, and closed her eyes. Felt the soft brush tickle her lids.

"Now you're Tinkerbell," said Julia.

Ruthie opened her eyes, looked in the mirror. The gold shadow was barely noticeable, just a thin sheen on top of the ordinary.

"Beautiful," she said.

It was easier just to pretend that she loved it.

As they walked toward the Haight, Ruthie eyed Julia surreptitiously. Ruthie knew she was being shallow, but Julia's purple tie-dye made her cringe. Teenagers didn't wear tie-dye in San Francisco anymore. They wore J.Crew, or they dressed Goth, or they went grunge, like Dara, who was forever wearing granddad cardigans and black Doc Martens. Or they donned vintage T-shirts, the cornier the caption the better.

The only person Ruthie knew in San Francisco who wore tie-dye was Abby Beringer's dad, an independently wealthy man who "missed his little girl so much" when she was away at school that he signed up as a substitute teacher at Hall's. An older dad with curly hair and a silver beard, he looked a lot like Jerry Garcia. Indeed, he was in a Dead cover band comprised of men in their fifties called More Than Just a Touch of Gray.

Though Mr. Beringer was nice, the Hall's girls rolled their eyes over what a hippie he was. Abby especially, who complained that her dad's Grateful Dead tie-dyes, which he wore with khakis on days he substitute-taught, broke the dress code.

Julia didn't look as goofy as Mr. Beringer, of course. She was young, slender, and pretty with her cloud of crazy auburn curls. Still, Ruthie thought Julia looked like she was trying way too hard.

Ruthie knew that to Julia, Haight Street represented freedom, a place where bohemia was on display both in the stores and out on the street. Where people could wear what they wanted, say what they wanted, smoke what they wanted.

To Ruthie, Haight Street was crowded, junky, touristy, and gross. In particular she did not like the groups of kids who congregated on the sidewalks in front of the shops, white kids mostly, with facial piercings and dreadlocks, dirty clothes, and mangy dogs surrounding them.

"Hey, man," one of them would say in a plaintive tone. "Can you give me some money so I can go get fucked up?"

And then, when he was ignored, "At least I was honest."

And collectively the group would snicker and laugh, as if they alone were in on the joke that the world was playing on humanity.

Despite Ruthie's dislike of Haight Street culture, there were a few stores, scattered between the head shops, in which she enjoyed browsing. There was a bath and body shop that sold yummy soaps and Japanese robes made of the softest cotton Ruthie had ever felt. There was an independent bookstore that had hosted Robert's last reading. There was a women's clothing store where Mimi once took Ruthie shopping, though the clothes were a little expensive for someone who was still continuing to grow. And there was a Ben & Jerry's ice-cream parlor, which Ruthie and Julia were fast approaching.

"Want to get ice cream?" Ruthie asked.

Ever since they had turned onto Haight, Julia had fixed a dreamy expression on her face, as if she expected soon to be greeted by a tribe of kids dressed for Woodstock, handing out flowers.

"Get some if you want, but I'm too fat," said Julia. She lifted her T-shirt and slapped at her flesh, revealing a flat stomach.

Julia was not fat. Julia was so skinny Ruthie imagined her

slipping right out of her jeans. If anyone was fat it was Ruthie, who had developed a little roll around her waist from eating all of Robert's good food.

"Is there any shop you are looking for in particular?" asked Ruthie.

Julia looked at her, snorted. "What are you, the cruise director?"

"Just asking," said Ruthie. She eyed a black and tan dog that lay beside its owner, who was slumped up against the side of a natural food store. The dog was not wearing a leash and looked mean. Ruthie stepped to her left, to put a little more distance between herself and it.

"Oh, Ruthie. You are so lucky to live here. I wish you could see where I live, what passes for excitement in the big V. That you live where you can walk to Haight-Ashbury, it's so fucking cool."

"People just call it the Haight. Not Haight-Ashbury."

Ruthie thought Julia would act pissed at being corrected, but all she said was, "That's good to know."

"There's a really cute store near here called Ambiance," said Ruthie. "It's got really cool clothes and fun jewelry and shoes and everything."

"Okay," said Julia. "Fine. Lead me to the consumption."

They were near, only half a block away. Ruthie recognized the cheerful black-and-white-striped awning of the store.

"Every time I've worn something from here on free dress day at school, I get complimented."

"That's really cute," said Julia, as if she were thirty years older than Ruthie.

Ruthie pushed open the door to Ambiance and a little bell tinkled above them. A woman behind the counter with dyed black hair cropped to her chin greeted them enthusiastically. All of the saleswomen at Ambiance were enthusiastic.

The store consisted of one long room with a loft upstairs. Every bit of it was packed with clothes. There were racks down the middle of the room, each packed so tightly it was hard to squeeze a hanger back in once you pulled a dress out. There were racks against the side of the store, also stuffed with hanging clothes. And in every corner, against every wall, there were baskets filled with scarves or tights or tank tops or slippers. There were several glass-front cases that formed the counter where the register was kept, packed with inexpensive jewelry, earrings, necklaces, rings, headbands. And even though it was only 11:00 A.M., the store was already filling with shoppers.

"How do you find anything here?" asked Julia. "It's like Loehmann's or something."

"It is *so* not like Loehmann's," said Ruthie. "Just start pulling stuff out. And don't be afraid to try on a ton of things. Mimi always says there's no hurt in trying."

Ruthie walked to the front rack and started looking through it. Something bright pink caught her eye. She grabbed its hanger and pulled it out, revealing a long-sleeve shirt made of fine cotton with a scoop neck and a little white heart printed on the front.

"Isn't this cute?" Ruthie asked, waving the hanger in Julia's direction.

Julia was standing in front of one of the side racks, a shirt in her hand. She was staring at the price tag and did not answer Ruthie.

"Earth to Julia. Isn't this cute?"

Julia glanced at the shirt Ruthie was holding up and nodded. "Very," she said. "Listen, is there a place nearby where I can get a cup of coffee?"

"You don't want to shop?"

"Dude, this just isn't my scene. Why don't you try on stuff and I'll get a coffee and we can meet in say thirty minutes?"

"There's a place down the street, not two blocks away," said Ruthie, putting the hanger with the pink shirt back in the rack. "I'll go with you."

"No, try that on. It's adorable. I'm just a little claustrophobic in here. I'm used to the spacious wonder of Belk's at our local mall. But no worries. I'll get coffee; you try on clothes. All will be well with the universe."

"Um, okay," said Ruthie.

Julia waved good-bye and was out the door.

And suddenly it was as if she'd never been there at all, as if the sight of Julia in San Francisco had just been a fantasy. For a second Ruthie felt panicked, imagining Julia disappearing down Haight Street and never coming back. But then Ruthie shook her head and focused on where she was, on what was really happening. She was in a clothing store and Julia was getting coffee down the street. It was no big deal. She would meet up with her sister in half an hour.

And then it occurred to Ruthie that with Julia not there, she could pick out some tops for her, put them on the emergency credit card Mimi gave her, and give them to her sister as a gift. Because really, Julia looked so ridiculous wearing that tie-dye. By trying to fit into her fantasy version of San Francisco, Julia simply looked as if she didn't belong.

It was the first time Ruthie had ever shopped alone. Before, she had always shopped with her mother, or Julia, and now Aunt Mimi and sometimes Dara. Ruthie felt sophisticated being in the store by herself, combing through racks, holding on to items she wanted to try on, being treated like an adult by the friendly saleswomen. (Sales nymphs, Mimi called them, because they were pretty and puckish with their little bangs and bright red lipstick.) For Julia she needed to find things that were a little hippie, a little "earth mama" without being a total throwback to the sixties. She chose a rose-colored shirt that had strips of rose-colored lace sewn down its front, a little revealing but also pretty. Feminine, her mother would have said. (How she had loved for her daughters to look feminine!) Ruthie also chose a soft white cotton top gathered around the chest but with loose, open sleeves, almost like a smocked dress a southern child might wear, but sexy. It had a poetess look to it that Ruthie thought Julia might appreciate.

Ruthie tried on the pink shirt with the little white heart in its center and, loving the color, the heart, the feel of the tissue-thin cotton, decided to buy it, too. At the register Ruthie asked the cropped-haired woman if she might use the phone to call her mom and make sure it was okay to use the credit card.

Ruthie had taken to calling Mimi her mom when talking to strangers she would probably never see again. It was just easier than having to explain things.

"It's a local call, right?" asked the woman.

Ruthie nodded yes and the woman handed her the phone.

She took one of Mimi's cards out of her bag and dialed Mimi at her design studio in Hayes Valley.

"Sullivan Design," answered Marc.

"Hi, it's Ruthie. May I please speak with Mimi?"

"Ruthie? Child of my heart? Love of my life?"

Ruthie smiled. "Yep."

"How's the sister reunion?"

"Great," said Ruthie.

"But maybe it's a little hard to reconnect with someone you haven't seen in so long?" Marc prided himself on his intuition.

"No, everything's great." She wasn't about to start spilling her feelings out to Marc while standing at the counter of Ambiance, talking on a borrowed phone.

"Well, that is so good to hear. Now let me get your wonderful aunt for you."

When Mimi picked up she sounded flustered. "Is everything okay?"

"Everything's fine. I'm just calling because I'm at Ambiance and I wanted to know if it's okay for me to charge some things to your MasterCard. I'm buying a shirt for myself and two for Julia."

"Oh good. I'm so glad everything is okay. I've just had this worried feeling all day, and then you called. . . . Anyway, yes, charge away. That's fine. Julia deserves a treat and so do you. Do I need to talk to someone at the store to give you permission to use the card?"

"Um, yeah, probably. Hang on."

Ruthie handed the phone to the cashier, who secured Mimi's permission.

Once off the phone, the cashier rang up Ruthie's items ("Great choices, sweetie!" she said), wrapped them in white tissue paper with black polka dots, and slid them into a paper bag, decorated with black and white stripes just like the store's awning.

Exiting the store, Ruthie felt a prick of irritation toward her sister. She just could not figure out why Julia was so enamored of Haight Street culture. The fact that Julia loved the Haight and did not seem to note any of its deep flaws made Ruthie suspicious of Julia's other choices, of her other preferences. Julia had always been her role model, her guide. But what if Julia had bad taste and Ruthie had just never noticed it before?

She walked down the street, keeping an eye out for the coffee shop. She knew it wasn't far but could never remember exactly where it was. She passed a meandering family of five, all wearing fleece jackets with SF printed on the upper left-hand corner of the jackets like a badge, a badge that marked them undeniably as tourists, same as Julia's tie-dye marked her as not really from around here. Ruthie guessed that the family was staying at Fisherman's Wharf—which Robert called the tourist ghetto—and that they hadn't packed warm enough for the trip, assuming the entire state of California to be perpetually seventy-two degrees.

She passed a shop that sold pipes and teddy bears wearing tie-dyed T-shirts. She passed a shop that sold crystals and juggling balls. She passed a shop that sold skateboards. Then she saw the coffee place, three storefronts down. Julia was sitting at one of the tables out front, drinking from a paper mug, and there was someone else sitting at the table with her. Someone with straight strawberry blond hair.

The hair was so straight and perfect it looked as if it belonged to a girl from Hall's. Ruthie wondered if someone she went to school with had recognized her face in Julia's, had asked Julia if she was Ruthie's sister. But no, what eighth grader would do that—would approach a random older girl?

As Ruthie got closer to the table she heard Julia laughing, loud and show-offy, the way she had laughed the night before whenever Robert made a joke, flirting with him a little. Ruthie realized, suddenly, that it was not a girl sitting at the table with Julia but a boy. A boy she was flirting with.

Ruthie was standing by the table now, and the stranger turned to smile at her. She was right. The strawberry blond was a he.

Julia caught Ruthie's eye, smiled. "Hey, spaz, what'd you buy?"

Ruthie had been feeling so grown-up, and suddenly, with Julia's nickname, she was a child again.

"Secret things," said Ruthie. She was trying to be playful, to not act as irritated as she felt, but her words came out clipped, making her sound defensive.

"Ruthie, this is Logan. Logan, Ruthie."

"Greetings and salutations," said Logan, lifting his hand.

Ruthie raised the corners of her lips in a barely perceptible smile. He was not bad looking, this Logan. He had a long slender nose on top of a long slender face. And then there was the hair, which would have been beautiful on a girl. Which was beautiful, even though Ruthie didn't like long hair on men. Around his neck was a thick necklace woven from hemp rope, dull little stones embedded every few inches.

"You ready to go?" asked Ruthie, still holding her bag from Ambiance, not wanting to sit down.

Julia grinned at Logan. "Did I not predict her exact words?" she said.

"Psychic sister power," he said. "Rad."

"Ruthie, they have the yummiest chai lattes here. You should totally get one."

Since when did Julia start drinking chai lattes?

"No thanks," Ruthie said. "I'll just wait for you to finish."

Ruthie remained standing beside her sister. It felt good to be temporarily taller than her.

"Jesus, Ruthie, sit down. You're making me nervous."

"Yeah, park it, dude," said Logan. "I'm not going to bite."

Ruthie sighed deeply and darkly before sitting down.

"Show me what you bought," said Julia.

"I'll show you when we get home."

But Julia had already grabbed the bag from Ruthie's hand and was pulling out one of the shirts wrapped in the white tissue paper with the black polka dots. She ripped loose the tissue paper, instead of gingerly prying open the gold sticker that held the wrapping together.

"You got the cute shirt! Good for you. And holy shit, it cost seventy-two dollars."

"Dude, let me see," said Logan.

Julia held the shirt up, unfolding it in the process, then put it down on the table. Put it on the dirty, scummy table that probably had cigarette ash all over it.

"You could buy some good bud for how much you paid for that shirt," said Logan.

Ruthie snatched the shirt off the table and stuffed it into the bag, resentful that it would be wrinkled and dirty when she got home.

"Can we go now?" she asked.

"Oh my god! Can you relax?"

"Maybe your sister needs a bite of brownie," suggested Logan. Julia laughed. "Good idea."

Logan pointed to the middle of the table, where a few remaining crumbs of a brownie rested on a piece of Saran Wrap. "Take some. I made them myself."

"No thanks," said Ruthie.

"Come on, dude. Who doesn't like brownies? Have some."

Though nothing about the brownie crumbs appealed to Ruthie, she picked up a small one and put it in her mouth. Just to show that she wasn't a tightass. Just to shut Julia and Logan up. The brownie itself had the telltale chemical undertaste of a mix, but riding on top of that was an unpleasant texture, as if Logan had mixed chopped-up pine needles into the batter.

"Wow, Julia, these are *really* worth the calories. So much better than Ben & Jerry's ice cream."

Logan let out a little laugh. "You are one intense little chick," he said.

He stood, stretched his arms above his head. "I've got to roll. I'm meeting some friends in the park. Stop by later if you want, Angelhair. We'll be by Sharon Meadow."

"Cool," said Julia.

They watched Logan walk down the street, toward Golden Gate Park.

"Thanks a lot for running off such a hot guy," said Julia.

"Are you kidding me? He's a total loser. Do you know how many guys there are like that around here? He's probably homeless, you know. He probably sleeps in a tent."

"Beats the shit out of sleeping in the middle of a Laura Ashley explosion in a split-ranch in Virden, Virginia."

Ruthie was beginning to think that she wouldn't mind Virden nearly as much as Julia. In fact, Ruthie was beginning to wonder if Julia made Virden out to be much worse than it really was. Peggy, too.

"That was the worst brownie I've ever tasted in my life, by the way."

"Well, the point of pot brownies isn't the taste. The point is they get you high."

Ruthie was stunned. She stared at her sister, leaning back in her chair, looking so smug in her stupid, awful tie-dye.

"That was a pot brownie?"

"Yep, though God knows it didn't mellow you out."

Ruthie started wiping her tongue with a paper napkin that was sitting on the table. "Why did you let me eat that?" she said, feeling panicked and teary.

What if she started hallucinating? What if she fell into a terrible trip she couldn't escape from?

"You had half a crumb. If *only* it were possible to get high from that small of an amount."

Ruthie glowered at Julie. A memory flashed through her head. She was eight or nine and Julia had tackled her to the ground and was sitting on her, knees digging into her chest. From Julia's opened mouth hung a thick wad of chewed-up Dorito. Periodically Julia would suck the wad in and warn Ruthie not to move.

"As long as you don't move, as long as you trust me, I won't let this drop on you," Julia said. And then she would dangle the chewed-up wad from her mouth again, until finally she let it drop, a warm ball of chewed-up corn and Cool Ranch flavoring landing on Ruthie's face.

That had been bad, but this was different. This was looking at the person across the table, the person you thought you loved most in the world, and wanting nothing more than to slap her. Ruthie had heard the expression "slap the smirk off your face" before, but she had never understood it. Now she did. She understood it because she wanted to make Julia sorry. She wanted to make Julia feel like shit. She wanted to make Julia cry.

"Robert and Mimi say that you're self-destructive because you don't know how else to deal with your grief."

(What she didn't tell Julia was that Mimi also said that she didn't blame her, that she understood Julia seeking chemical solutions for the position she had been put in.)

"What are you talking about, spaz?"

Julia was leaning back in her chair, eyeing Ruthie critically, challengingly, as if Ruthie were an unruly patient and she, Julia, was the wise doctor who knew all the answers. But Julia did not know all of the answers. Julia was pigheaded and wrong. Julia was selfish and stupid and self-destructive, and she couldn't even see it.

"They say you're self-destructive because you know that what happened to Mom and Dad is your fault. I mean, if you hadn't lied and told Mom and Dad you were going to Pawleys Island with Marissa, they never would have booked that trip. They never would have driven to the Grand Canyon. They never would have boarded that plane. But you already know that, right? I mean everyone else does."

Ruthie's words had struck. Julia appeared stricken.

"Jesus," Julia said, her voice calm, collected, though there were tears running down her cheeks. She stood, started gathering all of the napkins on the table into a ball, stuffing them into her empty chai latte glass. Julia's hands were shaking.

She walked inside the coffee shop holding the glass filled with dirty napkins. When she came back out she did not look at Ruthie, just turned right down the street, in the direction of the park.

A part of Ruthie wanted to call after Julia, to yell, "Wait! Come back. I'm horrible. I'm sorry!" But a stronger, stonier self let her sister walk away, turned, in fact, to face the other direction. And who was walking up to her but Dara and her dad, Dara carrying a paper bag from Haight Street Market.

"Ruthie!" she said.

They were standing by the table, looking down at her.

"Are you okay?" asked Dara's dad. "You look sort of shaken up."

Ruthie looked up at Dara's dad, who resembled a hunter from a fairy tale, with his green flannel shirt, his trimmed beard, his head of curly red hair. The expression on his face was one of pure concern.

"No. I'm not okay."

It was the first time she had said such a thing since the accident.

"Oh, honey," said Dara's dad as Ruthie started shaking and crying. He and Dara sat down at the table with Ruthie. Dara scooted her chair as close to Ruthie as possible, put her hand on Ruthie's arm. Dara's dad fished a tissue out of his pocket, and though Ruthie did not know whether or not it was new or just "nearly new" (as Phil used to say), Ruthie used it to blow her nose.

"What happened?" asked Dara. "Can you tell us what happened?"

Ruthie shook her head no, continuing to cry in long, shaky sobs. She could not yet say that she had lost her sister. That she had driven her sister away.

Part Three

Part Three

Chapter Ten

From *Straight,*
a Memoir, by Julia Rose Smith

CHAPTER ONE

The first thing you need to know about the Center is this: no one there looked like Winona Ryder or Angelina Jolie. Netted from the suburbs and rural outposts of Virginia, we were the dregs of American teens—a pasty, pimply assortment of losers—all swept into a series of low buildings with particleboard ceilings and oversized combination locks on all of the doors. This was not finishing school for bad girls. We did not inhabit a pseudo-campus with soft hills and architecturally significant buildings made of stone and mellowed brick. Nor did our daddies come and visit on the weekends, bringing us gifts of roast chicken and perfumed soaps.

No, we were on our own during our tenure at the Center, no visitors allowed, no contact with the outside world at all until we were deemed recovered, turned eighteen, or our parents' money ran out. Whichever came first. No health insurance covered the

Center. They were unaccredited. (Even Harvard, the brochure claimed, was unaccredited in its nascent years.)

I would like to believe that "Bobs Squared"—as founders Bob Mack and Bob Spurgeon jokingly called themselves—began the program with good intentions: to help out troubled kids, to channel teen anger into something other than drug use, to provide an alternative for when home life was no longer working. The Bobs were just so jolly, with their penchant for nicknames, their guayabera shirts. Surely they did not intend for the Center to become a sort of ground zero for sadomasochism cloaked in evangelical language. But if my theory is correct, if the Center was founded on good intentions, how did it become such an unholy place, disastrous to so many?

I only have to reflect back on my time there to know the answer, a trickle-down theory, if you will: The fundamentalist Christian viewpoint is one that embraces a strictly hierarchical universe, where those at the top have all the power. At the Center, the counselors were on top, and therefore were granted the power to do with us as they saw fit. And power corrupts, which in the case of the Center led to cruelty. And you better believe cruelty is contagious, especially when everyone—from the "Bobs" all the way down to the "Addicts"—is encouraged to participate in it. And most crucially, there was no one from the outside looking in. There was no one the Center had to answer to but God. And they were pretty sure they had him all figured out.

Everything that took place at the Center was shielded from the public eye. We could write as many letters as we wanted, just "to get things off our chests," but no postman ever delivered them. We telephoned our parents once a week—whether we wanted to or not—but never without a "Buddy" sitting beside us, making sure we did not go off the script we were given to read from during the call. Yes, were actual scripts, similar to the ones telemarketers read. I have a script sitting before me. A small miracle that I managed to hoard it away without anyone noticing.

Addict: [That was us. We were all referred to as addicts during our time at the Center, whether our "addiction" was sex, drugs, or general rebellion.] Hi, [name of parent or guardian]. I only have two minutes to talk, but I just wanted to call and say thank you for having the wisdom to get help for my addiction. I was in a bad place, physically, mentally, and spiritually, but now I am starting to heal. And though my addiction caused me to do terrible things, at least it has brought me to this place, where I can truly learn about Christ and what He has planned for my life.

And on it goes. With all sorts of "choose your ending" options. If a parent asks about the food, the addict can say: "It's delicious," or, "It's good but not as good as Mom's," or, "It nourishes my body just as Christ nourishes my soul." If the parent asks about Bible study, the addict can say, "I am becoming grounded in the word of our Lord," or simply, "I am learning so much."

If we veered from the script we were punished, and at the Center punishment was real. To Bob and Bob, the Bible was inerrant, and the Bible warned about sparing the rod, which at the Center was actually called Rod with a capital R, as in "I think you need a visit with Rod." As if the Rod were an actual person.

The lingo at the Center was filled with jokes and puns.

But before you get too worked up, before the details become the stuff of pulp fiction (Juvenile Delinquents Get Spanked!), let me say: I never visited with the Rod. I suffered my own humiliations, but that particular one was reserved mainly for the boys. Some overgrown kid would get really pissed off, would throw a chair or cuss out a counselor, and suddenly there'd be calls for backup. "We need some cowboys to come hold down a wild bull," the Buddies would say. And while he's down, might as well beat the shit out of him.

The Bobs would be pleased to know that being at the Center made me forever suspicious of Eastern religion. Not because

Buddhism is blasphemous, as they would have said, but because I came to understand that no matter how perfect your downward dog, no matter how long you meditate, no matter how many times you try to see the lesson in every single thing, you can never escape the fact of your physical body and what can be done to it. No matter how much you might want to.

But let me take you to those low buildings secured with padlocks, instead of just alluding to the worst of what I experienced there. And let me tell you that despite all of the stupid mean wrongness of that place, there were some funny moments. And good food, if you can believe it; the cafeteria ladies really knew how to cook. I wish to this day that I had their recipe for okra, which they split long ways, rolled in what tasted like salted cornmeal, fried, and served with homemade ranch dressing on the side for dipping.

"Better than drugs," they called it.

On the day that I was checked into the Center, I had just returned from a trip to San Francisco. Flew the red-eye back to D.C., where my dad and stepmom were waiting. For good reason they did not trust that I would board the puddle jumper that would take me from D.C. to Roanoke, which was much closer to Virden, our pretty but dull little town, surrounded by the Blue Ridge mountains. They greeted me at the gate, both stony and surprisingly reticent. I had expected my stepmother to be full of rebuke.

I had been in San Francisco visiting my little sister, whom I called Biscuit, who lived with our aunt and uncle. Biscuit was my half sister, and the year before, our mother and her father—my stepdad, Phil—had died in a small-plane crash. By some utter blindness on my mother and stepfather's part, they had decreed in their will that in the event of their deaths Biscuit, who at that time was the closest person in the world to me, would go live with Phil's sister out in San Francisco, while I would live with my dad in Virden. This separation would have been traumatic enough even if Dad hadn't married Peggy, who shall from here on be known as my mortal enemy.

(Ah, but I can just hear my favorite writing teacher *tsk-tsking* now. I must evoke sympathy for poor Peggy! I must make her real for the reader, and therefore lift her out of the one-dimensional role I have cast her in as "the villain." I must give you reasons for understanding why she came to be the way that she is. Well. I will have to receive an F in character development. I have nothing nice to say about my stepmother.)

I was arriving home in trouble. I was, at seventeen, fundamentally troubled. I had become convinced—not entirely irrationally, as you will learn—that my mother's and stepfather's deaths were my fault. I was trying to anesthetize the guilt in whatever way I could. Alcohol worked. So did pot. Acid not so much. Beyond that—who knows? I stuck with booze and weed. I had met a guy in San Francisco, a runaway from Ohio who slept in the van he had parked out by Baker Beach. I had run away from my aunt's house, from my little sister. I could not handle being there with her, with them. I could not bear to compare my life in Virden, with my awkward father and my resentful stepmother, to her life in San Francisco. My aunt and uncle adored her, sent her to a charming private school, stuffed her wallet with spending cash, let her loose in the city. And my sister, who had always looked up to me before, who had seemed to want nothing more than my approval, my little sister now looked at me with judgment.

She had grown so sophisticated after ten months of living in the city. And here I was, the big sister, aware that everything I did marked me as naïve. Before we were split apart, Biscuit had shared my addiction to junk food. Now she turned her nose up at Cool Ranch Doritos and Pop-Tarts. Now she and our uncle spent afternoons cooking elaborate meals that involved Dutch ovens and large cuts of meat, red wine, stock, and lots of garlic. On my first full day in San Francisco I played the Dead, danced around, pretended I was at Woodstock. My sister merely winced. I put on a tie-dye over old jeans and my sister tried to wrap me in a fleece before we left the house.

"You're going to get cold," she said.

When I told her I was fine, I'd deal, she looked at me pityingly and said, "It's just, people in San Francisco don't really wear tie-dyes anymore."

As if she was one of them.

I asked her to take me to Haight Street. I thought we would have fun looking around. I thought getting out of the flat might ease the tension. Plus, I was seventeen. I liked the Dead. I liked smoking pot. I imagined Haight Street to be the epicenter of cool. But my sister complained about going, claimed it was lame, boring, passé. Once there she took me to a clothing shop where a cotton T-shirt cost seventy dollars. In 1994. I felt like a yokel. I felt so disconnected, so uprooted. I was clearly not a part of Biscuit's San Francisco, but I certainly didn't belong in Virden either. I went to get a coffee while my sister finished trying on expensive clothes. And it was at the café where I met Logan, the Ohio runaway, a sweet kid who, when I think back on it, probably was gay.

And it was off with Logan I ran. Crazy now, thinking back on that. How impulsive my decisions. How destructive. Logan was part of a pack of runaways. He was better off than most, because he had his van. These kids carried sleeping bags on their backs and kept mangy old dogs for protection. They all had weed, all the time. They would shoplift for food, or dig through the garbage cans at Golden Gate Park, finding half-eaten hot dogs, half-drunk smoothies, bags of stale popcorn.

I try to remember what exactly I was thinking at that time, and all I can come up with is a sort of foggy memory of self-satisfaction, sitting in a circle of kids in Golden Gate Park, so far away from my unhappy home in Virginia, so far away from the judgmental eye of my little sister. That first afternoon I kept telling myself I would go back to my aunt and uncle's flat that night. I was just having a little adventure. I was just blowing off steam. But I kept thinking about my sister, about how much she seemed to dislike me now. And how finally I was with kids who understood me, kids who felt so alienated at home they decided it was better to leave. And then some guys built a campfire and it was so warm beside it. I was only wearing a T-shirt, had not taken my sister up on her suggestion of bringing fleece. And I thought, *I can stay here. I can bum around until I turn eighteen, seven months away.* At that point I would reappear in the real world and collect the trust fund money left for me by my parents, having already learned how to survive on my own.

I was missing for five days. Twice in Golden Gate Park I spied my uncle Robert and Biscuit looking for me. But I was always one step ahead of them. Always knew how to turn a fast corner, duck behind a tree, become obscured by a sea of Japanese tourists. Or maybe it was just that I'd colored my hair, using a box of dye Logan shoplifted from Cala Foods. My most distinguishing feature, my auburn hair, was swallowed by what looked like black shoe polish. I cried when I first saw it, but two weeks later, when my head was shaved as punishment for trying to run away from the Center, I was pleased that at least my hair was already ugly, at least I was not giving them the satisfaction of stripping me of my red hair, the color of my mother's.

On the fifth day Logan and I were walking alone on Baker Beach, looking for sea glass. It was unusual that we weren't a part of a bigger group. I was barefoot, having left my sandals in his van. I was proud of the calluses on my feet, proud I could walk over hot sand or prickly grass without feeling a thing. An older guy passed us, wearing a loose T-shirt over jeans. Steel blue eyes. Little goatee. Said he had some weed. Showed it to us, wrapped in a plastic Baggie. Let us smell that it was good. Logan asked how much, he quoted a decent price, and Logan reached for his wallet. As he was counting out the bills, the man told Logan that he was under arrest.

"I should arrest you, too," he said to me. "But I'm going to make you a deal. You've got five seconds to get out of here, and I better not catch you in public again without your shoes on."

He handcuffed Logan, as I darted away, hoping that Logan would know, by telepathy, that I planned to bail him out. I did not have keys to Logan's van, so I had to make my way on foot back to Sharon Meadow in Golden Gate Park, the de facto meeting

place for our group. It took a while. Sunny was there when I arrived, exhausted, my feet aching. Sunny was a petite white girl with
blond dreadlocks who wore scratchy wool sweaters on top of long
skirts made from hemp. When I told her what happened, she said
I needed to find Saint Joe, an older man who helped out runaways.
She said he worked at a used bookstore on Twenty-second near
Mission.

I had to take the 33 Stanyan bus, which seemed to stop at
every block. When I was halfway there one of the drivers noticed
I wasn't wearing shoes and kicked me off. I waited for the next
bus, entered from the back, got off at Eighteenth and Mission,
and walked the rest of the way. Finally I arrived at Twenty-second,
where I found the bookstore, a cramped and dusty space that
smelled of mildew. The man behind the counter wore a gray
T-shirt with a hole near the collar. He was probably in his fifties
though he had a full head of hair. I asked if he knew where Saint
Joe was, and, smiling, he said, "I'm Joe."

He had a chipped front tooth. He did not look like someone
who would have a large amount of cash on hand to bail out a
teenage runaway arrested for buying drugs. Not that I knew exactly how much cash I was going to need.

I introduced myself, told him I needed help. He took me to
the back of the store, and we stood in the corner, surrounded by
stacks of old books that had yet to be processed. He said he knew
Logan, that Logan was a sweet kid. Told me to make sure Logan
knew it was Saint Joe who put up the money. Told me Logan
could pay him back later, just make sure he knew who was owed. I
tried not to think about what payback would mean. I was relieved
he did not try to touch me. He pulled out his wallet and took out
five one-hundred-dollar bills. Told me to take it to the precinct by
Golden Gate Park.

"They won't press charges," he said. "They just like to round
up kids every now and then, just to shake them up."

It was late by the time I got there. As soon as I walked in the
station I realized I did not even know Logan's last name and hadn't

thought to ask Sunny or Joe if they knew. Hoping that the name Logan was unusual enough to identify him, I walked to the front desk and, affecting my sweetest southern drawl, asked about my friend. Just at that moment, a door from some back room opened and the arresting officer walked through it. Stopping halfway through the lobby, he turned to look at me. Looked me up and down, from my recently acquired jet-black hair to my bare feet.

"I told you not to let me catch you without shoes on," he said.

He didn't actually arrest me. Just gripped my upper arm tightly with his fingers and led me to the back, where he sat me in his office and demanded the number of my "parent or guardian." There was a photo on his desk of him with a little towheaded boy, riding on his shoulders. I complimented him on the photo and he grimaced. Told me all he needed from me was the number of my parent or guardian, no other comments necessary. When my aunt came and picked me up from the station, my bags were already packed and in the back of her car. She took me straight to the airport, told me that as per my dad's instructions, she had booked me on a red-eye back home.

Her last words to me at the terminal gate, where she waited until I boarded the plane, were, "I don't know what to say, Julia. I really don't."

I knew I would be landing in some serious shit. I knew my stepmother was mortified, would see my having run away as some personal attack on her. (It was through such a lens that she viewed all of my actions.) She hadn't wanted to let me go out to San Francisco in the first place, felt my aunt and uncle were too lax, felt San Francisco too corrupting a place. These were the same reasons she cited a year before, when I had begged my father and stepmother to let me move to San Francisco with my sister, to live with our uncle and aunt.

I expected to be grounded. I expected to have my car taken away. I even knew there had been some talk of getting me on Antabuse.

But somehow, the fact that I would not be taken home . . . that took me by surprise, though I suppose it should not have.

During the three-hour car ride home, everyone was silent. About thirty minutes into the drive, I dug my Discman out of my backpack and tried to play a CD before realizing that the batteries had died. I kept the earphones in. It felt better to pretend I was overriding their silence with music, even if nothing was being played. After another couple of hours we passed our exit, kept driving south on 81.

"Weren't we supposed to get off?" I asked.

Peggy turned around in the front seat, looked at me coolly. "Your father and I thought The Roanoker might be a good place to talk."

The Roanoker, an old-fashioned restaurant housed in a sprawling brick ranch, was famous for its country ham and biscuits. As its name implied, it was in Roanoke. It was true my father loved their country ham, but it seemed odd to drive an extra thirty miles south after having driven all the way from D.C. But I didn't say anything. Tried to be a good little lamb. And then Dad exited, miles before the exit for the restaurant, driving us past a couple of gas stations and a McDonald's before turning on a residential street I had never been on. I didn't even know what town we were in, though it didn't look all that different from Virden. Muted, with those beautiful mountains in the background. We passed brick ranch after brick ranch.

I must have known at that point that they were taking me somewhere, but I remained calm, quiet. We made two more turns, driving deeper and deeper into this unfamiliar territory. On our right was an undeveloped woods, the trees growing densely together, their trunks tall but slim. Dad slowed down, turning into a long drive marked with two signs, one saying PRIVATE, the other THE CENTER, the "t" in "Center" made to look like the Christian cross. And here is what I remember even as I was becoming fully aware that we were not stopping for ham and biscuits and I was not going home: the high morning sun slicing through the trees, casting shadows on the wooded acreage we were entering. The way the dust in the air sparkled when caught in a shaft of light. The calm of the woods.

I remained mute as we drove up the long road. I was looking around, trying to figure out where we were. Finally my father stopped the car in front of what appeared to be a series of trailers, the kind that overcrowded schools use for classrooms. In front of the middle trailer was a wooden cross, large enough to hang someone from.

"Now, honey," he said, turning to look at me. His lower lip was trembling like a child's. His eyes were glassy with tears.

And then I heard a click, the sound of the doors being locked, a sound I would hear again and again in different forms, in different volumes, but that first click came from Peggy, who was savvier than my dad, who realized that before you sentence a prisoner you had first better make sure she can't escape.

"What are you doing, Daddy?" I asked, trying to pretend Peggy was not there. Out of the corner of my eye I saw two jubilant-looking white men walking toward the car. Men in crew cuts wearing blue jeans and white T-shirts that showed off their muscular arms. Buddies, I would soon learn they were called.

My father began to cry without making noise, the tears collecting in the straight lines around his mouth. To this day I believe that had Peggy not spoken, or had I not answered the way I did, I could have convinced him to back out of the long driveway, past the trees with the light shining through, past the undeveloped woods, the streets dotted with brick ranches, the gas stations, and the McDonald's, and back onto 81 North, which would take us home. Dad wouldn't have been able to leave me there, I believe, if I hadn't provoked him into doing so.

"Believe it or not, we are doing this because we love you," Peggy said.

"Believe it or not, you are a fucking bitch."

(My god. What was I thinking? I was not thinking. One thing I have learned since then is diplomacy.)

Calling Peggy a fucking bitch was, of course, the coup de grâce. Was worse than having run away with a Haight Street kid, worse than having been involved in a drug deal with an undercover cop. My saying those words strengthened my father's resolve, allowed him to click open the lock for the "Buddies," who led me, twisting my head to babble desperate apologies at Peggy and my father before becoming subdued by their tight grips, into the front hall of the Center. My home for the next five months, until my father's money ran out and the Bobs declared me in recovery, if not yet saved.

Chapter Eleven

Fall 2001

On the first day of the fall semester, Gabriel Schwartz, wearing a white T-shirt inside out, walked into the senior seminar on Flannery O'Connor that Ruthie had been waiting three years to take. It took Ruthie a moment to figure out where she knew him from, but then she remembered. Remembered him from all of those years back in Atlanta—a lifetime ago!—when they were fifth graders together at St. Catherine's School and he was the classroom pariah. Every day he was teased, for his long hair, his sissy name, and the strange foods his mom packed for his lunch: leftover fried rice still in its Chinese take-out box, onion and cream cheese sandwiches on rye, an unidentifiable square lump in a Tupperware container, which, when asked, he said was vegetarian lasagna. And for dessert, perforated raisin bars. Ruthie still remembers John King snatching a raisin bar off Gabriel's desk and asking, "What's in there, Schwartz Wart, your ground-up boogers?"

The adult Gabriel Schwartz didn't look all that different than he had as a boy. He was still skinny, still had hair so dark it was nearly black, still had blue eyes framed with thick lashes. Only now he was tall, his curly hair cut short, and on his right arm Ruthie could make out the lower half of a tattoo, its design obscured by the sleeve of his inside-out T-shirt.

Their seminar professor, Dr. Finney, started the class by having them all introduce themselves. Ruthie glanced at Gabriel when she said her name, but he showed no recognition upon hearing it. Good. Let him not remember her from St. Catherine's. Let him not associate her with a place where he had been so incessantly teased. When it was his turn, he introduced himself as Gabe Schwartz. It had to be Gabriel. He must have just shortened his name. She wondered what he was doing at UC Berkeley. St. Catherine's kids, who often went on to be Coventry kids, typically didn't end up going to college in Northern California. And the rare ones who did went to Stanford, not Cal.

Then again, Gabriel Schwartz had not been a typical St. Catherine's kid. For one thing, he was Jewish, which put him in a tiny minority. Ruthie remembered his mother visiting their class to teach them about Hanukkah. Wearing some sort of flowing purple ensemble, her tight curls forming a thick halo around her head, she casually flipped potato pancakes on the electric griddle while trying to get the students to pronounce "latke." She was unlike any mother Ruthie had ever met. She made Naomi look normal by comparison. A hand on one hip, the spatula in the other, she leaned conspiratorially toward the students, telling them, "Officially my name is Norma. But Norma—yikes, right? My middle name is Rose, but I'm not really a Rose kind of a girl. So people just call me Schwartzy. Does that work for you guys?"

The good little southerners at St. Catherine's School had responded, "Yes, Mrs. Schwartzy."

To which she replied, "Mrs.? Ha. Just 'Schwartzy' will do."

Dr. Finney was a compact man, impeccably groomed, who spoke with an Irish brogue. When it was his turn to introduce himself, he told the class he was Catholic, which Ruthie already knew. Which anyone who was an English major already knew. Dr. Finney's Catholicism, which he referred to often, was part of his lore. It made him an oddity at Berkeley, whose faculty tended to be secular to the extreme. He explained to the twelve students in the seminar that in order to understand what O'Connor was "up to" in her stories, they must have a working knowledge of Catholicism. He would be their tour guide through her faith.

"Grace enters through the ragged hole left by the destructive yet redemptive power of the Holy Spirit," began Dr. Finney, and while Ruthie normally took umbrage at any sort of religious maxim, she found herself scribbling down every word her professor said, lulled by his beautiful accent.

She was walking out of class when Gabriel—Gabe—sidled up to her.

"Should we file a complaint?" he asked.

"Hmm?" she said, not wanting to seem too excited that he was talking to her. His jeans rode low on his hips. His arm muscles were ropey, and he smelled of burnt sage.

"I thought it was a requirement that professors be atheist, or at least agnostic," he said.

"He's a corrupter of youth, all right," she said, joining the joke.

They were outside now, passing under Sather Gate. It was a warm day, no hint of fall, though it would soon be September. The leaves on the old trees, their trunks patterned and knobby, were still dark green. Ruthie had a moment of self-consciousness, a moment of watching herself walk toward Sproul Plaza with this boy. It was as if they were in a movie about a college couple, the meet-cute scene.

"By the way," she said to him. "Your shirt is on inside out."

"I ran out of clean clothes," he said.

"Gross," said Ruthie, though in truth she didn't find Gabe gross at all. She found him alluring. She found herself wondering what kind of a kisser he might be.

"Basically, I'm a disgusting human being," he said. "Rude, crude, and socially unacceptable."

"Mrs. Strokes's famous words," she said.

She hadn't meant to reveal their shared history. But he had just quoted their fifth-grade history teacher, a woman who had never liked Ruthie, who once asked Ruthie if she was "deaf, dumb, or just disobedient."

"How do you know Mrs. Strokes?" he asked. He turned his head, studied her with those dark blue eyes. She felt a little dizzy being watched so closely by him.

"Wait, you said your name is Ruthie?"

"Yep."

"You didn't go to St. Catherine's in Atlanta, did you?"

"Guilty as charged," she said.

"Oh wow. That's bizarre. I never thought I'd ever run into any-one from there. It wasn't exactly my scene. But Schwartzy—that's my mom—was going through a stage where she felt I didn't have enough structure in my life. Enrolled me at St. Catherine's in the fourth grade. She got over it fast, though, and I transferred to White Oaks in the middle of fifth."

It made sense that he would leave for White Oaks, which had the reputation of being sort of a hippie school.

"I remember your mom. I remember her making us potato pancakes for Hanukkah."

Gabe laughed. "That was one of maybe four times in my childhood that she actually cooked. Schwartzy was a big fan of Stouffer's frozen dinners."

He glanced at his watch, which was black and utilitarian look-ing. "Damn. I'd like to talk more, but I'm actually running late for something. But I'll see you in class, right?"

Ruthie watched him walk away, not hurrying really but taking long strides. She wasn't ready for him to go. She wanted to keep talking. She wanted to find out more about him, about his life in Atlanta after St. Catherine's. She wanted to know where he lived, what his major was, whether or not he liked Berkeley. She wanted to see his full tattoo, not hidden by the sleeve of his T-shirt.

An image flashed in her head: she and Gabriel naked, bodies pressed against each other, his lips on her neck, her head tilted back. Such a contrasting picture to the actual memory of the few clumsy times she and Brendan, a kid from her class at Urban, had slept together. Both were still virgins their senior year of high school, and their coupling was fueled not by desire but by a mutual urge to leave for college having had sex at least once. They had it three times, none of them satisfying, at least not for Ruthie. She was so dry the third time that the condom broke without them realizing it and he came inside her. What followed was a horrible experience: the missed period, the positive e.p.t., having Mimi drive her to the appointment early one Saturday morning, standing after she awoke from the anesthesia used for the proce-dure—as Mimi insisted on calling it—and having what seemed like a gallon of blood splash on the floor.

The one silver lining: The night after the abortion was the one time since her sister went to rehab that Ruthie felt close to Julia. Julia who spoke with her for two hours on the phone, who reas-sured her that she was not a bad person, who told her that no one makes it through life without getting a little stained.

The following week Ruthie and Gabe sat next to each other in seminar, during which the class discussed the assigned story, "The Enduring Chill." Ruthie suggested that perhaps Asbury, the supe-rior young protagonist, represented O'Connor at an earlier age.

"It could have been a self-referential wink-wink. I mean, don't you imagine she was condescending to her mother when she re-turned from the writers' workshop at Iowa?" Ruthie glanced at Gabe while she spoke. He watched her, seemingly interested in what she had to say, though he did not seem to be interested in speaking himself. Indeed, during the three-hour seminar he con-tributed to the conversation only once, when he explained what the catechism was to a student who did not know. Apparently Gabe knew what he was talking about, because Dr. Finney nodded in agreement.

When class was dismissed Gabe stood by the door waiting for Ruthie while she packed her books into her messenger bag. She glanced up at him and smiled. They walked down the hall together, walked out of the building, and walked into a brilliantly sunny day.

"Do you have time to get coffee?" he asked, placing his hand over his forehead to block the sun's glare.

Ruthie checked her watch, even though she knew she had time. The O'Connor seminar was her last class of the day.

"Sure," she said. She reached into her bag and pulled out a pair of retro sunglasses she had bought at Buffalo Exchange for six bucks.

"Caffè Strada?" he asked. He had a little gap between his front teeth. She had forgotten about that. She found it endearing, reminding her of her mother's gap, which Naomi always hated.

"I'm a Milano girl myself," she said. "But I can do Strada. Especially because it's such a nice day." She pushed the pink-framed sunglasses onto her face.

At Caffè Strada they each got a cup of coffee and sat at a table outside. And there they stayed for hours, talking. It began with Gabe asking Ruthie how a St. Catherine's girl managed to land at Berkeley. And so she told him about the plane crash, and moving to San Francisco to live with Mimi and Robert, and being separated from her sister, Julia.

It was rare for Ruthie to bring up the accident, even rarer to bring up her sister. With new acquaintances she often didn't mention her dead parents or Julia at all. It wasn't that she lied. It wasn't as if she called Mimi and Robert "Mom" and "Dad." She simply didn't feel a need to interject the details of her tragic past into casual conversation. And yet she felt compelled to tell Gabe the truth about her life. It was the way he listened, the way he leaned in toward her while she spoke. He seemed actually to be interested. And she wanted to be interesting to him. She wanted him to think that she was a woman with an interesting story.

She told him about how hard it had been to connect with Julia, even that first year, before things got really bad. How different their lives became, just by virtue of Ruthie being in San

Francisco, Julia in Virden. How when Julia finally did come to San Francisco, to visit, the trip had been a disaster and she had ended up running away with some boy she met on Haight Street. How after she was found by the authorities and sent back to Virden, she was put in a drug treatment program for five months, which left her both bitter and subdued. Or at least that was how she sounded on the phone, during their more and more infrequent and dissatisfying calls.

And then Julia had surprised them all by not only being admitted to the University of Virginia—she was a disciplined student after her time at the Center and her SATs were astronomical—but by deciding to go there, even though it was little more than an hour's drive from Peggy and Matt.

When Julia called to tell her the news, Ruthie expressed surprise, saying she assumed Julia would want to go to college as far away from Virden as possible.

She remembered Julia's exact reply, and she repeated it to Gabe.

"'UVA is the cheapest good school I can go to, and I don't want to squander my money. The only thing I can count on in this world is my trust fund.'"

"You took what she said about counting on her trust fund to mean that she couldn't count on you?" Gabe asked.

"I know that's what she meant. I don't think she's ever forgiven me for having said—when I was fourteen years old—that she was responsible for our parents' deaths. Even though I wrote her a letter when she was in rehab, telling her how wrong I had been. Even though I tried to tell her the first time I spoke with her on the phone once she got out."

Gabe made a clicking noise out of the side of his mouth. "That's rough," he said.

"But all's well that ends well, right?" Ruthie said, fearing that she was being too much of a downer. So she told him about how Julia had been a star in the creative writing program at UVA, how she had gone on to get her MFA there, how she had polished her master's thesis into a true manuscript, which was accepted for publication by an imprint at Penguin. How Julia had sent her a bound manuscript, which Ruthie had read. How the pub date for her sister's book—titled *Straight*—was scheduled for March of the upcoming year, March 11, 2002.

"Is her book good?" Gabe's elbows were on the table, and he was resting his chin in his palms. They had pushed their coffee mugs to the side. They had already had several refills, and could drink no more.

"It is. It's sad. The place she was sent to, the Center, it was totally out of a made-for-TV movie. There was corporal punishment, and isolation rooms where they'd leave you—cut off from everyone—for up to four days. And every afternoon they had these sort of group therapy sessions, but if you weren't forthcoming enough, or the counselors thought you were lying about something, they'd yell, 'BS!' and someone would pull your chair out from under you and sort of kick you into the middle of the 'sharing' circle and they'd put a scratchy brown wool blanket over you and everyone would pile on top. It was supposed to symbolize that you were drowning in your own bullshit. Though they'd never go so far as to say the actual word. The initials were as risqué as they'd get."

"Jesus," said Gabe. "Makes my junior high experience look tame."

"Um, yeah, I'd imagine. Your junior high wasn't run by a bunch of fundamentalist sadists, was it?"

She experienced a feeling of slight irritation toward Gabe. Junior high was a universal hell, but no one's experience could compare to what Julia went through during those five months of being locked up and at the mercy of "Christian" counselors who thought suffocating a kid would put her on the road to recovery.

"I'm just talking about this crazy teacher I had at White Oaks. Crazy, but kind of great. He had us write autobiographical stories, and he rode you really hard if he thought you weren't committed, weren't putting in real effort. And he really went apeshit if he thought you were bullshitting. Or being maudlin or self-pitying.

"When I was in eighth grade I wrote a story about how I

wanted to slit my wrists because my mom drove me so crazy with all of the men she would bring over to our house. I swear to god I'd wake up each Saturday and Schwartzy would be toasting an Eggo for some new guy. Well, three days after I turn in the story Howard saunters in, tells us he's read all of our papers, and says that one of them was particularly nauseating. From his satchel he pulls out mine, looks right at me, and says, 'Shit, kid, if I wrote such whining, driveling crap I'd want to slit my wrists, too.' And then he chucked the paper at me."

"Are you kidding? He didn't make you go see a counselor?"

"He did. I had to talk to the school shrink. But what I remember about the experience is Howard making me rewrite the story. He told me he'd kick my ass if I turned in anything less than brilliant. I believed him, too, spent two weeks solid working on it. Skipped a couple of days of class just so I could focus single-mindedly on it. It was probably the best piece of writing I'd ever done. Might still be. And he knew it, too. He published it in the *Book*, which was a collection of the class's best stories, sold at the school's annual auction."

"They sold a story about you trying to kill yourself?"

"I was just being dramatic with all of the slitting-my-wrists talk. It was really a story about my mom. About how much I loved her but how mad I was at her for bringing home all those men. I mean there I was, this horny little eighth grader, embarrassed to death by my own boners, and my mom is flaunting her own extremely active sex life."

Ruthie pretended not to be flustered by Gabe talking about his pubescent erections. "What did your mom think about your paper?"

"Oh, she loved it. Thought it was genius. Thought Howard was genius. She was always saying he deserved one of those MacArthur awards."

Ruthie laughed. "I remember when she came to our class at St. Catherine's. She told us to call her Schwartzy and we all said, 'Yes, Mrs. Schwartzy.'"

"That sounds like St. Catherine's all right."

"Is she still in Atlanta?"

"Yeah. She bitches about it, says I'm so lucky to be on 'the best coast.' But she's not going anywhere. She's a defense lawyer, the court-assigned kind for the sorriest, poorest, saddest sons of bitches in the state. Does a lot of work for the Southern Center for Human Rights, too. She's too needed to leave. And she lives in Inman Park, which is its own little liberal ghetto. Has a great house. Reminds me of the bungalows around here, only she bought hers for nineteen thousand dollars. Of course that was in 1982 and there was a homeless man living in the basement."

"You come from a very different Atlanta than I do," said Ruthie.

"Ah, but at least we have St. Catherine's."

She smiled at him. "Hey, lift up your shirtsleeve. I want to see that tattoo."

Dutifully, he rolled up the right sleeve of his shirt. Tattooed on his arm, in blue ink, was an utterly realistic Christ on the cross, complete with nails through his wrists and his ankles. When Gabe flexed, the Christ's bare abdomen tightened.

Ruthie squinted her eyes at him. "What is a nice Jewish boy doing with a full-out crucifix on his arm?"

"I'm a Roman Catholic," he said. "Converted my sophomore year."

"What!?"

Ruthie would have been less surprised had Gabe said he was actually born a woman.

"I don't know. It just sort of suits me. I like the structure. I like the history—that it traces all the way back to Peter. I like going to mass. I especially like that half of the masses are in Spanish. I like Walker Percy, and Flannery O'Connor and Thomas Merton and Dorothy Day. And sure, maybe I did it at first to piss off Schwartzy, but it took. I'm a mackerel eater, as Owen Meany would say."

Ruthie knew very little about Catholicism and was not sure what Gabe meant by it tracing all the way back to Peter. She had read a lot of novels, though, so she got his reference to Walker Percy and John Irving.

"What in God's name did your poor mother say when you informed her that her Jewish son had converted to Catholicism?"

Gabe laughed. "She had the perfect thing to say, the perfect thing to deflate me of any notion that I have the ability to upset her. I remember her words exactly. She said, 'Well, I guess this is another one of your Alex P. Keaton moments. I just hope you don't stop using birth control.'"

"Ha! So do you?" Ruthie tried to make her tone as breezy as possible.

"Most Catholics do actually. It's especially important for me to be really vigilant about it because of the whole abortion thing."

"What, you're antiabortion?" Her tone was light, joking. She did not know a single person in Berkeley who was not pro-choice, except, perhaps, for Dr. Finney.

"I say 'pro-life,' but all of the language around that stuff is probably just designed to create wedges between people who share more in common than not."

Ruthie felt on the defensive. He was really pro-life? Why did he even think he could have an opinion on such a topic? It wasn't as if he could get pregnant.

"If you're antichoice, pro-life, whatever, I don't see how we can share much in common. At least not philosophically."

"Are you against the death penalty?"

"Yeah."

"Well, so am I. It's part of taking a sacramental view toward all of life—from womb to tomb. So why is it that instead of talking about what we agree on—being anti–death penalty, for example—we instead become polarized over the issues where we disagree? I'm always telling Schwartzy, if Democrats could just be a little more open-minded toward pro-life progressives, then that overgrown frat boy from Texas might not have won the election."

"I don't think he really won it."

"Okay, whatever, if there had been a critical mass of people voting Democrat, Florida wouldn't have mattered."

"Hmm," said Ruthie.

She thought about Dara, with whom she had lived all four years of college, first in the dorms and later in their apartment in North Berkeley. Dara volunteered at a Planned Parenthood clinic in San Jose every other Saturday morning. She left in the middle of the night in order to arrive by 5:00 A.M., when the appointments began. Her job was to escort patients from the parking lot to the front door of the clinic. To ensure that the first voice that greeted each woman, many of whom were poor and young, was one of support. Otherwise the only voices they would hear, walking through the parking lot, were those of the protesters yelling loudly from the sidewalk, "Mom, mom! Please don't kill your baby!"

If Dara knew that Ruthie was attracted to a man who was antichoice, she would give Ruthie hell. And even if Ruthie were able to "find common ground" with Gabe on such an issue, what would he think if she were to tell him that her deeply entrenched belief in a woman's right to choose was rooted in her own history? That at eighteen she had chosen. She had chosen not to remain pregnant.

God, he was so good-looking, so funny, so smart. But a Jew who had converted to Catholicism and was pro-life? What kind of deep neuroses did that reveal? Better to look at her watch, exclaim at the time, and quickly, before he could say anything to pull her back, dart away.

As she hurried down Bancroft, she had a feeling of averting disaster, like swerving the car to avoid hitting the child crossing the street.

She managed to avoid him the next week by rushing into class at the last minute and then dashing out as soon as it was over. He called her twice, but she, regretting that she gave him her cell phone number during their marathon conversation at Caffè Strada, did not answer. She could not help but steal glances at him during class, though, when she was sure he wasn't looking her way. She could not help still being attracted.

That Tuesday Ruthie awoke to the ringing of her cell phone. She turned, looked at the face of her alarm clock. It was 7:30 A.M., too early to answer. She put her pillow over her head, willed the phone to stop ringing. A moment after it did, the landline rang. She remained motionless for a few more seconds and then, figuring someone really needed to reach her—Mimi? Robert?— grabbed the cordless phone, which lay on the floor beside her bed.

"Ruthie honey, it's Mimi. Are you watching your TV?"

"No. I was sleeping."

"Turn it on."

"What channel?"

"Any channel."

The urgency in Mimi's voice forced her out of bed. "I have to walk to the other room to do it. What's happening?"

"Oh, sweetie, it's terrible. Terrorists have been hijacking commercial airplanes. They flew two of them into the World Trade Center, and both towers—the north and the south—are down."

"What do you mean, down?"

"I mean gone. I mean collapsed. It's horrible, Ruthie; there were so many people inside."

When she reached the living room, she noticed that the coffee table was cluttered with dishes from the night before. She found the remote, punched on the TV. Saw a haunting image. An airplane plowing into one of the towers, followed by a line of thick gray smoke rushing toward the sky. And then a newswoman was talking, saying that they had just watched a recording of the first plane that crashed into the north tower at approximately 8:45 A.M. Eastern time.

"Holy shit. Is this for real?"

"I'm afraid it is, sweetheart."

They were playing another clip, this one of the second plane hitting the south tower. Ruthie gaped at the twin lines of billowing gray smoke, the flames shooting out of the side of the building. Tears popped into her eyes, though she couldn't really make sense of the images. They did not compute.

"Oh my god. Have you spoken to Julia? Is she okay?" Ruthie asked.

Upon finishing her MFA at Virginia, Julia had moved to New York, to the Williamsburg section of Brooklyn.

"I tried calling, but I can't get through. I heard everything is down in New York right now, so it probably doesn't mean anything that I couldn't reach her on the phone."

Another image played on the news, this one of the north tower collapsing, starting at the top. It collapsed so quickly. As if it were a vertical sand castle, held together by a frame. As if someone had hit the sand castle on the head with a hammer. The idea that cement and steel were part of that building—it was almost unfathomable.

"Have you sent Julia an e-mail?"

"I have, but I'm guessing that connection is down, too."

"Look, I'm going to come to your house, spend the day with you and Robert."

"I would love that, sweetie, but I don't want you crossing any bridges. Not today. We just don't know what else might happen. There may be more attacks."

Ruthie was chilled, though she usually complained that their apartment was stuffy. Dara walked into the living room, her hair, which she had cut short, sticking straight up. She wore only a T-shirt and underwear, her usual sleeping attire. She was holding her cell phone against her ear, and she looked wild-eyed.

"Oh my god," she said as she looked at the TV screen, which showed New Yorkers on the ground, running away from the collapsing building, shirts, scarves, sweaters over their mouths to keep from inhaling the smoke.

"Dara just woke up," said Ruthie.

"Why don't you two keep each other company. I'll call you later. And I'll call the minute I hear from Julia. You do the same if you hear from her first, okay?"

Ruthie said okay, told her aunt she loved her. When she hung up, Dara was still talking on the phone. There went the plane into the first tower again. Apparently they were playing the image on a loop.

Julia was there, in that city under attack. Ruthie went back to her bedroom to get her cell phone, where she had saved Julia's number. So infrequently did she call her sister, Ruthie did not have it memorized. She scrolled through her contacts until JULIA came up. She hit the call button.

The line was busy, but it didn't sound like a normal busy signal. The beep was longer, haunting.

Ruthie knew that Julia lived in Brooklyn—Williamsburg—but didn't know what she did during the day besides write. What if she rented a writing office in downtown Manhattan? And wasn't there a restaurant on top of the World Trade Center? What if Julia had gone there for breakfast that morning? What if an editor from Penguin had taken her there? No. That made no sense. She couldn't become panicky, illogical. Why would a literary editor meet a writer at a pricey restaurant for tourists and Wall Street people? Julia was probably okay. Probably. But it wasn't as if Ruthie believed her family was immune to disaster. Taking her cell phone with her, she returned to the living room with Dara, who now sat, Indian-style, in front of the TV.

"Classes are canceled, I'm sure," Dara said, not taking her eyes off the screen. "And if they're not, it doesn't matter. We're not going."

The news showed the clip of the north tower collapsing again. Dara turned to look at her.

"Holy shit, Ruthie. This can't be undone."

They watched TV for seven hours straight. Seeing the same images again and again. The two separate planes going into the towers. The firemen in their black protective gear with the yellow stripes. The profile of a woman watching the towers in horror, tears in the corner of her eye. The people clutching shirts and bandanas against their faces. People running after each tower collapsed. Mayor Giuliani at a press conference.

Ruthie phoned her sister every half hour but never got through. She told herself not to panic, that all of the lines in New York were down.

There was nothing to eat in the house besides Cheerios, old milk, and a six-pack of beer, which she and Dara finished quickly. Ruthie had been planning on grocery shopping that day, but now the thought of going to the Berkeley Bowl exhausted her. It was 2:30 and they were starving.

"I want more beer," said Dara. "Don't you?"

They decided to go to Ulysses, an Irish pub nearby that had two TVs for watching sports. Normally sports bars were not the type of place Dara and Ruthie frequented, but they felt as if it was wrong to turn away from the TV. They felt that by watching the horrific images they were somehow showing their support for the people of New York, for the country. Ruthie had an urge to call Gabe, to see if he wanted to meet them at the pub, but she decided against it. Her earlier impulse to nip their budding relationship was correct. Were she to see Gabe on this day of vast destruction, she would lose all self-control.

Dara called Yael, asked if she wanted to meet them at the bar. Yael said she would. She was also living in Berkeley, working on her Ph.D. in comparative literature. Yael now spoke Hebrew fluently, along with German and some Yiddish. She was dating a much older man, a writer in his forties, who lived in a beautiful glass and wood house in the Berkeley hills. Ruthie and Dara had gone to dinner there once. It was strange to see Yael, whom Ruthie would always think of as a riot grrrl, at home in such a refined atmosphere. It was as if she had jumped over years and years of striving and landed in comfortable middle age.

People were smoking inside Ulysses even though smoking was not allowed. The bartender did not seem to be bothered by it. Both of the TVs were turned to CNN. Ruthie and Dara sat at the bar and watched, waiting for Yael. The same images as before rotated before their eyes, only now there were more images of firefighters, astonishing in their bravery. Ruthie and Dara drank Guinness stout, which normally Ruthie did not like but on this day found comforting. They ate sliders and fries, which Ulysses called chips. They glared at the man sitting next to them, the man who said, "I hate to say this, but America had this coming."

He was as noxious as the group of boys who came in a few minutes later, drunk, chanting, "USA! USA! USA!" As if they were watching the opening ceremonies of the Olympics.

Yael arrived an hour after they did, looking expensive in her thin cashmere shell, her black pants made of cotton and linen. Ruthie assumed Yael's man friend was now buying her clothes. She and Dara put their arms around each other and hugged for a solid minute, and as always, Ruthie felt envious of them. Felt that they had the kind of relationship she and Julia would have had, should have had, if not for the accident.

Yael ordered a Black and Tan, asked Dara if the pub had a pool table.

"In the back," said Dara. "But I think people are playing."

"I'll check it out," said Yael. "Put our names on a wait list if I need to. I don't think I can just sit and watch TV anymore."

As Yael walked toward the back of the bar, Ruthie hoped the wait list for the pool table would be long. She hated pool. She was terrible at it, no matter how many times Dara tried to coach her. She thought of it as geometry with balls, and she had never thought of math as fun. She was startled from her thoughts by the ring of her cell phone. Julia! Please be Julia, calling to say she was fine. But no, when Ruthie glanced at the screen she saw it was a 510 area code. She answered.

"Hey. I just wanted to call and check in."

It was Gabe. Gabe Schwartz. That low, warm voice.

"Hey. It's good to hear from you. Are you okay? Is Schwartzy?"

"We're all accounted for. How about you?"

She told him she was waiting to hear from Julia in New York.

That she had been trying her sister's number all day and couldn't get through.

"God, I hope you hear from her soon. What are you doing while you wait?"

"Drinking Guinness at a pub with my roommate and her sister. Watching CNN. Trying not to go crazy with worry."

"Have you ever heard of Taizé?"

He pronounced it like "tie-zay."

"Uh-uh."

"It's this meditation service. The one I go to is held at an Episcopalian church, but the service is ecumenical. What happens is this amazing singer leads the congregation in fifty minutes of simple prayer put to music. Basically you just sing the same prayer over and over, but it's in Latin, so it feels deeper. And then there's ten minutes for silent meditation."

"I thought you were Catholic."

"I am. But my church doesn't hold Taizé services, so I sleep around a little."

"Just don't get pregnant," said Ruthie, a bitter edge to her voice.

"Funny. Look, I've been watching TV all day and it's just—it's just too much. I keep watching because it feels weird not to. But I'm already starting to feel desensitized. I really need to go somewhere and be quiet. Anyway, I wanted to know if you might like to come with me. The service starts at six thirty."

Ruthie looked at the cold fries on the plate in front of her, at the bartender who appeared exhausted, at the smoke that surrounded her, at the bright TVs with their unrelenting images, at Yael motioning from the back room, presumably because the pool table was available.

She said yes to Gabe. She would meet him at the church.

She lied to Dara and Yael about where she was going. Told them she was going to drive up into the hills, just for the view, the fresh air, the perspective. Asked Yael if she would mind taking Dara home.

"You're sure you don't want us to go with you?" Dara asked. "You're just going to drive around by yourself?"

"You know how I am," said Ruthie.

The church was on Cedar, just a few blocks away from Chez Panisse, which amused Ruthie, because she thought of Chez Panisse as her house of worship. Much as she liked to analyze books for her literature courses, she liked thinking about food even more, and she would study the menus posted weekly at Chez Panisse as if they were poems to savor, meditating on each word. She was so jealous of Robert, who had been invited to the restaurant's thirtieth-anniversary celebration, held just a few weeks before. She had listened hungrily as he described his favorite parts of the meal: the Provençal fish soup, the spit-roasted lamb with chanterelles, the homemade mulberry ice cream. She could taste what he was describing, the char on the meat, the intensity of the berry tempered with sugar and cream. She loved food so much that she was considering enrolling in culinary school after graduation, so that she might become a chef.

Gabe was waiting on the sidewalk in front of the church, a weathered gray wood building with an arched doorway and stained-glass windows. He was wearing the same Levi's he wore that first day of class and a green T-shirt with the words BARTON FINK printed across it. His face brightened as she approached. His eyes focused solely on her.

"Hey," he said, hugging her. She could feel his muscles through his T-shirt. "I'm glad you came. I've been thinking about you."

"I'm kind of a wreck. I guess everyone is. I still haven't been able to get ahold of my sister. I keep trying her cell phone. At first I got a busy signal, now just nothing. And I've been so out of touch—I don't even know what she typically does in a day. I don't know where she was supposed to be this morning. I don't even know if she changed her number. What if she changed her number? But if she did, why hasn't she called me?"

"I've heard that all of the phone lines are jammed in New York. There are just too many people trying to get through. Your not being able to reach her probably doesn't mean anything other than that. I know you're worried, though. I understand."

"You know what else I realized? I didn't even call her after she sent me her book. I had this grand idea about writing her a long letter, but I never did. So now it looks like I just didn't give a shit."

"I think you're being too hard on yourself. Try to let it go for an hour, okay? Let's go on in. It's peaceful in there."

She let herself be led into the church. It was simpler than she would have imagined an Episcopal church to be, though truth be told, the last time she'd seen the inside of a church was at her parents' funeral. There was a font with holy water at the entry, in which Gabe dipped his finger before crossing himself. Ruthie dipped her finger in the water, too, though she just touched her wet finger to her forehead. There were lighted candles flickering in glass holders on the floor by each simple wooden pew. And at the front of the church was another set of votives, these placed on top of a wooden cross that was positioned flat on the floor.

About two dozen people were already seated, dispersed about the sanctuary. They were all different ages. White hairs and spiked hairs. While looking around the church Ruthie noticed the stained-glass windows, which depicted simple images: two fish circled by five loaves, a lamb with its feet crossed beneath it, Mary kneeling beside Jesus on the cross. On the wall behind the altar was a metal crucifix.

Ruthie sniffed. The air smelled of melting wax and burnt sage, same as Gabe had that first time she met him. He must have just come from a Taizé service. Either that or he didn't shower much.

"How often do you come here?"

"I try to come for Taizé every week. I go to mass a couple of times a week, too, at my church. St. Joseph the Worker."

"So you're a complete religious fanatic?"

"Define 'fanatic,'" whispered Gabe. He genuflected, then crossed himself before taking a seat in the third pew from the front.

Ruthie sat beside him. "I've never known how to do that. Cross yourself, I mean. I tried before when I used to go to church with my best friend's family in Atlanta. With Alex Love. Do you remember her, from St. Catherine's?"

"Blond and athletic? Tall?"

Ruthie nodded.

"I remember being intimidated by her."

Ruthie smiled. "Anyway, I could never remember how it goes: do you go up down or down up or what?"

"What do you mean?"

"When you cross yourself."

"Just remember 'spectacles, testicles, wallet, watch,'" whispered Gabe, crossing himself to demonstrate the order. "Of course that's only if you wear your watch on your right arm. And really, you tap your chest, not your testicles."

"That's a relief," said Ruthie. "Because I don't have testicles."

"Good."

She smiled at him, thinking this was the oddest flirtation she had ever engaged in. Turning talk of religious gestures into something dirty. On the day that terrorists hijacked four planes and flew them into the World Trade Center, the Pentagon, and the fields of Pennsylvania. Just then, from inside her purse, her cell phone rang. A Latino man sitting in front of her turned and frowned.

She fished out the phone and glanced at the number. It was from a 917 area code. Julia.

She punched the answer button. "Julia?"

"Oh my god, I'm so glad I got through. I've been trying to call you all day."

"Are you okay?"

"Yeah, I guess. Freaked out, a little drunk, but more or less okay."

"Can you hold on one second? I'm in a church of all places. I'm just going to go outside where I can actually talk."

Ruthie stood, walked down the aisle and out the church door. Standing in the crisp evening air, she put the phone back to her ear.

"Where are you?"

"I'm in Brooklyn. I'm on the rooftop of my building. I've been standing out here all day. I watched the second tower go down."

"Jesus. Is anyone with you?"

"I think everyone who lives in the building is up here. My landlord lives on the first floor. Her husband worked in the World Trade Center, and they hadn't heard from him after the planes hit. They thought he was dead. But he showed up this afternoon. He got out. Had to walk all the way from lower Manhattan. They were so convinced he was killed in the attacks; it was like a second coming when he knocked on the door. Anyway, they're up here, sharing their vodka. Oh, and this girl I've been seeing, she's here with me."

Well, that was news. Ruthie didn't know that Julia dated girls—was dating a girl. She took it as a good sign, that Julia was interested in someone. Ruthie had imagined her sister living as a permanent hermit, locked away in a room, scribbling away at her memoirs.

"I'm so glad you're safe. That's amazing about your landlord's husband. And I'm so glad you're seeing someone. That's great. What's her name? What's she like?"

"Molly. She's a therapist. She was my therapist, actually, until I tried to seduce her during one of our sessions. Then she kicked me out. It's a long story. I'll tell it to you someday. But she's good. Very domestic. Like, she knits. And braises things."

"If she knows how to braise, then she's a girl after my own heart. Not that I date girls; I just mean—"

"I get it, Ruthie; I know what you mean."

"I read *Straight*. I'm sorry I didn't call sooner to tell you. But it's really, really good. I'm proud of you. And I'm so sorry you had to go through that shit—the Center, I mean. I had no idea it was that kind of a place."

"Yeah, well, no one did. Thanks for reading it, though. You really thought it was good?"

"I thought it was great."

"God, Ruthie, I know this is not what I'm supposed to be

thinking about right now, but I am just so grateful that my pub date got pushed back. Originally it was supposed to come out October first of this year. Can you imagine? Who would want to read a memoir about rehab in the middle of all of this crap?"

"Hmm," said Ruthie.

"Oh God, I'm such a narcissist. I can't even believe I'm thinking about the book. It's just you work so hard. . . . Anyway, I'll shut up. I've had too much to drink. Everyone has. It's like, what the hell else do you do besides break out whatever hard liquor you have in the house? There were people up here with peppermint schnapps, Godiva chocolate liqueur. I think I was the only one who had bourbon on hand."

"Bourbon for sorrow," said Ruthie. "I spent the day at a bar. And now I'm at church. How odd is that?"

"Not as odd as I would have thought yesterday. Hey, did I tell you I'm going to be in Berkeley for my book tour? I'll be reading at Cody's. Sometime in late March."

"That's great. I'm so there. I'll bring friends, too, okay? And you can stay with Dara and me if you want. You and Molly."

"She's not coming on tour with me, spaz. She has an actual job. And it's not like we're U-Haul lesbians or anything. Anyway, I think my publishing house is arranging places for me to stay. But thanks. That's nice of you to offer."

It had been so long since Julia had called her spaz. It was nice actually, that Julia felt comfortable enough to tease Ruthie.

A woman was hurrying past Ruthie, headed for the church. When she opened the door Ruthie saw the flickering of the lighted votives. Someone was playing the piano. By the altar a corpulent woman, her arms lifted, palms toward the sky, was singing something in Latin, in a voice that filled the room. Was singing something about *pacem*.

"So you're okay. I'm so relieved. Is everyone you know okay?"

"As far as I know, but that's not saying much. It's been impossible to get in touch with anyone. All of the lines are jammed. And I don't want to further jam them up by trying to call friends. I'm kind of amazed I got through to you. It's so surreal, Ruthie. All day we've just been up here on the rooftop, watching the smoke from the towers and listening to the news on the radio. It's just relentless, this smoke. Just this solid line of gray, leaning toward the left. And no one knows what else is going to happen. If there'll be another attack."

"Will you call me again tomorrow? Let me know you're still okay?"

"Yeah, assuming my phone works. Listen, would you mind calling Mimi for me now? God knows if I'll be able to get through again once we hang up."

"Of course. I'll call her as soon as we get off."

"Okay. I should probably go. Giuliani is saying something—they're playing it on the radio. God, I've hated that guy for so long and today it's like, I'm really glad he's mayor."

"I know," said Ruthie. "He looked so together on TV."

"Okay, Biscuit, I'm going to go. Call Mimi! I love you."

"I love you, too, Egg."

Ruthie pressed end, dialed Mimi's number. She would tell her aunt it needed to be a quick call. Now that Ruthie knew Julia was safe, her thoughts flew at full speed to Gabe. She wanted to return to him, to sit by him, listening to the woman with the beautiful voice sing Latin words that she did not understand. She was thinking about the expression on his face when he first saw her, arriving at the church. She wanted to see that look on his face again. As if she were the only person in the world he wanted to see.

Chapter Twelve

After the Taizé service Gabe invited Ruthie back to his home. He had walked to the church—he didn't own a car—so she drove the two of them to his house in her little VW Golf. It seemed so natural to drive through Berkeley with him, stopping along the way at the La Med on College Avenue, where they each got a glass of retsina and shared an order of hummus with pita. It seemed so natural to park on the street in front of his rented shingled bungalow, to walk up its front path and in his front door. His roommates were in the living room, sprawled out on the two sofas, which looked like Goodwill finds. They were watching the news on a vintage TV, framed in brown wood. They lifted their heads in greeting, murmured hello, and returned their attention to the news. Details were being given about Osama bin Laden, the man thought to be the mastermind behind the attacks. The news was listing his past crimes, his past statements about America. There must have been a complete file on him, Ruthie thought, just waiting to be pulled should the need arise.

The living room smelled of stale beer and boy sweat. Empty Rolling Rock bottles littered the floor, and a cardboard box that contained one remaining piece of mushroom pizza sat in the middle of the room. Ruthie wondered how long it had been there.

She mumbled a shy "bye" to the roommates and followed after Gabe, who was already walking down the bungalow's center hall. He opened the last door on his right, which was on the opposite side of the hall from the kitchen. When Ruthie peeked into the kitchen she noticed the dishes piled on the counter by the sink, and the old-fashioned white enamel stove.

Gabe's room wasn't much neater than the living room had been, but it smelled better. Smelled of Irish Spring soap instead of stale beer. The bed—a twin-sized mattress—was unmade, and there was a lump of clothes on top of the dresser. A damp towel lay on the floor, on top of the braided rug, which looked as if it had started out red but had faded, so that in some spots it was pink. Scotch-taped to the wall were small prints, their edges curling, of paintings by—Ruthie was guessing here—Latino artists. Ruthie liked the one of a thick man and woman, dancing, his pelvis pressed into hers. She studied it, feigning a more acute interest than she actually had. She suddenly felt very shy to be alone in Gabe's room with him. He was standing by the CD player, pushing buttons. Ruthie heard the opening bars of "All I Want" from Joni Mitchell's *Blue*.

"Nice seduction music," she said. This was a tic of hers, to joke when she was nervous. Gabe didn't answer, just gave her a look that implied she was a little immature. She *was* a little immature, at least when it came to men. Her only sexual experience had been with Brendan, and that had begun badly and ended even worse. Ruthie worried that her inexperience would be obvious to Gabe. She hoped he wasn't too seasoned. She hoped the fact that he only had a twin-sized bed with a single pillow meant he was not used to bringing women in here. Then again, it would be good for him to have had a little practice. She certainly didn't want him to be a virgin. If he was a practicing Catholic, would that make him a virgin? But no. He said he hadn't converted until his sophomore year. And besides, hadn't he said he was vigilant about birth control?

Gabe interrupted her thought by walking to her, putting his

hand on her cheek, and kissing her slowly, taking his time. She had imagined his lips would feel like this, soft and full against hers.

"Do you want to spend the night?" he asked. "We don't have to do anything; we can just sleep."

She said okay, but that first she had to call her roommate, tell her where she was. She phoned Dara, feeling enormous relief when she got her voice mail. It would be much easier to lie on voice mail.

"Hi," she said. "First of all, Julia is fine. She called me around six thirty tonight. Her phone was jammed all day. Also, I'm really sorry, but I'm not going to be able to come home tonight. I'm such an idiot, I'm sorry. It's just I stopped at La Med after my drive, and I ended up running into a friend from my O'Connor class. Somehow we kept ordering glasses of retsina, and now I'm too tipsy to drive. I suck, I know. But my friend lives really near the bar, so I'm just going to crash on her couch. I'll be home tomorrow morning. Maybe Yael can stay with you tonight?"

It wasn't that she wanted to lie, but had she told the truth, that she was (quite soberly) choosing to stay with a boy she hardly knew instead of returning home to Dara, her best friend—on the day the U.S. was attacked by terrorists—Dara would have been deeply wounded.

Gabe loaned her a clean T-shirt and a pair of sweatpants to sleep in. She changed in the bathroom, passing one of his scruffy housemates on the way out, who gave her a quick nod before scurrying to the kitchen.

It was not the sexiest outfit to be wearing, that first night in bed with Gabe, but soon after the two of them squeezed into his twin bed her shirt was off and he was running his finger along the curve of her breast, telling her she was beautiful. Her response was to point to the few stray hairs that grew along the periphery of her nipples.

"A guy I knew once told me these grossed him out," she said, and immediately started berating herself. Why bring up Brendan's careless insult? Why insinuate that she had more sexual experience than she had? Why, after Brendan's reaction, had she not started plucking?

"That guy was full of shit," Gabe said.

They didn't have sex that night, just kissed and kissed. Later, having put back on his shirt, she nestled into him, and they talked sleepily about casual things: favorite movies, favorite singers, favorite candy bars. Hers were *Big Night*, Lucinda Williams, 100 Grand. His were *The Graduate*, a draw between Elvis and Johnny Cash, and Snickers. The next day, Wednesday, September 12, in pinking morning light, without any discussion of their nascent relationship or their past sexual history, without any discussion of whether or not a practicing Catholic should even be doing what they were about to do, with only the words "good morning" murmured between them, she asked if he had a condom and he answered by walking over to his dresser, opening the top drawer, rifling through its contents, and pulling one out.

He moved with her while she was on top, and she quickly had an orgasm, which surprised them both. Ruthie did not tell Gabe that this was the first orgasm she had ever had during sex, that he was only the second person she had ever slept with. She also did not tell him about the abortion. It was something that had happened in the past. It would do no good to share. If she were to get pregnant by Gabe, that would be a different story. If that were to happen she would allow him to help determine their course of action. She would see how much of a hold his relatively newfound Catholicism had on real life. (It certainly wasn't stopping him from having pre-marital sex.) But considering how turned on she was by him, she could not imagine that they would encounter the same problem she and Brendan did. Gabe made her so wet surely a condom could not break inside her.

After that first night sleeping at his house, Ruthie's life became all about Gabe, all the time. Every week or so Ruthie would decide that she had to take a (brief) break, she had to spend some time with Dara and catch up, she had to get a full night of sleep without staying up late having sex. So she would shoo Gabe from her apartment, or return to hers from his. She would put a load of laundry in the washer, take a shower, make dinner for Dara. She would try to pay attention to her roommate's stories, but her mind would wander to thoughts of Gabe. Thoughts of his eyes, his protruding clavicle, his strangely alluring tattoo that she had nicknamed "Jesus of the flexing abdomen."

She simply could not get enough of him. And it wasn't just sex, or kissing, or cuddling. There was something so familiar about him, so comforting. It was the Atlanta in him, she supposed, for even though they came from very different parts of the city, they held memories in common, and not just of St. Catherine's.

Like how they both loved going to the Krispy Kreme donut factory on Ponce, though Gabe thought it was ridiculous that Ruthie's family would not stop for donuts unless the HOT sign was on. Or how they both loved the Varsity onion rings, each a tangle of onions suspended in thick, salty breading. Or their shared memories of southern springs, the flowering dogwood trees, the pink and yellow tulips in everyone's front yard, the lengthening days of bloom and green, before the mosquitoes arrived and the heat became oppressive and unrelenting. Of course the last spring Ruthie had spent in Atlanta had been heartbreaking—all that new life bursting forth when her parents' lives had so recently ended.

Gabe asked if she had ever gone back, was surprised when she shrugged and said no. He asked if she would like to go with him to Atlanta over winter break, stay with Schwartzy in her bungalow in Inman Park. Ruthie surprised herself by saying yes. She wanted to experience the world he was from. It was Atlanta, true, but it was removed enough from the Atlanta of her youth, from Buckhead, to make returning there, if not easy, possible.

She spent Christmas day in San Francisco with Mimi and Robert, where they celebrated the holiday in a mishmash fashion, borrowing from Christian and Jewish tradition: unwrapping presents in front of the tree that morning, eating Chinese food and going to a movie that night. Julia called from Vermont, where she was spending the holiday with Molly's family. They had an easy conversation, and Ruthie was grateful that the terrible burden of their past seemed to be subsiding, that she could enjoy speaking with her sister again.

The next day Ruthie boarded a plane to Atlanta, where Gabe already was, where she would stay through the New Year, celebrating with him and his mom.

As the plane approached the city, she pressed her head against the small, cold window and took in the trees, miles and miles of them, interrupted only by skyscrapers. It was winter, and though there were some evergreens she saw mostly branches shed of leaves, sculptural in their bareness. She had forgotten just how dense Atlanta was with trees. Now it was coming back. She remembered being ten or eleven and going with her parents to the rotating circular bar on top of the downtown Peachtree Plaza Hotel. She had sipped a Shirley Temple through a thin black straw and marveled at the view as the bar turned slowly on its axis. Observing the other skyscrapers from up close was neat, but it was the vast clumps of green that awed her. When she commented on the trees to her parents, her father told her proudly that Atlanta was a city built inside a forest.

Once off the plane she was surprised by how many fat people she saw, fat men especially, lumbering past her with their wheeled suitcases, their soft bellies spilling over pleated pants. In San Francisco and Berkeley the gay community set the standard: men were expected to be lithe; women were allowed a little bulk. Here it was the opposite; here the couples looked more like Robert and Mimi, plump men with thin women. At least among whites. Black people seemed to have a kinder standard. Many of the black women were bigger, more fleshed out, and seemingly more confident in their bodies.

Ruthie noticed one black woman in particular, walking in the opposite direction from her, toward one of the boarding gates. Not walking, striding. Shoulders back, chest out. She was big, thick; and while a white woman her size might have tried to hide her weight beneath baggy sweats, this woman wore her stretchy red dress with an attitude that implied anyone who got a glimpse of her was damn lucky. (And she was right. Ruthie felt lucky just being witness to her stride.)

What a difference attitude made.

She had forgotten how racially mixed Atlanta was, and it made her proud of her home city, though her pride was not really earned. In truth the only black person in Atlanta Ruthie had known—despite the city being full of black professionals—was the housekeeper, Addie Mae. And could she even lay claim to having *known* her? Ruthie had never even seen Addie Mae's house, could not tell you what neighborhood she lived in, yet two days a week Addie Mae had taken the bus to the Peachtree Battle stop, where she waited for Naomi to come pick her up and drive her to 3225 Wymberly Way. She had known the insides of their closets, their drawers, their toilets. Had changed their sheets, had folded their underwear. Had called the girls Miss Ruthie and Miss Julia, though Ruthie and Julia had called her, a grown woman, only by her first name.

Oh God, the South. Ruthie had forgotten so much. Had forgotten the accents, the elongated vowels, the authority with which they were articulated. On the underground train that took her from the concourse to baggage claim, she overheard a mother scolding her child. "Kelsey, no ma'am!" the mother said. And then a moment later, "I've got two words for you, young lady: be-have!"

Gabe was waiting for her as she ascended the escalator from the underground train. Her heart jumped when she saw him, in his thin white T-shirt, dark jeans, and green Army jacket. What a miracle it was that this beautiful boy was attracted to her. His mother, Schwartzy, stood beside him, her dark hair still as wild and curly as it had been when she visited Ruthie's classroom in the fifth grade, though now her curls were streaked with silver. She wore a pair of brown cords and a long-sleeve blue T-shirt with the words CHICKEN BABY printed above a graphic of a little girl's body with chicken feet and a chicken head. Though Schwartzy's hair had grayed, her skin was still smooth and her body slender. She looked younger than her fifty years.

"Hey," said Gabe, brushing his lips against hers. "Meet Schwartzy."

As Ruthie turned to say hello, Schwartzy enveloped her in a hug, as if she were a long-lost child. "Darling! Gabriel has told me so many wonderful things about you."

Ruthie was taken aback by the hug, but she tried not to stiffen. She breathed in, breathed out. Tried to stay loose. Schwartzy smelled of something good, something warm and slightly sweet, like a yellow cake baking, like vanilla.

"We've actually met before. You made me my first latke," said Ruthie, though technically that was not true. She had first eaten latkes with applesauce and sour cream at the Snack and Shop deli, where Phil and Naomi liked to go after their adult Sunday school class. They would go to church only for the intellectual classes taught by Emory professors—classes with names like God and the Big Bang Theory or Jesus, the Buddha, and You—and leave immediately afterwards, while everyone else headed to the sanctuary for the actual worship service.

They were walking toward baggage claim, Gabe on one side of her, Schwartzy on the other. "That was me," said Schwartzy. "Have electric griddle, will travel. How was the flight?"

"I'm happy to be on the ground," said Ruthie. She hated flying, found it only tolerable if she took Xanax. And the flight from San Francisco to Atlanta was long, over five hours.

"I don't like to fly, either," said Schwartzy, linking her arm through Ruthie's. "I do not appreciate being thirty-five thousand feet above ground, in a metal tube, kept in the air through a sustained explosion."

Gabe turned to give Schwartzy a look of admonition. Her eyes widened in embarrassment. "Oh shit. I'm sorry. I didn't mean to sound so flip. Gabe told me about what happened to your parents."

"It's okay," said Ruthie, though in truth she found Schwartzy's straightforwardness a little unsettling. "It was a long time ago."

Ruthie wondered how soon she could unhook her arm from Schwartzy's. She was glad that Gabe's mom seemed to like her; still, it felt weird to be walking arm-in-arm with a virtual stranger. Ruthie wasn't really used to touching people all that much, even those she knew well.

"And Gabe says this is your first time back to Atlanta?"

"My aunt tried to get me to come when I was in high school, just to see old friends, but, I don't know. It didn't work out scheduling wise."

Another lie. Until now, until Gabe, what was left for her in Atlanta other than ghosts?

Schwartzy parked her ancient Volvo sedan on the street in front of her yellow wood bungalow, and she, Gabe, and Ruthie climbed out.

"It's beautiful," said Ruthie, taking in the house. "It's perfect."

Schwartzy lived on Sinclair Avenue, a long street of craftsman bungalows, a few dilapidated, but many renovated to pristine condition. Sinclair was lined with magnificent old trees, the bare branches dark and noble against the blue sky. Ruthie envisioned spring, the street canopied in green.

"It's not quite as Norman Rockwell as it looks," said Gabe, walking to the trunk to retrieve Ruthie's bag. "We're only two blocks from Little Five Points, where it's easy to get a pair of used Levi's, an album from the seventies, a healing crystal, a juice cleanse, a bag of pot, a bag of blow, and—oh yeah—mugged."

Holding the handle of her suitcase in one hand, her backpack slung over that same shoulder, he closed the trunk with a resounding clang.

"Oh hush," said Schwartzy, as they walked toward the house. "Little Five Points is fabulous. And Inman Park is the only Atlanta neighborhood I'd even consider living in. That is if we can keep the damn yuppies from taking it over."

"Those damn yuppies who have tripled the value of your home," said Gabe.

"Oh God, here he goes again, having one of his Alex P. Keaton moments."

Ruthie felt as if she were watching a comedy routine that had been recycling its material for years and years.

"Well, I think it's gorgeous," Ruthie said, stopping in the middle of the yard to really take it all in: the wavy glass windows that widened at the bottom, the black wooden shutters, the shingled roof, the large front porch with a swing and two rockers. The house looked as if it belonged on a Hollywood set, the perfect backdrop for a lighthearted family movie: falling leaves, gangs of mischievous but ultimately innocent children on bicycles, simple domestic disagreements that resolve themselves with a look and a quiet touching of hands.

"When was it built?" Ruthie asked.

"Nineteen twenty-one, we think," said Schwartzy, standing beside Ruthie, in open admiration of her place. "Cost me nineteen thousand dollars when I bought it, nearly twenty years ago. Of course it had asbestos in the attic and a homeless man sleeping in the basement."

"Gabe mentioned that," said Ruthie. "How did you get rid of him?"

"It turned out the asbestos was a blessing. They had to wrap and seal the whole house. There was nothing for him to do but move. I felt bad for the guy—bad for kicking him back to the streets—but I had Gabriel's safety to think about."

They climbed the three steps that led to the front porch. They stood on its wide wooden planks, looking at the black cat that slept on the swing.

"Meet Solomon," said Schwartzy. "The real master of the house."

The cat must have weighed twenty pounds.

"He's huge," said Ruthie, and then worried that she might have offended Gabe's mom. How was she supposed to act toward this person, this person who had raised the boy—man—that Ruthie was pretty sure she loved? (Though neither she nor Gabe had used that word with each other.) Was she to be completely herself, or deferential? It mattered that Schwartzy liked her. It was conceivable that Schwartzy might one day be her mother-in-law. It was too soon to think of such things, yet she could not help herself.

How strange. To have a mother-in-law but no mother.

"In his heyday Solomon was catching three or four rodents a day. But he's a lover boy at heart, aren't you, Solo?"

Schwartzy reached out her hand, her long, thin fingers laden with silver rings, and scratched the cat's back. The cat turned his head toward her and let out a plaintive meow.

"Yo, Schwartz," said Gabe, who waited by the door, holding Ruthie's suitcase and her backpack. "I don't have the key, and these bags are heavy."

"Why don't you have your key?" she asked, walking toward him.

"I don't know. I must have left it inside."

Schwartzy unlocked the door and then pushed it open, standing aside to let Gabe and Ruthie enter first. As soon as Ruthie stepped inside she noticed the smell of baking yellow cake that she had first detected on Schwartzy. The inside of the house was dark, save for a flicker of candlelight from above the mantel, which Ruthie was pretty sure was an aromatherapy candle, and the source of the cake smell.

"Oh shit," said Schwartzy, walking toward the mantel. "I forgot to blow this thing out before we left."

Gabe turned on the brass lamp that sat on the table by the front door and flicked on the overhead lights, revealing a room with smudged beige walls filled with well-worn but comfortable-looking furniture: a dark blue couch that sagged a bit in the middle of each seat cushion; a love seat covered in a floral damask slipcover that Ruthie could tell, even from a distance, was coated with black cat hairs; an old corduroy La-Z-Boy with a reading lamp behind it. There were no rugs on the floor, or curtains on the windows, only white vinyl blinds, which appeared to be dusty. In the center of the room was a heavy wooden coffee table that looked as if it was from the seventies, cluttered with loose papers, legal pads, and a half-filled coffee mug. Framing the fireplace was a painted brick mantel that housed, in addition to the scented candle, several picture frames and a brass menorah. On either side of the mantel were built-in-bookcases, each crammed full of paperbacks.

"We're so happy to have you to our home," said Schwartzy, beaming at Ruthie.

"Thank you. It's great," said Ruthie, hoping she was sounding enthusiastic enough. "I love it."

It *was* great, homey, and Ruthie did love it. But also, being there made Ruthie self-conscious. She was aware, for the first time really, that Gabe had grown up with significantly less money than she had. She already knew that, of course, but she hadn't thought about it concretely. Even at the age of twenty-one, almost twenty-two, she still could not escape seeing the world through the filter of her youth, through Buckhead standards. She forgot that most people did not grow up in huge homes designed by architects and cleaned by black women, flanked with wide green lawns maintained by Latino immigrants. And though she loved that Gabe was not from that world, not from Buckhead, she was embarrassed by her own blinders, embarrassed by the fact that she was surprised by the middle-class furnishings of his house. What did she expect, that Schwartzy, a single mom and defense lawyer for the poorest of the poor, would have decorated her home exclusively with Stickley's line of Mission furniture? (Yes, that was what she expected. That was what the aesthetic of both Phil and Mimi led one to expect.)

"Let me show you our room," said Gabe, glancing furtively at his mom, as if he was a little embarrassed to admit that he and Ruthie would be sleeping together. (And, Ruthie was aware, if Gabe and Schwartzy were from Buckhead, she would be offered her own room, for propriety's sake if nothing else.) "Then do you want to get something to eat?"

"Y'all don't mind if I tag along with you to dinner, do you?" asked Schwartzy. "All I've eaten today is a PowerBar, and I'm starving. I've been working on the Marcus Willis case all day, only stopping to drive to the airport."

Ruthie wondered if she was supposed to know who Marcus Willis was.

"Of course," said Ruthie. "Please come. Am I okay going out like this?"

She was wearing jeans and green Saucony sneakers, a cream-colored waffle-knit T-shirt with a long black cardigan on top.

"Are you kidding me? You're dressed nicer than most of the people in Little Five Points will be."

They walked two blocks to the Yacht Club, a dive bar in Little Five Points that served southern food. They sat in a smoky booth and drank Pabst Blue Ribbon beers, two dollars a can. Ruthie and Gabe sat on one side of the booth, Schwartzy on the other. They ate fried okra and pulled pork barbeque sandwiches, and then Schwartzy said, "what the hell," and ordered some wings. Several men stopped by to say hello to her, including a bearded guy with twinkly eyes who Ruthie was pretty sure was the owner of the place. Schwartzy was loose and at ease over dinner, her arm draped over the booth, asking Ruthie questions about her uncle (she had read *Chi Your Mind*), her major, her thoughts on what she might like to do when she graduated.

"I'm thinking about going to culinary school," said Ruthie. "My uncle taught me how to cook when I was thirteen and I've kind of been obsessed with food ever since."

"That sounds so wonderful! Not that I can cook for shit. Poor Gabe had to eat a lot of Stouffer's."

"I would rather eat Ruthie's cooking than go to dinner any-where in Berkeley," said Gabe. "She's that good."

Ruthie allowed herself the pleasure of the compliment. "Thanks," she said, glancing at him almost shyly. "That's so nice."

"It's true," said Gabe, his mouth full of pulled pork.

"I think you've got the right idea," said Schwartzy. "Choose a career that brings you pleasure. I mean, I find a lot of meaning in my work, I really do. But Christ almighty it can bring me down. Take the appeals case I'm working on right now: a death row case. This kid, Marcus Willis, was convicted of murder ten years ago, when he was eighteen, on the basis of two convicted criminals' testimony—men who were offered lighter sentences if they turned state's evidence, by the way.

"So Marcus's execution date is set for this March, and it's probably going to happen, despite the fact that both of the men who testified against him have now retracted their stories. And the damndest thing is, Marcus is pretty much ready to go. I mean, when you're on death row they keep you in solitary twenty-three hours a day. It's a hellish existence. So why am I busting my ass trying to get a stay of execution for Marcus even though I know in my gut it's hopeless?"

"Because the death penalty is wrong," said Gabe. "Simple as that."

"Sure," said Schwartzy. "But that's not why I'm doing it. I'm busting my ass for Marcus's mother, LeVanda Willis. Forty-six years old, and waiting for her son to die. She's who the state is really killing in March."

God, did Ruthie feel shallow. How could her culinary ambitions appear as anything but light, frivolous, next to Schwartzy's dedication? Gabe's mother had spent a lifetime fighting death row convictions; Ruthie wanted to beat egg whites for a living.

"What about the governor? Is he sympathetic to Marcus's case?" asked Ruthie, wanting to show Schwartzy that she had something intelligent to contribute to the conversation.

Schwartzy practically spit out her beer. "The governor? Sympathetic toward the plight of a poor black man from Grady Homes? No, we don't have him on our side. Now, if LaVanda Willis had wanted an abortion back when she was *pregnant* with Marcus, then the good governor would have been very concerned. Very concerned with the sanctity of life. Just like my son, here."

Gabe glared at his mother. Ruthie was too surprised to say anything. She was stunned by the bitterness of Schwartzy's tone.

Schwartzy shook her head, pulled on a strand of her hair, stretching it from a ringlet to a straight line. "Oh God, I'm sorry, sweetheart. That sounded awful. I'm too tense. You are nothing like those political assholes. You have a good heart. It just still surprises me, you know? My son, Gabe Schwartz, the Catholic."

Schwartzy looked pleadingly at Gabe. Gabe's jaw was clenched and he was staring down at his fried okra. Ruthie wanted to excuse herself, to hide out in the bathroom, to walk to the bar and order another beer, and yet she felt stuck to the seat, her discomfort with the situation keeping her glued down.

"Oh God, did I just reveal something that you two haven't even talked about yet? You know Gabe's a Catholic, don't you, Ruthie?"

"I do," said Ruthie, carefully. "I think it's great, the social justice work Gabe does."

"You do know that your biggest anti-death-penalty supporters are the Catholics, don't you, Schwartzy?" asked Gabe, looking intently at his mom.

"What do you think about his stance on abortion?" Schwartzy asked Ruthie.

God, Ruthie did not want to be in the middle of this. How irritating, really, that Schwartzy was pressing on the issue, especially when Gabe was so clearly upset.

"We've just agreed to disagree," she said, acting as if the subject were something they had dealt with long, long ago. In truth, she and Gabe had avoided the topic of abortion ever since that first conversation at Caffè Strada. Ruthie knew that if their relationship continued at its current intensity she was eventually going to have to tell him about what happened with Brendan. But for now she just wanted to enjoy being coupled without all of the messy remnants from her past leaking into the present. He knew all about Julia and her parents. For now that was enough.

"You're so full of shit, Schwartzy. You pretend to be all about free speech, the First Amendment, blah, blah, blah, when in fact you can't tolerate any opinion other than yours." Gabe was clearly on the attack.

"Oh, sweetie," mused Schwartzy. "I'm sorry. You're right. I know you are. You're entitled to believe whatever you want. It's just—"

"It's just what?" he asked.

Schwartzy reached across the table, squeezed Gabe on the forearm. "It's nothing. I love you," she said.

Gabe slanted his eyes at her, but the tension seemed to have dissipated, somewhat.

"Anyway. New subject. Are y'all going to go see Catfish at the WP tonight? I would, but I've got a dozen files to get through before tomorrow morning."

"You want to hear some blues?" Gabe asked Ruthie.

Ruthie smiled. "Sure."

What a relief to have the evening alone with Gabe. Ruthie hadn't realized how much tension existed between Gabe and his mom. They were close, obviously, but there was an angry center to the relationship. Funny, in Berkeley Gabe never shut up about Schwartzy. His love for her was so obvious. Ruthie had expected that in Atlanta it would be obvious, too, that she would be witness to Gabe treating his mother with abject adoration. Had expected, even, that she might be jealous of how close he and Schwartzy were. But no. It was Ruthie Gabe looked at adoringly.

The Westside Pub—or WP, as Schwartzy called it—was a run-down little one-story shack on Howell Mill Road. Growing up, Ruthie had a friend from St. Catherine's who lived on Howell Mill, though her house, a two-story white-columned estate near Trinity Presbyterian Church, was five miles to the north, in Buckhead proper. There were no columned ancestral homes near the WP, only the city's waterworks, an outpost of the Atlanta Union Mission, and the Atlanta Humane Society. Ruthie was pretty sure she wouldn't see anybody from Buckhead proper inside the bar, either. That was a relief. She did not want to have to make small talk with people who knew her from that other life, from before her world flipped upside down.

The parking lot was full, so they parked down a side street. As Ruthie and Gabe walked, holding hands, from the car to the bar, Ruthie glanced around furtively, sure they would soon be mugged. Gabe, wearing a plaid scarf with his Army jacket, looked completely at ease, not worried at all.

The inside of the Westside Pub was as low-rent in appearance as the outside. There were pool tables to the left, the stage to the right, the bar straight ahead. The band—Catfish—was on break, but they had left some of their instruments onstage, including a set of spoons and an old washboard. Drunk people, mostly white, ordered shots and beer from a plump woman with pale skin and red hair whom Gabe, walking up to the bar, called to by name.

"Eugenia," he said. "You got any food left?"

He turned to Ruthie. "Eugenia makes a mean chicken-fried steak, for those on her good side."

Eugenia flicked her eyes from the change she was counting to Gabe. She smiled. "Where you been hiding out, darlin'?"

"California," he said. "Don't you remember? I'm in my final year of college out there. And thank god for that, because you can *not* get a decent piece of chicken-fried steak in Berkeley."

"Well, you cain't get a piece of chicken-fried steak here, neither. You're too late. You know Catfish and them bring an appetite. Wish I'd saved something for you, though. You're too damn skinny."

Gabe laughed. "Eugenia, meet my girlfriend, Ruthie. She goes to school with me out in California, too, but she's a southerner at heart."

Ruthie loved that Gabe introduced her as his girlfriend, but she thought it was ridiculous that he claimed her to be a southerner at heart. If anything she felt like a Jew at heart, not that she was one, but Uncle Robert and Dara, the closest people in the world to her, were. Gabe was, too, at least by blood.

"Ain't you been feeding this boy out in California?"

"I've been trying to, believe me," said Ruthie, with an affected southern accent. It wasn't that she was trying to imitate Eugenia; it was just that the woman's way of talking was contagious.

"Well, darlin'," said Eugenia, turning to grab an empty beer mug off the shelf behind her before holding it beneath the fountain and pulling on the tap labeled BUDWEISER. "Try harder. And get this boy on back to Georgia as soon as you can. His mama misses him, and we do, too."

Ruthie wanted to say something about how much she would miss Gabe if he were to leave California, but she knew better than to try to turn this conversation into anything serious. They were just talking, just shooting the shit, something that came as a relief after their tense dinner with Schwartzy.

"Okay," she said. And then she ordered a Bud.

The band was great, loud and raucous, but the most fun occurred afterwards when half of the bar emptied out into the parking lot and someone started shooting off firecrackers.

"Where am I, Alabama?" asked Ruthie.

"You're going to see a lot of firecrackers going off this week," said Gabe. "Southerners get really excited about the New Year."

"There were no spontaneous firework shows where I grew up," said Ruthie.

"That's a shame," said Gabe, slipping his arm around her waist.

An older man with a white beard stood next to her, holding an unopened pack of Roman candles, bound together with plastic wrap. He said something to her, but she couldn't understand him. He had a thick accent and kept his cigarette in his mouth while he spoke.

"Excuse me?" said Ruthie.

He pulled out the cigarette. "You want to help me set these off?"

He held up the Roman candles.

"Take one," said Gabe. "They're fun."

Ruthie shrugged. "Okay."

The man tore open the plastic wrap and handed Ruthie the explosive.

It was over a foot long, a red and white cardboard tube with ROMAN CANDLE printed down its side. There was a bit of tissue paper wrapped around the wick at the top.

"Technically you're supposed to plant this baby in the ground and light it from there, but you get more leverage if you just hold it," the man said. He put the cigarette back in his mouth, inhaled, then released a line of smoke.

"Damn straight," said Gabe. "If you stick it in the ground you can't aim at anyone."

Ruthie turned to look at Gabe, rolled her eyes at his joke.

"You're sure it's safe for me to hold it?" Ruthie asked the man.

"Oh yeah, it's real safe. One of my buddies once taped together about one hundred of these things and lit them all at once. Made a Roman candle machine gun. Now that might not have been the safest thing in the world, but this sure is."

Gabe clapped his hands together, laughed. "Are you serious, man? That's insane."

This was a new Gabe, this man who delighted in chicken-fried steak and jerry-rigged fireworks instead of Catholic mass and social justice work. Ruthie sort of liked it. Sort of liked the southern Gabe. Or maybe it was simply that she liked Gabe in general. Who knew? She was a little drunk. She had imbibed three Budweisers, plus the PBRs at the Yacht Club. She wanted to set off the fire-cracker in her hand. The whole thing seemed surreal, to be out in this parking lot with all of these strangers, lighting explosives in the middle of the street, the Atlanta skyline glowing in the distance.

"So should I just light it?" she asked the man.

"I'll do it for you. Hold it way out in front of you, yeah, like that, arm's length, and when you're good and ready just give me the word."

Ruthie held the explosive as far in front of her as she possibly could. The night air cool against her exposed skin, she felt exhilarated, like anything could happen. Like she could take a risk and it wouldn't blow up in her face.

She imagined her parents, boarding the Ford Trimotor, giddy with their shared sense of adventure.

"You ready?" the man asked.

She said a silent prayer—of sorts—to God. *Try me*, she said. *Just try me.*

"I'm ready."

The man took the cigarette from his mouth and held it against the wick of her Roman candle. There was a flash of light, and then a sizzling sound, and then she felt the force of the explosive leaving the cardboard tube. *Thwump.* The star shot from the tubing and traced a streak of light against the sky, ending with a pop that came sooner than Ruthie had imagined it would. Another star followed, then another, and another, and another again. *Thwump. Thwump. Thwump. Thwump.*

"Now you're an official redneck," said Gabe, after the Roman candle released its final light.

"I want to do it again," she said.

Gabe leaned into her, whispered in her ear, "That's what you'll be saying later tonight."

He wiggled his brows at her, in an exaggerated motion. She punched him on the shoulder. Told him he was a dork.

She loved being with him.

They left the Westside Pub at 1:00 A.M., but Ruthie wasn't tired. It was only 10:00 California time, and besides, she was wired from the band's exuberance, from the illegal fireworks.

"Want to go to Krispy Kreme?" asked Gabe once they were back in Schwartzy's old Volvo sedan.

"Let's drive by my parents' house," said Ruthie, surprising herself with the idea. "I want to show you where I grew up."

"Don't you want to go during the day? When we can actually see things?"

"No. I want to go now."

She was feeling charged, feeling reckless, and besides, she thought it might be easier to see the house at night, after a few drinks, with Gabe driving the car. She directed him, and though they weren't far, she was surprised that she still knew the way.

"This is a beautiful neighborhood," said Gabe as he cruised down Peachtree Battle Avenue, even though in truth it was hard to make out much of anything. It was so dark, and the houses were set so far back from the street.

"Go slow," she said. "I don't want to miss the turn."

He slowed down, was creeping along. She remembered driving this same stretch of road with Julia, the day of her parents' funeral, when Julia let her take the wheel. She saw the green street sign in the headlights, WYMBERLY WAY. It seemed strange that the street still existed, that it had not vanished as soon as she did.

"Turn left here," she said.

They were on her old street, a place she had not returned to in nearly ten years. Wide lawns stretched on either side of her, each topped with a gorgeous home. If she thought about it hard enough she could remember the façade of each one, though not the insides. They had never really known their neighbors. Naomi had never really had any neighborhood friends.

Naomi. Her mother. Her mother who was so alive and then—so quickly, so finally—was simply gone. From matter to memory. Like that.

Ruthie felt something rising against the back of her throat. Gabe was driving so slowly, probably because he'd had too much to drink, was nervous about driving at all. It was the opposite of how Julia used to drive, used to careen, really, and yet it was as if she were back in Julia's car, in the Saab, approaching the drive of 3225 Wymberly Way, during those months after the crash when they were still living in Atlanta, when it was Julia and not Naomi who chauffeured her to and from school. There were afternoons when somehow—*how?*—she would momentarily forget that it would not be her mother waiting inside to greet her; it would be her aunt Mimi instead. And though Mimi was lovely, and though she was kind, she was never enough. She could never fill the loss. Still didn't, though that was not something Ruthie allowed herself to think about much.

She remembered the dread feeling of waiting, waiting to lose her sister at the end of the school year, and not being able to do anything about it. She remembered, with a startling intensity, that she had been angry at her parents during that time, so angry at them for leaving instructions to split up her and Julia, and yet it had seemed so wrong to be angry at them, when they were the ones who no longer got to be alive. When they were the ones whose bodies had burned after the crash. It was so wrong that she had forced herself to stop feeling it. Yet here it was again, that forbidden anger, from all of those years back. She thought of Mr. Z, her ridiculous eighth-grade English teacher, the man who made his girl students sit in a circle on the floor and hold "powwows." Who was upset with her for bringing in an orange instead of some meaningful memento from her past. Who warned her that whatever feelings she shoved down were going to have to come up again.

And then, even though she usually had an iron stomach, even though she had only drunk beer and nothing stronger, she knew she was about to throw up. Immediately. (Mr. Z was right! How annoying. How pleased he would be.)

"Pull over, pull over," she gasped, and Gabe did. As soon as he stopped the car she opened the door and, thrusting her head forward, threw up pulled pork barbeque onto the edge of someone's grassy lawn. Tears ran from her eyes. She spit several times, then lifted her head, remaining in the passenger seat, her body turned so her feet dangled out of the car.

"Are you okay?" asked Gabe, rubbing her lower back with his palm.

For a moment she was quiet, just letting the cold night air hit her face. She leaned over, spit again. The inside of her mouth tasted horrible.

She readjusted so she was facing forward in the passenger seat. She pulled the car door closed.

"Can we go home?" she asked. "To your house?"

"You just lean back and close your eyes and I'll get you home as soon as I can."

He put his hand on her thigh and she shut her eyes, leaned back against the headrest. She would just sit here, cool and quiet. Dignified. She would not say a word.

Except that she was crying. Blubbering, really, blubbering and drunk. And suddenly she felt overwhelmed by Gabe, overwhelmed by his kindness and care. What was he after? Why was he treating her so gently?

"Why are you so nice to me?" she asked, a wasted, slobbering mess of a girl who still had the taste of vomit in her mouth.

"Because I love you," he said. And though he had never before said these words to her, he was almost nonchalant in his utterance. As if his love were a fact, a mathematical solution that made everything simple: solve for x and unlock the equation.

Chapter Thirteen

March 2002

Ruthie, Gabe, and Dara carpooled to Julia's reading, arriving early, anticipating that it might be difficult to find parking in downtown Berkeley. Mimi and Robert were at that moment on a plane, returning from France, where they had gone on a research trip for Robert's new book on chocolate, tentatively titled *The Devil's Food*. They had promised Julia that they would be at her book event in Marin the following day. Ruthie planned on going to that reading as well. Afterwards they would all return to San Francisco and Mimi and Robert would take the girls to Zuni.

They drove by Cody's, knowing that sometimes a space in front of the bookstore—rock star parking—would suddenly appear. On this night they had no such luck. There was always the option of parking in a pay lot, but Ruthie felt like a sucker using one. She circled around the block slowly, scanning for a space. She had to brake suddenly when a guy on a bike sped across the street in the pedestrian walkway.

"Good thing you didn't hit him," said Dara. "That would have started a riot."

The bicycle rights people were very big in Berkeley. Every month they staged a "critical mass" and hundreds of cyclists, many in outrageous costumes, would ride together down the middle of the street during rush hour, blocking traffic.

"Do you want to jump out and I'll circle and find parking?" asked Gabe. He was wearing an old Braves T-shirt, tissue thin from years of washing, along with jeans and New Balance sneakers. New Balance sneakers always made Ruthie think of Dara's dad, who was devoted to the brand. Ruthie loved Dara's dad, that sweet man who still sent his daughter care packages filled with candy and sugary cereals, even though she was a senior in college. Even though she only lived across the Bay Bridge from him.

"Let me do one more loop," said Ruthie. "Readings usually start late, don't they?"

"Hail Mary full of grace, help us find a parking space," intoned Dara.

Ruthie glanced quickly at Gabe, to see if he was offended. He was frowning a bit, but Ruthie was pretty sure that was because he was concentrating on finding a space. Dara often said irreverent things in front of Gabe; she claimed it her duty to be a provocateur. She was flabbergasted by his conversion, and tried to talk him out of it. She had even implied that his becoming a Catholic indicated internalized anti-Semitism.

After meeting Gabe for the first time, Dara had declared to Ruthie, "He's a dirty boy. But he's sexy as hell. My prediction is you two will hole up and be dirty together, before he graduates and moves back to Atlanta."

"What makes you think he's going to go back to Atlanta?" Ruthie had asked.

"Are you kidding me? He went on and on about it. About the bungalow his mom bought for nineteen thousand dollars, and the 'holler' behind their house where all of the kids in his neighborhood would play, and the way he knew all of his neighbors growing up, and how his mom and some dude named Earl would share a joint every afternoon on the front porch."

"There's one," said Gabe, interrupting Ruthie's memory. A blue Toyota Camry was backing out of its spot. She put her blinker on and waited. The Camry had a bumper sticker that read: BARBARA LEE SPEAKS FOR ME.

Barbara Lee was the lone member of Congress to have voted against authorizing the U.S. invasion of Afghanistan.

"I'd send Schwartzy one of those," said Gabe. "But people in Georgia would probably just assume Barbara Lee is a country music singer."

Cody's was a great bookstore, cavernous and overflowing, with tables and tables of books up front and rows and rows of books in the back. There was a balcony level, too, where readings were held. It was only 7:10 when they arrived. While Gabe and Dara headed for the bathroom, Ruthie scanned the store for Julia. She didn't see her, at least not in the flesh, but there was a poster propped on an easel by the front display tables, announcing that Julia Rose Smith would be reading that evening from her "acclaimed" memoir, *Straight*. Julia's picture was on the poster. It was black-and-white and in it her eyes looked very shiny. Like they would reflect anything. She was not smiling in the picture but instead stared straight ahead, her mouth a straight line. Julia looked good, smart, but Ruthie wished her sister had smiled. She walked over to the table of new fiction on display and started turning over books, looking for the author picture. In almost all of them, the authors met the camera with a serious expression.

Suddenly she heard her name and her sister was rushing toward her. Before she really even had a chance to register what her sister now looked like, Julia was hugging her tight, then stepping back, looking at Ruthie from arm's distance.

"You look gorgeous!" Julia said.

Ruthie had spent a lot of time that evening getting ready. She used a flatiron on her hair so that it hung perfectly straight and shiny. She applied brown liner to the edge of her eyelids, and just below each eye. She even wore lipstick, a deep ruby stain that contrasted nicely with her pale coloring. And all that sex with Gabe must have burned the calories away, because she certainly wasn't dieting, yet she had lost five pounds, which made a real difference. Her jeans were loose on her hips. She wore a silky green tank top embellished with tiny white polka dots, and a button-up red cardigan that she had found on the street, over by Tilden Park. (Gabe was really big into wearing "recycled" clothes, and she found herself picking up his habits.) Dara had screamed at her for picking the sweater up off the sidewalk. But once it was dry-cleaned, it was actually quite cute.

Julia looked great, too, although utterly different than Ruthie expected. Mainly because she had cut her hair. Those long crazy curls were gone, replaced by a springy head of short ringlets, adorable, but not nearly as sexy as her old style had been. Having short hair did highlight her features, her delicate wisps of eyebrows, her dark brown eyes. Julia was dressed differently, too, a little edgier than before. Black jeans over a spiky heel, the front of the shoe covered in some sort of black webbing. The jeans were the highly stylized ones that had become so popular, the ones that looked worn but cost a fortune. She had on a blue ribbed tank top with no bra, revealing the push of her nipples against the fabric of the shirt. Ruthie hoped she had a jacket somewhere; it was chilly outside. Julia's necklace was made of a single piece of thin brown leather, which tightened around her throat and hung long from one end, as if she had escaped from a teeny-tiny gallows.

Out of the corner of her eye Ruthie saw Gabe, scanning a row of books. Probably books on religion. She waved him over.

"That's him," she said to Julia, as Gabe walked toward them.

"Nice," said Julia.

When Gabe reached the two of them he held his hand out to Julia. "Hi. Great to meet you. Congratulations on the book."

"Congratulations on banging my sister," said Julia, her eyes shining with mischief.

Ruthie gave her head a quick shake, not sure what she had heard. "Julia?" she said.

"Oh God, I'm sorry. Nerves. And, well, I have impulse issues, as Molly is constantly reminding me. And anyway, am I wrong?"

"We're really excited to hear you read," said Gabe.

Julia slapped Gabe lightly on the arm. "Oh, don't get all formal with me. What's the good of being a big sister if you can't tease your little sister? Right, Biscuit?"

Ruthie had a pressing urge for a drink. A beer, glass of wine, shot of bourbon, anything.

"What sections of the book are you going to read?" she asked.

Julia pursed her lips. Shrugged. "I don't know, either the bullshit blanket chapter, or chapter twelve, where I wake up to find one of the counselors standing above my bed, whacking off."

"I really loved the bullshit blanket chapter," said Ruthie. "But maybe you should read chapter twelve. That one gave me the creeps, and I mean, that was what you were after, right?"

"I don't know. Maybe I should stick with the bullshit blankets. Gabe here is already looking a little freaked out."

"I'm fine," said Gabe. "Believe me. If I look freaked out it's just that you really remind me of my mom. You could be her spiritual sister."

Ruthie couldn't figure out whether Gabe considered that a good or a bad thing.

Julia looked so powerful standing in front of the crowd—a small crowd, but still—reading and talking about the terrible things that had happened to her. She read the chapter about the counselor who used to stand beside her bed at night and masturbate, but she skipped around and read bits from other sections, too. She enunciated and varied her cadence. Laughed a lot. Joked about the b.s. blankets, how everyone knew "b.s." stood for "bullshit," but no one was allowed to use the actual word. Joked about the fact that the paddle they used to beat kids with was named Rod, as in "spare the rod, spoil the child."

After the reading the floor was opened to the audience for a Q&A.

The first question was from a woman with short blond hair. Ruthie was sitting behind her and couldn't see her face. "Do your dad and stepmom know about the book?"

Julia raised her brows and nodded solemnly. "They do. And

while I ended up portraying them somewhat sympathetically toward the end of the book—and especially in the epilogue—they are still pretty upset that I chose to write it. Let me put it to you this way: they have not called to congratulate me on publication."

The members of the audience murmured their sympathy. Ruthie opened her copy of the book, flipped to the back. She hadn't remembered an epilogue in the bound manuscript Julia had sent her. But there it was, "Epilogue: Seven Years Later . . ."

The next question came from a graying man in a plaid flannel shirt whose ears stuck out as if they were handles for his head. "This so-called rehab place? I'm thinking someone shut it down, right?"

"I'm so glad you asked that. And sadly, no, the Center is still in operation. I'm hoping that somehow this book might help to change that, that when parents are researching rehab programs for their kids this book might steer them away, at least from the Center's type of program. I speak about this at length in my epilogue. The epilogue was a last-minute addition—my editor wanted to kill me for springing it on her—but I realized it was really important to clearly articulate my intentions behind publishing this book."

Ruthie put her hand on Gabe's knee. Gabe turned his head to the side, smiled. He was flipping through the copy of *Straight* he had purchased, reading the chapter titles.

A woman in a UPS uniform raised her hand. She was young, pierced, a little punk. Ruthie wondered if she really worked for UPS or was just dressing that way to be ironic. "Okay, we know the Center really, really sucked, but, like, don't you think you needed some sort of help?"

Ruthie tensed in her seat. This was the question—perhaps phrased a little differently—that she had wanted to ask ever since she read the draft of *Straight* that Julia had sent her. Did Julia realize how reckless she once was, hiding out in Golden Gate Park with some runaway who hung out on Haight Street?

"At seventeen, when all of this happened, I was a pretty messed-up kid. I had recently lost my mother and stepfather, whom I thought of as my dad. Lost my beautiful sister, who's here tonight—wave 'hi,' Ruthie—because of the way our custody arrangement was set up. So I was very, very angry. The living situation I was put into happened to not allow for much expression of that anger. I needed help. I self-medicated with pot and alcohol. And I'm sure I was a royal pain in the ass to deal with. But did I need traditional rehab? Was I an actual alcoholic? I'm perfectly able to have one or two drinks every now and again without going overboard, so I'm not sure if that was my problem."

Julia fingered the long end of her leather necklace. "I needed some sort of help, that was for sure. But I don't think anyone benefited from the quote-unquote help the Center offered."

Dara raised her hand. "I read the copy you sent Ruthie. I was kind of shocked that there wasn't more anger in it. I mean there was so much humor. And no self-pity!"

Julia grinned. "Thanks, Dara! Everyone, this is Dara, my sister's roommate. Stand up, Dara."

Dara stood, waved as if everyone had come to see her.

"I'm not nearly as angry as I once was. Growing up will do that to you. And hell, I owe the center some credit for helping me to become a writer. You had to make up so much shit about yourself to survive there. Confession was demanded, every afternoon for five hours during 'Group.' That of course is when the b.s. blankets came out. But it was a catch-22 because once you confessed to—say—doing more drugs, they could keep you in the program for longer. So you had to confess in order to get out, to 'graduate,' but you also got stuck there longer and longer the more drugs you said you had done.

"Anyway, as I write about in the book, this catch-22 made me very crafty when it came to making up confessions. I stuck to one drug—pot—and I simply exaggerated the number of times I had used it. I realized at the Center that when lying the best thing to do is to start with a grain of truth and spin the story from there. Now when I wrote *Straight*, which is nonfiction, I was utterly meticulous about sticking to the truth. Or at least, the truth as I understood it. But I'm now working on a novel, and I find that often I start a scene with something that really happened and then I spin a new story out from there. So I guess in that respect I have to thank the Center for the 'lying' skills they engendered within me."

The audience laughed. Ruthie smiled. She was so proud of her sister, standing up there, speaking so candidly and with such confidence. Taking this horrible thing that had happened to her and somehow spinning it into art. It made Ruthie think of the kitchen alchemy Robert had taught her, how you could turn a tough old cut of meat, stringy and inedible, into something wonderful simply by braising it for hours in wine and stock and fat until it was fork-tender and delicious. Until it was something everyone wanted to eat right up.

After the reading Ruthie, Gabe, Dara, and Julia walked the five blocks to Le Beret, a cute little French bistro with copper-topped tables and Edith Piaf playing on an endless loop. The restaurant was crowded, but Ruthie had made reservations, so they were seated right away. Immediately Ruthie ordered a carafe of the house red for the table.

"You were so good, Julia!" gushed Dara. They did not have their wine yet, so she lifted her water glass instead. "Cheers!"

"Thanks," said Julia, raking her right hand through her short curls. "Strange to be reading about masturbation to a group of strangers. I kept glancing around, hoping no one was too offended."

"Don't worry," said Ruthie. "It's hard to shock people in Berkeley."

"Unless you said you didn't believe in evolution or something like that," said Dara.

Their waitress, cute and young, with a small metal butterfly pinned to her short, dark hair, returned to the table with the carafe of wine and four glasses. "Is everyone partaking?" she asked.

"We all are, right?" asked Ruthie.

Julia and Dara nodded and the waitress began filling their glasses. "What about you, Gabe?" Ruthie asked.

Gabe, who was hunched over the table reading the epilogue to Julia's book, looked up. "Oh sorry. Yeah, I'll take some. Julia, I'm loving what you added."

"Thanks, sweetie," said Julia.

Ruthie felt just the tiniest flash of irritation that Julia was calling her boyfriend sweetie, as if he were five, but she told herself to let it go. To let it all go. Everything. Looking over the day's specials, she noticed that they were serving the chicken liver pâté with Calvados. It was only occasionally on the menu, and Ruthie always ordered it when it was. She loved how buttery and rich it was, with just a hint of sweetness from the apple brandy.

"Should we get the pâté?" she asked, rhetorically.

"Yum," said Dara.

"Gross," said Julia. She looked up at the waitress. "No offense."

"Doesn't bother me," the waitress said. "I don't eat meat." She had finished pouring the wine and now stood with her pad out and her left foot balanced against the side of her right knee. Probably she was a dancer.

"Go ahead and order it if you want," said Julia. "I'm going to get the baked Brie to start. Y'all will help me eat it, right?"

"Double yum," said Dara.

"Do you guys want to go ahead and order your main course, too?" asked the waitress.

"I think we need a few minutes," said Ruthie, who hadn't had a chance to look over the menu thoroughly.

When the waitress turned away from the table, she bent her knee in a graceful plié.

Dara lifted her wineglass. "Now we can have a proper toast. To Julia, the only published author I know!"

"Wait," said Ruthie, not yet lifting her glass. "What about Robert? And isn't your mom friends with tons of authors? I mean, no offense, Julia. Just, you know, accuracy."

"Fine. To Julia, the only memoirist I know."

Technically, Robert's book about the foods he ate in Brooklyn as a boy, *The Carp in the Bathtub*, was a memoir. But Ruthie let it slide.

Ruthie, Dara, and Julia lifted their glasses, clinked them together. Gabe was still occupied reading Julia's book.

"Aren't you going to toast with us?" Ruthie asked, a little annoyed that Gabe was not even pretending to be interested in the group.

He looked up, obviously surprised at the interruption. Ruthie did not understand how Gabe was able to do this, to become so absorbed by whatever he was doing that he could just block out all other noise.

"Sorry," he said, looking at Julia. "It's just that I'm reading this really gripping memoir."

"Aw, Ruthie, I love your boyfriend! He's so cute and has such great taste in books!" said Julia.

Ruthie put her arms around his shoulders. "Isn't he?" she asked.

"Two thumbs-up," said Julia.

Gabe raised his eyes from the book. "Y'all are making me feel like a piece of meat," he said.

"We didn't say you were Grade A. We said you were two thumbs-up. That means you're a good movie," said Julia.

Gabe smiled at the joke, and then returned to the book.

Ruthie studied the menu. Sometimes in restaurants she would become so absorbed thinking about what had inspired the chef to create each dish that she would forget to choose something to order. But not tonight. Tonight she would keep it simple. She would order the hanger steak cooked medium rare with fries. Easy. Her decision out of the way, she could now concentrate on Julia, on this confident woman who was her sister. Ruthie felt abuzz with happy energy sitting across the table from her, neither of them upset or tense. And how wonderful that Julia got to meet Gabe, got to see how great he was, if a bit distracted. But it wasn't as if he were distracted by a football game on TV or something. He was distracted because he was so engrossed in her writing.

"What are you getting?" Dara asked Ruthie. Dara liked to order exactly what Ruthie did, claiming that Ruthie was a "perfect orderer."

"I'm getting the hanger steak with *frites*," said Ruthie.

"I'm having that, too," said Julia. "But I'm having fries, not *frites*."

"Same thing," said Ruthie. "One's just in French."

"I know that, you dork! I'm just teasing."

"Oh," said Ruthie, a little sheepish. "Wait. We can't all get the steak. We won't be able to trade tastes. Gabe, you have to order something else."

"What?" said Gabe, looking up from the book. He looked angry.

"I asked what are you having?"

"The steak."

"Well, shit. Then I guess I have to get the *boeuf bourguignon*," said Ruthie.

"Then I'm getting *boeuf bourguignon*," said Dara.

"Why don't you get the trout and I'll get the *bouef* and we can share."

"Will you trade with me if yours is better?"

Ruthie rolled her eyes at Julia. "See what I have to put up with?" she asked, imitating Phil from so long ago.

Julia smiled ruefully. "God, it's good to see you."

Even though Gabe finished the epilogue before his steak arrived, he remained quiet and withdrawn during dinner. This bothered Ruthie, who wanted her new boyfriend to be extra charming in front of Julia. Julia didn't seem to mind, though. She was obviously having a good time talking with Dara about what Brooklyn was like compared to San Francisco. All year Dara had been threatening to move to New York after graduation, but Ruthie didn't really believe her. Or maybe she just didn't want to believe her, didn't want to imagine day-to-day life without Dara in it.

"San Francisco is more livable, but New York is where the conversation starts," said Julia.

"Spoken like a true New Yorker," said Ruthie. "Which is to say, like a snob." She stole a fry off Julia's plate, dipped it in the *jus* from the steak, and popped it in her mouth.

"And when have you been to New York?" asked Julia.

"When I was in fifth grade and you were in eighth. Remember? Mom took us for a 'girls' weekend' and we stayed at that junky place in Midtown that Dad had gotten a deal on."

"Oh my god, you're judging New York based on a weekend you spent in Midtown when you were in fifth grade? That's like me going to Atlanta, staying overnight at the airport, and then making proclamations about the city."

"I had a layover in Atlanta once," said Dara. "It kind of sucked."

"Exactly my point. It wouldn't have sucked if someone who actually lived there had shown you around. Which is all to say that you need to come visit, Ruthie. It's ridiculous that you haven't been to my place in Williamsburg, or met Molly, for that matter."

It was ridiculous. Especially that Ruthie hadn't met Julia's girlfriend. But prior visits with Julia had always been so difficult. Ruthie had stayed with her in Charlottesville twice, once when Julia was a freshman at UVA and once for Julia's graduation. Both times had been awkward. The first time Ruthie visited, her sister got upset with her for using her towel to dry her face. "I put aside a towel especially for you," she had said. "Why are you junking up mine?" And when Ruthie came for Julia's graduation, Julia had gotten mad at her for making a long-distance call to Dara from the phone in her apartment.

Back then, it had seemed pretty obvious to Ruthie that her sister did not want her around, that her sister no longer had warm feelings toward her. But now they were relating as if they were girls again. Affectionately teasing each other, laughing, bringing up old jokes. Ruthie wondered if maybe publishing the book had unleashed Julia's old, fun self.

"Want to go to Williamsburg?" she asked Gabe, who was eating his steak rather speedily, as if he were trying to see how fast he could choke it down.

"New York is overrated," he said, not making eye contact.

He didn't appear to be joking, teasing. He was simply being rude, and Ruthie had no idea why.

"When was the last time you were there?" asked Dara, her tone still jovial.

"I went to visit Columbia my senior year after I was admitted. The people were pushy and the city was dirty."

"Whereas you are known as Mr. Clean," joked Ruthie. In fact, Dara referred to him behind his back as "dirty boy."

Gabe fished his wallet out of his back pocket and pulled out two twenty-dollar bills, which he tossed into the middle of the table. "Look, I'm exhausted. I need to call it a night. I'm going to walk home."

He stood.

"What?" asked Ruthie. "We're not even halfway through with dinner."

"Julia, it was really nice meeting you. Your book is wonderful. The epilogue was particularly illuminating."

Julia's brows shifted and for a moment she looked worried, concerned, but then she broke into a smile and acted as if Gabe's walking out in the middle of the meal were a perfectly normal thing to occur. She remained seated but gave him a little wave. "Thanks so much for coming. And it's great to meet you, too."

"See you, Dara," said Gabe, and without saying good-bye to Ruthie he walked toward the door.

"What just happened?" Ruthie asked, looking at Dara and Julia in astonishment.

"I have no fucking idea," said Dara.

"I'm sorry, I have to find out what's going on. I'll be back in just a minute."

She rose, walked through the restaurant, and made her way out the door. Once on Shattuck, she looked to her left and saw Gabe, about a half block away, walking fast.

"Gabe!" she yelled. "Wait."

He kept walking.

"Gabe! Please. Stop."

She saw him stop. Turn. She ran to him, slowing as she neared, seeing that his face was clouded with judgment, anger. She walked the last few steps, until she was standing close enough to touch him.

"I don't understand what's going on. This was a really important night for me, and you just, you just flaked."

She was so embarrassed by his behavior. She was so confused.

"I don't like being lied to," he said, his voice devoid of its usual warmth.

"What are you talking about?"

"Look. I'm not going to get into it with you right now. I don't want to say anything I might regret. Go back to your sister and Dara. Finish your meal. When you get home, read the epilogue of your sister's book. Shit, just read the second-to-last page of the epilogue. You'll understand."

He turned and continued walking. Away from her.

She did not call after him this time. She knew he wouldn't stop. Instead she slowly walked back to Le Beret, aware even in her confusion and anger of how refreshing the evening breeze felt on her face. How it helped hold back the tears pooling in her eyes.

When she reached the restaurant, she paused a moment before opening the door. Took a breath. Ran her fingers through her hair, straightening it. As soon as she pushed the door open, she was greeted by the cacophony of happy diners eating and talking, and Edith Piaf singing, "Je ne regrette rien."

She walked to the table where Dara and Julia were quietly eating their dinners, exchanging twin looks of concern.

"Is everything okay?" asked Dara.

"I don't know," said Ruthie. "Apparently I need to read the second-to-the-last page of your epilogue to find out."

She watched Julia while saying this, saw that Julia stopped chewing for a moment, as if by doing so she could also stop time. Ruthie grabbed Gabe's copy of the book, which he had left on the table, and flipped to the end. She found the epilogue, turned to the second-to-last page. She scanned it quickly, looking to see what it was that had so upset Gabe. There was something about another girl at the Center, a girl named Ashley, a girl whose mother found out about her abortion by reading her diary. During group therapy Ashley was referred to as "the murderer." The counselors would debate whether there was any possibility for her to be saved. Ruthie kept reading, her chest tightening, and then, *Oh. Oh fuck. Oh God.* Well, no wonder he had stormed out. There it was. She was reading her secret, the one thing she did not know if Gabe could accept about her, printed in her sister's book. Contained within a parenthetical statement, no less. Written as an aside. Right there.

> (Compare the Center's treatment of Ashley to my aunt's reaction when my sister found herself pregnant at eighteen, the summer before she was to head to college. First thing my aunt did was tell her: "Whatever your decision, we will work this through." Sat down with her at the kitchen table, talked through options. Scheduled the appointment with a trusted doctor, drove my sister to the hospital. Held her hand in the waiting room and was there afterwards, to drive my sad and emptied sister home. Fixed homemade macaroni and cheese for dinner that night, understanding when my sister chose to eat her serving alone in her room.)

She looked at Julia, whose eyes were round with worry. "I cannot believe you would put this in here without asking me."

Ruthie's voice was low, still, like grease in the skillet, heated past boiling. "It's most dangerous when it's still," Robert always warned.

"Sweetie, did you read the whole thing? It's important that you read the whole thing. It's a tribute to Mimi, really. To what real compassion looks like. It is written with love."

She was going to lose Gabe because of this. She was going to lose Gabe over a buried secret of hers that Julia had decided to include in an epilogue she handed in at the last minute. Or at least that was what Julia said, but maybe she had long intended for the epilogue to be there and had simply sent Ruthie an early copy in which it was not, so as not to upset her.

What other secrets of hers might Julia have added to the pages of her book?

The tears were falling. Ruthie wiped them away angrily with the back of her hand. She looked at the half-eaten mess on her plate, the soft carrots cut into coins, the translucent onions, the chunks of rich meat, almost purple from the wine. She felt faintly nauseated. She could not eat another bite of this food. She dug her keys out of her bag, worked the Golf key off the chain, slid it across the table to Dara. "I'm sorry. I've got to get out of here. You take the car."

She stood, just as Gabe had a few moments earlier, and took a step toward the door.

"Ruthie, come back," pleaded Julia. "You need to read the whole thing. You'll understand if you read the whole thing. Plus, we don't even share the same last name. No one will know you are the sister I was referring to. I never once refer to you as 'Ruthie' in the book."

Ruthie turned. Stood still, in the middle of a crowded restaurant, surrounded by the sounds of boisterous people eating, of Edith Piaf's nasal intonation. She looked at her sister, whose entire face leaked regret.

It was too late.

Ruthie did not try to be heard above the noise that surrounded her. She did not speak at all. It did not matter whether or not Julia knew her exact thoughts, which at that moment were, *Gabe knows, and that's all that matters, you narcissistic bitch!* It occurred to her that nothing she uttered was safe with her sister. Everything could be used for material. This exact moment could show up as a scene in Julia's next book. It occurred to her that when it came to Julia, the best thing to do was to say nothing, to reveal nothing, to give one final stony look and then simply walk away.

Chapter Fourteen

After aimlessly walking up and down Shattuck, feeling bereft and trying not to cry, knowing she needed to talk to Gabe but wanting to be more in control before she did so, Ruthie finally just sat down on a public bench and let loose her tears, scaring away a homeless woman who sat on the bench adjacent to hers. The crying fit was brief. Afterwards she fished from her purse a Kleenex (barely used) and the copy of *Straight* that she had bought at Cody's, so much more a "real" book than the bound manuscript Julia had sent.

Reading by the light of the lamppost that glowed above the bench, Ruthie flipped to the dedication page, a dedication that up until a few moments ago had pleased her inordinately: "To my darling Biscuit: though we were flung apart too young, and remained that way too long, I will always treasure what we had and have."

Ruthie closed the book quickly. She did not want to experience a flicker of love, or sympathy, for her sister. Yes, the Center was and remained a nightmare. No, that did not give Julia the right to write about Ruthie's past. And then Ruthie's mind, trained to be ever judicious, betrayed her and she considered the situation from Julia's point of view. (This tendency toward empathy was a lasting and often frustrating inheritance from Naomi, Naomi who used to claim that almost everyone was deserving of some amount of empathy. Even murderers. Even rapists. "Knowing that everyone has a story," Naomi would say, "I find it very hard to judge.")

And so she mulled over the fact that her sister had no way of knowing that when *Straight* came out Ruthie would be dating someone who staked a religious claim against abortion, and that Ruthie would have kept her own past abortion a secret from him. She considered the fact that her sister had taken pains not to acknowledge her by her real name in the book, referring to Ruthie only by her nickname, Biscuit. She pondered the question: were she dating someone else, a normal Berkeley boy whose politics aligned completely with hers, would she care that her sister "outed" her as having once ended a pregnancy? Was it simply because Gabe was furious with her that she was furious with her sister?

But no. No, no, no. No! Even if Gabe had been unaffected by what he read, she would still be angry. Julia had betrayed her, had taken something private of Ruthie's and shared it with whoever was willing to hand over twenty-five dollars for a book. Fuck embracing the inheritance of her mother's endless empathy! Julia did something wrong and Ruthie had every right to be upset. Ruthie was allowed not to have to parse out the myriad ways in which the situation was complicated. Ruthie was allowed to draw a line around her private life and kick the shins of anyone who tried to cross it.

Bile rose in her chest, and she felt a need to move, to walk. She rose from the bench, took aim, and attempted to toss Julia's book into a wide metal trash can that was missing its lid. She aimed poorly, and the book bounced off the can's side. She bent down, picked *Straight* off the sidewalk, and threw it away.

She had to see Gabe, had to talk to him face-to-face. Dara had her car key, so she had to walk the twenty blocks to his house, even though it was dark and the streets were mostly empty. Beneath her jeans she wore knee-high boots with two-inch heels, not intended for traversing such a distance. By block seven her feet ached. She kept walking. Past a yard of older black men standing in front of a Weber grill. Past her favorite wood bungalow, green with white trim and a shingled roof, with a rose garden in the front that scented the entire block with its sweet perfume.

She walked, fantasizing about one day living with Gabe in a house like that. A house where at night they could sit on the front porch swing, sipping beers and watching their children catch fireflies, just as she and Julia used to do during the summers. Not that there were fireflies in Berkeley. They would have to be in the South for fireflies. And Gabe would have to have forgiven her.

She walked past a falling-down home, its windows covered in newspaper. She walked past the rust-covered bungalow with the chain-link fence that contained Maizey, a yellow Lab, who was always outside, even at night.

"Hey, Maizey," she said, as the dog bounded to the fence. Were Ruthie with Gabe, he would have some sort of a treat in his pocket for the Lab. He kept a box of Milk-Bones at his house for the next-door neighbor's dog and always took a few with him on walks. He told Ruthie that he couldn't wait until he could get a dog of his own. As soon as he was more or less settled. He had smiled when he said that, and Ruthie imagined he was smiling at the idea of settling with her.

She walked and walked. She had to see Gabe.

Except when she got to his house, and rang the doorbell, no one answered. She rang the bell again. Waited. No one came. Usually at least one of his three housemates was there, watching TV or studying. It occurred to her that Gabe might be home and he simply wasn't answering. But no. All of the lights were out, including the front porch light. Gabe wouldn't just hide out inside, in the complete dark.

Was he at his church? Was he at a bar? Was he sitting in a cozy booth with some other, prettier girl, throwing back shots and shooing Ruthie from his mind? She dug her cell phone out of her purse, dialed his number. It rang four times and then his voice mail picked up. His recorded voice sounded warm and open, so different a tone from when she last spoke with him outside the restaurant. She waited for the beep and then, unsure what to say, hung up. She dialed again. The voice mail picked up after one ring. Again she listened to the greeting, listened to the beep. This time she spoke.

"It's me. I'm at your house, but I guess you're out. Look, I'm so, so sorry. I should have told you—it's just . . . It's hard. I wanted to tell you, but then, it doesn't really have anything to do with us. Or, maybe it does. I don't know. I've never done this before—I've never really been in a relationship. I don't know what's expected. Please. Just call me; just come home. I need to see you. I just want to hold you. If I could just see you I think we could figure this out. I'm sorry. I'll be here, waiting."

She sat on the top step of his front porch and waited, wishing she had a book or a magazine to read, something to occupy her, something to keep her mind from spinning with worry. (Did couples break up over things like this? She did not know. She had no prior experience.) She thought wryly of Julia's book, which she had thrown in the trash. She could have read that little charmer again. She considered checking Gabe's mailbox, just in case a *New Yorker* or something had arrived that day. But then she remembered that the mail was put through a slot in the door. Whatever mail he and his roommates had received was already inside.

And that was when she remembered the time that Gabe got locked out and unscrewed the mail slot's brass cover. How once the brass cover was removed, the rectangular hole in the door was wide enough for him to slip his arm through and unlock the door from the inside. He had used the screwdriver from one of those glasses repair kits, purchased for two dollars at the drugstore. Ruthie did not have a glasses repair kit, but she did have a Swiss Army knife that Mimi had placed in her Christmas stocking a few years ago. The blade of the knife had her name engraved across it, which Ruthie thought was delightfully sinister.

She retrieved the Swiss Army knife from her purse, pulled out the screwdriver arm. She was not sure it would match with the screw on the door. She tried, and though it wasn't an exact fit, with enough pressure she was able to loosen the screw. In this way, she managed to get all four off and then pull off the brass cover. She reached her arm through the rectangular hole in the wall, just as Gabe had done, and felt around until she found the doorknob. She turned the lock in its center, and then turned the knob. The door opened, with her hand still inside it. She pulled out her hand, checked the outside knob to make sure it was now unlocked, pulled the door shut, and reattached the cover to the mail slot.

When she had finished she walked inside and was greeted by the smells of stale beer and boy sweat. Familiar smells to her now. The living room was almost entirely dark. She thought of turning on a light but did not want to disturb anything else. Doing so, somehow, would make what she was doing feel more invasive, even more like a break-in. She tiptoed down the hallway, going slowly until her eyes adjusted to the dark.

Once in his room she pulled off all but her underwear, put on his Barton Fink T-shirt, which was crumpled on top of the dresser, and got into bed. His pillow was redolent of him. The sharp clean smell of Head & Shoulders, the mustier smell of oil and body grease. He was a dirty boy all right, just as Dara joked, but to Ruthie his smell had become home. She imagined him entering the room quietly, slipping into bed with her, and then slipping inside her, easily, the trust between them restored.

She wasn't sure when she fell asleep, but she awoke to find the overhead light on and Gabe standing above her, still in his tissue-thin Braves T-shirt, reeking of smoke and booze.

"Hi," she said, rolling over so that her back touched the bedroom wall, making room for him in his narrow bed. "I broke in."

He looked at her coldly but didn't reply, just grabbed the extra blanket from the foot of the bed and walked out of the room. She rose, followed him down the hall and into the living room, where he flicked on the light, revealing a surprisingly clean space, with no dirty mugs on the floor, no crusted plates on the coffee table.

"Did you clean up?" she asked.

He sat on the sofa, put the blanket over his knee, and looked up at her wearily. "John's mom is in town," he said. "I'm pretty sure she did it."

"Where is everyone?"

"She took them to Chez Panisse. And then to Yoshi's for a concert."

"They invited you, too, didn't they? And you said no because of Julia's reading."

"Yep."

"Bet you're glad you made that call," she said.

He didn't smile at her attempt at a joke. He was sitting on the far left side of the couch, not making room for her to squeeze in beside him. She walked around the coffee table, to the other end of the couch, and sat down, a few feet away from him.

"You know, a lot of things happened to me before we met. Like my parents dying, and all of the shit that happened between Julia and me. And then when things finally seemed to be settling, Julia was doing okay and I was heading to Berkeley, I got pregnant. And it wasn't like I was in love with the guy. He was just a kid from my high school. We were both virgins. That's why we slept together, to get it over with before we went to college. Which was really dumb, I know, but it seemed like a good idea at the time. Anyway. It was just too much. Too much for me to have a baby right then."

Gabe leaned forward, put his head in his hands, rubbed his forehead with his fingers. "Why didn't you tell me? Why did I have to find out about it by reading a book your sister wrote?"

"I had no idea she was going to publish that. I don't understand how she could have done that without talking to me."

He straightened his back. Turned his head to look directly

at her, his blue eyes projecting confidence in his rightness. "You should have told me."

She knew that she should just agree, apologize again, move a little closer to him, put a hand on his leg. But there was a part of her that could not. A part of her that was fierce and stubborn. That refused to lie even though she knew that by not lying she might forfeit the relationship.

(But would she want a relationship that required her to submerge her fiercer parts?)

"Listen to me. If somehow I got pregnant from us having sex, I would not hide it from you. I promise. And I would be open to—you know—to your concerns, your desires about what steps to take. Or not take. And that's a big fucking thing to promise. But what happened to me when I was eighteen, it's my past. Mine. It's as if you're upset with me for not showing you my past medical records, my dental history."

"Telling me you had an abortion is a little different from showing me your dental records."

He sounded tight, petulant.

She studied the ring on her right ring finger. A gold band with a flower in its center, each petal made of a tiny amethyst stone. It was her mother's ring, though Naomi hardly ever wore it. Naomi said it was too youthful for a woman in her late thirties to wear.

"I don't know what else I can give you," Ruthie said.

"Would you ever have told me?" His voice was softer now.

"Yeah, I think I would have. Eventually. I mean, if we were to move in together or, I don't know, one day get engaged. I would have told you."

"You mean once I was too invested not to walk away."

Her heartbeat picked up. And again she broke with her father's advice about not asking a question unless you knew you wanted the answer.

"Are you going to walk away now?"

He shrugged. "I don't know."

She felt a rush of anger. "I have to tell you, I don't really get it. I mean, your womb-to-tomb sanctity of life argument, it's a very pretty idea. It's very sweet. But it doesn't really apply to the complications of real life. Like, what if a fetus, in utero, is horribly deformed—I mean a desperate case—and it's an impoverished woman who is going to have it and she doesn't have health care. Should that fetus be born?"

"It's not about the individual cases. It's about the soul of humans in general, as a society. If we just zap out all that is painful and hard, we're going to lose our souls. We need to learn to care for all incarnations of human life."

"That is a very lovely sentiment. Now let me ask you this: do you think I lost my soul when I chose, at eighteen, not to allow a cluster of cells to grow into a baby?"

"I don't think it's my place to judge any more than it's our decision as humans to decide which clusters of cells get to live and which don't."

"Jesus, Gabe. I really don't think you'd feel this way if you were a woman. I think you've just romanticized this nineteenth-century view on life."

"Well, Schwartzy would agree with you. And she certainly exercised her twentieth-century freedom of choice."

Ruthie looked at him. Remembered the boy he had been at St. Catherine's. Shy, long-haired, teased.

"She had an abortion?"

"At least one that I know of. I was seven. I overheard her talking on the phone to her best friend. Said she was pregnant, throwing up every morning. Said it was shitty timing, but then laughed. Said, 'What can you do?' I was thrilled. Thought I was getting a sister or a brother, someone to play with. Someone else to have Schwartzy as a mom. But that sibling never came. I just kept waiting, kept waiting for Schwartzy's stomach to get big and then for a baby to arrive. But nothing changed. Schwartzy stayed skinny. I stayed an only child. Later I figured out what must have happened, though I never asked her about it."

"I'm sorry. That's really sad."

"Yeah, well."

"Do you think that's why you became a Catholic? Because if Schwartzy had been a Catholic she would have had the baby?"

He laughed, a little ruefully. "Schwartzy says I converted because I was embarrassed as a kid to be Jewish. That I wanted to be one of the little *goyishe* southern kids who shoot squirrels in the backyard with BB guns and assume everyone puts up a tree at Christmastime."

Ruthie didn't say anything, but she thought that Schwartzy was probably on to something.

"But if all I wanted was to fit in, do you really think I would have become a Roman Catholic in Berkeley, California?"

Ruthie laughed and Gabe smiled, a little.

"You know, I don't want to get pregnant right now, obviously. But if I did, I think we'd have a really cute kid."

Gabe looked at her, sighed. "Oh, Ruthie."

It was not an utterance of acceptance, or even forgiveness. He sounded pained. He sounded like he didn't know what to do.

She scooted a little closer to him on the couch. Rested her palm on his thigh. They sat like this, heads leaned back on the couch pillows, absorbed in their own thoughts, their own pasts, until the front door burst open and the living room was filled with Gabe's drunk and sated roommates, one of whom put in a videotape of recorded *Simpsons* episodes, which Ruthie and Gabe watched with him until Gabe fell asleep in the middle of an episode and started to snore and Ruthie woke him up, telling him it was time for them to go to bed.

Part Four

Chapter Fifteen

Winter 2009

Ruthie pulled into the driveway of the yellow craftsman bungalow on Sinclair Avenue in a bad mood, having received yet another "helpful" Post-it note from her boss, Chef A. J. Aiken, owner and creator of Pasture, the acclaimed Atlanta restaurant, where practically every item diners put in their mouths—including the ketchup that accompanied the black truffle burger on challah—was house made from sustainably sourced ingredients.

Whether it was the failing economy, or the fact that Ruthie's signature dessert, her "Elvs" (peanut butter cookies, filled with roasted banana ice cream, the sides rolled in crumbled caramelized bacon) was listed in *Atlanta* magazine's "100 Things You Must Eat Now," while Chef A.J.'s signature chicken legs *sous vide* stuffed with homemade sausage were not, the chef was on the warpath. Every day when Ruthie arrived at the restaurant to make that evening's desserts, she would find a yellow Post-it note waiting for her. Across the top of the note the words "Tip o' the Day!" would be jauntily written. Beneath lay that day's missive.

Today's "tip" had read: "20 Elvs left unsold last night. This equals money in the garbage. Try to budget better, okay?" Yesterday's was: "We can't afford to buy new ingredients for every dessert. Be creative with leftovers!"

That "tip" especially rankled. Ruthie *always* included a bread pudding on the menu, made from the leftover sourdough bread they served at the beginning of each meal. And today's tip—about the extra Elvs? Chef A.J. *knew* that the ice-cream sandwiches weren't assembled until ordered and that the peanut butter cookies left over from the night before would be perfectly fine the next day, wrapped tightly as they were in waxed paper and stored in the refrigerator.

And was it Ruthie's fault that reservations at Pasture were dwindling, that in the terrible economy of George Bush's twilight days (only six more days until he left office!) people were cutting back on lengthy and expensive meals? Indeed, customers often came into the restaurant just to sit at the bar and order coffee and dessert. Ruthie was helping the restaurant stay in business, goddamn it, not running it into the ground with frivolous spending and bad kitchen economics! If anyone was hurting Pasture's business it was Big Steve, the house manager who once took a photo on his cell phone of a steak sent back to the kitchen by a diner who said it was overdone. Cell phone in hand, Big Steve crouched by the offending diner and showed him the picture, saying, "It's cold now, so we'll fix you a new one, but I want to show you that you sent back a perfectly medium-rare steak."

Ruthie released an audible sigh, put the car in park, and, though she no longer parked on hills, engaged the parking brake. Six months of living in Atlanta and she still couldn't get used to parking on flat ground, not after so many years of driving, and parking, in San Francisco. (Though she was in Berkeley for four of those years, she returned to visit her aunt and uncle in the city so often that her San Francisco parking habits never died.)

Stepping out of her ancient Volvo sedan—a gift from Schwartzy, as evidenced by its many bumper stickers advocating a Bush-free White House and a nuclear-free world—Ruthie was immediately greeted by Solomon, the big black tomcat who had refused to leave the house on Sinclair when Schwartzy moved to the Artisan condos in Decatur.

Schwartzy had lured Ruthie and Gabe back from San Francisco to Atlanta by promising to sell them her bungalow for half of its assessed value. Little did Gabe and Ruthie realize that by the time they actually took ownership of the house the real estate market would have crashed. Still, getting the bungalow at half its assessed value, even in the bad economy, was a real deal.

"A once-in-a-lifetime deal," Schwartzy had declared that past spring, over salads at Café Gratitude, the raw vegan restaurant she always insisted on going to when she visited Gabe and Ruthie in San Francisco. Gabe, who had been looking for any excuse to move back to his hometown, who had in fact already sent his résumé to the White Oaks School, in case they were hiring, looked so pleadingly at Ruthie that she knew she was going to have to acquiesce.

Solomon waddled up to her and stretched his front paws against the chocolate-stained leg of her pants.

"Come here, buddy," she said, scooping him up with a grunt. Solomon snuggled into her, wrapping each arm around her neck, purring maniacally.

She walked toward the front porch, still carrying the cat, stopping to open the back of the old-fashioned metal mailbox that had a swinging door that locked with a key. Schwartzy (of course!) lost the key years ago and Gabe and Ruthie (of course!) never bothered to replace it, so the door could only be closed, not securely locked. Ruthie pushed it open with one hand, holding Solomon with the other. There was lots of mail, including several envelopes that looked like bills, a couple of catalogs, and one large blue envelope that looked promisingly personal but was probably just some gussied-up plea for money from one of Schwartzy's many activist groups.

It was too much to hold both the mail and Solomon, so Ruthie dropped the cat onto the ground and gathered all of the mail in her hands. Giving a closer look to the blue envelope, she recognized the slanted script—which included the instructions DO NOT BEND. Ruthie was shocked. The letter was from Julia. It had been years since Ruthie had last received a letter from Julia. The two of them were hardly in touch. An e-mail or two every year or so to keep each other informed on major life changes: that Ruthie got an externship at Chez Panisse after culinary school, that Julia published a second book, this one a novel, which, to Ruthie's secret delight, sold rather poorly, that Julia and Molly moved to Red Hook for the cheaper rent, that Ruthie and Gabe moved to Atlanta.

Ruthie knew she should be over it by now, that it had been years since the betrayal, but she never forgave Julia for writing about her abortion, for "outing" Ruthie to Gabe. Even though Ruthie and Gabe had worked through it, even though it was important that they did work through it, Ruthie had lost all sense of trust in her sister. Ever since she read the epilogue to *Straight*. And apparently Julia had lost her warm feelings toward Ruthie, too. Perhaps because Ruthie accused her of having "narcissistic personality disorder" when Julia telephoned to apologize again for referring to Ruthie's abortion in her memoir. Or perhaps because when Ruthie and Gabe got married, two years after they graduated from Berkeley, they eloped in order not to have to invite Julia. In order not to have to deal with her.

Once on the porch Ruthie noted that the Christmas wreath was still hanging from their front door. She was pretty sure that if left to Gabe, the wreath would remain until Christmas 2009. She dumped the mail on the front swing, lifted the wreath off the nail it hung from, and walked it to the trash. She should have driven the wreath over to the chipper at Agnes Scott College, where it would be chopped into mulch and used to landscape people's yards, but she just didn't have the energy to do the environmentally responsible thing. Besides which, she was pretty sure that she was too late, that the chipper had been put away for the season.

Instead she dumped the wreath into the Herbie Curbie, first peering inside to make sure that the baby opossum that sometimes nested there was gone. If she and Gabe could find the lid to the Herbie Curbie, the opossum wouldn't be able to climb inside it, but being who they were, Ruthie knew that the lid would remain missing, in perpetuity. And Gabe being who he was (a fanatical animal lover), Ruthie could not call animal control to take the opossum away.

"He's adorable," Gabe had said the first time they spotted the marsupial.

"He's disgusting," said Ruthie. "Like a white rat. Do *not* bring him into the house."

Ruthie walked back to the porch, scooped the mail off the swing, balanced it in one hand while unlocking the door with the other, and stepped inside. Gabe was in the living room, lying on the couch, their chocolate Lab, named Berger (short for Scharffen Berger), settled on the floor below him.

"Honey, I'm home!" said Ruthie, an ironic nod to the fifties couple they had not become.

Berger jumped up to greet her, and Gabe, following the dog's lead, jumped up, too, running toward her, putting his hands in front of his face as if they were paws, sticking his tongue out and panting like the dog. This was all part of their shtick, a routine they performed often.

"Down, boy," she said to her husband, which was also part of the shtick. "Let me just put this stuff down, and I'll give you a real hello." Walking into the kitchen, she dumped the mail on the counter.

"What's this white crap stuck on here?" she asked, knowing the answer. It was dried-up blobs of Greek yogurt that Gabe had smeared on the counter for Solomon to eat. Gabe had a thing about not eating in front of the animals without sharing.

"I'll get it up," said Gabe, following her into the kitchen and walking to the sink to get a sponge. "How was your day?"

She told him about the latest missive from Chef A.J., trying not to get too worked up in the telling, for Gabe became upset when she got too riled.

"Tell him if he keeps messing with you, I'll kick his ass," Gabe said pleasantly, dabbing at the counter with the sponge.

(Gabe used to try to reason Ruthie out of her fits of agitation, which only ended up agitating her further. "What do you want me to do?" he had asked when she barked at him to stop minimizing her feelings. "Tell you that if people don't stop messing with you I'll kick their ass?" "Yes," said Ruthie. "That's exactly what I want you to do.")

He glanced at the mail, noticed the blue envelope with Julia's slanty script. Picking the envelope up, he studied the Red Hook address in the upper right-hand corner.

"This is a surprise," he said. "Are you expecting anything from her?"

"Nothin' but trouble," Ruthie said, as if her feelings about Julia were breezy.

"Perhaps it's an essay she plans to publish detailing our dilemma over whether or not to have a baby."

Ruthie humphed at his gallows humor but was relieved that at least on this particular day he could joke about Their Big Issue.

"I think it's a photo," she said. "See the DO NOT BEND?"

She walked to the refrigerator and took out a Sweetwater 420 lager. Ruthie was just a tiny bit concerned that she depended too much on her evening drink (or two, or sometimes—but not very often—three). Indeed, having to cut out alcohol for nine months was just one of the many reasons why she was ambivalent about having a baby.

She always had thought she wanted to have a child with Gabe, but now that it was time to actually do so, she was deeply resistant.

"Are you going to open it?" Gabe asked.

"My beer? Why, yes. Yes, I am."

"Ha. The letter—or whatever it is—from Julia."

Ruthie twisted the top off her beer and took a long sip. "I will later. I can't deal with it right now."

"Oh, come on, Ruthie. You have to see what she sent." He picked up the envelope, breaking its seal with his pointer finger.

"At least let me do it," she said, grabbing it from him.

She opened the flap, turned the envelope upside down. Two photos landed on top of the wood counter. The first was of Julia and her. Ruthie couldn't be older than five in it, which would make Julia eight. They were standing in the dining room of Wymberly Way. (All of these years later and Ruthie still recognized the elaborate moldings on the crème-colored walls, the green marble fireplace with the brass screen in front of it.) Julia, her auburn curls pulled into two pigtails, wore shorts and a yellow-and-pink-striped Izod shirt. She stood behind Ruthie, her hands resting on her little sister's shoulders. Ruthie, her hair parted on the far side and held back with a green barrette, wore an emerald bathing suit with pale green stripes. Her hands rested, embarrassingly, along the sides of her crotch.

The second photo was of Ruthie and Naomi. Ruthie was younger in this one, only two or three. She had on a blue-tiered dress with tiny Swiss dots, each tier trimmed with white lace. Naomi was holding her, wearing a yellow silk shirt with an over-sized collar, a black sweater-vest on top. Both Ruthie and Naomi had variations of a bowl cut, though Ruthie's hair was plain and brown while Naomi's was auburn and vibrant. Ruthie looked so tiny in her mother's arms, almost as if she were a little doll. On the back of the photo Julia had stuck a Post-it note that read: "Was going through old photos and found these. Thought you might like. Will talk soon. XO, J."

"Why do you think she sent me these?" asked Ruthie.

"Maybe she misses you," said Gabe.

"Look at her hands on my shoulders in this one. Like I'm hers."

Gabe took the photo out of her hands, studied it. "She looks like she's being protective of you. Like she's your bodyguard."

"That was Julia. My protector." She put the photos back in the envelope. Shook her head as if to rid herself of them. "Weird. Anyway. What do you want to do for dinner? Pasta or go out?"

On days when Ruthie worked at Pasture she was never up for cooking much at home. The same had been true when she was at cooking school at Tante Marie, where she learned everything from butchering large cuts of meat to pressing thin layers of butter into a dough made of flour and water in order to make puff pastry. For most of that year all she ate at night was plain pasta with a little butter and Parmesan cheese.

"What do you think, Berger? Huh? Should we have pasta or go out?" Gabe pulled on the dog's ears while he spoke to him. Ruthie knew that Gabe did this in part because he wanted Berger to be desensitized so that if they ever had a child ear and tail pulling wouldn't rile the dog.

"Let's go out," she said.

They decided to eat at Mofongo, a Latin American restaurant nearby on North Highland. Mofongo would have been a splurge, but in the last few months Ruthie had become friends with the chef, Armando Sanchez, and he often gave them free food. Indeed, they received free appetizers, drinks, and desserts at many of their favorite restaurants now, because the Atlanta chefs—with the notable exception of her own boss—were supportive of each other. Her friend Billy Allin, whom she had known from Chez Panisse, had opened a great restaurant in Decatur the previous year. It killed her to think that if the timing had been right, she could have worked with him.

Even though it was January, the night was pleasant. Gabe suggested walking, but Ruthie said no. Just a week ago a man was walking home from a bar in Little Five Points when a car came to a screeching stop beside him. Two young men—boys, really— jumped out, one waving a gun, while the third stayed inside the car, keeping the engine going. The boys took the man's wallet, made him lie facedown against the pavement, and sped away.

"Did you not read about it on the Inman Park Yahoo! group?" Ruthie asked.

"I stopped reading that thing," said Gabe. "You should, too."

"Yeah, 'cause that will make the crime stop."

Gabe shrugged. "There's crime everywhere. Though I swear, there were no armed muggings when I was growing up here. Plenty of people asking for handouts, but no muggings."

They drove the Volvo because it had more gas in it than the Camry. Not that it mattered. They were only driving half a mile. It made Ruthie crazy how much they had to drive now that they lived in Atlanta. In San Francisco they had only owned one car—the Camry—and they only used it once or twice a week, to go grocery shopping, or to drive to Ocean Beach.

Sometimes Ruthie missed San Francisco so much it made her chest ache. As if San Francisco were a person, one in a series of people that she had lost.

Once at Mofongo they sat at the bar and ordered *mojitos*. As soon as the bartender plunked her drink down before her, Ruthie found herself wishing that she could just hide away in this welcoming place forever, just suck down sweet rum drinks stuffed with mint and avoid ever facing another Post-it note from her boss or an unexpected mailing from her sister.

Her drink safely in hand, she turned to Gabe, eager to further discuss their days.

"How was school?"

"My students are fucking geniuses. Every single one of them is smarter than me."

"You don't really believe that."

Gabe grinned. "You're right. But they *are* really, really smart."

Gabe taught high school English at White Oaks, his alma mater, so to compliment his students was, in a way, to compliment himself.

Ruthie sucked down more of her *mojito* and, knowing that they took a few minutes to prepare, signaled to the bartender that she would like another.

"And why don't we get some of those bacon-wrapped dates, and those little Cuban sandwiches, and maybe a salad, the frisée with the poached egg and the *jamón*. . . ." She looked at Gabe. "Do you want to try the pineapple chicken wings?"

"Sure, whatever you want."

"And the pineapple chicken wings."

"Can I get you another drink?" the bartender asked Gabe, but

Gabe shook his head. He didn't drink nearly as much as Ruthie did.

"Do you ever feel as if you've regressed by going back to White Oaks?" she asked, knowing that the question was a little mean but not being able to help herself. The day had left her in a punchy mood.

Gabe looked down at his T-shirt, which he got at an REM concert Schwartzy took him to in 1992. "I'm a regressive sort of a guy," he said. "When I find something good, I stick with it."

He looked at her and smiled.

She kissed him on the cheek, to acknowledge that he was referring to her as well as to White Oaks and REM.

"So Ruthie, anything interesting happen at the restaurant today besides A.J.'s usual passive-aggressive Post-it?" she asked.

"So, Ruthie, anything interesting happen at the restaurant today?" he asked.

"The big news is, last night Big Steve kicked out a couple who were a no-show two weeks before. He recognized their name from the reservation list, and he told them they weren't welcome."

Gabe grinned. "You're kidding me. First of all, couldn't they have had the same name as the no-show but been different people?"

The bartender placed Ruthie's new drink before her. She took a generous sip. God, if it weren't for the hangover, she'd drink *mojitos* every night.

"The guy's name was Luther Giovinazo, which is pretty unusual, so it probably was the same person as the no-show, but that's not really the point. The point is: why in God's name is Steve turning away people when our reservations are down thirty percent? And you can bet A.J. didn't say a damn thing about it, either. He's convinced that Big Steve is this major asset to Pasture, even though he's totally abusive to customers. He keeps giving him more and more power while I keep getting these maddening Post-it notes blaming me for slow nights."

Ruthie sucked down more of her drink. A server arrived with the bacon-wrapped dates and Cuban sandwiches. Ruthie grabbed one of the dates, popped it in her mouth. There was a salty little bite of manchego cheese stuffed in its center.

"He's an ass," said Gabe, biting into a sandwich. "Do you remember how I had to stuff my leftover pork terrine into my cloth napkin because Big Steve wouldn't stop bullying me into eating all of it?"

"He does that to everyone. It's his little song and dance. He says that the pork terrine is a labor of love and to not eat it all is an act of aggression equaling war. And A.J. has such a fat fucking ego he lets him get away with it! Honestly, it's Big Steve who is driving the customers away more than the shitty economy."

Ruthie realized she was getting too worked up. Her heart was beating fast and she was tearing her cocktail napkin into little bits.

"Why don't you just quit?" said Gabe.

"And do what?"

Gabe pretended to rock a baby in his arms.

"Nice," said Ruthie, genuinely annoyed. "So glad you brought that up. Just the discussion I need to have at the end of a shitty day."

She ate another date, trying to remain calm. She smiled at the server who dropped off their frisée salad and chicken wings. She took another sip of her drink. She didn't want to get in a fight with Gabe, didn't want to risk that this would be one of their big ones, after which they would be prickly and short with each other for days. But why would Gabe bring up their unresolved baby dilemma in the middle of her venting work frustrations? And on the same day that Julia made contact for the first time in nearly a year, since she had e-mailed to share news of her move to Red Hook and the fact that her novel was being remaindered?

"I just think we should go for it. You're about to turn twenty-nine. You've been to culinary school, you've worked at Chez Panisse and Quince, and now you can add Pasture to your résumé. You're established, babe. After you have the kid and go on maternity leave, you can write your own ticket. Start your own café, be a caterer, write cookbooks, whatever."

"And how would we pay for this kid during the time I quit my job?"

"You've got your trust fund."

"Yeah, and that's great, but twenty thousand dollars a year doesn't exactly make me Paris Hilton," she said.

Gabe ran his hands through his hair, excited by his plans. If he sensed her irritation, it didn't show.

"The point is there's a cushion. We'd figure it out. And since you're dissatisfied with your job and Big Steve isn't going anywhere, why not take this opportunity to, you know, start a family? Besides which, I heard Paris Hilton isn't worth all that much."

He smiled, teasing, but Ruthie was in no mood to riff on his joke.

"Really? This is the pep talk you want to be giving me? On this day of all days?"

She picked up a chicken wing, tore into the meat.

Gabe put his hand on her thigh, and when she looked down at it, looked down at his raggedy nails and the silver wedding band that matched her own, she realized that she was still wearing her chocolate-stained pants from work.

"Ruthie, I really, really want to have a baby."

Dara had a child last year, and when Ruthie went to San Francisco to visit Mimi and Robert a few months ago Dara drove over from Berkeley with little Theo. She brought so much baby paraphernalia with her that it took up the entire trunk of her car. As Dara unfolded the stroller so they could walk Theo to La Med on Noe, Ruthie found herself thinking, *Thank God I don't have to lug one of those around all of the time.* After Ruthie returned to Atlanta she tried to express her feelings about Dara's transition into being a mommy to Gabe. She told him of the heaviness she felt in her own heart watching Dara unfold that baby stroller.

He pooh-poohed her. "We'll get a BabyBjörn then," he said. "Hands free."

Gabe was rubbing her leg with his hand, using too much pressure.

"Ruthie, I really need for us to take this step."

It was at that moment that Chef Armando, rotund, bald, and effusive, came bounding out of the kitchen to say hello. He and Ruthie kissed on both cheeks and he asked how she liked the wings, which were new on the menu.

"They're amazing," she said. "So sweet and meaty. I could eat another dozen of them, easily."

She had turned as far as possible away from Gabe and was directing all of her energy onto Armando.

"How's business at Pasture?" Armando asked.

Ruthie shrugged. "It could be better, but I don't think we're in danger of closing or anything. Why? You need a new pastry chef?"

"You'd be the first I'd call," he said.

Gabe stared at the floor while they talked, not even pretending to be interested in their conversation. Armando told Ruthie about his upcoming trip to Nicaragua, to suss out new Latin American recipes. Ruthie finished her second drink while listening, envious of his adventures.

"You want another?" asked Armando, motioning toward her empty glass.

Ruthie shook her head. She had to work tomorrow, and she was already feeling tipsy.

"Well, listen, it's so great to see you. Congrats on the *Atlanta* best-of mention."

"You, too!" said Ruthie, remembering that Mofongo had won for best brunch.

"Good to see you, man," said Gabe to Armando, holding out his fist for a bump. The fist bump had become de rigueur for him ever since Barack and Michelle did it after securing the Democratic nomination. At first Gabe did it ironically, implicitly acknowledging his dorky whiteness whenever he held out his fist. But now it was just what he did when signing off.

After Armando returned to the kitchen, Ruthie was left with a dread feeling. Now she had to resume her fight with Gabe, and she was not even sure she could articulate her feelings clearly, because she was feeling woozy from the booze.

Gabe jumped right back in.

"You know, you accuse me of being regressive, but you're the one who is terrified to take the next step, to move forward in our marriage. We always said we'd have a kid—we talked about it from early on. And now we're at the end of our twenties. If we want to have more than one—which, believe me, we should; it sucks to be an only child—I just think we need to get on it."

Maybe it was the alcohol, or frustration over A.J.'s Post-its, or the rumbling of nerves set off by Julia's having sent photos, or simply the fact that her husband was using her age to guilt her into having a child, but whatever the cause, Ruthie erupted.

"Are you kidding me? I gave up everything—everything!—to move with you to Atlanta. I am now thousands of miles away from Mimi and Robert, and Dara, and all of our friends from college, and I am living in your childhood home in a city I *never* meant to return to, and you are telling me that I can't move forward? That *I* am regressive? We are living in *your* childhood home, Gabe. You are teaching at the same school you went to. And I'm the one that's regressive. And my problems at work—problems I would not be having had I stayed in San Francisco, by the way— my problems would be solved if I just popped out a kid. Jesus, Gabe, you're such an asswipe!'"

In moments of marital strife Ruthie's vocabulary reverted to that of a foulmouthed middle schooler. Once in a fight she had called Gabe a "fucking fuck-head."

She glared at him, sitting across from her so calmly, so imperiously. Well, she could be imperious, too. Rising from her bar stool, she walked outside, stood beneath the restaurant's awning, trying to breathe deep. She would calm down. She would return to Gabe and tell him she was sorry. It had been a long day. She was rattled by Julia. She watched as a homeless man, someone she recognized from the neighborhood, a broad-shouldered transvestite wearing a sequined top and an ill-fitting black skirt, approached her.

"Diva," said the transvestite, "love the earrings!"

Ruthie's earrings were round and delicate, made of intricately carved white bone, and though she loved them, too, Gabe once told her they looked like two round tortilla chips hanging from her ears.

"Thanks," said Ruthie, giving just a flicker of a smile before staring straight ahead, hoping this person would just mosey on down the street and not try to talk to her anymore.

"Look, I have HIV—don't worry; it's not catching—but I really need fifteen dollars for my medication, so if you could just help me out . . ."

He tried to hand Ruthie a crumpled sheet of paper, a document that would "prove" his HIV status. It was bullshit. He might be positive, but the document he was holding was the exact same thing another man had shown her earlier that week. Right down to the name at the top and the dried coffee stain along its perforated edge.

Ruthie looked at the man, at his dripping black eyeliner, the slight stubble on his pale cheeks, his long nails, painted black, that looked as if they could scratch. Had she been living in San Francisco, she probably would have given him some money, figuring that she shouldn't punish him for his dishonesty, that he was obviously in need of help, regardless of his recycled documentation. But here in Atlanta, where the fence behind her bungalow had twice been burned by vagrant men starting fires, where she was scared to walk half a mile at night because of armed muggings, where she often witnessed drug deals taking place when she walked through Little Five Points, her compassion had shriveled, just shriveled right up.

"Sorry," said Ruthie. "I don't have any cash."

"Hug then," said the man, and held his tracked arms open for her.

"No," she said, and then again, more emphatically, because he was still leaning toward her, "No!"

"Then at least a handshake," he said, holding out a hand with his long, pointy nails.

She was yelling at him now, yelling, "I don't know you! I don't know you! I don't know who you are!"

The man popped his eyes, murmured, "Diva," one more time, and sashayed away.

Ruthie began crying in earnest. Crying because of her outburst. Crying because she used to have a tender heart toward the down-and-out, she used to, in fact, wonder if the homeless might all be Jesus in disguise. Crying because of Chef A.J.'s hostility and Big Steve's aggression, because of the failing economy and the dwindling customers at Pasture. Crying for her old life in San Francisco, for streets populated by pedestrians—day and night—and breathtaking views at the top of every hill, for Mimi and Robert, who still lived in their old flat on Mars, for trannies who were happy and well adjusted and did not try to hug you for spite.

But mostly Ruthie cried because even though her parents had been dead for nearly two decades, she still missed them. Naomi especially, who held her so tightly when she was just a little girl. Missed them even more so, now that she was back in Atlanta, so close to where she grew up, but in such a completely different world. Only a few miles away, and yet she hadn't returned to Buckhead, not once.

And Julia. She missed Julia. Her sister who used to place her hands on her shoulders so protectively, who used to run after Ruthie any time she was banished from the table for childish behavior, who used to let her sleep in her room when she would get scared at night. She missed the big sister she once had. A lifetime ago.

Chapter Sixteen

The next morning when Ruthie, hungover, checked her Gmail account, in addition to a note from Robert about his and Mimi's upcoming trip to Atlanta, an e-mail from Dara that included a jpg of baby Theo, several pleas from the Democratic Party of Georgia, and an announcement of a winter sale at J.Crew, there was an e-mail from Julia. She knew it! She knew she would be hearing from her sister. There was a reason why Julia sent the photos—she was surely up to something—and Ruthie felt certain that Julia's e-mail would explain. Still, she waited to read it last, as if receiving a note from Julia were a casual thing.

> Hi! It's been too long. So my agent says it's time for me to go back to writing memoir, considering that The View from Williamsburg was far from a "box office smash." I think she's right—and I've decided to take the plunge and finally write about our family, about what happened to us, starting with Mom leaving Dad for Phil and going through the accident and beyond. And listen, I promise to show you what I'm going to publish before it goes to the printers, so we can work out whatever issues you might have. (I can't promise to cut anything, but I promise to work with you on whatever might make you uncomfortable.) But first I've got to write Mom's story, and what I'm trying rather desperately to figure out is: how did a

good girl from Union City, TN, have the temerity to leave her first hus-
band, child in tow, to be with Phil, who was still married at the time? (Our
mother was nothing if not an interesting woman, huh?)

Any insight you have into her psychology would be great. But also, here
are some more pedestrian questions that I need help with:

1. *Do you remember the name of the nail polish she used to wear? I re-*
   member it was a deep plum, but I don't think it was called plum.
2. *Did she used to eat cottage cheese and fruit for lunch or was it plain*
   yogurt? I'm thinking it was cottage cheese, but I'm not positive.
3. *Did they call you at all when they were in Las Vegas, during those days*
   before the crash?

Oh, and I need any old letters, pictures, etc. Do you have any? And
did you get the two I sent you? Priceless, aren't they? Let's talk soon. I'll
be on a plane all afternoon—headed to North Carolina to get some serious
writing done. I'm going to be staying at a friend's house for a bit while she's
away on sabbatical from her teaching job at Davidson. Apparently the only
company I'll have for the next three weeks are the ducks that live on the
pond behind her house. Which is great, because solitude equals productiv-
ity! But of course I'll still have e-mail, and assumedly I'll get cell service
there, so please be in touch.
Love,
J

Ruthie had no idea what color nail polish her mother wore,
though she remembered once knowing, remembered how thrilled
she was when her mother would paint her nails, too, just for fun.
It was cottage cheese and not yogurt that her mother ate. Alex
Love used to make fun of it behind Naomi's back, saying that cottage cheese looked like something you coughed up, like phlegm.
And yes, they had called the day before the crash. Ruthie, annoyed
at being stuck with Mother Martha while everyone else was on
vacation, had been sullen and the call had been brief.

Not that she was going to tell Julia any of this. Why in God's name did Julia think Ruthie would aid her sister in the writing of another memoir? As if that first one hadn't been painful enough, as if that first one hadn't revealed enough. Now her own private family stories were to be interpreted through Julia's eyes and then put out for the world to read? And because Julia would fix her version of their story to the page, hers would become the truth. Julia's memory, Julia's sensibility, Julia's philosophy would trump Ruthie's because Julia's would be the one that people read.

Ruthie felt terrible. Not just from the e-mail, but from the alcohol the night before. She had dry mouth; she was hungry; her head ached. She decided to take a shower, get dressed, and drive to Chick-fil-A, to rely on that time-tested combo of grease and salt to cure a hangover. She would get a Chick-fil-A sandwich, douse it in Texas Pete hot sauce, and wash it down with a lemonade, maybe drive around listening to country music afterwards, just for the full southern experience.

But when she got in the Volvo after showering and dressing in jeans, a T-shirt, a long cardigan, and an intricately patterned scarf Mimi had brought her from India, instead of heading to the Chick-fil-A in Decatur, which was the one she always went to, Ruthie instead drove to North Highland, and from there she turned onto Freedom Parkway, the lusciously landscaped road that led to the interstate. She passed the Carter Center on her left, reminding herself that she really should go sometime and see—well, whatever it was Jimmy Carter kept in there. She continued on the parkway, stopping at the red light at Boulevard. Standing at the corner was a black man holding a handmade sign that read: I HAVE CANCER. PLEASE HELP.

Ruthie, who had resolved to give her money to organizations, not individuals, stared straight ahead while hoping that the side door of the Volvo was locked. Deciding that if it was not that was just her own tough luck. She would not insult the man by leaning over to lock the door in his presence. (The Volvo, which was built in 1980, did not have power locks.)

When the light turned green Ruthie drove toward the interstate entrance, the downtown skyline bold on the horizon, a skyline that was most impressive if viewed from a distance and preferably at night. Up close Atlanta's downtown was a mess of ugly hotels built in the eighties, corporate office towers, and third-rate storefronts that sold cheap suits, fake gold watches, and sweatshirts advertising the ATL.

As soon as she entered the highway it split, one half going south, toward the city's predominantly black neighborhoods, one going north, toward the white ones. Or at least, that was how the city's demographics used to be. Now things were changing, sort of. A lot more whites lived in the city, and many black families had moved to the suburbs. Inman Park had become so gentrified in the past ten years that Schwartzy could hardly stand it, which was why she had moved to Decatur.

"What happened to the hippies and rednecks in rusty pickup trucks?" she had lamented.

Ruthie continued on I-75/85 North. She passed the steeple of All Saints' Episcopal Church, where she used to go with the Loves after spending Saturday night with Alex. It was at All Saints' where Alex's little sister, Amy, pointed out that Ruthie was wearing white shoes after Labor Day. They were standing in the vestibule, waiting for Mr. Love to come out of the men's room so they could go to their pew, when Amy pointed to Ruthie's shoes, declaring, "You're not supposed to wear white shoes in the winter."

"Shush, Amy," said Mrs. Love.

Ruthie stared at her scuffed white ballet flats, wondering who else at church had noticed them.

Amy, only seven, protested. "But, Mom, you always said it was tacky to—"

The look Mrs. Love gave her daughter shut her mouth.

Just across the street from All Saints' was The Varsity, where the Loves used to get lunch after church, a greasy treat for their piety. Once Ruthie told Mr. Love that she did not like Varsity hamburgers, that she found the meat too soft and greasy. He acted shocked, proclaiming her "un-Christian, unsouthern, and unpatriotic."

She was pretty sure he was joking.

She passed the new Atlantic Station development on the left, a place that depressed her, for though it was heralded as a model of New Urbanism, she viewed it as nothing more than an oversized mall with apartments. Just past Atlantic Station the highway split again, the four far left lanes becoming I-85 North, the three far right lanes I-75 North. She had been driving in the exact middle lane of the highway, as if she wasn't sure which way she would go once the highway split.

Of course she veered right, toward 75, toward Buckhead. Immediately she had to merge and merge and merge again, as the exit for Northside Drive was coming right up, almost without warning.

She made the exit. She was off the freeway, back on the northwest side of town, the area where she grew up. She turned right on Northside Drive, a street made of three lanes, the middle one reversible. Atlanta was hilly and Northside Drive was no exception. The street ran over a series of steep hills, up and down, up and down. Coming up on a hill, you couldn't see over the curve until you were at the top, so if you were driving in the middle lane and someone coming from the opposite direction messed up and drove in the middle lane as well, their car and your car would crash at full speed on top. Because of this many drivers avoided Northside's reversible lane altogether.

Not Ruthie's father. Phil *always* drove in the middle lane on Northside Drive. He said it was quicker.

"They call this the suicide lane, you know," Naomi would say.

"Relax, babe. I've got it under control."

Sometimes he would glance in the rearview mirror and make eye contact with Ruthie. "See what I have to put up with?" he would say. His old refrain.

Driving in the far right lane meant waiting forever at the stoplight at Collier Road, where everyone seemed to want to turn right, and yet there was no right turn on red and so the going was slow, slow, slow. Ruthie considered turning right on Collier and driving to Ardmore Park, where Julia used to go with her old boyfriend Dmitri to make out. The train tracks ran straight through that park, and sometimes Julia would drive Ruthie over there and they would walk on them.

Ruthie kept going straight on Northside, passing the Bobby Jones Golf Course on her right. She remembered how she used to bicycle around the paved paths intended for the carts. What a discovery that was—all of those smooth, traffic-free paths amid the shorn green grass of the course. She had wondered why others didn't bike there, too.

The answer came one day when a golf ball whizzed by her, just barely missing her cheek. A white-haired man wearing pants stitched from multiple patches of madras plaids lumbered off the course and onto her path. He stood about fifteen feet in front of her, stretching out his arms in order to block her from passing as she biked up to him.

"Stop, lassie, stop," he said.

Lassie? Was he calling her a dog?

Though she was scared of him, she stopped. What else could she do?

"You're going to end up with a concussion if you keep riding around while we are trying to hit balls," he said.

"I'm sorry," she said, her voice soft. "I didn't realize."

"Well, off with you then," he said. "Leave us to our golfing."

On her left was Memorial Park, where she and Julia went to swing the day of her parents' funeral. Where Julia told her she didn't believe in heaven. The park's perimeter was 1.8 miles, a fact she recalled from when she and Julia used to go there to jog. Julia always had more stamina than she. Ruthie would usually give up in the middle, would start walking right where Howell Mill intersected with Peachtree Battle. There were always lots of joggers there, fit and groomed men and women, wearing T-shirts that proclaimed their Greek affiliation. When Ruthie was in seventh grade she was enamored of the women in their sorority T-shirts, women who so obviously belonged to the world of the pretty, the fit, the few. Back then she wanted nothing more than to go to Georgia and be in Kappa Kappa Gamma sorority, the sorority Mrs. Love was in when she was an undergraduate there.

Once when they were jogging Ruthie told Julia that after going to UGA she would like to buy her starter house near Memorial Park.

"Your *starter* house? Your *starter* house? Lord, chile, you sure drank the Kool-Aid."

Ruthie didn't know what Julia meant by this and Julia wouldn't explain, but now as Ruthie passed the park she knew exactly what "drinking the Kool-Aid" referred to—Jonestown—and exactly what Julia was implying about Ruthie's inherited Buckhead values.

What a funny world she was from. A starter house that started at half a million dollars.

Yet was she really *from* it? She had lived over half of her life in the Bay Area. There she really had "drunk the Kool-Aid." By the time she was eighteen she would have no more applied to the University of Georgia than she would have voted Republican. She would have no more rushed a sorority than she would have proclaimed Hershey made better chocolate than Scharffen Berger.

It occurred to her that Hershey owned Scharffen Berger chocolates now. It bought them in 2005. So what did that mean? That all of the careful distinctions she made were ultimately meaningless? That they all had a way of collapsing into each other?

At the corner of Northside Drive and Peachtree Battle, where Ruthie turned right, sat a two-story, pale pink columned house that had once been portrayed in a line drawing on the cover of the Atlanta Junior League cookbook. Ruthie's mom was not in the Junior League. She had never been asked to join, nor had she ever pursued an invitation. Alex's mom, Mrs. Love, had been a member. Which went without saying. And there, just before the intersection of Peachtree Battle and Woodward Way, was Alex's old house. Those white shingles. That pale blue door. Did the Loves still live there? What would they do if she were to pull into their driveway and knock on their door?

(Invite her in for a drink, and a plate of cheese straws, that was what they would do. Invite her in and exclaim again and again how absolutely wonderful it was to see her after all this time. Tease her about what a serious child she had been; call her Max.)

She was approaching Wymberly Way. She remembered the last time she was on this street, during winter break of her senior year of college, when she had first visited Gabe in Atlanta and had wanted to show him her childhood home. She hadn't even made it to the house. She had become so anxious she had vomited.

She turned left onto her old street.

God, the houses were impressive, each one more so than the last. How could the owners of these—these manors—keep everything about them so impeccable? There was no lawn that needed mowing, no exterior that needed painting, no flower bed that needed tending. Everything sparkled. The houses were old, but the copper gutters, the roofs, the cars parked out front (though most cars were parked discreetly in the back) were brand-new, or, in the case of the ancient Rolls, perfectly restored. They shone, they gleamed, they screamed: *Money is no object here!*

She passed the white wood house with the two-story columns, the wide porch, the black rockers. It looked like the admissions building of a southern university. She passed the brick monster flanked by wings that looked as if it could hold the entire Mafia. She passed the brick Tudor-style house her father had always loved, the one he said was second in beauty only to theirs. And then she slowed down completely, for she was in front of 3225 Wymberly Way, the house that seven years earlier she had not been ready to face.

But today she was.

Chapter Seventeen

Ruthie pulled into the driveway, as if she belonged, parking next to a black Mercedes. The Mercedes looked as if it had just been waxed. Ruthie marveled once again at how everything in Buckhead managed to stay so clean, as if rust and dust and wear were part of some other, lesser world.

From the exterior, the house was as elegant as ever. Symmetrical, stately gray stone. Two manicured boxwood trees, each in a blue glazed pot, framing the black front door. A Palladian window above, its glass wavy, as was the glass in all of the windows, which must have been recently cleaned, given how the afternoon light reflected off them so brilliantly.

As she walked to the front door, she remembered the feel of the driveway's irregular round stones against the soles of her shoes. Once the pointy heel of her mother's pump got stuck in a crack between two of the stones. Naomi was able to slip her foot out of the shoe but could not loosen the heel. Finally Phil went inside and retrieved the can of WD-40, sprayed some around the heel, and managed to yank it loose.

The only thing Phil really knew how to do around the house was spray WD-40.

Ruthie's heart rate was elevated, she was perspiring even, but she did not hesitate. Boldly she walked to the front door—a door her family had rarely used, always going in and out of the back—and pressed on the bell. She heard chiming inside, heard the scurry of a dog's nails against hardwood, and then heard the sound of barking just on the other side of where she stood.

She waited. Wondered if whoever drove the Mercedes was home but was choosing not to answer, for fear that Ruthie might be a burglar scoping out the place, or at the very least someone trying to sell something. She remembered selling Girl Scout cookies on Wymberly Way when she was in fourth grade. How hard it was to get people to come to the door, but once they did, how competitive the neighbors were with each other, scanning the order list, seeing how many boxes others had ordered and then ordering that many plus one more.

She rang the doorbell a second time, which started the dog barking again.

There was a voice coming from inside, scolding the dog, calling it "Shugah," telling it to hush.

"Who is it?" the voice asked, and Ruthie saw a woman with a helmet of coifed hair the color of the inside of a pineapple pressing her nose against one of the windows to the side of the door.

Ruthie stepped in front of the window so that the woman could get a good look at her, could see that she was not dangerous. Ruthie smiled, gave a little wave.

The woman opened the door.

"May I help you?" she asked in a gravelly lockjaw.

She was elegantly dressed, wearing creased black pants and a starched white shirt open at the neck, the collar framing her preserved face. In her fifties, or possibly her early sixties, her skin was smooth and nearly wrinkle free, the result, surely, of very expensive surgery. Wrapped around her right wrist was a thick gold cuff, and on her earlobes were little knots of varnished gold. Her wedding ring was gold, too, no longer the fashion but surely the fashion back when it was given to her.

"I'm so sorry to bother you. I'm Ruthie Harrison. My family used to live in this house, from 1979 to 1993."

The woman made a little O with her lips. "We bought the house in 1993," she said. "And have been here ever since."

Ruthie nodded, stoic. "My parents were killed in a plane crash. My sister and I continued living here for a few months while the custody details were sorted out, but then I ended up moving to San Francisco with my aunt. This is the first time I've been back—not to Atlanta but to the house—since then."

"You poor thing," said the woman. "Of course I remember the details of your parents' death. So very, very sad. Gave Spencer and me second thoughts about buying the home, to be honest, but then we decided the best thing we could do would be to move in and love it, bring life to it again."

Ruthie wanted to object, to tell this woman that life had never left Wymberly Way, that she and her sister had filled the home with life even after her parents were gone. But that would be a lie. Those few months after her parents had died were mostly somber, a waiting game for an unwanted outcome.

The woman glanced at her watch. "My manicure appointment is in just about an hour."

"I don't want to hold you up. I just happened to be in the neighborhood—"

"It's a standing appointment. My husband, Spencer, is a surgeon. Works with his hands, and for that reason, I suppose, he's always liked for me to keep mine in good shape, too. It's our thirtieth wedding anniversary today, if you can believe it. We're going to Eugene's."

"Happy anniversary. Enjoy Eugene's. Linton Hopkins is an amazing chef."

"Oh, he's the best. The absolute best." She glanced at her watch, which was metal and shiny and surely expensive. "I suppose I don't have to leave for another forty minutes. Would you like to come in for a moment? Look around? Have a little drink?"

Ruthie felt compelled to say yes, even though she generally found it difficult to make small talk with strangers. But she was here, wasn't she? She might as well go all the way through with it.

She stepped inside, onto the walnut floors, floors she once slid on in socks, before her father bought the Oriental runner. She took it all in: there was the ornate banister with the wrought-iron scrolls and the cherrywood rail, there was the curved archway that divided the entrance hall from the dining room, and there was a curved archway again (an architectural detail that would echo throughout the house), leading from the hallway down the three stairs and into the living room.

But the colors on the walls, the paintings, the furniture—all were different. It was obvious to Ruthie, after being there for only a moment, that the couple who lived there now fit into Buckhead, were comfortable in this world. Naomi never was. Their possessions implied a confidence, a boldness of those so deep within the inner chambers of society that they were allowed to make statements. Point in fact: the walls of their dining room were painted a deep, fiery orange, startling and intense.

There were antiques everywhere. Oriental rugs adorned all of the floors. Phil had bought Oriental rugs for the floors, too, but these were older, the colors faded in a telltale sign of inherited wealth. These rugs had been passed down. Across from where Ruthie stood was an enormous glass vase, resting on an antique chest. The vase was filled with blossoming branches from a cherry tree, imported, surely, for it wasn't yet the season. Sitting by the stairs leading down to the recessed living room were two porcelain dogs, each painted a shiny white with little red swirls.

"I'm Evelyn Edge," the woman said. "And you said your name is Ruthie?"

"Yes, ma'am," said Ruthie, slipping back into the old southern manners, the manners her parents did not enforce but Alex Love's mom did. (Ruthie's mother had not liked to be called ma'am, said it made her feel old.)

"What may I get you to drink? An iced tea or something stronger?"

"Something stronger would be wonderful if you don't mind," said Ruthie, hoping she wasn't being too forward but not caring enough not to be. She needed a drink in order to handle being back in this house.

"Wonderful. I've got white wine and I've got the makings for a gin martini. My husband almost always insists on a martini when he comes home from work."

There was a part of Ruthie who adored the Evelyn Edges of the world, these throwback women who seemed to have no ambivalence about being their husband's helpmate, the keeper of the home, the raiser of the children, the maker of the drinks.

Ruthie felt ambivalent about nearly every decision she ever made—major and minor. Even on her wedding day, she had experienced doubt, a feeling that had troubled her deeply, that caused her to wonder if she was making a mistake. Ruthie knew that her mother, though she felt guilty over leaving her first husband, never, ever doubted her decision to marry Phil.

"White wine is fine," Ruthie said. "Thank you so much."

"Make yourself comfortable in the living room and I will be right back with some. Is sauvignon blanc okay?"

"That's perfect."

She pointed Ruthie to the living room, though of course Ruthie knew where it was. Then Evelyn walked through the orange dining room and toward the swinging kitchen door, the door that once killed Ruthie and Julia's new kitten when it swung back just as the kitten was trying to dash through its opening. It had smacked the animal hard on the head, breaking her neck. It had been Naomi who—accidentally—let the door swing back on the kitten, and who had to deliver the sad news to her daughters, who were upstairs getting ready for school.

Ruthie walked down the three steps to the recessed living room, with its wood-beamed ceiling and shiny walnut floor, covered in yet another faded Oriental rug. There was a grand piano in the corner of the room with photographs in polished silver frames atop its closed lid. She thought of her father, proclaiming, "Addie Mae *loves* polishing silver!" She sat on one of the sofas, which was covered in a linen slipcover the color of sand. There were bright decorative pillows on top of it, splashes of yellow, red, and orange. Shugah made her way into the living room, and Ruthie, immediately, wondered if she was allowed.

During the few years that Ruthie's family had owned cats— they kept getting run over, and then the kitten was killed and Naomi said no more—their animals had never been allowed in this room. Phil always kept the doors closed for just that reason.

It was in this room that Phil and Naomi had entertained their (infrequent) guests, in this room where they set up the Christmas tree, in this room where Santa had come that one Christmas Eve, bringing with him soft peppermints that you chewed instead of sucked.

Ruthie never knew who that Santa really was. The most logical guess would have been that it was her father, dressed in a red suit and white beard, except Phil was in the living room the entire time Julia and Ruthie were, grinning at his girls. When they demanded to know who Santa was, Phil had said, "Ask me no questions and I'll tell you no lies."

Evelyn returned to the living room, holding two stemmed glasses of wine, each filled nearly to the top. "This is what we call a country club pour," she said, in her modulated accent.

A country club po-or.

She sat in an upholstered chair catty-corner from Ruthie, crossed her legs at the ankles, and lifted her glass.

"Cheers," she said, which came out as "cheer-ahs."

Ruthie raised her glass vaguely in Evelyn's direction, though they did not clink rims.

"Spencer and I grew up in Atlanta. He attended college here, at Tech. I went to Hollins for my first two years and then to Vanderbilt, where my daughter Lauren also went."

"My father went to law school there."

"What was his name again?"

"Phillip Harrison. But he went by 'Phil.'"

"Oh yes, I knew that. From the documents when we bought the house." She looked thoughtful for a moment, and then shook her head. "But no, I didn't know him otherwise."

Ruthie remembered being at a Christmas party at the Loves' house, when she and Alex were eleven. It was a party for adults, but Mrs. Love insisted the girls put on dresses and come be seen for a little while before going back upstairs to watch *Dirty Dancing* and consume the mini quiches they had pilfered from the buffet. Again and again Ruthie was asked by the Loves' guests who her parents were, and again and again the guests would, upon hearing her answer, shake their heads and say, "No. No, I don't know them."

"When Spencer and I first married we lived in a little starter house in Garden Hills. On Sundays we would drive around this neighborhood, making a game out of pretending we lived in one of the big, beautiful homes on Habersham, or Peachtree Battle, or Wymberly Way. This house was always one of our favorites. But the first time it came on the market, when your father must have bought it, we were still building up our nest egg and couldn't yet afford it."

Ruthie did not say anything, but she imagined that most likely Evelyn and Spencer could have always afforded Wymberly Way. Evelyn, with her lockjaw accent and utter certainty of self, dripped old money. Probably she just had some idea of protocol, a planned order of how life should unfold. First the starter house, then the babies, then move into the big one you'll never leave.

"You've done a beautiful job designing the interior," said Ruthie, who knew from Mimi to say "design" instead of "decorate."

"My mother loaned me her eye. She was always wonderful with interiors."

"My aunt has a real gift for it, too. She's the one who took care of me after the accident, she and my uncle. She ran an interior design firm in San Francisco. Still does, actually, Sullivan Design."

"Is your aunt a Sullivan?" asked Evelyn. "I did know some Sullivans growing up."

"She's not from Atlanta. And Sullivan is her business partner's last name. She's my dad's sister, a Harrison. But her married name is Wolanksi."

"I suppose Sullivan was the right choice for the name of the firm then," said Evelyn, emitting a knowing laugh.

They each took a sip of their wine, Ruthie musing that old Evelyn Edge probably hadn't socialized with too many Wolanskis in her life. Ruthie imagined that if she were to mention Coventry, or the Loves, or even the fact that Mimi had been a Tri Delta at Vanderbilt, she and Mrs. Edge would probably discover a whole world of people they shared in common. Or rather, once shared. It had been a long time since Ruthie was in touch with anyone from this side of Atlanta.

In one hand Evelyn Edge held the stem of her wineglass. The other hand rested on her lap, her deep plum nail polish bold against her black pants. The polish looked perfect, and Ruthie wondered why Evelyn was getting a manicure. The polish, in fact, looked similar to the color Naomi always wore. What was it called? Vintage Cognac. Estée Lauder Vintage Cognac. That was it. That was the name Julia was looking for. As a child Ruthie had believed the name Vintage Cognac to be the utmost in sophistication.

"Would you mind if I used your restroom?" she asked. She actually did need to pee, but she also wanted to see more of the house.

"Of course not, but I'm afraid you will have to use one of the ones upstairs. Do you remember the toilet that used to be in the downstairs bathroom? Ancient, with that old-fashioned pull chain? Well, my daughter has become absolutely fanatical about conservation. And charming though that old toilet was, apparently it used gallons and gallons of water per flush. Lauren badgered us about it until we finally agreed to have the old toilet replaced with a high-efficiency TOTO. Of course it wasn't until after the plumber ripped out the toilet that he informed us that the TOTO we wanted was on back order."

"I'm sure that replacing the old toilet will be a good investment in the long run."

This was what Ruthie had learned to say to anyone in Atlanta who spoke of home renovation projects. That whatever the project was, it would be a good investment in the long run. That seemed to be what everyone wanted to hear.

"If you go up the front stairs and turn left, you can use the one in John's old room."

"That was Julia's room," said Ruthie.

Evelyn Edge gave a sad smile. "Isn't it funny how even when things change you hold on to how they once were? It's been years since Johnnie lived at home and I still call it his room. I suppose I always will."

Ruthie put her wineglass down on the coffee table before rising. As she made her way out of the living room, she noticed Evelyn putting a coaster beneath it, even though it was a stemmed glass that would not sweat. Ruthie walked up the three steps that led to the entry hall, turned again, and walked up the front stairs. Running her hand along the smooth wood of the banister railing, she remembered how Julia used to dare her to slide down it. She never took Julia up on the dare. She was afraid she would topple over the wrong way and smack her head against the marble table where her father kept his antique music box that played "Frère Jacques" every time you turned the crank.

At the top of the stairs she saw that the wall-to-wall carpeting Naomi had installed had all been removed, revealing beautiful wooden floorboards. As she turned to enter Julia's room, she remembered how it used to be: the pale pink walls, the mounted lamps with their decorative pink metal bows, a Playboy bunny decal dangling from one of them. The wooden dresser that had held Julia's clothes and secret things, the heavy wooden bed, the green and pink floral coverlet.

Everything had changed. The walls were now painted kelly green. There was a pair of twin beds with plaid bedspreads, and a glassed-in case holding some sort of sports trophies. In the corner of the room was a set of free weights. Framed and hanging on the wall, centered between the two twin beds, was a blown-up photo of a boarding school campus. EPISCOPAL HIGH SCHOOL, where Johnnie must have gone, was printed at the bottom of the photo.

Ruthie walked to the bathroom, now painted tan, pulled down her pants and underwear, and sat on the toilet, staring at the tub in front of her while she peed.

A memory swam to the surface.

It was in this very tub that she had once urinated, after Julia had drawn herself a warm bath. Ruthie must have been four or five, and when Julia left the room to get a clean towel from the linen closet she had climbed right in and relieved herself, just because the water looked so inviting.

"What are you doing?" Julia had asked, when she returned, holding a fluffy, folded towel in her hands. "Why are you smiling like that?"

Ruthie could not remember whether or not she actually told her sister she had peed—though she would have said "tinkled" at that point in her life—or whether Julia just figured it out, maybe by a shot of yellow dispersing into the water. What she remembered was how surprised she was by Julia's angry reaction. How silly she thought it was of Julia to make her get out, drain all of the water, wipe the tub with a washcloth, and fill it back up again.

Ruthie smiled at the memory of such innocence.

Still sitting on the toilet, she reached for the shower curtain and pulled it back, revealing a collection of toiletries propped on the corner of the tub. A brown bottle of Crew shampoo, a green bar of Irish Spring soap, a striped can of Barbasol shaving cream, a rusty disposable razor.

What was she doing here, peeing in a stranger's toilet, peering at the items in a stranger's tub? And what had her family been doing here all of those years ago, smack in the middle of Buckhead, in this grand Philip Schutze–designed house that was intended to be occupied by the likes of the Edges?

The door swung open and for a moment she thought Evelyn was barging in on her until she realized it was just the little dog, just Shugah, nosing her way in through the crack.

"Hey, pretty," said Ruthie, scratching the dog's neck underneath her thick leather collar.

Ruthie wiped, flushed. Pulled up her pants, stood.

This was somebody else's house. Had been for almost twenty years. What was she trying to accomplish by using her old toilet? By comparing the way things were to how they are now? Life went on. There was nothing anyone could do about it.

She scooped Shugah into her arms, but the dog wriggled and kicked until Ruthie put her back down on the floor. She ran the water in the sink and pumped two squirts of liquid soap into her palms. Her training as a pastry chef had made her forever vigilant about washing her hands. When she walked out of Julia/John's old room, instead of turning to go back down the front steps, she opened the door that led to the back stairway, wanting one last look at the chair that moved up and down its metal ramp with the press of a button that looked like a doorbell.

Except there was no chair, no ramp, not even the button. It must have been taken out. Ruthie examined the wall; it had been smoothed and sanded where the button once was.

How many times did Alex Love make her ride that thing up and down, up and down, though Ruthie had long grown bored with it?

She was going to become emotional if she didn't watch out, discovering all that had been changed about her old house. And she had been gone far too long from her hostess, nearly ten minutes, much more time than it takes to use the bathroom in a lady-like way.

She peeked very quickly into her old room—utterly different—Laura Ashley print wallpaper, four-poster bed with a white eyelet bedspread, silk curtains, jute rug, photos from sorority events tacked to the pink-framed corkboard in the corner of the room.

Though she really needed to go back down, Ruthie quickly walked over to the corkboard so she could see which sorority Evelyn Edge's daughter had been in. It was a good one, she was sure. Girls from this world were almost always invited to join the good ones. She studied a picture of four tall blondes, all wearing black tights and leotards, bright toothy smiles on each of their faces. The caption below the picture read: "Delta Delta Delta, *Delta Underground.*"

Just like Mimi.

Ruthie hurried out of the room and down the stairs, trying not to feel a ping of melancholy over the absence of the antique grandfather clock ticking time away in the downstairs hallway. Phil had loved that clock, had treated it like a treasured son. He used to explain to Ruthie in detail how to care for it, which included winding it every eight days. In the will Phil had left the clock to his first grandchild. And since at the time of his death no such grandchild existed—still didn't—the estate lawyer decided to sell it at auction, along with most of Phil's other antiques. Mimi considered buying it, but it would have overwhelmed her flat and at the time she had no clients interested in an eighteen-thousand-dollar clock.

The money received from its sale had gone directly into Ruthie and Julia's trust. As had the money from the sale of the house, once the considerable mortgage was paid off.

Ruthie stepped back into the living room. Evelyn Edge was sitting same as before, ankles crossed, though her wineglass, with its "country club pour," was now empty.

"I thought you might have gotten lost up there," she said. "But then I remembered that you know your way around."

Ruthie blushed as she sat back down on the sofa. "I'm sorry. There are so many memories here. It's hard not to get pulled in."

"Your parents' marriage, it was the second time for each of them, yes?"

Ruthie nodded yes, surprised that Evelyn Edge remembered this detail about Phil and Naomi.

"You have a half sister, Julia, who was your mother's biological child?"

How shiny Evelyn's eyes had become.

"I do. I'm impressed that you know all of this."

Actually, she was more alarmed than impressed. Hadn't Evelyn only minutes earlier had trouble remembering Phil's name? Evelyn Edge was morphing into a different person, right in front of Ruthie's eyes. She was smiling but trying not to smile. She looked like a mischievous child, delighted by her own naughtiness.

"Don't be alarmed. It's simply that I found some of your mother's personal papers a few years ago. There's a little hiding place in the closet of the master bedroom. A secret door that gives access to a hidden storage place. So discreet it took me years to notice. It's for storing fine jewelry, I suppose, but it also works for hiding things you don't want others to read or see. Your mother kept a stack of letters back there, along with journals and some photographs. Some of the photos might be a little embarrassing for you to look at, dear, but remember, she was a woman before she ever became a mother."

Evelyn Edge had a hidden stash of letters and journals written by her mother? Ruthie reached for her wineglass. She was not sure, but it didn't seem as full as it had been when she left it with Evelyn.

"Did you read my mom's letters and journals?" she asked.

"Wouldn't you have?" asked Evelyn, leaning back in her chair, amused.

Of course she would have. It was human nature—wasn't it—to be curious about others.

"Do you still have them?"

Evelyn Edge nodded, her eyes glinting.

Letters and journals of her mother's. And pictures, too. Ruthie thought she knew what the pictures might be like. She had found a sexy one once of Naomi, a Polaroid that Phil must have shot. In the picture Naomi was staring at the camera from the bathtub, looking a bit annoyed. The lower half of her body was covered by bubbles, but her breasts were exposed. Without a bra they hung heavy, and her nipples looked like raspberries.

Ruthie had taken the photo from her mother's jewelry box where she was poking around, and held it in front of Naomi, who was trying on clothes in front of the full-length mirror.

"What's this?" Ruthie had demanded.

"Give me that," said Naomi, snatching the picture out of her hand. "That's nothing. That's nothing for you to see."

But of course it had been something. Back then Ruthie thought it was further proof that her parents were strange and other. Alex Love, she was sure, never found pictures of her mother naked in the bathtub. But now Ruthie considered it further proof of her parents' love, hard evidence of their unabated lust for each other, even after so many years of marriage. Astonishing, really. How their desire never seemed to fade. After only four years of marriage it was difficult to remember the time when her passion for Gabe had felt like an addiction, so much had it mellowed. And while Robert and Mimi mostly got along, their relationship seemed to be grounded in compatibility, not passion.

In truth, Ruthie had never known anyone who had a long-term relationship that matched the romantic intensity of her parents' feelings for each other. It occurred to her that perhaps her parents' romance set too high a bar. For her own marriage or for anyone's marriage. Phil and Naomi's relationship had been a special thing, and perhaps she should treat it as that, a rare bird not often sighted.

"Your mother's letters changed my life," said Evelyn.

"They did?"

"Your mother was a brave woman. Brave and selfish, I'd venture to say. How hard it is to be selfish as a woman! At least it was when I was young. Today that's all you young women know how to be, isn't it?"

Ruthie ignored the undeserved jab. What did Evelyn Edge know of Ruthie's life? Of her dedication to her job, her craft? Of her dedication to her husband, despite the fact that their relationship had been a struggle this past year, ever since Gabe had become obsessed with having a child?

"How did my mother's letters change your life?"

"Before I read her letters, Spencer was the only person I'd ever slept with."

Ruthie couldn't help herself; she giggled. And not because what Evelyn said was amusing—though it was, a little. It was just the way she said it, so grave, as if she were giving Ruthie the nuclear code.

Evelyn looked hurt.

"I don't mean to laugh. I just didn't expect for us to be talking about, about any of this. But go on. Please. I'm very interested. What happened after you read the letters?"

"Well, I wouldn't say that I had an affair." As Evelyn waved the word away with her right hand, a ray of sunlight reflected off her gold cuff, temporarily blinding Ruthie.

"An affair implies some sort of sustained period of time. Mine was nothing like that. Mine was simply a finishing of something I began long before Spencer and I got married. A romance I never forgot. One that made me—occasionally—question the choices I had made early in life. I read your mother's letters and I thought, well, if she can do it, why can't I? Why don't I just contact this person? Why don't I just phone? Spencer works all the time, anyway. And the children are gone. What harm will a phone call do? And this person that I once knew, he doesn't do the sort of strenuous work my husband does. His job is walking to the mailbox."

"He's a postman?" Ruthie asked.

Evelyn looked amused. "Hardly. His job is to receive a check. His family was quite wealthy. He's never really had to work. He's dabbled, of course, but never had a true career.

"So. We arranged to have a weekend together. I told Spencer I was going to Highlands, where we have our mountain house. Instead I met my old beau in New York City. It was heaven. We picked right back up where we left off. Just talk, talk, talked into the night. Among other things. We stayed at the Carlyle, which is a pleasure in itself with all of its gorgeous, original artwork. Seeing those Calder prints alone made the weekend worth the risk.

"Well, sooner than I could imagine, our time was over. I returned home. It wasn't like your mother's relationship with your father—it wasn't anything that could come to be. But it was lovely for that brief time. And even though I missed this person terribly, even though I won't be surprised if someday before we both get too old we arrange another meeting, I returned home feeling better about things between my husband and me. I was no longer so bothered by Spencer's absence. I had this—this secret self that he would never know about. I had a secret self that he would never see. Most of my secrets I don't think he cares much about. But this one. This one mattered."

Evelyn sat tall in her chair, the expression on her face that of a cat who had just licked the last bits of cream off her whiskers.

"I don't really know what to say," said Ruthie. Did Evelyn want her congratulations?

"I'd like to give your mother's things to you," said Evelyn, standing. "They're yours after all. And then I'm afraid I must run if I'm going to make it to my manicure appointment on time."

Evelyn left the room and Ruthie heard her climbing the stairs, headed toward Naomi's old closet with the hidden door in the wall.

How had she and Julia not discovered that door? With all their games of hide-and-seek, with all the times they played in their mother's closet, dressing in her clothes? Or when Mimi cleaned out Naomi's closet, after the funeral. How had she not noticed a door in the wall?

My god, thought Ruthie. I am going to see my mother's handwriting again for the first time in years. In her bedroom closet in Inman Park, Ruthie had a paper hatbox stuffed with old letters, but most of them were between her and Julia, during that first year in San Francisco when they still frequently wrote. The only letters she had from her mother were ones Naomi had written while Ruthie was away at summer camp, the one that turned out to be run by Southern Baptists. Only a few of those letters remained. Back then she had not thought to save them. She had never imagined there would be a time when a letter from her mother, written in that perfect round cursive, would be precious to her. Back then she found her mother's letters boring and unremarkable, filled with endless detail about what errands she ran that day and what she was planning to fix for dinner. Ruthie used to read them aloud to her bunkmates. " 'I'm just sitting down to a little fruit and cottage cheese for lunch,' " she would read, and everyone would groan at how boring their mothers all were.

She heard Evelyn Edge's footsteps, coming back down the stairs. She rose from the linen-covered sofa and went to meet her in the front hall. It was time for Ruthie to leave. Certainly she was returning home with more than she had bargained for.

Evelyn held an oversized yellow mailing envelope, large enough to hold a manuscript. It reminded Ruthie of the envelope that had delivered the bound manuscript of Julia's book, *Straight*, all those years ago. How she had sat down on her couch and read it right away, feeling so very sad for Julia, for what she had been put through at the Center, that sadistic place that claimed to rehabilitate. And then how angry Ruthie had become months later, when she read the epilogue of the finished book, the epilogue that revealed to the world—or at least to Gabe—that she had once had an abortion.

She could have lost Gabe over that. And it wasn't as if that piece of her history has just gone away. It still haunted their relationship. Even more so lately. Beneath his outward cheerfulness ran a current of resentment. He wanted a child, and the knowledge of her terminated pregnancy from years back only added to his anger at her for not being willing to grant him one.

(It had been easy to say that she had the abortion because she was too young to be a mother. But if she pressed deep enough on her feelings, she knew that she might not ever feel comfortable taking on the responsibility of a child. How could she, knowing how it felt to lose her own mother so young? How could she subject a child of her own making to such a risk? At the age of thirteen Ruthie had internalized the unsettling knowledge that just because she had thought the world was safe did not make it so. "So what?" she could hear Gabe argue. The world was never safe—that wasn't the point. And besides which, there were plenty of women who, having lost their mothers young, tried to become mothers themselves as soon as possible. Gabe had a friend from high school who lost her mom when she was ten. Now, at twenty-nine, his friend was pregnant with her third child. Ruthie wished she had this impulse—to re-create what she lost—for her husband's sake if nothing else.)

"Read these and then go have yourself a hell of an adventure," said Evelyn Edge, handing Ruthie the stuffed yellow envelope.

"Maybe I'll go to the Carlyle."

Evelyn squinted a little, then reached out her hand and patted Ruthie on the right side of her face. "Cheeky girl," she said.

She walked Ruthie to the door, turning the lock at the same time as she pulled on the door handle. It was a stubborn door, impossible to open if you didn't know the trick. Ruthie's friends never could figure it out, yet all these years later Ruthie still remembered how it was done.

"Thank you," said Ruthie. "I'll treasure these."

"Wonderful of you to come by," said Evelyn, as if she and Ruthie were old friends.

Stepping outside, Ruthie was surprised by how light it was. She glanced at her watch. It was only 3:30. The Wymberly Way house never let in enough sun. She walked to the car, eager to get home so that she could read whatever it was Naomi had written. She would share Naomi's writing with Gabe, too. Let him "meet" her mother. And Julia. Julia would be ecstatic over the discovery. These writings of Naomi's would be pure gold for her memoir.

Yes, Julia would be thrilled. Would eat Naomi's words right up. Would, in fact, take Naomi's story, her "selfish bravery," and turn it into her own. Would cannibalize their mother's words, would lock them in print, would say to the world, "Here. This is our mother. This is who Naomi Harrison was. Take her."

And Ruthie wouldn't have any choice in the matter. Julia would get to decide what to leave in and what to leave out, because Julia had a publisher and this gave Julia a power and authority that

Ruthie did not have access to. This had allowed Julia to publish Ruthie's own private history, without asking her permission. And surely Julia would not really ask Ruthie's permission for what she might publish in the new memoir she was writing. What was it Julia had said: she couldn't promise to take anything out but they could "discuss" anything Ruthie might have a problem with?

Well. There was nothing she could do about the fact that Julia was writing another memoir. But she could keep her mother's journals and letters for herself. Who said she had to surrender all pertinent material? She could make sure that some things remained private. She could claim her mother's words for her own.

Chapter Eighteen

As soon as she got into the car and pulled the door shut, she opened the large yellow envelope given to her by Evelyn Edge and slid its contents onto her lap. Two black-and-white-speckled composition notebooks fell out, along with several Polaroid pictures (including the one of her mother Ruthie had seen all of those years ago) and a white envelope, "Julia" written in blue pen across its front. She flipped through the notebooks, filled with Naomi's perfect round cursive, the entries dated, starting with 1978. She was hoping that somewhere, caught between the pages, she would find a second envelope, this one marked: "Ruthie."

She did not.

Overcome with what she knew was probably irrational hurt and jealousy, she raised her hands, palms open, and started talking to herself, to her mother.

"Really? Really? You leave behind one letter and it's addressed to Julia and not me? That's fantastic, Mom. Fantastic. It really is. Thanks. Thank you so much."

Irrational though she was being, she was so consumed by a sense of posthumous betrayal that she started making little noises. Little snorts. Little "ha's!" Was this some idea of a cosmic joke, that after she decided to block her sister from having access to their shared past her mother would "send" a letter Ruthie's way, addressed to Julia?

Evelyn Edge remained at her front door, watching Ruthie talk to herself in the car. Ruthie imagined that Evelyn was probably having second thoughts about having given her the documents found inside the secret door. Or maybe she was having second thoughts about letting Ruthie into the house, into the upstairs rooms. Perhaps she was wondering whether or not Ruthie was really who she said she was, was perhaps an imposter, faking her history in order to case the joint for a future break-in. Evelyn did not budge from the door frame, even though she had said her manicurist was waiting. Probably she would stay there until Ruthie drove away.

Fuck.

Ruthie put the keys in the ignition and turned on the car, wiping at her eyes with the sleeve of her cardigan. She put the clutch in reverse, backed up to the driveway's curb, then put the car in first and drove forward, turning the wheel. Reverse, forward, turn. Reverse, forward, turn. She did this until the nose of the Volvo was pointed toward the street.

She made a left onto Wymberly Way, no longer paying attention to the houses she passed. She could hardly pay attention to drive. She was crying in earnest now, driving and crying—just like the name of that band Julia used to listen to, the one that sang "Straight to Hell," which became a sort of anthem for fraternity boys all over the South.

Music. She needed music. Or voices. Something else, anything else, besides this terrible anger she felt, this anger that exceeded all proportions. She switched on the radio. The station was programmed to 90.1, NPR, just like her mother used to listen to. Well, good. Maybe the calm, rational voices of public radio would soothe her.

Only the voices weren't soothing. They were talking of a plane crash, a plane that just crashed, moments ago. US Airways Flight 1549 had left New York's LaGuardia Airport en route to Charlotte, North Carolina, when both engines went out. It was thought to be a flock of birds that killed the engines, but no one yet was certain. There had been an emergency landing. On the Hudson River. And somehow, the pilot landed the plane smoothly—as smoothly as possible—on top of the water. Witnesses said it looked as if the landing was intentional. The plane did not break up into pieces, or tailspin, or flip. So far there were no known fatalities. People were calling it a miracle.

Ruthie began to sob. Never before had she heard of a plane crash with a happy ending. She could not keep driving. She could not keep listening to this story while trying to drive. And how could she turn it off? There were passengers waiting on the wings of the plane. It was only twenty-two degrees in New York. She had to see what would happen to them.

She was back on Peachtree Battle Avenue, that long stretch of road that cut a curvy line between some of the great lawns of Buckhead, each topped with a distinguished manor. The road that she drove on when she was only thirteen, on the day of her parents' memorial service, when Julia let her take the wheel. What if the plane crash her parents were in had ended with a miracle? Until the exact moment of his death, her father was probably expecting just that. Hadn't he experienced a miracle forty-two years earlier, when he had sailed out of his mother's lap and through the front window of their Ford Custom Deluxe sedan? The medics had pushed the bloody baby out of the way, presuming him dead. But he had lived. Had thrived even though the doctors predicted that if—*if*—he were to make it he would be permanently brain damaged.

Phil had told Ruthie and Julia that his aunt paid no attention to the doctors. She knew he was a child of God, saved for a reason. She held him and loved him for the first two years after his mother's death, while his daddy was in Korea, fighting in the war. She picked out the pieces of glass that rose from deep within Phil's skull and surfaced on the flat spot of his head, the spot where he hit the windshield, where his hair would from then on grow in a strange cowlick, until it stopped growing there at all. At night his aunt would pick out that glass, ever so delicately, while humming hymns.

And he had survived. Not only survived but thrived. Always an excellent student, he was named valedictorian of his senior class. Was voted "Best Boy Citizen" by the Union City Press for his oration "I Speak for Democracy."

And the 155 people, the passengers and crew who were on US Airways Flight 1549, it sounded as if they were going to make it, too. The radio announced that a commuter ferry had already made its way to the starboard wing. Those standing there, shivering in the twenty-two-degree weather, were being pulled aboard, were being draped with the coats and sweaters of the paying ferry passengers. And more ferries were on the way; more help was to come.

At the traffic light Ruthie turned left onto Northside Drive. Saw Memorial Park to her right. She turned onto Wesley, one of the streets bordering the park. She could not keep driving. She was too overcome. How angry she felt at Julia on the day of the funeral, when she had refused to entertain the notion that maybe there was life after death, that maybe Ruthie would see her parents again, even if it were in some unknowable form. On that day she had needed her sister to acknowledge the possibility of heaven.

At twenty-eight Ruthie no longer had much faith in an afterlife, though she still held on to a stubborn faith in some sort of God. If Gabe had remained a Jew she would have converted, been a Jew with him. Officially joined the tribe of Robert and Dara and Schwartzy, who were her tribe already, who constituted her family as much as anyone. Joined a faith that held the story of Jacob wrestling with God as a supreme example of engagement with the divine. A faith that would allow her to wrestle with God, too.

Oh God. Why couldn't Julia have given her the hope of heaven when she was only thirteen and had just lost her parents? Why did her sister insist that—at most—Phil and Naomi were cosmic dust gathering in some distant galaxy, cosmic dust that might one day become a minuscule part of a star?

Ruthie had parked the car, but the engine was still on. The voices on the radio were still talking about the crash. And why shouldn't they? One hundred and fifty-five people should have died, and yet they had not. Instead they were veritably walking on water: standing on the wings of that plane, floating on evacuation rafts, swimming away from the downed jet, bright yellow life jackets hugging their necks.

The voices on the radio were calling the pilot, Captain "Sully" Sullenberger, a hero. What if a hero had been flying the tiny plane that her parents had strapped themselves into in order to have a grand adventure over the Grand Canyon? Would it have made any difference?

She couldn't think about that. She turned the key in the ignition, turned the car off. The radio went silent.

She wondered if those people who nearly died in the crash would grow to see themselves as invulnerable, the way her father did after being pushed aside for dead as a baby. Or perhaps they would have the opposite reaction. Perhaps those 155 survivors would live the rest of their lives cognizant of that thin, thin line separating the living from the dead.

She stuffed the speckled notebooks and the letter to Julia back into the yellow envelope, which she pushed inside her purse. Taking her purse with her, she stepped out of the car. Closed the door. She would walk across the dewy grass and make her way to the swings, where she and Julia had gone after her parents' funeral. She would read her mother's letter to her sister, though she would not be the first one to do so. Evelyn Edge had already broken the seal on the envelope. Evelyn Edge got to it first. She would read her mother's black-and-white-speckled notebooks, which with their dated pages surely were journals.

Funny, Naomi never spoke of keeping a journal. Perhaps it was a habit she kept under wraps. Or maybe she wrote in them only during that time when she was leaving Matt for Phil, when she destroyed her reputation among her friends in Virden, her family in Union City. Naomi once told Ruthie that when she left Matt her own father thought she was out of her mind. Thought she was crazy. "If he could have put me in a mental hospital without further damaging his reputation, he would have," she had said.

Ruthie reached the swings. They were empty, which seemed

strange, considering it was the middle of a Thursday afternoon. Well, maybe the media was right. Maybe kids no longer played outdoors. Maybe they were all being raised by videos, starting with Baby Einstein and going from there. She sat on one of the U-shaped swings, made of black rubber, with chains on the side to hold on to. She remembered Julia telling her that if she swung too high she would flip over the bar and fall to the ground.

She used to believe all of Julia's stories.

She pulled her mother's letter from the envelope with the broken seal. Unfolded it. Saw her mother's handwriting, round and pretty, though the words were more tightly squeezed together than her normal script, as if Naomi had been writing while agitated, or in a hurry.

November 5, 1978

Dear Julia,

I don't know if you will ever be able to forgive me for what I am doing, taking you away from your father when you are just a little girl. I don't know if I'll ever be able to fully forgive myself. But I suppose what I'm hoping is that by writing this letter I can at least try to explain what was going on inside of me during this tumultuous time in my—in both of our lives.

Probably you will never read this. Dr. Zachery told me that was okay. When I first left Matt, Mother and Daddy insisted that I go see a psychiatrist. I think they were hoping he could give me electroshock treatments, zap me back into sanity. Instead Dr. Zachery gave me the book I'm OK— You're OK. *Told me it was time to discover my "inner adult." Told me to start writing things down. Told me to write to you. Pretend you were grown and old enough to understand how a person can simultaneously love her child, love her child fiercely, while doing something that will, irrevocably, damage her.*

Ruthie's cell phone began to ring from inside her purse. She ignored it.

If you ever do read this letter, I hope that you will be grown (my little girl, a woman!) and well past the age I was—only twenty—when I married Matt.

I hope you will be able to recognize how very young I was. And on top of that, I was a young twenty, immature. Take the fact that the only alcohol I had ever tasted was in vanilla extract. I was that good of a girl. I had signed a temperance pledge at United Methodist, and I was not one to break the rules. So even though all of my sorority sisters at Meredith College would drink beer or a cocktail at fraternity parties, I stuck with ginger ale.

Julia, at that time in my life I didn't know how to be anything but a good girl. Ever since my sister Linda got pregnant at sixteen—when I was only thirteen—I had been making up for her transgression. I made A's. I went to church and MYF every week. I never stayed out past curfew. I did not drink. I did not smoke.

It's funny. I was so good at saying no to things that ultimately did not matter—whether or not I drank a Tom Collins, whether or not my miniskirt was more than three inches above the knee. Yet I was horrible at saying no when the answer had real consequences. Like when Matt proposed.—

Her cell phone rang again. *God!* It was probably Gabe, home from White Oaks and wanting to know where she was. She ignored the ring, kept reading.

In truth he and I never should have even dated. He's a good person, Julia, and a wonderful father, kind and loyal and sweet. But as long as I said that initial "yes" to him, to being with him, he never said no to me. Never. If I were to say the sky was green, he'd say, "Yes, it looks pretty green today."

We were a bad match. Dr. Zachery said that in my own quiet way, I dominated him. I was so frustrated with his passivity that I would be mean just to let my frustration out. And he would show me—by a look, a sigh, a drop of the shoulders—how wounded he was. Wounded. He was always so wounded.

But he would never say anything to openly rebuke me. Would let me do anything I wanted, as long as I didn't leave him. And you have to remember, sweetheart, this was long before we were married and—

For the third time Ruthie's reading was interrupted by the phone ringing. *Jesus.* Why was Gabe so pushy? But then it occurred to her that it could be Chef A.J. from the restaurant. Though technically it was her day off and technically she was a pastry chef and not a "hot" chef, Ruthie was expected to fill in for last-minute emergencies. And Chef A.J. had been run-down these past few days. Which probably helped explain his parade of pissy Post-it notes. What if he was sick and desperately needed Ruthie? Answering the phone was the last thing she wanted to do, but she was scared of A.J.'s wrath. And really, who but A.J.—or, god, Big Steve—would have the audacity to call three times in a row?

Grabbing the phone out of the side pocket of her purse, she flipped it open without even looking at the caller's number.

"This is Ruthie," she said, using her "professional" voice.

"Oh god. I'm so glad you finally answered. It's me."

Julia. It was Julia, though she did not quite sound like herself. She sounded sad, and full of wonder.

"Oh. Hi."

"Are you sitting down?"

"Um, kind of. I'm sitting in a swing at Memorial Park."

"The park we used to run around?"

"Yeah."

"Why are you there?"

She would not tell her sister about visiting Wymberly Way. She would not.

"I was visiting a friend who lives in the neighborhood."

"Are you with her now?"

"No. I'm by myself."

"Ruthie, you're not going to believe this, but I was just in a plane crash. I was just in a plane that crashed. We landed in the Hudson River. We were supposed to die. I was supposed to die. But I didn't . . ."

The hair stood on Ruthie's arms and a thousand tiny bumps popped up on her skin. "You were on the US Air flight, that just crashed?"

Julia drew in her breath. "My god, how do you know?"

"Oh my god, Julia. I heard about it on the radio, when I was driving over here. Are you hurt? Are you at the hospital?" She imagined Julia on a stretcher, bandaged, broken.

"I'm fine. Whatever that means. I was sitting right by the wing. I was one of the first out. I stood on the wing, pushed up against all the others, and then a commuter ferry came and there was a ladder off its side and one by one we climbed aboard. A few people who were more badly hurt had to be pulled onto the boat, but they got on. Someone threw a coat over me. I was only wet up to my knees, but I was shaking, shivering. We all were. It was so cold. They took us to Pier 79. There was a triage unit waiting. I think they were expecting a lot worse. All I really needed was dry socks, another blanket. I wasn't cut; nothing was broken. Not even my cell phone. It was in my jacket pocket. It's completely intact."

Julia couldn't have been in an airplane crash. It was impossible. Impossible that Ruthie nearly lost all three members of her immediate family by virtue of heavy machinery falling from the sky.

"Wait," said Ruthie, trying—somehow—to negate Julia's story. To make it not true. "They said that plane was going to Charlotte. Why would you be going to Charlotte?"

"I was going to stay at a friend's house near there. She teaches at Davidson, but she's on sabbatical in France. I was going to use her house as a writing retreat."

"Oh. That's right. You told me about that in the e-mail you sent. Oh god. Julia. You almost died. I'm so glad you didn't die."

Ruthie glanced up to see a pretty woman walking toward her, toward the swing set, wearing jeans and a khaki-colored barn jacket, her dark hair pulled into an efficient ponytail. She held the hand of a young girl, three or four years old, who wore a red coat with Paddington buttons over leggings and tiny brown boots. Mother and daughter, surely, come to use the playground. Ruthie looked at them with a mixture of irritation and envy. She did not want her conversation with Julia interrupted or overheard—and yet she couldn't help but notice their easy contentment. To wonder, briefly, what it might feel like to hold your own child's hand.

"Listen, Ruthie, I need to tell you something. I need to tell it to you right now. Before this moment passes and something happens to make you hate me again."

Ruthie started to cry at Julia's use of the word "hate," though Ruthie knew it was true, accurate. For a long time now it had been easier just to hate her sister. Easier to try to define the relationship with that simple emotion than to live with the conflicting set of feelings Julia brought forth.

The mother and her child were standing by the swing set now, the mother looking quizzically at Ruthie, who was clutching the phone to her ear, snot hanging from her nose, her face wet with tears. Ruthie did not look up but shielded her forehead with her hand, as if she were trying to block out the sun.

"Let's go on the slide, sweetheart," the mother said.

"Why is that lady crying?" asked the little girl.

"Shh," said the mother. "Come on with me."

They walked toward the curvy plastic slide. Ruthie heard the girl ask her mother if they could ride it together, heard the mother say that she had an even better idea: she'd be waiting at the bottom to catch her daughter when she came sliding down all by herself, like a big girl.

"Remember how we used to try to imagine what Mom and Phil's last few moments were like? On the Trimotor? Well, now I know. I mean I know what happens when a plane is going down. When the engine is silent because it's no longer working and the smell of gas is so strong you can't ignore it. And you look out the window and see a fire coming out of the engine. And then the skyscrapers are coming toward you, or you are going toward them, and the pilot comes on the loudspeaker and says, 'Brace for impact.' And the flight attendants are telling you, 'Feet flat on the floor! Heads in your laps! Seat belts tight as they will go! Link arms with each other!'"

"Oh God," said Ruthie, crying harder. She felt sick, nauseated. That Julia had to live through this.

"And the funny thing is part of you is still in denial. Part of you is thinking, 'This can't be happening.' But on a physiological level, you know. I knew I was experiencing a plane crash. I started hyperventilating. The woman next to me, whose arm I was linked with, an older black southern woman, soothed me. Murmured, 'It's going to be okay, baby. Keep praying to Jesus. Everything is going to be okay.' But things were not going to be okay. We were about to die, and I imagined it was going to be an excruciating death by fire, or drowning, or, God forbid, having our bodies dismembered when the plane broke into pieces on impact."

"Julia, I can't—"

"No, listen, the crazy thing is, in the midst of that terror, I experienced a brief moment of peace. I was so scared, and so sad that my life was going to end just like Mom's—"

Julia's voice broke, and for a moment all Ruthie heard was her sister crying, while in the background the little girl at the bottom of the slide was saying, "Do it again, Mama. Let's do it again."

After a moment Julia spoke again. "I'm shaken up. I'm sorry."

"It's okay; of course you are. It's okay."

"What I'm trying to tell you is that in the middle of that surreal terror, when my mind finally caught up with my body and I knew *this is it*, I was given a moment of grace. I don't know of any other word to describe it. It was like, even though I was about to die, some distant part of me realized that it was okay, that the world would keep right on spinning. It wasn't that I wanted my life to end—I did not—but in a very impersonal sort of way I knew that what was about to happen to me, death I mean, was basically unremarkable. That eventually it happens to everyone.

"And then my brain turned to you, and to Molly, and I felt a sickening sort of grief again because I didn't want either of you to have to go through losing me. You especially, Ruthie. I wasn't sure if you could survive another person lost. And then the terror returned because now I was fighting the outcome again."

Ruthie watched the mother standing behind her daughter, holding her arms protectively near but not on her daughter's legs, as once again the girl climbed the ladder to take her to the top of the slide.

"So what does that mean about Mom and Dad? That they died terrified?"

"I don't know how to explain this, Ruthie, without sounding really New Age, but I know that Mom and I experienced the same thoughts during those moments of knowing we were going down. I know it. I've been writing so much about her, it's almost as if she's become a part of me. And I know that in the middle of her terror, Mom reached a sort of peace with death. And then her thoughts turned to us, and she was overcome with grief that she was leaving us behind. She died thinking of us, Ruthie, hoping that we would be okay without her. That we would live good lives."

"What if you had died, Julia? What if I had lost you and Mom and Dad, in two separate plane crashes? How messed up would that have been?"

Julia laughed, and then Ruthie laughed, too, because there was no way to articulate her dismayed wonder at what might have been without sounding trite.

"I guess I should have known I was going to be all right," Julia said. "That the gods would have protected you from such a fate."

"Me but not you?" asked Ruthie.

"I've never felt more grateful for my life than I do today, but I think it's fair to say the gods have put me through some shit."

It was Julia's old claim: that she was dealt a worse hand than Ruthie. It had always maddened Ruthie when Julia implied this. She heard it as a judgment, a put-down, a negation of the tremendous loss Ruthie had incurred when she was only thirteen. A way for Julia to make herself feel superior, a way for Julia to remind Ruthie again and again of how much better off she had had it after the accident. But today she took Julia's statement for what it was. The truth. Besides her parents' deaths—and that was a doozy—Ruthie had been blessed again and again with love and opportunity. And her sister, starting from when she was just a little girl and Naomi's love for Phil had taken Julia away from her father, well, Julia had been through some things.

Yet she had survived. Again and again, she survived. And on

the day Julia had come closest to death, she was calling out to Ruthie. She needed her. Three times she had phoned on this day.

Her sister needed her, and she needed her sister. Her sister, who had always been willing to live on the edge, to skirt near the precipice she might one day tumble down. And Ruthie had always backed away, stayed in the middle, tried to be safe. But surely there were cracks in Ruthie's middle place, cracks she was too near-sighted to notice.

And Julia could slip off the edge again. . . .

Once Ruthie had believed she could catch her falling sister, save her from herself. Now she wondered if she had the capacity to save anyone. Certainly not the homeless men who slept behind her back fence on Sinclair Avenue. Certainly not the neighbor who was mugged while walking home from the bar in Little Five Points, who was made to lie facedown on the sidewalk while two boys stood above him, one brandishing a gun. And certainly not her sister, who couldn't be saved by Ruthie, who could never have been saved by Ruthie, not today on a plane to Charlotte, and not even all of those years ago, when she had walked away from Ruthie on Haight Street, when she had headed toward Golden Gate Park and Ruthie had not called after her.

But Julia was calling her now, turning from the edge to find her, like a child scanning for her mother's face in the crowd.

"Ruthie?" her sister said. "Are you still there?"

Ruthie answered, echoing the words of the mother nearby. "I'm here," she said. "I'm here."

Acknowledgments

Heartfelt thanks to Suzanne Gluck, and a million red velvet cakes to Rebecca Oliver at William Morris Endeavor. Thank you so much to Trish Grader, who launched this project. And a huge thank you to my editor, Trish Todd, whose enthusiasm and support for this book, along with her fine edits and general loveliness to work with, have put me in a permanent good mood. Thank you also to the amazing Marcia Burch, the wonderful Kelly Bowen, and the rest of the team at Touchstone.

My talented writing group, Sheri Joseph, Peter McDade, Beth Gylys, and Megan Sexton, held extra meetings this summer when I was working under deadline, and provided much-needed insight and companionship. "Uncle Ken" talked with me about airplanes. Will Becton gave me invaluable help with chapter eleven. Dixon and Stephanie made sure my description of Roman candles was copasetic. Ellen Sinaiko stopped me from placing Ruthie and Dara in a coffee shop that had yet to open in San Francisco in 1993. Jessica Handler taught me how to research a novel as if it were a piece of journalism, and Kitty and Todd provided sympathy and laughter.

Had it not been for my parents, I don't know how I could have written this book. Thanks to my mom who—among other things—told me about the Ford Trimotor, and helped me figure out the ending. And thanks to my dad for his boundless love and his seemingly boundless supply of pertinent details, from where Naomi would have bought Phil's ties to the name of the Peachtree Plaza Hotel. Thank you to my sister, Lauren, who continues to inspire, both in writing and in life. And finally, thank you to my husband, Alan, who serves as fact-checker, mentor, shrink, friend, and love. I am forever grateful to whatever divine force brought him to me.

A Soft Place to Land

Description

After their parents are killed in a plane crash, half sisters Ruthie, thirteen, and Julia, sixteen, are shocked to learn of the instructions left in the will. These tight-knit sisters, who grew up in the shadow of their parent's romance, will be sent from their Atlanta hometown to separate coasts, to live with very different families. Cautious Ruthie adjusts to a new life with her generous, fun-loving aunt and uncle in San Francisco, but rebellious Julia struggles against the conventionality of her birth father and disapproving stepmom in a small town in Virginia. The vast differences in their new lives strain the sisters' relationship to the breaking point, and they drift in (but mostly out) of each other's orbits for the next twenty years, until an unexpected turn of events brings them together again.

Discussion Questions

1. Why do Ruthie and Julia so obsessively imagine their parents' ill-fated Vegas vacation and the airplane crash that killed them? Julia feels "to tell the story was to control it, somehow." Do you agree?

2. White gives clues early on as to pivotal events in the girls' futures: that Julia will become a writer, that Ruthie will have

an abortion. Why does she include these flash-forwards? How did anticipating these events change your reading of the story?

3. When she hears there has been an accident, Ruthie's first fear is that Julia has been hurt, not her parents. Discuss the sisters' bond. Why are the sisters so intensely connected? Do you think Julia and Ruthie would have been as close if their parents had not been so centered on their romance with each other?

4. Was Phil and Naomi's romance worth the pain it caused others, particularly the pain it caused Julia? Ruthie realizes she "had always viewed her parents' story through their eyes, the eyes of the victors." How do you think Julia viewed Phil and Naomi's relationship?

5. Did Naomi and Phil have any choice but to leave instructions in their will that in the event of their deaths Ruthie and Julia would go to separate guardians?

6. How does San Francisco shape Ruthie? How does Virden shape Julia?

7. Were you angry with Julia for writing about Ruthie's abortion in her memoir? Are you able to see both sides of the issue?

8. As girls, Ruthie and Julia's relationship is filled with games of Julia's imagining. One simple but meaningful game they play is "Biscuit and Egg." As children, what are some of the games you played with your siblings and friends? Retrospectively, what insights about your childhood do these games reveal?

9. How did you feel about the book's ending? What do you

think happens next, for Ruthie and Julia, and for Ruthie and Gabe?

10. How do you think the sisters' lives would have turned out if their custodial arrangement had been switched?

11. Discuss the title of the book. Think about where Ruthie and Julia have "landed," both physically (Atlanta, New York), in their careers (chef, writer), in their relationships with others, and in their relationship with each other.

Enhance Your Book Club

1. Play "Seven Steps to an Unlikely Outcome" or "Who the Hell Is He?"

2. Ruthie becomes a chef, and the book includes many delicious descriptions of cooking. Reread the Thanksgiving dinner preparations in Chapter 8, and try making one of the dishes Ruthie and Uncle Robert create together. Or make Ruthie's signature dessert, "Elvs" (peanut butter cookies filled with roasted banana ice cream, the sides of which are then rolled in crumbled caramelized bacon).

3. *A Soft Place to Land* focuses on the relationship between two sisters. Talk about your relationship with your own siblings and family members. Is there anyone you feel compelled to reconnect with?

Author Q&A

What inspired you to write *A Soft Place to Land*? How did you choose to include real-life events, such as 9/11 and the plane crash on the Hudson? Did you begin with the end in mind, or did those elements simply find their way in?

Frankly, I was inspired to write *A Soft Place to Land* because my mind is filled with morbid "what ifs." These morbid thoughts especially come to play when I'm on an airplane. Now on a rational level, I know that air travel is actually the safest form of transportation. And on a spiritual level, I think travel is a sublime practice—it's important to experience new places, new cultures, new foods. But these are all thoughts my mind only allows on the ground. Once airborne, my rational thinking flies right out the pressure-sealed window. I think it's because airplane crashes, while rare, are so dramatic. Usually everyone on board dies, and the last few moments are a horror. Add to that the fact that if parents are on the same plane, a child's family can be wiped out in one swoop. And what if those parents had daughters, and the daughters were actually half siblings, and one still had a biological parent living . . . ?

I'm going to jump ahead to the third question and then work my way back to the second. I had no idea what the ending of this story would be when I started writing about Ruthie and Julia. All I knew was that I was going to tell of half siblings who were split apart after their parents died in a plane crash. In fact, initially I had four siblings in the story, but the more I wrote, the more I realized I needed to boil the sibling relationship down to its essence: that it needed to be about a particularly intense relationship between two sisters. I knew, too, that after the crash the girls needed to land in very different places, and that those places needed to have a profound impact on who they would become.

In terms of incorporating real life events: well, 911 occurred during the time span of the book (1993–2009), and it was such a terrible and defining event with such long reverberations. I don't think there was any way *not* to include it. Especially because the actual day of September 11, 2001, was one where so many former grievances seemed petty. It was a day when people reevaluated their lives.

The "Miracle on the Hudson" was, for lack of a better expression, a strangely happy accident. (Not to diminish the horror experienced by those on the plane as it went down; still, the outcome was astonishing.) I first heard about US Air Flight 1549 while driving in my car. They were talking about it on the radio, how a plane had crashed but it looked like everyone on board might survive. I burst into tears while driving. It was just so poignant. Here was this hope, this proof that doom was not always inevitable. It was such a powerful story; I couldn't stop thinking about it. (Who could?) And then it occurred to me: let Julia be on that flight! That way she could experience what her mother went through in the last moments of her life, an experience that would allow her to try for true reconciliation with Ruthie.

I know that you have a sister; can you tell us a bit about your relationship? Are there any parallels between you and your sister and Julia and Ruthie?

I actually have two half sisters and three half brothers. I have many memories of being the youngest of all of those kids, being caught in the giddy and chaotic swirl of a big family. But my oldest sister Lauren and I did have a special bond. She was, simply, a great deal of fun, and she and I spent an enormous amount of joyful time together. So yes, I absolutely based the love and intimacy that Julia and Ruthie have in their early years on Lauren's and my relationship. Lauren was a fantastic inventor of games and stories, and I wanted to create that sense of childhood play on the page. (Full confession: Lauren and I did play "Biscuit and Egg," and if she were beside me now she would insist I tell you that she was the one who made it up.)

That said, Ruthie and Julia are invented characters. And they change so much after they are separated by thousands of miles. So pretty much once the Grand Canyon crash occurs, and the girls are split apart, the resemblance between my fictitious sisters and Lauren and me evaporates.

You include great descriptions of both Atlanta and San Francisco. You grew up in Atlanta, and currently live there. You also spent time living in San Francisco. Did you need to do much research for the settings of your book, or were you already well versed in these cities?

Though I know mistakes happen, I really strive for verisimilitude in my stories. My feeling is that if I want my characters to seem as if they are made of flesh and blood, then I need the world they inhabit to match the world as it is, or as it was during the time the story takes place.

While drafting the book I didn't do much research about Atlanta, but I did go to San Francisco for about a month, just to reconnect with the feel of the city. During that time I spent a couple of afternoons at the San Francisco public library, researching newspaper headlines from 1993, mainly so I could figure out what Mimi and Robert might discuss during dinner. After I finished a draft of the book I did a *ton* of research, to make sure that I was accurately describing the way Atlanta and San Francisco would have been over fifteen years ago. It's amazing the changes that a decade and a half bring.

Here's a minor example: initially when I wrote the book I had Dara and Ruthie meet at Peet's Coffee on Market Street in the Castro neighborhood of San Francisco. (This is the scene during which the two friends play "Who the Hell is He?") But then I called my friend Ellen Sinaiko, who has run a café in the Castro since the early eighties, and I casually asked whether or not Peet's had been there in 1993. I was fully expecting her to say yes. But it had not! So I had to change the location to Café Flore, which, in fact, I think works better as a meeting spot for the two girls. So serendipitously, by fact checking I actually found a better place to set the scene. Or maybe serendipitous isn't the right word, maybe this minor example just proves how good things will come from sweating the details.

There are great descriptions of meal preparations in the book. Do you cook? Did you invent Ruthie's signature dessert, "Elvs"?

I love to cook. I think of it as my second passion, behind writing. I read cookbooks for pleasure, and spend time imagining which foods might taste good together.

I did invent "Elvs," but I was greatly influenced by two sources: 1) the "phatty cakes" at Cakes & Ale restaurant in Decatur, Georgia, which are sandwiches of two spicy ginger cookies with a marscapone cream filling, and 2) a dessert I had at Woodfire Grill in Atlanta. I don't remember the exact specifics of the dessert, but I know it included caramelized banana, caramel sauce, and bacon crumbles. It was both earthy and sublime.

You've mentioned that you have a fear of flying. What made you decide to tackle that fear by incorporating two plane crashes into _A Soft Place to Land_? What do you imagine your last thoughts would be?

Wow, I wish I had tackled my fear of flying by writing this book. Unfortunately, I have only intensified it, especially after researching the details of the "Miracle on the Hudson" flight. That said, I think it's important for me not to give into the fear, so I've learned to deal with it by 1) getting a prescription for Xanax for flights, 2) adopting the mantra, "It's probably going to be okay," and 3) making sure I have a charged iPod before I go to the airport, because listening to familiar music really soothes me on the plane.

I have some idea of what my last thoughts might be because I was once on a pretty intense flight that I thought was going to crash. Now, granted, I have an active imagination. Probably we were just going through severe—and I mean severe—turbulence. But there was a moment in the midst of the turbulence—I was hyperventilating, mind you—when the plane must have dropped 1,000 feet and I suddenly became very calm. I thought, *Oh. This is it. This plane is actually going to crash.* And suddenly, I was more or less okay. I was distantly sad that I was going to die but I realized that—as Julia says—it happens to everyone. I was glad that I had experienced such a great love with my husband, Alan, and I hoped the crash wouldn't make the rest of my parents' lives too sorrowful.

Eventually the turbulence subsided, and I realized we were going to be okay, and I felt panicky all over again, felt like I had to get off the plane *that instant* even though it was an international flight and we had about six more hours to go. But in those few moments when I honestly thought my death was imminent, I experienced a strange and comforting peace, which I allowed Julia to have during her own experience on Flight 1549.

Julia's memoir incorporates personal details that Ruthie would rather not share with the world. Julia's writing seems to be cathartic for her, but it has almost an opposite effect on Ruthie. Do you believe Ruthie is right to want to hold back details she remembers about their childhood? Which sister do you side with?

I don't side with either. I absolutely understand why Ruthie felt betrayed and I absolutely understand why Julia included the detail about Ruthie's past abortion, especially because in her memoir she never refers to Ruthie by name, only as "Biscuit." My showing both sides of the story was probably my way of wrestling with what it means to be a writer.

Have you ever considered writing a memoir?

While I love my life, and feel immensely grateful for it, I'm not sure it warrants a memoir. Basically all I do is read (a lot), write, teach, cook, eat (a lot), walk the dog (not as much as she'd like), spend time with my husband, and eat meals with friends. And do laundry. In the summer I garden. Occasionally I go to the movies. And I'll take any opportunity I can to escape to New Orleans or New York for a few days. (And in New Orleans and New York what do I do? I read, I spend time with my husband, I eat meals with friends . . .)

Which is all to say that the stories I make up are probably more interesting than my own life.

What are you working on next? Would you ever write a sequel to *A Soft Place to Land*?

I have just started working on my third book, and while I'm not yet ready to talk about the details of the story, I will say that cooking plays a huge role in it, and a good portion of it is set in New York City during the late 1940s.

Right now I'm not planning on writing a sequel for *A Soft Place to Land*, but who knows how I'll feel later. I certainly imagine I'll continue to explore its themes in my writing.

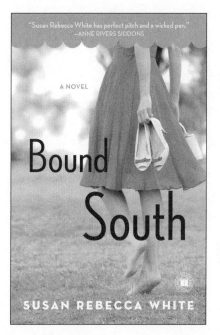